Praise for *The Remedy*

'[Michelle Lovric] reveals in carefully-crafted prose, the dark side of the Enlightenment – while managing to enchant us with a surprising love story . . . From first page to last, Lovric transfixes one with her superb language, imagery and twists of plot. At no time does the confidence or quality of narrative falter. Thrilling' *Mslexia*

'The language is opulent and sensuous and the setting intriguing' *Historical Novels Review*

'Fresh, graceful prose' *Publisher's Weekly*

'*Remedy* is a ravishing, meticulously authentic buffet of words and sensations' *Entertainment Weekly*

'Told in lushly beautiful prose, Lovric's dazzling new novel conjures up a world of dangerous secrets and shadowy pasts' *Image*

'An intriguing and sometimes sinister tale' *Sunday Times* (Australia)

'A rollicking read that evokes the squalor and danger of eighteenth-century Europe as well as it does the glamour' *Daily Telegraph* (Australia)

Also by Michelle Lovric

Carnevale
The Floating Book
The Virago Book of Christmas
Venice: Tales of the City

The Remedy

A novel of
London & Venice

Michelle Lovric

Virago

VIRAGO

First published in Great Britain in March 2005 by Virago Press
This paperback edition published in May 2006 by Virago Press

A CIP catalogue record for this book
is available from the British Library.

ISBN-13: 978-1-84408-137-0
ISBN-10: 1-84408-137-0

Typeset in Baskerville, Cochin and Dante by M Rules

Printed and bound in Great Britain by Clays Ltd, St Ives plc

Virago Press
An imprint of
Time Warner Book Group UK
Brettenham House
Lancaster Place
London WC2E 7EN

www.virago.co.uk

Love lends its name to countless dealings which are attributed to it but of which it knows no more than the Doge knows what goes on in Venice.

FRANÇOIS, DUC DE LA ROCHEFOUCAULD (1613–80), *Maxims*

As far as I am concerned, no sweet thing is evil.

AVICENNA (973–1037)

Part One

So at fifteen, spread belly-down upon the floor, a black sheet hunched over me and candles at my foot and head, my lips pressed on stone, litanies in my ears, as the priest broke and entered my shocked fist to slide the ring on my finger, I promised to take no other husband than Christ. I almost meant it. In that heady moment the vow itself seemed no great sacrifice: I'd never known a man, but I had tasted chocolate.

Venice, 1768

· 1 ·

An Anodyne Epithem

Take Brandy 4 ounces; Camphire half a dram; Opium 2 drams, dissolve.

It comforts the Nervous parts, by its warmth appeaseth the raging Spirits, penetrates deep, sets open the Pores, attenuates, dissipates, obtunds the dolorific Matter, and drives it off by Diaphoresis.

I was an unwilling nun, bundled into the convent by a family that had briefly lost its head over a trivial adolescent melodrama. My ultimate crime was such a negligible one that it's not worth the recounting. One day I was the pride and idol of my parents, roaming freely around the family *palazzo* with my tribe of high-bred she-dogs, having my hair dressed, clowning adorably at my dancing lessons, having my portrait painted. I believe I was a little wilful with the artist. That's all. Yet the next day I was in San Zaccaria, which was by way of being our family convent, as at least six unmarriageable aunts had been deposited there and a number of my plainer cousins. At first I thought it just a brief punishment, a warning, some time to cool my heels. There was no problem of conjuring a dowry for me, and I was far from ugly, being a piquant blonde of the kind that precociously detained male attention. But after a few weeks I began to suspect the dreadful truth: that my parents meant to keep me there.

And I realised that it had been in the planning for some time.

I already knew the inside of San Zaccaria all too well. And my parents had every excuse to feel satisfied in their consciences, despite my protests, with this destiny they had thrust on me.

For the nuns had caught me early by my sweet tooth, hanging sugared almonds, balsamic lozenges and candied fruit in the humid swoop of the orchard branches whenever we went, in my infant days, to visit two or three aunts Catarina, our family's Christian name for girls. No one remarked upon the lovely crop or stopped me snatching jellies from their strings or cracking pink-nubbed nuts against my milk-teeth. So I was free to think that in convents such things grew on trees, whereas at home they must be prayed for. A happy mouth does not forget what once befriended it.

In Venice, the noble dynasties were recorded in our so-called 'Golden Book'. And each Golden Book family stored its female shadow, like its conscience, in a nunnery: seventeen Contarini at Santa Catarina, a score of Moresini at Spirito Santo, the Balbi at Sant'Andrea de Zirada. And the unwanted Foscarini and Querini women were interred in our own living crypt at San Zaccaria.

At ten, I'd joined the boat when my cousin Paola made her bridal tour of convents, to salute her sisters sealed in chastity. This archaic ritual was long out of fashion, yet my uncle persisted with it, for the sake of the family nuns who loved company, and whose isolation was a constant source of inadmissible guilt. *They'd* been given to God, who asked the merest thousand-ducat dowry, this so my Uncle Paolo could spend thirty thousand on a Gradenigo bridegroom for Paola and a new infusion of old Golden Book blood into his grandchildren.

Her confined cousins blessed Paola with dead eyes, forked almond crescents through the grille into her violable mouth, for while they might feed her, they were not allowed to touch the bride's naked hand. Meanwhile, for me, there were buckwheat wafers thin as hosts but interleaved with honeyed whipped cream, still-smoking fritters brisk with powdered musk and spiced *panpepato* such as I was not allowed at home.

When I was twelve, the nuns asked me would I like to see the kitchens? A noble girl, I'd never seen one, so why not? Down I went, and there I found such red-cheeked happiness pulling such trays of sweet warmth from gnashing ovens, such lucent bottles of Seville syrups staining the glass of the windows, such a hot and blissful hub of softening, folding, melting, lubricating, rising, turning, glazing, and stacking in painted boxes destined for fine tables that I cried when they made me go home. I wasn't bred for such low labour myself, but I was partial to watching it.

And so I continued to visit San Zaccaria regularly and felt myself at home there. I even boarded at times as a schoolgirl, sleeping in the rooms of my aunts while my desultory education continued in a classroom next to the refectory.

I called on the convent kitchens as a sparrow calls on a bird-table, taking what I wanted and flitting off. No one could bake marzipan cakes like those nuns at San Zaccaria, except perhaps those at Sant'Alvise. Most certainly no one made such frothing chocolate or served it in such elegant caudle cups. I came so often to drink it that a special cup was reserved for me.

It seemed such an agreeable place. One of the loveliest gardens in Venice was San Zaccaria's. Still more pleasing was the orchard, with its delicate swathing of trees. The convent was more like a pleasure house in the country than a fortress for God's brides. Terracotta enfilades laced with arches of white Istrian stone led to two graceful cloisters, one even ornamented with a loggia above. From the door of their cells the nuns saw the church cupola rising above them in harmonious composition with the apse and campanile. Just beyond our southern wall lay the Riva degli Schiavoni and the basin of San Marco: a fresh salt air purified the cloisters even in the summer, though in the winter, being at a low point of the city, they were sometimes briefly transformed into dismal lakes, and, once or twice, into mirrors of ice.

The convent was to the south of the church. At the necessary hours, the nuns filed there quietly and positioned themselves in severely grilled galleries. From behind those grilles they fixed their blinking eyes on the coal-black marble on the floors or rested them on Giovanni Bellini's transcendent *Sacra Conversazione*. Or they sat in the wooden niches of the choir like so many carved saints, observing one another and the five gilded chairs which were reserved for the Doge and his party on their annual visit to the church.

It was a small life, without privation but without any variation.

It was not for a person such as me.

When my parents delivered me to the convent after my misdemeanour with the artist I was quite within my rights to assume the banishment was temporary and that shortly, after a period of demonstrable good behaviour, I would be restored to my former freedom and privileges, with due reparations paid for the affront to my dignity. To this end, at first I behaved as dumbly as a trained bear, docile as you please. It was hard to keep my temper; yet I did. I would earn my free passage home, no matter what. And there were those marzipan cakes to console me in the meantime.

But the days flowed into weeks, and still I was at San Zaccaria. When I might not leave the place, it seemed suddenly far less attractive. I winced at the noise of keys turning in locks. I shivered in the shadows of the high walls that I had previously perceived as cooling refuges from the Venetian sun.

I wrote to my parents, alternately apologising, grieving, berating. They did not come to see me as the other parents did. I suspect that the sight of my misery would have shaken their resolve. Only once did my mother come, and I performed such a climacteric in front of her that she departed, biting her lip, without saying a word to me. I heard nothing from them after that.

Yet still I hoped they would relent. How could they leave me there?

The first sign of the finality of their decision was the arrival of my *cassa*. When the painted wedding box was delivered to my cell I lay on the floor and wept, for it meant that they had resolved that I was truly to be married to Christ. I wrenched open the lid, looking for the luxurious trousseau that had been accumulating for many years. My parents had replaced the gay

10

silks and linens with cloth no humbler but in drab colours. There was one more thing: a gilded casket that was intended for my blonde hair.

Even as a child, I had never thought my parents perfect in wisdom. Now I began to think them mad. Did they realise what they were doing, confining me against my will? Did they not realise how badly such an attempt must end?

I had not a breath of a vocation for the Church.

Until that moment the deepest religious experience of my life had been praying to God to uncreate Sundays, the most tedious day of the week. Now my every day was to become a Sunday, and repeated without mercy, not merely with the passive endurance of my previous life, but an active participation in rituals that I saw as degrading antics.

Now, under the eye of the *madre di consiglio*, I was sworn in as a *monaca da coro*, a proper choir nun, and not a mere *conversa*, the lower order of sisters who acted as our menials, who ate only what the refectory supplied and were always given the dark meat of the chicken. The poor *converse* wore wimples and chafing habits taken from the communal wardrobe. They kept their hair lopped and invisible. But the Golden Book girls like myself might be regarded indulgently if we chose to display our curls about our temples, wear jewellery (if we cared to – I did not) and silk stockings. We adapted our habits to fashion.

You may ask why I agreed to become a professed nun when I so hated my confinement at the convent. It was because I kept my eyes open and saw how the *converse* were treated. While I never accepted that I would spend the rest of my life in the convent, it seemed expedient to take my vows and exist on the superior plane. All Golden Book girls did.

In the preparations for this moment, the convent's rituals were truly bridal. Those of us about to take our vows were cherished, fêted, the subject of whispered admiration. The atmosphere was heightened in those days; my own skin felt like fine glass bottling hot blood. There was breathless giggling in the corridor outside my cell, and fine white sheets were laid on my bed. In it, I fell asleep with the melt of special cakes, sent up expressly from the kitchen, in my mouth. I awoke to tender smiles and reverent fingers untying the ribbons of my chemise.

I married Christ in a delirium spun of sweetened wine.

I was only bitter later, when I saw little girls dreambound in the smell of almonds and burnt sugar in the orchard. For by then of course I knew full well that real nuns might not freely come and go from there and that God did not make such trees.

· 2 ·

An Emmenagogue Decoction

Take roots of Smalage 2 ounces; Calamus Aromaticus, Bay-berries, each 2 drams; Zedoary, Cubebs, each 1 dram and a half; Mace 2 scruples; Galingale, Grains of Paradise, each half a scruple; Dittany of Creet, Pennyroyal, each 1 handful; boil in Water 1 quart and white Wine 1 pint to 28 ounces; when it's strained add Tincture of Saffron (made in Treacle Water) 1 ounce; Syrup of Stechas 3 ounces, mix.

It excites a new Orgasm in the Mass of Blood; and forcing it briskly into the Uterine Arteries, opens the Extremities of the Vessels.

Other girls of my blood and station found the life of the convent quite convivial.

Not I.

I soon found out my mistake and regretted it bitterly. The seductions of God were short-lived in my hard little heart. Worse, I realised that now I had professed myself as a nun my parents had every excuse to leave me there. I lacerated myself with rabid recriminations. How had I been so stupid? So blind?

Despite my high status and kind treatment I chafed against everything. I could not bear to be there. I began to play them up, to behave as badly as I dared. I was forcibly escorted by differ-ent nuns to Prime, Tierce, Sext, None, Vespers and Compline. Impeccably devout nuns were made responsible for shaking me awake in the dead hours for Matins. The nuns who accompanied me to the choir-stalls chanted continuous, breathy meditations on the glories of the virginal state.

Some had their hair cut off and kept for them until their death in caskets such as my parents had sent me. I shuddered to conjure the image of that moment, when the nuns' aged corpses would be reunited with their young hair, for it would be buried with them. This so that they might go to their wedding night with God all intact. I could not rid myself of the grotesque vision of their avid, aged faces, toothless as lampreys, curtained by their thirteen-year-old curls, awaiting their deflowering at His hands.

They were all thirteen, in their minds, for ever, sealed into adolescent behaviour. The natural appetites which were arising in them then were trapped just at the moment when they should be set free. With their primal urges stoppered up inside them, and not even softened by familial affections, they lived the rest of their lives enacting highly charged little melodramas, setting up rivalries and unleashing trails of poisoned whispers, just like a cancerous cluster of spiteful schoolgirls.

One morning, I lost control of myself and confronted two of the smuggest nuns, eyes uplifted and faces alight with their own superiority over fleshly things.

I hissed at them, 'Chastity! All it means is that you think continually about the opposite!'

They cast their eyes down, refusing to meet mine. They exchanged glances under the demure shadows of their lids – they would take pleasure in reporting my unseemly outburst.

Yet I knew that there were others like myself among these women: unwilling nuns who had taken no internal vow of chastity. And, like me, they were all perfectly aware of the fact that the sexual enclosure of the Venetian convents might, with a little cleverness, be ruptured; and in no nunnery more so than at San Zaccaria. The city would have preferred a little more virginity in her nuns, but shrugged her shoulders. Those unruly instincts, if they could not be contained, must be managed. Blind eyes were turned where open eyes might lead to inconvenient scandal.

Everyone knows that a man is the only way out of a convent, and after two months as a *monaca* at San Zaccaria, with not the merest sign of mercy from my parents, I was already making my own plans. I would be happy to leave on the arm of the first man who proffered one. A Venetian, a Frenchman, a Turk, for all I cared, might own that arm. I would have tripped out of that convent even on the withered elbow of the dread Hermippus, rumoured to have lived a hundred and thirteen years already by constantly inhaling the breath of young girls and who scoured Europe looking for recruits to his boarding school. It was being said in those days that he was in Venice, on the hunt for little nuns, for he wanted to indulge in a practice prescribed by Marsilio Ficino for prolonging youth: to drink from the opened veins of young women. Yes, I swore to myself, I'd open my veins to a blood-sucking old man, if it would get me out of the living death of the convent.

So it was scarcely a problem to me if my saviour turned out to be an Englishman who spoke Italian like a native and even Venetian like a Venetian, with only his little glint of northern coldness to mark him out from us.

He was visiting Venice on some business matter or other that was never made clear to me, quite possibly because I was not listening.

Who can listen when there is so much to touch and taste as this man offered me, even from his first glance, when he came to the *parlatorio* to see the girls, prattling like cloister parrots behind the wall of metal fretwork that contained us, barely, from the world. I saw him and something cold and vivid immediately congealed in my stomach. I rose from my seat and pressed my nose against the grille. He laughed at my frank interest and stepped forward, caressed my nose with a slow finger, as if picking me out from a litter of puppies.

This one.

How was I to know that was all it was to him?

Nor, in all likelihood, was it the first time.

Retrospectively, I have no doubts that my Anglican lover made a habit of cuckolding the Popish God by inducing brides of Christ to commit adultery. For him it was just another form of illicit commerce, of the style he liked so much. He was a man who revelled in delinquency and malfeasance. Far more than plain dealing, he enjoyed dubious business pacts sealed in dark taverns and dangerous negotiations on deserted bridges in the early hours of the morning. So smuggling me out of a convent spiced the regular joys of love-making with a little risky free-trading.

I guessed none of that at the time. I simply rejoiced that this picking out met entirely with my own plans.

I knew almost nothing about him, and I liked it that way.

Some love is like gangrene, I told myself, *it does not require the oxygen of information in order to thrive.*

This love would be of that variety.

· 3 ·

Emmenagogue Pills

Take Venetian Borace, Myrrh, each 45 grains; Birthwort Root,
Saffron, each 15 grains; Oil of Pennyroyal, Savine, Cloves, each
2 drops; with Syrup of the 5 opening Roots make 18 Pills for 6
Doses.

The Title tells their Design. Let them be given about the
Menstrous Time, when Nature is slothful and wants Stimulation,
twice a Day.

I never knew whom he paid to have me let out in the middle of
that sultry night: at San Zaccaria, at all levels of authority, certain things were to be had for cash. I only knew this: an older,
humbler nun came and shook me awake, dragged me, stumbling, yawning and protesting to a room where a ewer of
steaming water and a bowl of perfumed soap were waiting, with
an ostentatious dress of thin silk worn almost to transparency,
but of a vivid orange colour.

'Wash,' she said, curtly, 'especially there, and in your mouth.'
I could not look at her sallow, tragic face. She was clearly moved
by the occasion, but I could not distinguish whether it was jealousy or mere ill temper at the extra chore that kept her lips
working in breathless oaths. Blushing, I commenced to wash,
trying to keep my chemise lowered. Impatiently, she ripped it
over my head and I stood before her naked. I whimpered and
covered myself with my hands, not able to meet her eyes for
shame. She was sorry for me then, and spoke more kindly.

'Learn to do this. It won't be the only time tonight.'

When I was clean and decked in the dress, which covered me
as barely as a sigh, she took my hand, as a nurse might take a

little child's, and hurried me through long, airless corridors to a barred door that opened straight into the orchard. We passed through the trees to the second door where the *ruota* was inserted. This wheel – half in the real world, half in ours, enabled food, money and – at times – unwanted babies to be passed through a hatch, while concealing the identities of the people at either side. I wondered if some kind of illicit transaction was about to take place and how it could concern me. But instead the nun drew back a black cloth which screened the gate's iron grille and looked out. She seemed to be expecting someone.

Outside I glimpsed the gold of his hair illuminated by a lantern. His face, not at all anxious, just amused and pleased, was not even staring at the door, but looking up at the stars as if reading their portents and finding them much to his satisfaction – just as was to be expected, for in his case, all plans were blessed and all promised things delivered. It was the man I had seen at the *parlatorio* grille, who had touched my nose through the bar. His smiling complacency made my own discomposure and ignorance feel ridiculous.

The nun whispered to him and he came closer to the door, which she opened, and then bundled me into his arms. I was oddly gratified to find them trembling a little. He reached over me and handed her some money. I knew then what was to happen.

I had been a prudish child. I never liked to see my parents show any affection to each other. Once I had beheld two servants kissing, and I screamed all kinds of murder, drawing people from all over the *palazzo* to witness this disgusting orgy. Afterwards, when my mother explained certain matters to me, I vomited. The naked facts were too bare for my taste. Despite my feelings on the subject, current circumstances made me see my forthcoming telescoped seduction in an optimistic light. I think God made me a cold young woman, for I was easily able to conquer my scruples about the act itself by thinking about the reward of freedom that I would thereby procure. I almost looked forward to it, though I felt fear as well.

I looked at the nun, wondering if I might appeal to her –

should I wish to – and opened my mouth, but then I felt his hands on my breasts.

Believe me, it is not necessary to love the man who takes your virginity, even if he does so with scintillation. My former prejudices against the act itself were dispelled that first night in his rooms in a *palazzo* near Rialto. And I liked to hear the words that accompanied all stages of the business. It seemed too good to be true, that my saviour could also provide such subsidiary pleasures as compliments that raised me to a peak of warm satisfaction about myself. But I felt nothing for the man himself.

It seemed to me that he had awakened my senses without touching any deeper notions of romance that might be lying dormant in me. Perhaps I lacked them entirely?

Then, at the end of our first night together he knelt and kissed my feet and fed me some sweet cakes he dipped first in a goblet of wine. By this time my lips, eyes, fingers and sex were all replete, and with that almond crescent and the kiss that followed it, I think we both knew he had found the casement of my glassy heart, though he had not yet entered it.

When I came back from him the first time, the other women asked me, *So what kind of man is he?*

Is he rich?

Does he . . . appeal, as it were?

What did you smell of his character?

And then, when they saw I was too far gone for that, they loosed their more difficult questions:

Has he given you his real name?

And –

Has he softness to him or will he be hard as ice when the time comes?

But who can listen to questions like this, in the first fever of contagion, and who wants to hear the answers, either?

Not I.

There followed three months of hard love-making and days

19

drained of thoughts, except hazy recollections of our most recent assignation. It seemed the very essence of a superfine thing to be bundled in his arms each night, or rigged out in some lustrous gown he'd supplied for the pleasure of unlacing it. I was ecstatic as a prophet at this change to my life.

I could not too much admire this miracle of passion that made the walls of San Zaccaria both transparent and permeable.

When I knew that I was carrying his child, I came to him full of hope. What man does not want a son, even one fathered outside of marriage with a woman who is not of his tongue or kind?

And indeed, upon hearing the news, my lover mimicked delight and mimed all kinds of shows of tenderness, protection and ever-after happiness, without actually uttering the words. I settled into his arms, observed the golden tinge of those English hairs on his wrists, and allowed myself to think of nothing.

I refused the Emmenagogue pills offered by the nuns and adopted the important personage of a cherished mother-to-be.

So this is love, I declared to myself. But I knew that I was lying. My lover and I performed all the duties laid down in the statutes of pure romance, but the thing did not come to its natural conclusion. My rapture was threadbare, venal – and short-lived.

Balsamic Lozenges

Take fine Dragons Blood (in drops) 2 scruples [sic]; Flowers of
Benjamin 16 grains; Balm of Gilead 24 grains; fine Sugar searced
4 ounces; Mucilage of Gum Tragacanth as much as requisite,
make Lozenges according to Art.

They are good for such as are in danger of a Consumption, to
be carried always about, and taken frequently.

God did not design me for a mother.

The early pregnancy was terrible. I retched my innards into
a basin every morning for weeks, confirming that the foetus,
conceived in the hot, dry *tramontana* wind, was male. I sent
my regrets to my lover, and he responded tenderly, that he
would wait. I believe he returned briefly to London in this
period.

After a few weeks the ignominy ceased, and I resumed my
nightly visits with him.

By day, at the convent, I gazed complacently on Palma il
Vecchio's *Madonna col Bambino*, happily reflecting how much
prettier I was than she – all spaniel-faced and drooping. And
her baby – a gingerish and fat-lipped little gargoyle. But the
shapely relief of Mary and Jesus on the archway to Campo
San Zaccaria – that was elegance indeed! And Bellini's
Madonna, I always thought, was pleasantly endowed with good
looks not unlike my own, and she also suited blue. Our son
would be much more like Bellini's infant Christ, a refined and
exquisite creature, whom I would always clothe with elegance
and raise to be a heartbreaking little gentleman. I did not plan
to succeed him with any more babies, however. My sisters in

carnality at San Zaccaria had by now explained a few robust facts neglected by my mother, and I would not be so careless again.

None of the paintings showed women with the ungainly outlines of late pregnancy, and I did not anticipate that state with any pleasure. Worse, I imagined that it would render my lover more paternal, less passionate, less desirous of giving pleasure. And my burgeoning shape would make it more difficult for him to spirit me away from Venice.

I never found out, though. For, needless to say, by the time I reached a visible amplitude, he was gone.

Some time into the fourth month he tired of me.

I speculated endlessly on the change in him, unwilling to pin the blame on what had really caused it.

Fear of losing his youth by becoming a father? Fear of my Golden Book blood and the indelible connection he would make in marrying me? When I first saw him examine the altered profile of my belly, his eyes became unreadable.

There was another reason. There's no point in concealing it now.

You see, we fought. Not just the fervid arguments of lovers, but something darker. It was as if the devil in him – for it was there – and the devil in me were passionately in love with one another too. I had skirmished with other girls in the convent, with my parents who had placed me there, but the quarrels I knew with him were of a different order altogether.

It mattered not at all what subject inspired the war. It was the style of the combat that was so terrifying.

I discovered this when we argued for the first time. I remember that he *ridiculed* me, and how that stung, for no one had ever done so before. He called me stupid. He laughed at me, called me a brainless eel, a silly cod.

Then we were divided by a dense viscous silence spangled with fulminous glances, during which each of us, I'm assured, wished himself and herself dead if only so that the other might be impaled on a shaft of sharpest guilt. When he brushed past me I

22

felt bristles of anger scraping my skin with intent to damage. He wished me ill, I could see that: not just misery but physical harm. Confronted by his anger, his adoration of me disappeared without a trace.

As a man who was enchanted by me, he was undeniably attractive. As a man who didn't love me, he was simply – repulsive.

It was a cruel blow to see him in this antipathetical light. My plans for liberty were pinned upon him. It was painful to force myself to acknowledge in this instance not that I must renounce him but that I must mount my hopes upon a lesser object, yet still housed in that same disappointing carcass.

And so, while he waited for my apology, I was engaged in an entirely different *fatica*. I was cauterising my green hopes, sealing in the still useful sap.

So, I reflected, *this man I thought so beautifully formed for my purpose, has improvidently hardened into a disagreeable shape that revolts me. I am trapped here with my attraction for that other incarnation. Am I to attach myself to this brutal new circumstance?*

I told myself that it was merely a convenience that he had once – moderately – pleased me. In my difficulties I would have acted as I did with him, were he a very goblin.

So now, I must steel myself to make pretty to him, to make him forget I ever showed him the least morsel of rebellion, make him think I slavered for his love, that this precious balm was all I sought. By then I had learned some things from the other 'sportive' nuns that could make a monkey of the cleverest man. Why, all the truncheoned beasts turn their eyes up and roll over at those things they taught me, so even a mere Englishman must respond. Dogs of all races wag their tail when you finger them aptly.

So, with sand in my heart, I set about winning the bastardly worm back. I bent my head to kiss his hand, subtly tonguing it so that it seemed that the cool sting of a tear was left behind. *That* stirred him, and even while I felt a tremor in his fingers, I was sinking to my knees before him, my eyes cast down, kissing his knees, his calves, the tops of his boots, all the while not insensible to the mandolin effect of my proffered rear-quarters and waist.

'Forgive me,' I whispered, 'though I so little deserve it. I am so ashamed.'

Inwardly I spat words of an untranslatable Venetian character, which, if he had heard them, would have assassinated him and haunted his corpse with their vile resonances. But I continued aloud, soft as a dove, 'I prostrate myself to you – take me back to your bosom, my beloved one.'

And I ran my finger from his boot to his breast, now fixing upon his small blue eyes my own large green ones, piteously laden with unspent tears that I had conjured up not from remorse but from fury.

'Just a gesture,' I begged. 'Anything to show me that you allow me back into your heart.'

'You may do as you wish,' he said, stiffly. 'It's nothing to me,' yet I knew he was already half-beguiled.

'You are extraordinarily . . . good,' I murmured humbly.

Then he raised me upon his knees, whereupon he commenced his usual flashy fiddling with my ribbons. And kissed me with the usual hard lips, and turned me upon the bed and took me with the usual speed and skill.

On the *divano* while he mounted me I, all unseen, made the most vile grimaces and gestures and silently insulted his every move. Although I had known no other lover, I was ready to attribute great deficiencies to him in their comparison. Knowing how he would abhor it, I imagined other men in his place – all of the pitifully few adult male faces I could conjure from my limited experience, from our priest-confessor to the butcher's delivery boy who came bashfully into the kitchens at San Zaccaria. In the dark, I scraped the inside of my cheek to my lover. I dilated my nostrils and my sphincter at him. Against the pillow, I bent the nail of my thumb back at him till it broke. I turned myself invisibly inside out to show my hatred. I pushed my curls into my ears to filter the hateful sounds of my lover's pleasure.

But I was gratified to see that as he spent himself a grateful tear hovered on his nose before it dropped on my own lid.

I lay panting and whimpering my false admiration and satisfaction and then lifted my head to kiss his eyes and lips, those parts of him that I had much rather score a dozen times or so with my nails, were this body of his not the only vehicle for conveying me out of my prison.

· 5 ·

A Refrigerating Expression

Take Male Pimpernel 3 handfuls; Borage 6 handfuls; Roots of Borage cut into thin Rundles 2 ounces; Pippins 3; Salt Prunel 2 drams; white Sugar 1 ounce and a half, stamp, and pour on them Meadowsweet Water 3 pints; when they have stood cold a night's space, strain out the clear Liquor.

It's dedicated to the service of such melancholy Persons, as are of an Adult, hot and dry Temperament, for it corrects atrabilarious Blood, qualifies its Ebullitions, tempers flatulent Estuosities of the Hypochondria, refrigerates the over-heated Brain, condenses rarified and restrains boisterous Spirits, precipitates Salts, and carries them off by Urine.

Too late came to me the realisation that this dark ribbon of nastiness that flowed through him was as habitual and crucial to his doings as the *cloaca maxima* to Rome. His temper purified him: he excreted all unwholesome emotions in this way.

If he felt any inner pain, he simply bludgeoned someone else, and that took the pain away for a while. No wonder he enjoyed such a smooth face, and dispensed such an uncreased smile. His lines and scars were surely worn by the people who had loved him. So that even when I was oh-so-discreet and flattering, unrolled myself like a carpet beneath his feet, he still felt the need to stamp on me, cursing and spitting in his jakes-breath, at the times when the venom overspilled.

So though I still somehow enjoyed him physically in my cold-hearted fashion, for he was undoubtedly endowed with all the points of masculinity that are universally in request, I now hated him with far stronger intensity. After that first display of vitriol, there came others, until it happened that every word he said, even on neutral subjects, fell vilely on my ears. By then his endearments were as welcome to me as if kicked up from a puddle of street slime; yet if they did not come, then I fell into a despairing panic that I might never leave San Zaccaria by his agency.

When he waxed vicious, I just stood dumbly, listening to things about myself that my bitterest enemy could not hope to devise. He insulted my appearance so intimately that I bit my cheeks to stop myself from crying out. When he hated me I was always, at some point, 'dowdy'. I realised he probably did not know the true meaning of the word in Italian, well though he spoke our language, but I imagine he knew it was an evil thing that women said of one another, so it must be eviscerating.

There were times when he lost command of himself. Strangle-eyed and teeming with spleen, baffled in all his schemes, his resentment was also expressed in shoes, bottles and other missiles.

'Not my face!' I begged him at times like that, for I could not endure to be humiliated in the convent. The bruises on my hips and thighs were bearable because they were invisible to others.

What I could not withstand were the threats. When he was beast-eyed and breathless, numb-toothed with all the poison that had spurted from his mouth, that was when he began to speak dangerously, in a low voice, of how – very soon – he would not want me any more. This was my undoing, for it robbed me of my prospect of escape. Then I gasped and wept honest tears, and then he strode about the room, shouting that he saw through my melodramatic trickeries and that I should be not in a convent but on the stage.

When I sobbed a protest, he snarled, 'Why don't you set it to music?' His lips disappeared and his eyes became opaque.

But I do not doubt it was a kind of love we had for each other. What the poets call 'love' is made up of need and desire, is it not? And ours was that. I needed him. He desired me. But it was also the kind of love that when he raised his hand I knew not if it was to strike or caress me.

He found yet another device to humiliate me. When, in a roundabout way, I was making for the vital subject of our marriage, he would always say, with a perfectly controlled expression, 'We don't talk about that.' In this way, he made himself the emperor, inquisitor, judge and lord of all the emotional commerce that passed between us. And like all people who live under the yoke I felt a bitter resentment towards the person who had set me in this position of inferiority.

Were all women as loathsome to him as I was now, I wondered, once their brief mystery had been exposed as mere coquetry and their fears as melodrama and their insecurities as selfishness?

He had tactlessly talked of a few of my predecessors when his gullet was silked with wine and his brain addled with repeated spendings. At first, listening to tales of these unworthy women, I had felt it my place – and my only path to my own salvation – to soothe his way forever forward. He certainly believed the world owed him something. Were these women really such shrews? Did they truly commit these grave offences? Or had they in fact merely responded in kind to the disparagements he dished up for them? A little respect and a great deal of pity for those unknown women began to throb in my thoughts.

Eventually, at the end of each of his broadsides, I would apologise and he would tell me how unhappy he had been feeling, and I would comfort him until he snored. And I would slip back to the convent.

In terms of a great love, it was a mockery, but until he took me to a priest and married me, then this was how it would have to be.

But after we married, what a luxury of revenge I planned for myself. What foul epithets I had stored up for him, what cold shoulders I would turn upon his pestilential caresses, what sluttish housekeeping would I inflict and what violently laxative juices would I slip into his drinks! For every offence I had its just dessert planned out in the same minute.

And these fantasies took away the sting of every blow and insult, until he did the one thing that I had not planned against.

· 6 ·

A Consolating Mixture

Take Sherry Wine half a pint; strong Cinnamon Water 4 ounces; Rose Water, white Sugar Candy, each 2 ounces; Juice of Kermes strain'd 1 ounce; Species called Laetificans Galeni 2 drams; Leaves of Gold 4; Oil of Nutmeg 4 drops, mix.

It helps Concoction, corrects Crudities, dissipates Flatus, cherishes native Heat, specifically recreates Women with Child, when drooping and languid, comforts the weak, feeble Foetus, prevents Miscarriage from dejection of Spirits, and cold flaccidity of the Womb, and supplies desir'd Strength, Vigour and Ability for the happy performance of the great work of Child-birth.

I was a poor species of idiot not to guess that it would happen.

I was so green that when he failed to call for me one night I was genuinely surprised and shocked. My former procuress was no longer required to urge me to the grille, and I was glad she was not there to witness this first instance of my abandonment and humiliation.

I stood for a long time, listening for the steps that did not materialise. Alone, in the shadows, my self-assurance soon faltered. After a small half-hour I knew in my stomach that he was not coming.

I imagined all kinds of reasons: a business meeting, an encounter with a *bravo*, an *acqua alta* in the parts of town he must traverse. But the image that I settled on was of him at the grille of another *parlatorio*, in another convent, choosing another young nun to amuse him now that I had ceased to do so. I was ill-tempered, and I was already swelling with his child, so that soon I would cease to be a lover and become more of a mother in his eyes. There was a vacancy for the lover. Perhaps he had already filled it. Perhaps he was filling it now.

So long as he set me free, I did not care how he amused himself. It occurred to me that he did not even have to marry me, so long as he left me a purse to endow my freedom. It was the least he could do, especially if he planned upon leaving me here with his child in my belly. He could afford it; I knew little of his business, except that it thrived, and entailed many visits to the apothecaries, wine shops and the boatmen of Cannaregio.

Waiting by the *ruota*, I wondered if he would long punish me like this. I decided not to wait for him, and so preserve the fragments of my dignity.

On my way back to my cell, I noted bitter smiles in my wake. How quick were the other nuns to mark my misfortune! I whispered unconvincingly, 'I have mistaken the night. It was to be tomorrow.' Yet still I heard a little knot of gossipers confer in the hall outside my cell, and my name mentioned, and one long, dry laugh. I had not made any friends among the nuns: there was no one to defend me, even among those who had shared their amatory adventures with me. We were only co-conspirators; there was no warmth between us. In the refectory next morning, seventy pairs of eyes were lifted triumphantly above my head to gaze at a point just over my left ear.

My status would diminish fast if I did not quickly recapture my lover's affections. By our usual messenger, the butcher's boy who came daily to the *ruota* for his orders, I sent him a tender letter. I promised to do better. I assured him of my passionate, faithful, subordinate love. But still the next night I waited in vain. And the morning after that the butcher boy stammered the news that my lover would not pay for the delivery of another letter from me.

On the third night I crept out, making my way out of the gate and disappearing to the Riva degli Schiavoni. My lover had long since arranged things so that I had my own key, and could meet him in the shadow of the church. But I had no safe haven in which to pass the requisite hours. I could hardly go all the way to his rooms at Rialto. I had no money for a gondola and I flinched at the thought of what might await me there. So I walked up and down the street, pausing to watch the monster-mongers and the retailers of strange sights touting their hermaphrodites, pygmies, mermaids taken on the coast of Acapulco and ambulant Egyptian mummies, all such things that appealed to the imagination of the Venetian crowd. My spirits, however, were too low to be enticed into credulity, so this enter-tainment soon palled, and I turned my attention to the mountebanks selling their nostrums from their swagged and painted platforms.

I felt nostalgia for my old life, when my parents dressed me up like an elegant doll to attend the theatre, where we sat in the family box, attended by liveried servants. Now I was reduced to seeking free amusement from the theatrical charlatans of the *riva*, just like any poor peasant or foreigner newly arrived in Venice. Yet I stayed out among them for three hours, enjoying the shows, even forgetting myself as I listened to the quacks' speeches about their Balsamick Dew brushed from a banana in the Gardens of Babylon, or their vials of Restorative Snow col-lected in the crags of the Caucasus. One brandished a pure white candle, embodying, so he declared, some precious oils extracted from a Royal Spermaceti Whale that had sacrificed itself upon the shore of the River Thames in far-off London, at a place charmingly denominated Blackfriars. Some of these nostrums had even attained the dignity of printed handbills, which I col-lected with relish and stuffed into my pockets. It was a long time since I had been given anything other than religious tracts to read, and I looked forward to the diversion that these ridicu-lous high-flown texts would afford me later in my cell.

When I slipped back into the convent just before midnight, I made sure that my happy sighs and yawns could be heard all down the corridors. I washed noisily and I cried out my lover's name, as if in the ecstasy of a dream, in the middle of the night.

And so I did for the next three evenings, trying to forget my plight among the crowds of the *riva*, mingling with the strangers and Venetians, taking solace from the unaccustomed press of carefree bodies and the colourful entertainment on the mountebank stages. On the third night I took some coins with me and bought a Consolating Mixture against the troubles of childbirth. I knew that it was unlikely to help me, but the fact of having bought it was consoling in itself. I hid the bottle behind a curtain on my window-sill.

On the fourth night I was followed. Someone must have learned something or perhaps I had performed my part with too much feeling. As I slipped out, I felt a shadow detach from me and when I entered the narrow *calle* that leads to the *riva*, I heard the unmistakable slither of discreet feminine footsteps behind me. It had to be pure coincidence; no one suspected me. But all evening, as I wandered among the tooth-pullers and fortune-tellers and those colourful purveyors of magical potions, I had an uneasy sense of company. And when I returned to the grille, the abbess was waiting for me there, with a contingent of her flunkeys. Her face was grim, and without ceremony she gripped my shoulder and rubbed a rough hand over my belly.

'I thought as much,' she said, coldly, and then she kicked my feet out from under me so that I fell forwards on to the stone.

It was then I knew that he had betrayed me. My heart fell immediately into that state that cannot be repaired, and it continued to beat only by grace of mechanical habit.

· 7 ·

A Julep for Child-Bed Women

Take waters of Baulm, and Black Cherries, each 3 ounces; of
Barley Cinnamon, and Dr Stephens's waters, and Syrup of
Meconium, each 2 ounces; Liquid Laudanum 40 drops, mix.

It's a blessed and well-experimented Remedy for Puerperal
After-Pains: And none here need fear stopping the Lochia, for
that most frequently is occasioned by intense Pain, which by
troubling the orderly Motion of the Spirits, convulsing the
Fibres, constringing the Membranes of the Uterus, and Vagina,
and pursing up the Mouths of the Vessels, suppresses the efflux
by these ways: And therefore, Opiates that take off those
Pains, hurry of Spirits, and Constrictions of Fibres, must
needs promote the Purgation, and render it placid and
plentiful.

My belly swelled hard as a barrel and my complexion flowered,
my right nipple turned darker first, and I also favoured my right
foot when walking. All this confirmed what I already knew: the
baby was a boy. When my time came near, the midwife told me
with evident relish that my natal passage appeared too slender to
allow the great babe an entrance into this world. The nuns threw
up their eyes and clasped their hands piously, as if it were a
godly act for me to sacrifice my life for his brat.

I gulped my sweet Consolating Mixture the night my pains
began, hoping for oblivion.

I remember little of my travails, for they continually spiced my
water with more sedatives, hoping to quieten my screams. In the
end I fell unconscious, and believed, on leaving the bloody scene
in spirit, that I would never again wake up in the flesh.

33

My thoughts were confused and angry. I had not seen my lover again, after our last great fight. He had evidently 'handled' the problem of me remotely, paying the nuns to shelter and midwife me, and to keep my condition secret from my parents. Instead of springing me free from the convent, he had me imprisoned there in a worse state than before. Even so, I could not renounce hope entirely. Every day of my pregnancy I had asked the nuns: 'Is there any message? Do I go to him today?' They pursed their lips and looked away, until I ceased asking.

The nuns concealed my stomach in shapeless gowns. I had no visitors in any case: my last tirade through the grille of the *parlatorio* had so offended my mother that she had decreed that none of our relations might come to see me. My cousins and aunts within the convent shunned me entirely. When my pains started, I was as usual alone in my cell, and it was there that they brought the midwife, whose sweating, ugly face was the last thing I saw before I slipped from consciousness.

When I awoke, I was again alone, weak and sore. There was a smell of blood, sweat and soap in the room, all unpleasantly fused. I felt my belly: it was lumpy and tender, but clearly emptied of its burden. I raised the sheet and saw that my nether parts were bound up in tight clean linens from beneath which bloomed great dark bruises halfway down my thighs. I looked around for the little creature that should be resting somewhere near by. There was nothing. Not even an empty cot, or swaddling clothes or a feeding horn, or any sign of maternity whatsoever. I could not raise my head. I tried to call for help, but my throat was raw and painful.

I lay still, whimpering with resentment. How dare they leave me alone? And I a Golden Book daughter, owner of a name a thousand years old! I screamed piteously that they had stolen my child and intended to leave me to die. Eventually I wore myself out and passed into sleep again, still sobbing.

When I next roused, they were changing the damp and bloody linens around my privities. To lessen the shame, I still pretended at sleep until the dry rags were fastened and my shift pulled down over my thighs. Then I opened my eyes and beheld the midwife and two nuns whispering by the door to my cell. I tried to speak but my throat was still constricted. I stared at them with imploring eyes until they noticed that I was awake. They began to speak to me in cool, impersonal tones. In chorus, as if rehearsed, they told me that my son was dead. They explained, all three looking at the floor, that he had tried to emerge with his face and not the crown of his head to the fore, increasing the difficulties of a near-impossible birth. With his large head he threatened to tear me in half. They had been instructed to spare me rather than the child, should the choice arise, and so they called in a doctor who had used the cranioclast on him.

'What is that thing?' I croaked. 'Cranioclast?' Still looking at the floor, they described the instrument, an iron tool used to reach into the birth cavern and break the skull of mother-splitting babies. The doctor had pushed the cranioclast inside me, the pain being almost unnoticeable amid the tearing contractions. But in hearing of it, I thought I remembered a man's voice and the sensation of cold metal inside me.

'That was when I fainted?' I asked.

They nodded.

'What happened then?'

Unwillingly, they told me. All within the theatre of my womb, the doctor had sliced the child's skull in two halves, sucked out the contents with a syringe and squeezed the broken bones together. The crushed, dead baby was then pulled out with a hook. All this had happened while I was still unconscious.

'And my throat?' I whispered. 'Why does it hurt so much?'

'We were obliged to insert a tube to keep you irrigated with laudanum. Had you woken or moved while he worked the cranioclast and hook then you would have been in the greatest danger.'

My wits being capable of absorbing no more horrors, I fell asleep, for many hours, and when I awoke, I had been freshly dressed below. I licked my lips and found the traces of oat pap on them: they had also fed me while I slept.

For days this was my life. Deprived of my own baby I had

indeed returned to being one myself. I allowed myself only infant feelings: those of heat, coldness, satisfaction and voiding.

Later they told me that my absent lover had returned to London, and I asked for the money he had left for my new life outside the convent.

They claimed that these funds had already been exhausted in the care of me during the birth and after. The doctor with the cranioclast was the most expensive in Venice. He fee'd extra for such emergencies. The drugs lavished on me during my recovery were also of the costliest kind, they added coldly, as if they considered this a poor investment.

'You have lived,' they told me sternly. 'You may count yourself fortunate.'

And so they robbed me of my last portion of freedom, having already murdered my son.

· 8 ·

A Camphorate Electuary

Take Conserve of Rue 3 ounces; Venice Treacle 1 ounce; Camphor 8 grains; Oil of Amber 16 drops, mix.

It reprimands the Animal Spirits when too furious, and ready for Tumult and Explosion, disciplines them into order again, shakes off their heterogeneous Copula, and sometimes expels it quite. Upon these Accounts, it's found by Experience to be very serviceable to Hysteric Women, howbeit some cannot away with the odious Ructus, which Oil Amber causeth.

I myself cared little whether I lived or died, but the pull of life was not to be resisted.

When my brain recovered some of its vitality, I acted frailer than I was. Mutinous thoughts were stirring. I was not going to be confined in the convent for ever, despite what they told me. I lay on my pallet, pondering a viable plan for my subsistence in the world outside.

My lover had frequently taunted me that he had rarely seen better melodramatics on the stage. As I had indeed manufactured much of my behaviour in his presence, I confess I fancied myself a very adequate actress.

So this was my hazy ambition: that I would escape the convent – the walls of which had already proved themselves porous to such plans – and become an actress at one of the theatres in Venice. It seemed ludicrously simple. When I regained my health I would slip out on the pretext of an errand, or secretly, using my key. My accent and aristocratic features would ensure me any theatrical interview I desired. I thought my charms

37

invincible and my confidence remained boundless despite the painful setback I had just endured.

I had reckoned without my new loss of status. While other sportive nuns might quite easily leave the convent for their adventures, I alone was now guarded every hour of the day and night. My key to the outside world had disappeared during my confinement. I was given to believe that my parents had somehow been informed of my recent adventure and had commanded more rigid supervision. I did not believe it. There were times when I asked my guards if my lover had paid them for their vigils, and they always shook their heads.

'It is your Mamma and your Papa,' they grinned. 'They are worried for their little girl.'

Then they saw tantrums that were real: screams, tearing of my clothes, even the beating of my head against marble door-frames. They remained impassive, turning the vast rusty keys in the three locks that were thought necessary to contain me. There were never fewer than two nuns outside my door, and, when they came to bring me food and water, they were always attended by a third.

And I never heard a word from my lover. I guessed that without the baby to bind me to him, I was even less safe in his regard. I was just another troublesome lover. Perhaps he even resented me for the incompetent birth that had robbed him of an heir.

Whatever his motives, he never manifested himself in person or by letter. Yet still I talked of him brightly, as if this temporary absence had been agreed between us. I saw them shake their heads, which were split with bitter little smiles. I informed them loftily that my key to the gate by the *ruota* had been stolen by some jealous nun while I slept. When I asked for it, they met my imperious request with pitying smiles that raised a turmoil of bile and fear in my stomach. When I screamed insults at them they told me they were not sorry for me personally, but, from the superiority of their virgin state, they pitied foolish, weak womankind, prey to debilitating lusts and therefore clever men. I was an example of such a degraded object, wasting my shuddering heart on a man with all the tenderness of a brandished hammer. How they enjoyed their righteous miniature sermons! How I abused them, and with what foul language! Until they backed away, blushing and tearful.

After that, they sent a *conversa* to lie in my cell with me, presumably to report on the words I muttered in my dreams. I could not sleep with her in there. I found loathsome both the idea and the very odour of her . . . She was not a kinswoman, the *conversa*, and, being of the lower class of sisters, she wore no perfume or pomade. Her naked smell of milk, soap and musty skin operated repulsively upon my nerves: I told her so. I demanded exclusively Golden Book women around me, insisting that I was used to a greater refinement. My guard slipped away, mouse-snouted, to inform on me. The abbess herself came all the way up to my cell to lash me with her tongue.

'There is a difference between being exclusive and being refined,' she told me, her voice flat and harsh. 'These humble women are of good character. You, who have been docile to every vice, have no pretensions to being their better. It ill behoves you to demand company that smells sweeter than your own conscience.'

I thought I had nothing left to lose: I was not afraid of her.

'Are we not in Venice?' I asked sarcastically. 'Have we been transported to Heaven, where blood counts for nothing and all women are equal, and none more noble than others?'

Trembling with rage, the abbess regarded me. Her mouth moved, but no words came out. She swept out of my cell and I heard her galloping with undignified haste down the corridor, a noise accompanied, as ever, by the rasp of poor nuns chafing with rags at the wainscoting already bare with such punishment. No doubt the abbess wished she might put me to such ignominious work. But no matter how bad my behaviour, my family name set me above that fate. After this confrontation, I was left alone in my cell, dwindled to a creature that was fed and watered, but ignored.

Soon a new torture emerged: when I asked after my lover, they shook their heads as if they did not know what I was talking about.

I screamed out his name, again and again. They mimed complete ignorance of him, smiling as if I played some childish game with them. I screamed more, and they turned away, saying, 'There is no such man.'

They would not allow me to purge my bitterness by expressing it to them. As soon as I began to bewail my situation they disappeared and I was left to tell my sorrows to the damp, leprous walls, down which indeed clammy tears trailed in the only semblance of compassion I ever saw at San Zaccaria.

As soon as I was well enough to walk, I was dragged before the *capitolo delle colpe* to confess my sins of lust and disobedience. I shouted at the sisters, 'When I was committing them, you never bothered to caution me!' When they moved to silence me I hissed, 'It's only now I've stopped that you condemn me. How much did he pay you? Did you turn away the money?'

A gag of linen infused with bitter herbs was put over my mouth and I was led back to my solitary cell. From that day forth my one remaining pleasure was denied me: no more sweet food was brought into my room. Just unsweetened porridge, salty bread and unspiced meats. But I could smell the convent kitchen and I could still make out the fragrant steam of every different cake as it billowed through the air. Those cakes became my calendar for I had no other way of marking the days. On Mondays there was *panpepato*, on Tuesdays marzipan cakes, on Wednesdays tarts made with fruit preserves, on Thursdays *biscotti* with honey and pine-nuts, on Fridays ginger wafers, on Saturdays *fritelle*. On Sundays, there was no smell at all, except of candle grease, and just one cruel Sabbath, the warm perfume of chocolate, when some giggling sister left a cup of my favourite beverage on the deep sill outside my window, just beyond reach.

My baby died in the spring.

Summer passed, then autumn, and I never left my cell. I never ate anything that was not merely a tasteless fibre. I drank only water from a chipped cup. My own Murano glass goblet had disappeared. I never spoke to anyone except purse-lipped nuns who clapped their hands rather than speak to me, as if my breath contaminated the air. I amused the gloomy hours of my incarceration with practising my pretty voice. I sang all the songs I knew, dwelling bitterly on those that spoke of betrayal. My voice grew sweet and strong, its echoes haunting the corridors. Draped rather than dressed in white rags, I sat hunched in my cell like a mummy, my head down, my mouth open, my eyes blank, singing my unholy dirges. I frightened myself to think how I looked; a spectre of evil and misery; inhuman and repulsive.

Winter came, sealing the convent in snow. My cell was icy. When I beat the door, screaming for blankets and a fire, they whispered through the keyhole that my parents had refused to spend on such trappings for my cell, in order that I might learn humility through fortitude.

I shrieked until a delegation of nuns came and opened the door, ready to chastise me. Even that they did in whispers. No one knows how to whisper like a nun. No woman can make her face as immobile, her eyes darting all the while!

'We will make you behave like a proper nun,' one simpered, and pulled her habit open a little to show me the hair vest she wore.

'Whatever gives you pleasure,' I suggested maliciously, and they filed out in silence, giving the key an extra turn as they left.

As the metal groaned in the lock, I snapped an icicle from the window of my cell. I cut open a vein in my calf and let a pool of blood throb into my water cup. I tore the linen from my bed, dipped my forefinger in the cup and wrote his name in blood, in letters as long as my arm. Then I bound up the wound with a strip torn from the same sheet.

Still clutching the icicle in my hand, I screamed at the top of my voice.

When the nuns came bustling through the door they were confronted with the banner draped over my window, with the faint light behind it blackening the blood that spelled out my lover's name. *Then* they showed some emotion. One cried out and another fainted. The third stood rooted to the spot, mouthing the word I had written.

It was the first time I had heard his name in a year.

I could not breathe.

But I hardened my heart, and I took my chance then.

· 9 ·

A Draught for a Bruise

Take Canary 4 ounces; Oil of Turpentine 10 drops; Sealed Earth,
Dragon's Blood powder'd, each 1 scruple; white Sugar 2 drams,
mix.

It absorbs acrious, extravasated Serum, preserves the due
mixture of the Blood, impresses on it a Balsamick Consolidating
Character, and stints inward Bleeding.

I did not mean to hurt the nun. I intended only to terrorise her
into immobility, to permit my escape. It was not my fault that she
ran into the icicle I still brandished in my hand. It was to be a
warning, not a weapon. But, in the dimness of my cell, the
translucent ice must have been invisible to her when she ran
towards me shouting threats. I felt it meet her eyeball and penetrate its jelly. In God's name, I did try to pull it out then. But it
slid out of my hand and deeper into her eye until the makeshift
hilt snapped off and fell to the floor. I was left looking only at my
own fingers, slick with blood and melted ice.

For a moment all of us stood motionless. But as she collapsed
to the ground and the other two nuns rushed to her, I glimpsed
the open door to the stairs at the end of the corridor, and I ran
out of the cell before I even had time to think of what I had done.

Trailing blood from my calf, weak from my long incarceration,
I staggered down to the source of cold light in the first cloister
and limped along its periphery. Seeing no one, I boldly ran
across the second courtyard and rushed to the orchard of the
convent. At the far end of the trees was another door, the one
with the grille and the *ruota* beside it.

There was the remotest chance that the door might be open.

But I found it locked against me. I raked my hands over its surface, pocking my fingers with painful splinters. I threw my weight against it. I beat my head on it. I knelt and scrabbled at its base. Finally I spat at it, again and again, as if some venom in my saliva might dissolve it. By then the throbbing in my leg had spread through my whole body which was at the same time devoured by a fever.

That was how they found me, spitting at a door and screaming. By then, they had summoned some serving boys from the nearby tavern. My pursuers had tracked me by the blood that gushed from my wound. I was soon restrained and tied to a wooden plank which they rested between two tree stumps in the orchard. There they left me, in the cruel cold, for many hours, to cool my murderous rage, they said. They made no move to clean or dress my leg, perhaps hoping that I would die without their further intervention and that they might then say it was of natural causes, that I had hidden myself in the garden and frozen to death in the night.

I almost wished to satisfy them. I felt no guilt for harming the nun, though she must have been suffering unspeakable agonies from the wound I had inflicted: someone had come to whisper the news to me, to tell me that the contusion had spread and both eyes were thought beyond repair. My informant took this opportunity to empty a pitcher of foul water over my head. The water soon turned to ice, so that my hair hung down in whitened stalactites. Eventually the cold brought on a pleasant kind of delirium. I fancied myself toast-warm in front of a fire with my lover and I murmured lewd words to him. I imagined us engaged in amorous congress and I raised my frozen hips to meet his again and again. Perhaps it is in this way, by keeping in motion, by not succumbing to torpor, that I stayed alive.

As the birds began to open their throats in the pearly darkness just before dawn, I started to feel the cold again, and to ponder the consequences of my act. I was so young, so ignorant, that I had no idea if the nuns might commit me to a summary justice of their own, perhaps stoning me to death, or if I would be bundled into a carriage and sent to Rome to be quartered and burned in the Campo dei Fiori.

I began to be conscious of sounds and smells: the unmistakable rustle of a large rat, the stale stench of the dirty water thawing in my hair. The darkness was leaking by increments from the sky to reveal the black tracery of winter-stripped branches overhead, those same branches from which the nuns had hung sweet jellies to tempt me when I was a child. I licked my dry lips and tried to swivel my head, but they had bound me cruelly across the neck and forehead, even tying string, ignominiously, around my ears.

I was falling into delirium again when five of the *signori di notte* came to take me away, four to carry me and one to guide our way with a flaming torch. They bore me, still on the plank, through the gate held open by the abbess and two of her hench-women, who saluted me with grim smiles.

First we crossed the *campo* of San Zaccaria diagonally. The church leered up like an Oriental ziggurat. There was nothing of Christian kindness in its barbarous frontage. We left it behind and proceeded into the throat of the *calle* that led towards San Provolo. Passing under the arch, I glimpsed the exquisite relief of the Madonna to whom I had once compared myself. After a moment, that was gone and I heard one of the guards grunt. The night sky then swung round and I was semi-upright, looking on stone: they were carrying me over a bridge. From the top of the bridge, where they levelled me again, I had a glimpse down the canal all the way to the lagoon, which loosed on me a spiteful tongue of gelid air. I was tipped backwards as we descended again. My stomach rose up in rebellion and I choked on bile. Then I was righted, and we continued on our way.

Above me the first tatters of dawn light struck the sneering snouts of stone lions on marble balconies. Beneath them the ivory-coloured teeth of the cornices gnashed in and out of the shadows. In serried stone arches wrought-metal lanterns dangled from their chains like hunting spiders, as our silent passage disturbed the dead air around them.

I stared on my city as if it was a dream. The dark canals, the Gothic windows, the courtyards and the bridges all appeared unreal to me. I looked up at towering walls, everything distorted by my strange viewpoint so that the *palazzi* loomed over me like

44

bewitched trees in the dark-hearted forest of a nightmare in which a black-clad, hooded troop of men carried a girl with frozen hair on a plank.

The crust that had formed over my leg wound broke open. I felt the warm trickle of blood – we must have left a trail of drops in our wake. In time to the officers' steps I whispered, 'Please, please, please, please.' They looked away. I continued to keen, 'Please don't hurt me.' They marched on like enchanted toy soldiers. I soon lost my bearings and eventually closed my eyes.

When I woke I was inside a large room and a man was looking down on me with a kindly expression. My leg felt tight: in the warmth the wound had sealed itself again.

He must be the torturer, I thought, wary of his smile, for it is well known that these men love their work, and therefore the beings on whom they practise their arts.

But he was elegantly dressed, well shod and did not stink of beer or urine. His hands were beautifully kept, I noticed, as he brushed the hair from my forehead. He was of my own class. I did not know if this was better or worse for me.

'So this is our saintly little vixen,' he said. 'You have put us in a considerable dilemma.'

His voice was smooth, his accent patrician. I wondered how well he knew my parents. Did they wait outside to beg for my life? But if they cared not whether I froze to death in the nunnery, why should they want to save me now?

I was soon enlightened. My companion explained that my parents were even now being woken with the news that I had died in the struggle with the nun I had stabbed.

It had been decided that this was the best course. A Golden Book daughter, he told me sternly, could never be brought before the court for a violent act. The whole city would be destabilised by such an event. Golden Book daughters were not permitted to be guilty of such crimes. And if I were to be cleared: why, that would be worse. Not just noble nuns but also the daughters of merchants and the daughters of glassmakers would get it into their heads that they might take a knife – or an icicle – to anyone who displeased them.

My companion shook his head sadly. 'You see what difficulties you present,' he said, gently.

For the first time I spoke. 'Why don't you strangle me now and burn my body? It is the only solution.'

I had blurted out my worst fears, hoping to have them assuaged. He smiled again to let me know that my fate would be otherwise.

'It is not the only solution. We can offer you another.'

The room was growing hot. My hair was melting and water trickled from it, noisily striking the floorboards, forming a glistening puddle that glowed like blood-flecked gold powder, reflecting the fire that roared menacingly in the grate.

'But of course, you are in discomfort,' he said kindly, 'and in no condition to consider our proposal sanely.' He rang a bell and two women appeared. They cut my bonds with little stiletto daggers and helped me rise. I stood unsteadily, and peered around the luxurious room, which was decorated with frescoes of a grandeur I had not seen since my parents expelled me from our home. Meanwhile the man gave instructions to the women, who regarded me with blank eyes.

They took me to an antechamber, pushed a chamber-pot beneath me. While I sat on it they filled a large tub with jugfuls of warm water and gently removed my clothes. They washed my aching limbs and my matted hair, leaving me to soak for many minutes. The warmth of the water rinsed all thoughts from my tired mind, and soon the room grew dim about me. I smelled the rich clot of an ointment gently rubbed into my wound. I closed my eyes then and when I opened them again the water had grown cool, and the room had been lit with dozens of candles.

Twelve men surrounded me. I felt their eyes on my nakedness, on the pale curls that had dried in a cascade that spilled over the edge of the bath. My nipples, rising above the water, were puckered in the cold air. I was unable to move or speak.

Among the men I detected my recent companion. He told me: 'You have no reason to feel afraid.'

I said nothing. How could I answer such a patent lie?

Part Two

Sweet Glyster

Take New Cows' Milk 6 ounces; Melassos 2 ounces, mix.

This Glyster is to be made use of, before the bitter one, whilst the Worms lying in the small Guts bite and gnaw and cause the Belly-ache. For they will greedily make to the Milk, which is sweet and delicious to them, and so leaving off biting, will come out of their lurking Holes, and crawl downwards and lie ready easy to be cast out by Siege.

When they murdered my Pa, that was a good day for me.

For a start, I was made ward of the handsomest man in London, my Pa's best friend, Valentine Greatrakes.

And after that there were plenty of treats with Uncle Valentine, very nice indeed, even with his long face about my Pa's passing.

He kept all the details prodigious snug, as if I were a little girl. So, soon as I could, at Don Saltero's Coffee House, I went foraging in the pockets of his greatcoat while he went out to buy a newspaper, and that's when I found the letter from Smerghetto, the man who conducts the Venetian end of their business.

Smerghetto had identified my Pa's body on the slab in Venice, and this was his report.

I scanned the letter quickly and replaced it in the pocket before my guardian returned. I resumed cheering him with choice conversation. The day proceeded to our joint satisfaction, including a vastly good spread of cakes and two cups of spiced chocolate. Then we went to Madame Cornelys' in Knightsbridge for some sweet Asses' Milk, which is always so renovating to the appetite. Afterwards we ate cutlets and damson pudding. I like to think that I consoled Uncle Valentine considerably. He really was very finely cut up about my Pa's death.

'Poor little Pevenche,' he whispered sorrowfully, when he took me back to the Academy. For some reason he had not invited me to go to the theatre with him. Yet it seemed to me that he could scarce stop himself weeping at our goodbye. You see, they were of the same age, and my Pa's cut-short life must have made him think to himself. Also, my Pa was in Venice on their mutual business. You *could* say Uncle Valentine had sent him to his death. I saw all these thoughts soaking through that remarkable face of his when he turned it in my direction.

Then he was gone, not before thoughtfully reminding Mistress Haggardoon to administer my Sweet Glyster without fail.

Later, over supper, I reviewed the contents of the letter, which listed every wound on my Pa's body in a businesslike way.

Only the last words puzzled me: 'And his face was raped with fish.'

Smerghetto wrote as if it was clear, but for me the words conjured only blurred visions of thrashing fins and white eyes marbled with blood. I supposed that Smerghetto had botched the translation.

He did not put forward any theories about why anyone would want to do away with my Pa. But that didn't require too much thinking about. Apart from the matter of the fish, this kind of end is not uncommon in his line of business, which of course they all think I know nothing about, living genteelly as I do at Marylebone, in Mistress Haggardoon's Academy for Young Ladies.

I know plenty. I know about the rolls of nun-made lace smoothed inside the packets of chocolate. The wax figurines faintly gurgling with stashes of taxable liquors. The glass daggers vertebrating candles in wooden boxes. The hollow glass eyes, the painted bottles of holy water, the finest nostrums quackery can distil, cunningly packaged. All these things pass through Venetian hands before they make their way to the grand depository of Valentine Greatrakes at Bankside, on the wrong side of the Thames.

There must have been one among them who thought his palm not greased as fatly as it should be?

On the other hand, knowing my Pa, it was as like to have been a husband.

London, late November 1785

· 1 ·

A Traumatic Infusion

Take green Twigs of woody Nightshade (cut like Sarsaparilla) 4 ounces; Cochineal 1 scruple; White-wine 1 quart; infuse hot and close, all Night; then, having strained out the Liquor, add Syrup of Ground Ivy 4 ounces; Venice Treacle half an ounce, mix.

It's a singular Experiment in a Contusion; for it dissolves extravasated Clots of Gore, after a marvellous manner, drives it again into the circulating Mass of Blood; and there, partly by Diaphoreisis, partly diuresis, and sometimes by Purging, throws it out of the Body.

Sometimes a man goes to the theatre just to bury his troubles for the duration. And sometimes he comes home with new ones.

Valentine Greatrakes, poached in hate and no wonder, cuts through the throng. Toes wince under his ebony cane. Theatregoers flitter like ashes in front of his livid eye. Yet what he wants is to inter his raving self, every Irish atom of it, among living souls.

Like when a man whispers a blade between two ribs and lets it lie quiet there awhile in the meaty midnightish redness.

There's nothing else to be done with his great heart-broken self tonight. He needs the close company of others to sheath the stinging vision that's driven him out of the house.

'The wounds were not done with artistry.'

That's how Smerghetto, sparing of sentiment, phrased it in the letter that still stiffens the pocket of the heavy coat Valentine presently drops upon the buckling cloakroom attendant. He disdains the proffered ivory ticket. The clerk will not be forgetting him.

That final insult Tom did not deserve. His own finesse with the knife is living legend round Bankside.

Yes, several's been the funerals of one of our enemies where the widow shyly complimented me on his neat work.

One such once-wife had caught Valentine's eye this May past and he had an entire mourning bed delivered to her, black posts, black pall, black blankets; even black sheets and before long he his own great self was enjoying the black pleasures between them with her. But a widow is an exacting species of woman, and when that one grew needsome, not to say a little venal, he'd had the bed removed to the house of a pretty wife Tom had more freshly bereaved for him.

Tom.

There were no cuts on the dorsal plane of Tom's right hand: he had not even tried to fend off his assailant. Nor were there lesions to his palm: so after the murderer fell on him, he had no time or power left for plucking out the knife himself. The fatal wounds to his neck and side were both inflicted while he was still alive, for there was a fast flow of gore and a rim of coagulated blood between the lips of each incision. Blood stops flowing after death, Smerghetto explained.

As if I did not know that for myself.

Tom was probably two days in dying.

And all that time he was alone, behind the bridge at Rialto in the desert wakes of a Saturday night. So the body lay undiscovered until Monday morning, hidden under fish waste and, by that time, mingling with it. The sepsis, the report continued, started slowly and then came the gangrene, which requires no air to breathe but obstructs the blood to the affected organs. And then the mortification, the discolouring of the skin flagging the massacre of Tom's inner particles.

When they had finally found him, he was melting into the canal. Drop by drop, the gangrene had liquefied his flesh. No one could say, Smerghetto had written, when he had lost consciousness, for how long he suffered the pain of his wounds, if he could smell his own putrefaction, if he had time to ponder on his murderer's identity or motive. Evidently, he had been too weak to scrawl the name

54

in his own blood, the code of their kind, to help those who will avenge him, not least of whom is Valentine Greatrakes. No one could tell Smerghetto what poison was used on the tip of the blade; the murderer must have pulled the weapon out and made off with it so that it could not be examined.

Valentine flows with the crowd into the gilded barrel of the theatre.

It simmers hot as a glassworks inside. The lace at his wrist wilts, embracing his fingers in a corpse's handshake. Gasping candles despatch gouts of wax down the walls, clotting the carpets below. The mumble of voices hustles the air around in clammy arcs. Upstairs in the five- and three-shilling galleries they must be fainting like flies. The ladies and the so-called ladies flap their fans with such hectic energy that the stalls look like the breeding grounds of an enormous species of moth. The fans throb the faint stink of theatre drains into a living pungency. Something is on the fret deep below the stalls.

Valentine makes his way to a ten-shilling seat in the front of the aristocrats' enclosure. Who would dare deny him? His new neighbours flick him uneasy glances and then gaze intently in another direction, hiding the nervy drumming of their fingers in downturned palms. Even this, inaudible beneath the whining and cavilling of stringed instruments tuning up, feeds Valentine's fury. He loathes all these people calling out to each other in stage whispers, stupidly lifting their heads like birds drinking to gaze round the honeycombed galleries, or prematurely becalmed in slackmouthed spectators' passivity.

Why don't they ever get started on the stage? It's well after seven.

He's sweating like a tumbler of iced beer, rubbing his back against the seat like a riggish dog. A woman behind him sniffs and he turns to fix her with a look that makes her recoil in her chair, her cheeks sucked in like paper bags and the whites straining out of her eyes.

This is of course by no means the normal state of play with the ladies. It's just that Valentine's pleasing features are temporarily deranged. Otherwise she, like all women, would have grown astoundingly fond and flirtish merely at the sight of that lean face and the shapely nose that lists very slightly to the right. The amiable slant of his eyebrows lends him a habitual expression of irrepressible good humour, and he can arch them independently, and frequently does so, in a way that never fails to endear. He wears his own auburn hair, even to the theatre, and it grows so fine and gleaming soft that no one misses the wig. The offended woman is already hoping that he can feel her regretful sigh caressing his neck.

At last the velvet shuffles up on the stage. A breath of dusted air belches out from a radiant slit in the pall. The first true note of a violin makes a wet punch through the flabby chatter of the theatregoers. Officious people start shushing, and others mock the shushers with exaggerated shushes of their own. The curtain lifts on a rustic Italianate scene and the actors burst into ragged song and shabbier dancing.

Now he's more than willing to be pleased, but this is not enough for Valentine, not by a long way. He shifts endlessly in his seat, unsticking his thighs from its hot embrace.

It's the usual mediocre fare, he thinks, *there's no relief to be had here.*

He's about to rise and push his way out of the stalls when the leading lady makes her entrance.

She does so as the virgin of the piece. This is spelled out, as if in a printed caption, by the fact that she's dressed in white gauze (fitted to her body with the utmost niceness), fever-spotted in the lily cheek, and subtly rouged at the tender point where her breasts meet. Each step is hesitant, childlike, but all the same avid. And every male actor she now encounters, for she straightaway does the rounds of them on a pretext of some inquiry, is pictured in the minds of the audience violently astride her. Yes, definitely the maiden: this does not happen in the case of actresses impersonating married women or widows.

At first sight I cannot endure her looks, she's nothing to me, I wouldn't go next or near to her, and nor would Tom have given her a second backways glance, much less the clicket she's offering gratis to every man in this hall with that look over her shoulder.

The thought of Tom affixes Valentine to his seat again.

Is Tom's murderer still at large in Venice or has he come to London now to continue his massacres? Does Valentine himself know the poxed dog that did it? Will his revenge be more savoury if he does?

You'll not be going on alone, Tom.

He scans his memory for sundry Venetians black-affronted by any of their little enterprises or by Tom's being so very nimble in the act of friction with their ladies. But no known face, merchant, spouse or father, is conjured in Valentine's mind by these ruminations: just the anonymous silhouette of a monster raising the dagger again and again over Tom's cringing form.

From up on the stage the Italian actress tugs at his attention. Suddenly, she has it all. The jaws of the music are snapping around her. Now she parleys with the man who will save her from ravishment. And there's the would-be ravisher himself, a fine pinguid specimen, hair black as a sooty raven, staking his claim with a lewd motion of the hips, forcing into Valentine's unwilling mind the memory of those inexplicable and unbearable words in Smerghetto's letter: 'And his face was raped with fish.'

A snake is eating his heart. He cannot bear it. He half-rises to leave.

Then the heroine utters a raw-boned cry of agony and commences to weep utterly genuine and copious tears. Valentine drops back in his seat.

Damn me if she's not the most delectable woman I ever saw in a public place.

In that moment, every flea, satisfied or not, departs from Valentine's electrified body and finds other accommodation in the pit. He fumbles with the playbill, unwrapping the crushed ball of it in his hand. She goes under the soubriquet, he reads, of 'Mimosina Dolcezza'.

Well, she would, wouldn't she? Her breasties mouthfulling even from this distance, neat as a bee's toe in that dress. You could run a mill with those tears.

By some freak of passage, a plump tear shaken from her lash flies suddenly across the pit and lands upon Valentine's own mouth, slips in through that astonished hole, jackets his tongue in its salty melt and kisses his tonsils like linctus.

Would you listen to that lady? In the blue yonder of my wildest dreams I never heard a voice like that.

The other actors on the stage are marionetting through their roles, and yet *she* puts flesh and blood into every word, butters every morsel of a body's feelings with that creamy voice. Her song reaches out to Valentine and fondles his ears, runs a finger down his sensitive back. He feels a great heat in his heart and the parts adjacent to it.

And his head's a-smoke with the ember of an idea.

His hands prickle as he looks back at the programme. And by a grim and curious coincidence it turns out she's Venetian herself, or so it suits the entrepreneur to style her in his fulsome biography of the actress.

And when she must show herself unhappy she makes like a cat that is unwell, a dolefulness that loses nothing of its grace. No, really, she's too dear for an ordinary body.

Something of her bearing brings to his mind the image of Tom's orphaned daughter, now his ward, who Tom always insisted, had conversation so original as to still a party quite to rigor mortis, so intent did one become not to lose one mere word by interrupting the torrent with a reply. And such forest-floor ideas too as to give a body the lockjaw just to hear them. And she a large size of child and never let out of school to be interfered with by anyone!

It's going to stay that way, too. That, at least, I can do for Tom.

The moustachioed villain menaces. There seems a real danger that the *ingénue*'s purity will be extinguished by the villain. Soft and languishing, she pleads her case, in breathy whispers and delicate coloratura. It is to no avail. He *will* debauch her. The actress faints. Her torso dips into a spillage of petticoats and she concludes with her head coddled in a hand, ringlets splayed about her so her face is like a luminous egg in a soft nest. Valentine suddenly feels the comprehensive sensation of lying behind her, cradling her hip against his own. *Astonishing.* He glances at his neighbours, both men breathing hard, gripped by the same fantasy.

The difference between those chinless toothpicks and myself is that I could be there if I wanted. I know the manager of this place and it would be the work of a few minutes to have him owe me a tangible favour.

The story onstage plays itself out to its inevitable conclusion. The heroine averts her sweet eyes as the hero delivers the villain, swaddled in chains, to her feet. She even throws herself on her knees to beg mercy for the man who had desired to ruin her.

It must be the pain of Tom's dying that has wedded my eyes to this woman, and it must be lust for life, provoked by his stark lack of it, that gives me such a sheer molten need to have her.

After all, the preliminaries have already been played out on the stage. It but rests with him to conclude the act, to perform the act of generation itself upon the woman. It is natural; it is fitting. He is panting ripe to have her. He'll briefly rub off the sadness upon this actress, this cunning little piece of Venice, this Mimosina Dolcezza.

It's a fine idea, with some handsome curlicues upon it.

There's the clatter of hands rising. The opera is over. Valentine simmers in his chair while his neighbours jump to their feet, clapping their hands at her like twinned castanets. They call the actress back, again and again. She feigns reluctance and the stage manager is forced to march her back onstage and to hold her in front of him, where she droops with downcast eyes, as if she is too fragile to withstand the power of their rampant adoration. Yet, from those lowered lids, she shoots off grateful glances like sparks in a foundry. Men caught in their direct trajectory jerk with pleasure, ducking their heads and shrugging bashfully.

Valentine gazes up at her now, and thinks rapidly: *How many men before me? Will she cry out someone's name? I wonder if she speaks God's own English. Does it matter? Tom would have loved those green eyes.*

· 2 ·

Spleen Ale

Take Barks of Tamarisk 4 ounces; of Capers and Ash-tree,
Woods of Guaiacum, Sassaphras, each 1 ounce; Herbs of
Agrimony 4 handfuls; Wormwood, Dodder, each 2 handfuls; cut
and boil these in 6 gallons of new Ale to 4 gallons, into which
hang Filings of Needles half a pound; Crude Antimony 4 ounces.
   When it hath Fermented enough, and is become clear, give
half a pint twice a day.

So the thing is, how to get her.

Stepping out under the star-stuttered sky, Valentine is pum-
melled by a bitter wind. He feels the sudden tiredness of a man
who has fought a battle and changed the landscape. It is true. In
the scenery of his heart, his rage and pain have smelted down
into something else entirely.

*Mimosina Dolcezza, the pride of Venice, the miraculous beauty who has
enchanted courts and Royal Families from Russia to Naples* – so declares the
playbill he still holds in his hand as he strolls west of Drury Lane,
his carriage following at a discreet distance. He halts under a lamp
to smooth it out and look at her likeness etched on the paper.

The delicacy of her has already informed Valentine that it
would not do to send a purse and scrawled card to her dressing
room, the coachman curling his whip like a dog's tail in his hand
and averting his eyes while she read and felt for the purse's bulge.

He has no scant feeling that this lady is of the type that requires
to be forcibly adored all the way from her high horse to her last,
grateful whimper.

*And this meets nicely with my own feeling that a quick once is not going to
give more than brief respite from all the hurting.*

No, he wants a sought-after coupling, one that costs him something and so is worth something. He craves a spending that is waited for, hoped for, not even inevitable. The more intricate the plot of getting her, the more he can soak his mind in it, the more it will crowd out those insupportable images of Tom.

He had no small eye for those Italian ladies, Tom, unpetticoating them by the dozen, with a great tongue on him for their lingo. Sure, no woman was safe from the fellow, not on the Thames or the Grand Canal, and all and every one of his ladies kept in Turkish ignorance of her rivals.

Valentine Greatrakes takes himself for a promenade around the Seven Dials, for a restful eyeful of tarts. Some men like to go to the sea when they want to think profoundly. Or to the countryside. Or the inside of a tavern. But Valentine holidays his worries best on a flutter of Covent Garden nuns.

Of course the sight of all those willing women and the fact of their availability does not bypass the trout, the rig, the handsome pissworm of Valentine Greatrakes but communicates directly with it. So often the result of a quiet contemplation is indeed a quick, refreshing clicket, though it is rarely the main object of his going out on such perambulations.

He strides along Monmouth Street and pauses at the Seven Dials, the delta of the local streets, and the richest pickings of whores in all London, where there are situated any number of convenient places to buy love ready-made and kept warm at all times. At the sight of the girls strewn around the seven corners, in his trews the friend of Valentine Greatrakes and his friend's two friends yollop about.

'You hungry, boy?' he asks out loud, looking at what's on offer. 'You on for your greens?'

A twitching *yespleasenow* fetches a smile to his lips and he resolves to make a speedy selection. This new enterprise, the winning of Mimosina Dolcezza, is not something to work on from a point of sensual famine. Better to contemplate that special copulation from the relaxed state that comes with an intermediate satisfaction. He considers one whore after another, a blonde, a brunette, a redhead, some proud in the theatre-glow of the lanterns that adorn every tenth frontage, others eschewing the revelations of the light: many here are wrinkled and some scarred, and some indeed no kind of lady, but male-misses, for every taste can be accommodated here at the Seven Dials.

Pausing in front of each genuine female, Valentine silently asks his friend, 'This one? Her? You want to go a-goosing in Hairyfordshire?'

He wanders about, letting his imagination sample what the various whores suggest verbally and with gestures. They sink before him, as if he winnows through a cornfield of women, each raising her skirts to one side in the time-honoured gesture to confirm her availability. Some speak to him in winning, confidential tones. Trembling quirks of music beckon from lady accordionists with subsidiary talents. Others writhe briefly like rashers on the griddle as he passes, or mince a few dance steps of the highest quality.

He does his devoirs to each proffering lady: 'Lovely', he smiles encouragingly. But none tempts him sufficiently. He strays to the less populated fringes of the street, the territory of the girls less in demand, who loiter almost apologetically, like paltry coins left contemptuously on a counter, not even worth the counting.

At last he spies a fake flower-seller, who, with the travesties of a profession, mimics not to be a harlot. She displays a poor stock of flowers, and she is outstandingly incompetent with her wares: they slide through her hands all the time, the blooms all wearied from being twice handled. A knot of men has collected around her and they cannot bring themselves to move on because it is somehow delicate and indelicate, this mauling of the flowers, and the tiny wan girl wilting herself.

'Now that's the one,' he says, looking at her taut little face.

Hey-up lass, he winks at her, and she drops the entire drooping stock of flowers on her feet. He pulls a silver coin out of his pocket and waves it in the air. The other men shrug their shoulders and melt away. She walks, dreamlike, towards the guinea. He is amused, and moves the coin to the left and then the right. Her whole face follows each manoeuvre.

She's hungry, he realises, and is pleased to think that she'll dine well later.

Valentine summons the carriage that crawls behind him and draws her into it with his silver coin.

A few circuits of St Giles and still it is not done. Valentine Greatrakes fumbles but fails. The girl is encouraging and blames herself. This predicament is unknown to him. She gently suggests that a glass of warm wine will set him up. He shakes his head, rebuttons, stares straight ahead. Passing another stall, he leans out and buys the girl a new bunch of flowers to maul and deposits her back at the Seven Dials. He assures her discretion with the additional tribute of a shilling.

His head is far from clear. This is not at all what he intended.

Worse, his eunuched encounter with the flower-girl gives him cause for worry about the Venetian woman. He does not like to envision her similarly available for such use.

I don't want to be throwing apples into an orchard.

He shrugs off the thought and orders the carriage back to the theatre, where he is unsurprised to find the manager still at his desk, working by a mean rushlight. It is a desk that hosts two sets of books: one that records the ingoings and outgoings of the theatrical side of the business, and another that keeps record of the items 'free-traded' into London in the costume coffers of the troupes he imports from Italy, often in alliance with his esteemed colleague Valentine Greatrakes of Stoney Street, Bankside.

'Greatrakes, you great scoundrel, how goes it? *Tutto bene?*'

Massimo Tosi, bulky and fragrant as a hay-bale, lumbers from his desk. Seamed into his cushioned face is a mixture of pleasure and apprehension. It's a finely judged thing, to call Valentine Greatrakes a scoundrel. And it seems Massimo has miscalculated tonight. His visitor regards him coolly, greeting him: 'And what can you do for me? Isn't that right?'

'Exactly, exactly,' simpers Massimo. 'All was well with the shipment? You need a box for some of your foreign colleagues? Champagne buffet? Some girls for after?'

'Maybe you'd do me the courtesy of thinking sweeter, Massimo.'

The manager's face grows troubled. 'The leading lady's not . . . available this time, Valentine.'

'Soon you'll be telling me she's a nun! An actress? An Italian actress?'

Valentine makes the appropriate voluptuous gestures, pouring a torrent of enthusiasm into the motions. Even his large hands are almost musically attuned.

It is a pleasure to watch him, thinks Massimo. *What a shame the business is impossible.*

Aloud, he responds: 'She is not like the others. She's – she's a genuine oddity. I don't know what it is with her. Never came here before, and she was substituted at the last minute. The original was taken with child or some such thing. She is competent, as you saw, but there's something not quite right about her, anyway. Don't waste your time on her. You are not the first to come to me with an interest in her.'

Valentine feels a lurch in his stomach at the unforeseen presumptuous bastards who have attempted to get there first. His mind's eye drenched rosily with images of revenge, there's a buzzing in his ears.

But the manager is explaining that no man has obtained what he sought from Mimosina Dolcezza, that the actress does indeed live, most unusually, a blameless existence when she's not on the stage. She seeks no dalliances, not for pleasure, nor for gold: that purses are regularly sent back to their owners and there are no late suppers in her rooms. Those rooms are not in the usual garish quarters in St Giles but in Soho Square, a salubrious area more favoured by foreign ambassadors than actresses. She does not let her creditors' notes decay. To add to this strangeness, she is always quiet and modest in her bearing; she makes no outrageous demands, not even upon the patience of the dressing women. She seems afraid of everyone greater or lesser than herself: in fact, in all ways she appears to resemble the trembling and virtuous maiden she plays, though – Massimo Tosi lowers his voice – she is of course a trifle older than the part she performs. She shuns the other actors as if they offend her delicate sensibilities. After each performance she quickly resumes her own simple clothes and returns – in an irreproachable sedan chair – to her rooms.

She has been in London but a few days and already she is a cult. Men are asking for her likeness to be painted on snuffboxes. Some are willing to pay monstrous sums to be seated where her glance falls meltingly at certain stages of the play. There are grand polemics about her special allure; some say it is her skill in performance, for she excels in comical attitudes but is also well capable of pathos. Others say it is her offstage virtue that heats their blood and has them waiting like dogs under the windows of her apartments which she is not seen to leave except on guiltless errands. It is, all in all, an extraordinary departure from normal behaviour and the entire company is mystified by it.

Massimo Tosi has shaken all possible insinuations out of his sack. Ducking his head, and turning saintly eyes to Valentine, the theatre manager mourns the hopelessness of the situation, as a brother. After all, if an actress is co-operative with well-to-do admirers, Massimo too stands to gain, as his dear friend must see.

Valentine remains silent when this performance is over. He seems to be waiting for more satisfactory news. The features of the manager tighten in rictus. Massimo has omitted mention of one thing: the troubling existence of the wordless Venetian man who has accompanied the actress to London, who haunts the theatre at all times, and, while he is never seen to come into actual contact with her, is never far from her side and who is rumoured to have taken rooms in a street that overlooks her own.

Watching Valentine's face, Massimo is already scribbling the address on a piece of paper and holding it out to him.

Valentine lets the hand stay suspended in the air. In five seconds the pleasant gesture of offer has become one of abject imprecation. They both look at Massimo's outstretched hand. The manager's face crumples. 'Craving your condescension and saving your grace, Valentine, there is nothing else I can do.'

'You are her employer. You'll be having a small word with her on my behalf. She would not be at this work if she did not need the money. Or something else you're offering her. No, I don't want to know the details. I shall be joining her at home for a twosome kind of supper tomorrow evening after the play.'

Valentine turns on his heel. He does not take the address: not for him a pathetic vigil in the cold street outside her rooms. For Valentine Greatrakes, Massimo Tosi can do better than that.

Massimo falls back in his chair, his face in his hands.

Striding through the shadowy corridors of the theatre, Valentine fails to see a small woman veiled in grey. She watches him from an alcove next to the door of the manager's office. Then she slips in through the open door and says a few words to her employer, who thinks to express his grateful surprise in an embrace but is repulsed with a surprisingly robust slap.

The echo of that slap reaches the ear of Valentine Greatrakes as he approaches the outer door of the theatre and he pauses a moment. He wonders briefly if a duel has erupted among the actors, but he's not long distracted from a more pressing conflict.

He is quarrelling with himself.

The words of the manager gnaw at him. He had resolved to win her slowly, but this coyness on her part has aroused in him an urgent desire to speed the proceedings. He can imagine his competitors now, all equally provoked by her unwillingness, some even skilled in the acquisition of such women, some perhaps as keenly interested as he himself. It is to be expected. She has transformed herself into something else: no longer a mere actress, the currency of the pleasure trade, she has elevated herself to something much more refined. She has claimed the contraband quality of chastity.

Contraband is something that Valentine Greatrakes understands with all his heart, to which all his faculties are perfectly honed, and for which all his considerable resources are available. To this end, he whistles up his carriage to take him back to his Bankside depository.

· 3 ·

Horse-Dung Water

Take Brooklime. Water Cresses, Harts tongue each 3 handfuls;
juicy Orange peels 3; Nutmeg 6 drams; succulent fresh Horse
dung 3 pounds; Whey 9 pints; juice of Scabious, Dandelion and
Hyssop water, each 1 pint. Draw off the Water gently, in a cold
Still, for three days in an Alembic (which is used for
expedition's sake).
   'Tis used in Juleps, in the Pleurisy, Scurvy, and vagous Pains.

For a man of his genre, Valentine Greatrakes is a great pacifist. He
hates to do a body violence, positively tries to avoid it, and when it
must happen he sincerely regrets it. But there is one war he fights
gladly, with relish and with glory.

Only to press him lightly on the matter is to be rewarded with a
sturdy barrage on this theme, at the core of which is this: *It's a
party's downright duty and not just his inalienable right to fight against horse-
dung taxes.*

Just such a flight of eloquence – not a little inspired by another
blockade, that of Mimosina Dolcezza – is the treat bestowed by
Valentine upon his driver, jolting by moonlight over luminous cob-
blestones back to the place where he conducts his personal
vendetta against unjust harvesting of revenues.

'Iniquitous!' he bellows, 'infamous!', as he calls the roll on the
taxes that snack on every article that comes in at the mouth, or that
shelters the skin, or is placed underfoot; taxes on all things that are
lovely to see, hear, feel, smell or taste; there are taxes upon light
itself, upon warmth, upon methods of locomotion; taxes on the
raw materials; taxes on those things enriched in value by human
labour and ingenuity; taxes on all things that stimulate the appetite

67

and all things that satisfy it, on the judge's ermine and the criminal's noose, on the pap and the spoon of the baby, the toys of the child, the horse of the man and the road he rides it on, the ribbons of his bride, the brass nails of his coffin, and the marble of his tombstone.

To each item the driver assents with a great flourish of his whip and so they progress down the Strand at a cracking pace. The horse anoints the cobbles with a superabundant stream of piss.

The mullioned water of the Thames winks from between the riverside buildings. Valentine and his driver lean forward to examine a squat vessel that weaves towards St Mary Overie Dock. At dawn it will unload the bales of hops with which Valentine Greatrakes quite legitimately supplies the Thrale brewery at Bankside, the brave parapets of which he salutes with a wave as they pass over London Bridge. Those bales are looped by rope twined with smuggled tobacco. They lie next to feathered heaps of headless geese, whose innards have been replaced with bottles of rum that shall be discreetly removed before the birds are delivered to the butchers of Smithfield and crates of living parrots destined to amuse affluent homes, having been schooled in speech by sailors on long journeys aboard illicit slavers' ships.

Occasional forays by the excise-men into the tenebrous vaults of the depository of Valentine Greatrakes reveal nothing to incur a penny of duty, but plenty to baffle and torment the dreams of the officers. For their lanterns discover many unblinking drawers of glass eyes, hard clutches of false hands made of leather, racks of wooden leper-clappers, trays of artificial ivory noses for syphilitics, and miniature anatomical models of pregnant women with removable parts peeling back to reveal a foetus or two in residence.

The Revenue never stay long. Cupboards specially hinged to utter dying groans swing slowly open to reveal rows of pink Bohemian tincture bottles, hallmarked silver nipple shields, earthenware posset pots, tin-glazed bleeding bowls, iron scarificators for blood-letting, and pewter enema syringes. Strung up in cloudy luminescence are necklaces of dentures fashioned from hippopotamus ivory (less liable to stain than that of baboons and goats). Lifting a trembling lantern, the excise-men then gasp at the vision of a biblical plague of locusts apparently come to life – only to be reassured by their genial host that these creatures, mounted on velvet screens, are merely a craze of recent years: Algerian amulet brooches in the shapes of locusts, studded with what might credibly be described as, and is, purest turquoise from the mines of the Americas.

And not a single item of it culpable for duty.

The dim catacombs of Bankside are suddenly lit up by a providential shaft of pure moonlight, as if to welcome home its most illustrious son. Late as it is, men tip their hats to him and women bob as the carriage of Valentine Greatrakes passes by.

The horse goes like an eel down the slyest alleys. Valentine surveys his domain with a certain amount of smugness. What he slips in and flushes out has made Bankside what it is today. No public house rollicks without the illicit life-blood he porters to it. Every local magistrate, if he does not sup off the discreet back-handers of Valentine Greatrakes, at least dines on the affordable commodities he has free-traded all the way to his kitchen door. No babe is born without its mother first partaking of his Maternal Wafers. No man goes to his marriage bed unfortified by his excellent preparation, the Husband's Friend. It is these last two items, and many related confections, that please Valentine above all items of commerce, that raise him higher than all other gentlemen free-traders in London, and not just in his own eyes. For Valentine Greatrakes, while not disdaining Ginevra from Amsterdam and Bohea from India, has taken it upon himself to specialise in certain liquid and powdered pharmaceutical substances that come only from the tiny aquatic Republic of Venice: universal balsamick cure-alls for the people of London.

The quack doctors of Valentine Greatrakes thrive richly on the credulity of London's afflicted. And such lovely nostrums, so sweet and grateful on the throat, are those he provides to ease them of their money. And if their narcotic or purging qualities do sometimes prove destructive to the patients, why, his quacks will always mention that this is because they have been taken in insufficient quantities. A man killed by taking thirty of these wonder-pills would have been saved by the thirty-first. If only he had not lacked of courage at the last moment: why, then his vital spark would not only have been prolonged but fully renovated.

And how picturesque are these potions, these Balms of Gilead, these Macassar Oils, these Odontos and these Infallible Balsamicks. Their labels are the poetry of the streets, and the stanzas are their lists of fantastical ingredients. And indeed they appeal infallibly to that majority of Londoners who bear a love of the incredible and marvellous. Sometimes it is no mere congenital deficiency of brain that sends people scurrying for these nostrums but a special form of blindness: they might read any newspaper with all the cynicism of a Frenchman, yet, when they scan the quacks' handbills, they respond as if to an article of the catechism, with an instinctive and deep belief.

And the trade is all the smoother for one fact that became apparent to Valentine when he was just a young entrepreneur, thin as a shotten herring and half hazy on the excitement of it all. Bankside, as he has known since childhood, is excellently attired to be the disseminating headquarters of the business. For Bankside is the Murano of London, the site of a hundred glassworks, all churning out clear containers for the soothing and uplifting liquids that must be free-traded through the city, commencing their journey in the capillaries of passageways communicating secretly between friendly houses.

They pass on to the baker's and Valentine hulloes his platter-faced friend already at work inside, on a batch of hollow loaves for the concealment of whatever morsel's currently attracting the interest of the Excise. Cooling in his storerooms are trays of the aforesaid Maternal Wafer, excellent business at a penny each.

One of Valentine's quacks passes in his trap pulled by a white donkey painted with purple spots. He brandishes a bleached female femur at his employer and indicates, with his hands, the airy lightness of his cart: today he has sold many dozens of his bottles of nostrums, each one enriched with brandy poured from kegs damp with the slime of Romney Marsh. Valentine scowls and the quack lowers his head. Too late, the man has remembered the effect of his proprietary escharotic ointment on the sensitive back of his patron. Despite the application of a cabbage leaf, the caustic salve has caused a weeping lesion that still troubles the laundrywomen beating the linen shirts of Valentine Greatrakes. When he sees the quack who is the author of his discomfort, the delicate skin of Valentine's back contracts painfully, and he is forced to remember the words of the advertisement that he himself had written: 'It prevents Inflammations, Festerings, and Running of Matter, in any of which cases this great Vulnery has never yet been known to fail of effecting a perfect Cure in a few Days.'

The public girls are out on the streets still: all faces and figures he knows well one way or another. For Valentine frequently sends the skimpy south London prostitutes on jaunts across the Channel so that they might return crinkled and snowswept with lace: apparel in use upon a living body is not liable to duty. Moreover, he most heartily enjoys the unwrapping of his lacy girls when they come home to him, dipped in cognac and juicy for the tasting. Those more lively in their wits double up as assistants to his quacks, posing as deathbed cases who are instantly revived by the latest miraculous nostrums.

Now the carriage is drawing into the depository in Stoney Street and two of his sleepless men, having observed his arrival through a spyhole, open the discreet gates and close them again behind him.

Valentine vaults down from the carriage and runs up the stairs into his office where his assistant, Dizzom, hunched over a burner, worries a piece of hemp into charred segments that will be sold for a guinea an inch as hangman's rope, which is known to be efficacious against the earache. Behind the man a row of bottles glow hellishly in the firelight: the heat agitates the liquid inside them, so that slow and graceful ballets are now performed by the corpses of rats and mice preserved in their death throes and other, less familiar, abortives put up in syrups. Dizzom's experiments with embalming fluids have proved grimly and unexpectedly useful: this week nine gallons of them have already been despatched to Venice, so that Tom's body, packed in a lead-lined coffin, will soon be on its way back to them, without growing inconveniently ripe. Valentine wants Tom's remains laid out in state at Bankside, for all their friends to pay their last respects.

'What's new?' Valentine asks affectionately. Since Tom's death he takes the lives of none of his manor for granted.

Dizzom smiles. Due to a tendency to taste his own potions and resultant encounters with dental quacks, he displays a giddy rush of forward-leaning wooden and gold teeth at the front of his mouth.

In the pleasure of seeing his master, Dizzom has forgotten the task at hand. A segment of rope catches fire, releasing sharp tarry fumes into the room. He plunges the rope into a jar of something that makes it fizz and spit. Some drops splash Dizzom's low forehead, which is oppressed by a coarse pinkish wig that is heavy with grease and waved in stiff little peaks like innumerable tiny ears. His hands are delicate rose-pink on the inside, hornily skinned and heavily downed with grey hairs right up to the second joint of each finger. Dizzom has long adopted a habitual posture in which he holds his digits curved to his breast with the roseate skin upwards. When he must use them he turns away from any witnesses and busies himself with astonishing rapidity, so that, as now, all that may be seen is a shadowy blur about the ends of his wrists, as if someone were scribbling above them with a soft lead pencil.

Valentine takes a step forward, and puts his arm on his employee's shoulder.

'What can I do for you, my dear?' asks Dizzom fondly. 'I see you have an idea about you.'

He lays down his task and stands up to look his master in the eye.

'Well, indeed, and it's about a woman,' declares Valentine a little shyly, and at this Dizzom chuckles aloud, revealing the full treasury of hollow back teeth, in each of which, on certain business trips, he may lay up a ruby or an emerald. Or even a tiny phial of poison or sleeping philtre.

It is something between the latter two that Valentine Greatrakes requires.

· 4 ·

Antiphthisic Decoction

Take Ox Eye Daisy flowers dry'd 1 handful; Snails wiped clean 3; Candied Eryngo Root half an ounce; Pearl Barley 3 drams; boil together in Spring Water from 1½ pints to 1 pint, and strain it out.

It smoothes and restrains the saline turbulent Particles of the Blood, so as to hinder it from rushing impetuously through the Canals.

The next morning opens the sky like a bank vault. Valentine reads the crackling golden light as a good omen, but cannot decide whether it instructs him to take in one more stage show by the actress before he allows her to perform intimately for himself alone. To do so might dilute or it might enhance the effect she achieved the previous night, and he is perfectly happy with the sherbet of excitement that currently enlivens his blood. In a strange and pleasant way the certain prospect of her, confirmed in an oblique note from Massimo, makes it easier to concentrate on the demanding business of the day.

With Dizzom, he despatches some Venetian glass daggers to St Giles, and oversees the packaging of some Antiphthisic decoctions for a Mayfair destination. He checks the inventories of their nostrums, finds a certain depletion in the Balm of Gilead. He has himself composed some alluring texts for the bottles of their latest confections from Italy, borrowing from Shakespeare and Galileo, melting down the language of literature and science and fusing them for his purposes.

Perhaps it is the Irish in him, but no one can match Valentine Greatrakes in the kind of wordsmithery that provokes a rumpus in the chitterlins, a sudden thirst for the contents of a petite green bottle and the conclusive symptom of the opening of the purse.

The luminous words of Valentine Greatrakes are rarely read in the newspapers, for since 1712 a scurvy law has placed a duty even on advertisements. But in the depository at Bankside he has his own small press, where handbills by the hundred are printed, full of learned miniature essays on the latest scientific discoveries, with many references to the great physicians of the day and the arcane past. Valentine knows his audience, he knows that they long to hear not of homely garden cures but of atoms charged with the Quintessence and Virtues of Chymical Oils, and secrets unearthed from the tombs of Pharaohs.

Here at Bankside he also prints and stores the labels for his quacks' potions. These square tickets may be indifferently applied to any bottle of their cures, to flatter the needs of each separate market. So, arranged in neat piles, are labels that bear the legends, Digestive Bolus for Aldermen, Sublime Elixir for Poets, Consolation Cordial for the Bereaved, and solutions for many other retail opportunities. These colourful labels Valentine sells to his quacks at almost no margin at all, just for the joy of their manufacture.

Errands of mixed sociability and profitability detain Valentine around Bankside until late evening: even if he had chosen to do so, there is now no time to see the actress reprise her role on the stage. From time to time, the thought of her suddenly rinses all other thoughts from his mind and he must stammer apologies to his colleagues and friends. He wonders if she speaks English. He would like to ask Massimo, but he somehow scruples to send a messenger, lest this interest drive up the cost of the favour.

Returning to his desk, Valentine is already dragging the cravat from his neck in preparation for changing into his evening dress. He greets his assistant, immediately aware that something is wrong. From the pink rims of Dizzom's anxious eyes he knows that there is a new communication about Tom to be found there among the papers. Sure enough, here it is, atop everything: the news that Tom's body is now approaching Basel and that all goes safely with the couriers appointed to bring it, but the delays continue with the paperwork. It occurs to Valentine that it is easier to bring contraband back to England than a dead Englishman with expensively immaculate papers. For once, everything about Tom is above board, something that never happened in his lifetime.

Valentine approaches the theatre to the thunder of the final applause, and remembers how last night Mimosina Dolcezza was held up to the crowd, impaled on the arms of Massimo Tosi. He hears the drumming of appreciative feet and the cries of pleasure from the audience, if anything louder than the previous evening.

Of course he already knows the rear entrance and all the passageways to the female dressing rooms. He enters the dim back hallway that stinks of the cheapest tallow candles – backstage Massimo has no need to maintain an illusion of luxury – and strolls without hurrying down the threadbare floorboards. He knows, from experience, that Mimosina Dolcezza is at this very moment walking towards the same dressing room, though from the other end of the theatre. He can almost hear her light tread and the whispering drag of her gown. If he maintains a leisurely pace then she should arrive a minute or two before him, have an interval to restore any dishevelment in her person, attend to any bodily functions, indeed discard any distracting preoccupations of the day, so as to be ready to meet her short-term destiny – that is, Valentine Greatrakes – in a state of pleasing expectation.

Young dancers start to helter past him, not bothering to change their gowns before falling into the arms of the beaux waiting for them in the street. He smiles, noting the comfortable fullness of several faces more familiar in an emaciated state. He often places lace-girls of his own with Massimo when they have done a few too many errands to France and their looks have become known to the excise-men. One girl stops and looks at him, jerking her head back in the direction of the dressing rooms with an interrogative expression. She looks concerned and opens her mouth to say something, but another dancer rushes past and seizes her wrist: she disappears with a light clatter of heels. He tries to remember her name, but such memories are swallowed up in the all-consuming thought of what awaits him.

Valentine reaches the corridor where the more elegant dressing rooms are to be found. He is uncharacteristically unnerved and slightly light-headed. His back itches painfully – he has, of course, forgotten to apply a buttercup decoction – and he pauses to rub it against a plaster column.

What does he know of this woman except that she dissembles professionally? And that she is a Venetian, and therefore capable of any amount of subtlety. He is starting to shake off his enthusiasm for her company. Too much has been made of the occasion, and it's putting him off the prospect.

But then his trout tickles hard at its cloth encasement and Valentine realises that no one else will ease him tonight, though he might spend himself – if he can manage it, a shuddering blush recalling last night's failure with the flower-girl – a dozen times in different women. He continues to pad towards the room he knows at the very end of the corridor, the one with two windows looking into the well of the courtyard, both swathed in silk and hung with Venetian glass baubles he himself has supplied, for Massimo Tosi considers the dressing room of his leading lady the very front of his house. Indeed, sometimes it proves more profitable than the stage: a wealthy patron who enjoys himself with one of Massimo's protégées is usually inclined to pleasant flights of generosity when it comes to subscribing to new productions.

This very thought jars Valentine so that he stops in his tracks. Massimo, who will lie as soon as pick his teeth, may well have invented the story of the Venetian ice maiden. The production is three days old. Perhaps he has already sold her on a nightly basis to different clients.

Isn't the wish of the world to be in her arms? – Massimo'll not have been backward in auctioning off the pleasure.

The notion of being gulled by Massimo Tosi raises a trembling in the bowels of Valentine Greatrakes.

If the swarthy little parasite has misspoken, he thinks, *he'll be laughing at me now.*

The thought is intolerable.

I'll be eating the head off him if he's sold me some midden of a girl here.

76

His hands have commenced to shake and he feels a tear of sweat peruse the blistered hieroglyphs of his back on the way down to the cleft of his buttocks.

Valentine has secreted about his person a phial of one product he distributes with great success. 'Quietness' is a tincture with one grain of morphine per ounce of sweet crimson syrup. This bottle is intended to still the nerves of Mimosina Dolcezza, who after all must be mightily unsettled by the prospect of an evening with so important a gentleman as himself. She'll be nervous, no doubt, with a hungering wind excavating her belly, and her heart battering away at her lungs. He feels for her. He will distract her momentarily and decant a few drops into her glass: afterwards she shall feel calmer and happier, and matters will move more smoothly towards their natural conclusion.

But what is this? Valentine Greatrakes, who has been turning the bottle in his hand, suddenly stops in a dark corner, lifts it aloft and removes the miniature cork with a deft tooth. He swigs briefly on the bottle, checks the level (half full) and recorks it. Whistling, he moves on towards the fateful door.

He is struck then by a sudden horror that perhaps his breath is no longer of the sweetest. He rummages in his pocket for one of his new bolus creations that is currently awaiting a patent. Dizzom has proofed up the handbill already, and he remembers all the maladies it cures: Mal-assimilation of Food, Coated Tongue, Bad Taste in Mouth, Bloating, Belchings, Sour Risings and Restless Nights. *Restless nights!* He clamps his teeth on a bolus and identifies the sharp and infallible bite of rhubarb and cubeb.

His tongue soft and clean, he taps at the door once, and courteously awaits the formality of her request to enter. A baffling silence ensues. He taps again, a little more forthrightly, and yet again she fails to acknowledge his presence. Without any consciousness of doing so, Valentine reaches into his pocket and withdraws the 'Quietness'. He is tipping the dregs between his lips when he feels a faint, humid breath at the back of his neck. A few livid pink drops of 'Quietness' spill on to his white shirt and the pale brocade waistcoat as he spins around, the bottle still upraised, to see who dares to menace him in this way. In his other hand he clutches at the tiny glass dagger sewn into the lining of his frock coat against any unpleasant eventualities. Only Valentine Greatrakes knows how to liberate the miniature weapon without lacerating his own fingers, knows how to find the hilt, fragile as a sparrow's breastbone, and where to thrust the beautiful sliver so as to launch it on a fatal voyage through human flesh.

For a dagger like this one has a special feature: on impact the skilled user simply twists the hilt so that it snaps off. The glass blade then sets sail through the nearest organs and nothing can stop it: no victim can reach in through the wound to clutch the blade, for on contact it slices his probing fingers. Slippery with blood and the slime of punctured organs, it tunnels deeper into the flesh. The more the victim thrashes in agony, the deeper voyages the little dagger. If the victim lies still, then so does the dagger, but even an intake of breath will send the knife on its way again, like a breeze lifting the sails of a lake-bound boat. No surgeon can reach the victim in time to stop the onset of gangrene. Even an unconscious patient starts to melt within a few hours of ingesting the glass through his skin.

All these images pass through his mind even as he spins on his left foot. His eyes must have snapped shut a moment, for now he opens them. He is astonished to see that his supposed attacker – still in translucent white and faintly haloed with dust from the stage curtains – is none other than Mimosina Dolcezza herself, who has stolen up on him from behind on her tiny slippered feet.

And it's out of his mouth before he can stop it, an ignominious piece of Irish: 'Holy Jesus, it's herself. I nearly had a canary!'

Instantly, he blushes hotly, hating himself, every Cork corpuscle.

But her face is expressionless, allowing him to paint upon it the sentiments that best suit himself. She stands still. Her only movement, and that propelled by the hot breath of his exclamation, is the jitter of the bird-trembler ornament worked into the silver-gilt of her feathered hair clip.

She didn't understand a syllable of it, he tells himself. *And of course the poor creature is a-tickle with the nerves herself.*

'Don't be afraid, my dear,' he says gently, barely suppressing his breathless palpitations. 'I have only come to take you to have supper.'

She smiles and fixes her eyes on his. She does not visibly notice the stains of 'Quietness' on his rising and falling shirt.

Then she half curtsies, half bows, humbly indicating not only her agreement to his proposal but also her gratitude for it. The bird-trembler in her hair nods vigorously. As she rises she fixes upon him a look that could break more marriages than a war.

Thus shall all be as it should be, he tells himself. *There's been no one else at her; I can see it at a glance.*

His breathing judders to a slower rate. He is even pleased that she shows no desire to change her costume, the same persuasive item low-cut in white, or clean away her paint. Her hair is still dressed as for the performance, fanned out in a graceful puff around her face and trailing in long curls down her back. She opens the door to her room, and without looking in the mirror simply draws on a ruffled cap and throws a cloak, also evidently from the theatre's wardrobe, over her dress. This shows a becoming degree of compliancy and eagerness. She walks quietly beside him down the corridors to the door where his carriage is waiting. Neither her footsteps nor her breath make any sound and he is forced to steal many glances to his side to make sure she still accompanies him. Each time he is more captivated by her sweet profile. It is but lightly swathed in stage paint, and he chooses to find it all the more modest for not being naked to his inspection.

As the carriage moves away a white face appears under a lamp: an Italian face, subtle and attractive. It watches the actress settling back under the furs provided by her new companion, and it registers a look of intense, though refined, displeasure.

Valentine Greatrakes sees nothing but the woman gazing up at him. Even without touching, she has a caressing way with her. He is already becalmed in her soft, wet eye.

· 5 ·

Consummate Broth

Take a Capon (pick'd, drawn, and cut into pieces); Sheeps
Trotters and Calves Feet, each 4; Shavings of Hartshorn and
Ivory, each half an ounce; yellow Sanders 3 drams; Dates 20;
Raisins of the Sun stoned 4 ounces; Pearl Barley 1 ounce; boil
these in Spring-Water 1 gallon to 2 quarts, adding when it's
almost boil'd enough, Ox-Eye Flowers dried, Herbs of Colts
Foot, Maiden Hair, Sage of Jerusalem, each 1 handful; Mace 2
Blades; 1 Nutmeg; Malaga Sack 1 pint; strain it out.

It's a commodious Prescription ... Digested with little
trouble, assimilated without effervescence, easily distributed,
soon agglutinated, and not presently dissipated by the Heat of
the Body. Moreover it yields such a soft, kindly and glutinous
Juice, that it qualifies the saline, hard, pricking Particles of the
Blood ...

Her rooms are luxuriously appointed and the maid discreet in a
way that can only be expensive. The girl curtsies once, lowering a
head clad in a round-eared cap, and disappears instantly.

Valentine is gratified to see that arrangements have already
been made for the supper. So he shall have no need to send out to
a cookshop for food of which neither is likely to enjoy the consuming. Not that he begrudges the expense. No, he'll not be
stinting on the hundred thousand ways he'll show he's grateful. But
he would have mourned the haemorrhage of time spent negotiating over her delicate appetite and the wait while the servant was
instructed, the dishes procured, portered, laid out and served,
taken away. Valentine Greatrakes is not a man who likes to bury his
nose in the ceremonial trough. He prefers to eat a little, here and

there, and that something simple that may be despatched without ceremony in order to proceed swiftly to more interesting matters.

A table is decked out in the Continental style. Pure spermaceti candle flame hovers over crystal and porcelain arranged like the board of a complicated, risky game. The wine has been decanted and the rosy tints of two glasses tell him that it has been aired as well. He is impressed, and a little apprehensive.

Mimosina Dolcezza speaks for the first time.

'Please,' she says, smiling towards the more elaborate chair at the table, and forever after Valentine will remember that this is the first word she said to him, and that she offered him the better place.

In his pocket, his fingers push the disgraced 'Quietness' aside and close round the other little phials he has brought as a precaution. For the fish course: a little Black Drop, opium dissolved in wild crab juice; for the dessert course, a tranquillising elixir of paregoric, alcohol, opium, benzoic acid, oil of aniseed and camphor: strangely the very same concoction his quacks sell to mollify scrotal tumours in chimney-sweeps, a very frequent hazard of their occupation, but also known to be a great soother of tense ladies. He has discreetly taken a drop while she was moving her shawl, not that he's tense himself, of course, just properly tensed for pleasure.

It's lovely here. In the whole of my natural-born life I've not seen a room as sweet as this. She has a way with the hanging of a curtain, and the choosing of a flower.

But his belly soon seizes up when he sees the feast her servant lays before him. In succession, he is forced to frame his lips to a thick and glistening soup of unknowable provision, to strange protuberant vegetables dressed in piquant oils. The fish lies glaring on the plate with three slender eels plaited around it. And for the meat, no pie but mysterious yielding nuggets soaked in some kind of perfumed cream.

And the drinks – everything but honest ale! Everything infused with swarthy flavours of something else. And finally a glass of brandy with an egg yolk beaten into it.

She says almost nothing while they eat. Just 'Please' again, and again, pointing to the new dishes arriving and then again to make sure he takes a second helping. She smiles at his evident amazement, taking it, no doubt, as pleasure.

The sight of his hostess is more appetising than the dinner. And clearly the fascination's mutual. She notifies him of the fact in bodily language. From the way she looks at the food travelling into his mouth, he can tell that she longs to kiss him. From the fluttering of her eyelashes as he takes a long swig of the flavoured water he divines her desire to have him do the same with her. And from the lustre of her eyes he realises with a flush that she desires not merely the deed of kind with him, but that she already feels something else for him: a tenderness, a welling affection.

He is not even sure if she is painted, after all. Her coral lips have left no imprint on any of the glasses at dinner. The delicate shadows that enlarge her eyes are naturalistic in colour. If she is painted, then it is as if her paint has united with her skin instead of merely lying atop it.

With soft gestures, she mimes a question. Would he like her to sing? A private performance, in the intimacy of her own room?

Why not? It can only delay things a little, and give him time to digest the difficult food before the main part of the evening's entertainment. He smiles and mimes the applause that she will soon merit, holding his large hands up to his face.

And so she sings. Her voice, without accompaniment, tinkles in volleys of delicate notes. It is an Italian love song. That is, it can only be a love song, the way her face glows and her eyes fill with dew. Even her tiny ears are translucent with love in the candlelight.

She really means it. The thought cuts through him.

She's singing about me.

It can only be that famed phenomenon, thinks Valentine, his belly swilling alarmingly and a multitude of bats beating their wings in his chest, love at first sight.

Love at first sight, that the women sigh for and the poets find such good meat for their productions. He knows he is a handsome man, and that his height and figure are worthy of admiring attention, but he feels in his heart that even after such a short time this discriminating woman has fallen for something more visceral, that she has divined the pure animating soul of Valentine Greatrakes and that she alone of all the women he has known has found just the right things about him to love. He does not know if her extraordinary perceptiveness comes from a kind of native intelligence of her own, or if he has suddenly, perhaps as a result of Tom's death, become transparent, and the coincidence of their meeting so soon after – why, he saw her first the same day he heard of the murder – has rendered him permeable to the sudden adoration of an unknown woman.

He has been in Venice many times, known not a few Venetian women, and her repertoire of subtly beckoning gestures is familiar to him. But there is something quite different! There is no doubting the genuine passion that is being enacted in front of him, albeit softened by a becoming modesty. Valentine thinks of Massimo Tosi and his description of the actress as a kind of nun. He understands now what the inarticulate fellow was stumbling at.

Suddenly he is anxious to lead her to her predestined altar: the bedroom. He is afire to unwrap and suckle her breasts, slide over her belly and to heave himself into her peach-fish, her warm place, and not stop, not for a very, very long time.

He's known lust before, but nothing like this. All previous desires seem by comparison mere bridesmaids of feelings, bystanders to a main event, palavering about trivialities, nothing but dust to this.

It seems she feels the same way, for as he shifts in his chair, she too is wriggling and frowning slightly, and they rise as one and turn to the archway which must only lead to the bedroom. They have not yet touched but the air between them hangs slackly. It seems they both feel weakened by their passion for they too sag on their feet and walk limply towards the open door of the chamber.

Valentine feels a great commotion in his trews and a terror at the thought of hurting her, for the desire he feels is fierce enough to tear the woman in half. A dizzying parade of images passes swiftly in front of him, in which he mounts her in every position, from the nun's habit to the dog's marriage, in swift and unrelenting succession, and yet he cannot be satisfied and keeps turning her over and over and over, juggling with her on his fifth limb, aching to spend himself and yet unable to forgo another variation.

And I've not even put a finger on her yet.

83

The bedroom is dramatic, hung with heavy purple curtains at both bed and window. But it feels troublingly insubstantial, like a stage set. An anxiety befalls him that the walls are false, concealing giggling boys with ropes, and he takes another swig from the cloudy brandy glass still clenched in his hand.

She makes gestures to indicate that she must leave him a moment, no doubt to make some intimate preparations to welcome him. She disappears along a curtained passageway. He hears a noise that tells him no expense has been spared in her equipage – the latest Bramah water closet has been fitted here.

He wonders if he should undress himself completely, or if she has reserved that pleasure for herself. He imagines her fingers plucking at his buttons and feels as if they might burst beforehand.

When she returns to the room, still in her gown, there's no time left. He doesn't even want to undress her. It would be too intimate. He's unwilling to be naked in front of her. He doesn't want to touch her hair.

He picks her up around the waist and carries her to the bed, slides his fingers through the minimum number of his own buttonholes with the speed of a laundress and mounts her, finding what he wants instantly and embedding himself there. And it's archery, it's racetrack, it's falling down a well, but at the last moment it is more like a slow smile, utterly complicit.

It is over in a few minutes and he is too shy to kiss her flushed, grateful face. He waits, poised above her, for a second wave of desire to hoist his rig again. But after several moments it has not come, and he can no longer look down on her face, lest he meet her eyes.

His mind still reels and he remembers that she called out 'Signore!' at the last moment. As far as he knows, this means 'my lord!' and he is most gratified by it, for it signifies that Mimosina Dolcezza sees him as a nobleman, and not as he is, a parentless snipe of the gutter, risen in his fortunes but not in his blood.

He dismounts with tender care. They lie side by side on the bed. He realises that he still does not know if she speaks English. But he wants to tell her things about his childhood, to be kissed sweet and comforting for them, about how it smothered the heart in his breast the night he saw her in the theatre, only yesterday. He wants to compliment her face and figure (though the latter he has not yet unwrapped, and in the brief congress there was not time even to find a nipple or a buttock to squeeze). He wants to tell her about Tom, and to have her console him.

For the first time in his life, he doesn't want to leave the bed he has just enjoyed. His fingertips flitter at his sides but he dares not reach out to touch her. He wants to stay and hold her; just to feel her breathing in his arms.

But he does not know how to tell her this. Like a dog with a docked tail he strains ineffectually to demonstrate his delight in her. The unaccustomed words fail to rise in his throat. He does not even know the gestures for them. Instead he stares and smiles in the dark, nodding like a madman.

He dozes briefly, wakes to find her looking at him, and he rouses himself to a second mounting, slower and sweeter this time, but still he is too shy to remove either his clothes or hers. In the early hours he rises and kisses her, dresses and slips out to his carriage, waking the coachman with a smart tap on his cap, and together in companionable silence they drive back to Bankside.

· 6 ·

An Electuary of Satyrion

Take candy'd Satyrion root 2 ounces; candy'd Eryngo root 1 ounce; candy'd Nutmeg half an ounce; Juice of ground Kermes, Spirit of Clary, each 2 drams; long Pepper powder'd 16 grains, mix.

It's an Aphrodisiac, and after a singular manner, restores People that are Consumptive and Emaciated. The Dose 2 or 3 drams, Evening and Morning with a glass of old Malaga or Tent Wine.

He awakes with a single thought in mind: a diamond brooch for Mimosina Dolcezza.

He sends for Dizzom and relates his requirements in as calm a voice as he can conjure. He wants one hundred diamond brooches so that the actress may have a choice of all the most scintillating sparklers London has to offer. By early afternoon the news has saturated the light-fingered fraternity: all the thieves of the manor know that they would be well advised to supply one not-paltry diamond brooch to the Bankside depository inside the week if they wish to stay on cordial terms with Valentine Greatrakes.

Even within a day, diamonds from Golconda to Brazil are raining on Bankside like a fall of stars. They arrive concealed in sleeves, handkerchiefs, under caps and in one case inside a wooden leg, which is also left as if integral to the jewel's setting. So many diamonds arrive that Valentine draws pleasing comparisons between his own fortunate mistress and the Queen of France, who has recently convulsed all Europe with the purchase of a necklace of a mere six hundred and forty-seven dazzlers.

Dizzom labels the brooches carefully with enigmatic signs and pins them in pleasing sequences to boards padded with velvet. A carpenter skilled in the false linings of coffins is commissioned to build a display case and it is made known that the final date for delivery of jewels will be the following Friday morning, promptly at noon.

Looking on the glittering contents, Valentine is suddenly reminded of Tom, who always loved diamonds, the hard glitter of them, and their easy disposability. It was Tom's old list of favoured jewellers they had worked through: every one of the local thieves knows that a true connoisseur of diamonds is employed by Valentine Greatrakes, though few would guess it had been Tom.

On a table in the apartments of Mimosina Dolcezza, that Friday night, he sees the papers bewailing the raids on noble jewellers all over the city. He wonders why she takes the *Daily Universal Register* and its strident ilk: her English is probably so poor that she must struggle with their inflated prose. But she must understand something, for he sees that she has cut out some of the advertisements for female products and that she studies them with an enlarging glass. And she has acted on the publicity, and sent out for what it offers. Godfrey's Cordial, Hooper's Female Pills, Dr James's Fever Powders all bestrew her table and there is evidence that the packaging has been broached.

Certain that she will not note the coincidence, he lays down the display case in front of her, opens its velvet-lined door and explains, with signs, that he could not be sure of choosing one exquisite enough for her, so she must make her own selection of the diamond brooches here.

Her eyes widen and she abruptly closes the lid of the box, overwhelmed. He opens it again, and gently guides her fingers over the cool faceted surfaces. Her hand is smooth as a tulip, blatantly ringless, vulnerable under his.

She looks up into his face, as if to ask, 'Is it really true? These are for me?'

He kisses her and then turns her face back to the box with a caressing finger.

Delicately, almost reluctantly, she points to the smallest brooch in the collection. So modest! So far from the greedy whores of his previous intimate acquaintance. He thinks how they would have weighed the brooches in their hands for worth, how they would have bargained with him for a second gift.

'You like this one?' he says fondly, lifting it off the velvet and holding it out to her. He is pleased to see that she has been discriminating. The emerald-cut diamonds, while petite, are perfect and lustrous. She lowers her eyes as if his generosity is almost too much to bear. She does not immediately pin on the brooch but lets it rest in his hand where she still stares at it in disbelief.

He turns it over to read Dizzom's label and is gratified to find that this robbed jeweller is one already known to him. He makes a mental note to send Dizzom off with a proposition: will this craftsman kindly take on the matter of removing stones from some hundred discarded brooches and creating a tiara, parure, earrings, almost any goddamned thing that can be sprinkled with sparklers? Not a ring, though.

That would be putting too much weight on the thing.

He will follow up this gift with gowns, furs, milk-white pearls, anything that women want for the buying in London! The town is a paradise for women with retail inclinations. He thinks of his ward, Pevenche, who has very recently taught him a great deal on this extensive subject.

In Venice, he thinks, he will buy the actress an island in the lagoon, something of a manageable size with a simple pavilion for summer love-trysts. When things are difficult, he will imagine that pavilion, hung with diamonds.

The evening proceeds as those before. Hard and sweet.

Tom's body is now in Paris. Valentine has received the news this day and his mind turns over the now-familiar agony: should he allow Tom's daughter, Pevenche, to see what is left of her father, as she shrilly demands to do, or should he lie to her and say that the body has been buried in Venice? He is inclined to allow her to see Tom. Dizzom's contacts report that the embalming has been scrupulously done, and the cadaver has travelled exceptionally well.

Valentine had the mistress of her school break the news of the death to Tom's daughter. He could not trust himself to do it, and by the time he comes to take her to tea she has composed herself enough to talk freely of her father and his passing. There's something strange about her attitude. There is an absence of delicacy in her curiosity. She wants to know all the details, demands that he draw the murder weapon for her, asks how long her father took in dying, grows ominously quiet when he refuses her this information. He excuses himself a moment on the pretext of fetching a newspaper. When he returns, she chatters bright and brainless as a parrot. It is horrible. She is too old now to assume the ruthlessness of childhood. It is not becoming in a twelve-year-old – or whatever she is – he never remembers – expensively educated and sheltered from the world.

She is so unlike Tom in this. Tom was subtle, charming, clever, usually.

And so unlike Tom she is in her looks, though she shares his notable bulk. Pevenche, young as she is, stands awkwardly at an inch over six foot, and she's generously endowed widthways too. Today she is dressed to the gills in tawdry black flounce like a Bartholomew Baby, a costume of her own choosing, of which she is immensely proud. However, she is incommoded by ruffles in tight crevices to the extent that she moves stiffly like a doll, and he sees how cruelly the seams cut into her plumpness by the rolls of fat that blossom wherever the fabric relaxes its grip.

Valentine has not hesitated to make Tom's daughter his ward and has already settled a sum on her, making it known to the simpering Mistress Haggardoon who runs her boarding school. What will happen to her in the periods of holiday is something he shall worry about later. Tom himself never took the girl home, preferring to visit her at the school. Valentine is faintly amused and at the same time slightly horrified at Pevenche's blatant lack of gratitude for his help. She expects to be taken to elegant teas and luncheons, and on the very day she heard of her father's death, she shamelessly asked for an increase in her allowance.

She takes his intervention for granted, saying, 'I'm too big for you to send me to the Angel-Makers, I suppose,' and before he

89

realises that this is her childishly incompetent idea of a drollity he is racked with worry that she even knows about the women who take in babies for a fee, and despatch them as soon as possible to a world where they will no longer trouble their parents with expenditure. Indeed the parents and the Angel-Makers, who often subscribe to several Burial Clubs that pay out for funerals, can even profit from a murdered child. Pevenche cannot know it, but this subject is personally dolorous to him. For yes, Valentine has some of these nurses in his pay too, though under strict supervision, and he is the patron of more than one Burial Club, because there are those among his lace-carriers and cure-victims who are afflicted with fertile wombs but lack the wherewithal to get rid of their own unwanted babies. He deplores the need but he is fond of his girls and he'd rather they did not have blood on their hands.

Pevenche too is childishly excited by the great diamond drain on London's jewellers.

'It's nawful, ain't it, Uncle Valentine?' she says happily. 'Worsen the Queen of France.'

She is full of theories, some uncomfortably close to the truth, and knows the day's tally by heart, can list the leading establishments and has added up the value of all the gems stolen this week. Mentally, Valentine Greatrakes makes a note to let Pevenche have one of the diamond brooches rejected by Mimosina Dolcezza before the others are despatched for refashioning. In this one thing, the extreme fascination with diamonds, the girl does indeed resemble her father, he thinks fondly.

Half listening to Pevenche's harsh voice, Valentine is almost tempted to share the truth, such delectation would she take in it. She might have some ideas to freshen the game, for that is what all this is to her: a game. Even the death of her father she seems to see not as a tragedy but a swingeing stroke in an exciting drama. She has presented to him two ready-formed plots for avenging Tom.

Valentine tells Pevenche that the matter of her father's murderer is in hand, and she purses her lips. 'Why do you not tell me what you are thinkin', Uncle Valentine? Why must you keep it so prodigious snug?'

He smiles nervously and rises to his feet, reaching for his hat and cane. No one else questions him like this.

'When do you come to me again, Uncle Valentine?' she asks, with her head on one side, and her hand insinuating itself into his. Just for a moment, she creates the peculiar illusion of diminishing in bulk to the proper childlike proportions of her age.

'Soon, dear heart, very soon,' he promises.

'I live for your visits you know,' she whispers. 'Since my Pa died you are all the world to me. You know I have nothing else.'

Valentine knows that a declaration of her preciousness to him is now required but he backs away, stammering, disengaging her hand and grasping for his cane, which slides between his legs and trips him up.

She is by his side all the way to the front door, pressing against him in the narrow hallway. He steels himself not to flinch away, but he cannot help it. As he leaves the building he hears the strum of her ukulele shredding the air with tuneless misery.

For Pevenche is not afflicted with the itch of making actual music. She has never needed to finish a tune before tickling the ear of her listeners to such a disagreeable frenzy that whatever she wants is given to her on the instant, so quickly that all she desires is achieved without even disturbing the cerebral processes of her benefactors.

Valentine does not know why he does so, but he finds himself turning on his heel.

He goes back in and summons the headmistress, handing her a packet of cash.

'Buy something nice for the girl,' he says gruffly, loud enough for Pevenche to hear. 'Spend it all.'

The music dies away on the instant, and the young votress of harmony is heard to sigh happily.

St Giles' Greek, the tongue of the street, styles ready cash as 'gingerbread' or 'balsam', and Valentine Greatrakes is pleased with the nourishing and healing implications of these words. It is his experience that money soothes and smoothes over a great many harmful things.

The Decoction Called Sacrum

Take Virginia Snake Root powder'd 6 drams; boil it in Water 1 pint to half a pint; strain and reserve the Liquor by itself: boil the remaining root in a pint more of Water to half a pint as before (adding when it is near boiled enough, Cochineal half a scruple); strain it, and having mixed together both the Liquors, dissolve in it Venice Treacle half an ounce; Honey 1 ounce; and then strain it once more for use.

Here I present you with a most desirable Alexipharmack, second to none, for it inspires as 'twere, the Blood and Juices flowing in the Vessels and Viscera with a new Ferment; and by moving them gently, and keeping them in an equable uniform mixture, frees them from Coagulation and Putrefaction. By the same kindly Agitation it dissipates the Poison Particles that begin to gather in tumultuous Clusters, and hinders their coming to Maturation; and then so occupies, animates and confirms the Blood and Spirits, as to defend them from taking the Venomous Impression.

Valentine Greatrakes is taking his time with Mimosina Dolcezza. Gradually, they start to remove their clothes when they make love. Each time, another garment is finally discarded and another small acreage of flesh revealed to the eyes and fingertips of the other.

No one would believe it if they saw the angles that lovers see, thinks Valentine. *That's why love conjures so many metaphors.*

An upside-down view of a slightly puckered thigh half turning away, a shadowed nipple like a fisherman's knot . . . even when he cannot be with her, such images crowd his shuttered retinas and paint them with a hot and shadowy pink palette.

He knows there have been others before him. Not many, and none such as he, of course. He thinks of her sentimentally, as his little soiled dove, but this only draws him closer. He himself has been far from chaste in his life, and yet he feels his virginity renewed by this love. It must also be so for her.

He has never known a woman so intimately. Within a week he has made love to her more times than to any other woman he has ever known. Her narrow body is delicate as a petal. Her eyes are pure candlelight. She is never looking away from him. He has never experienced such attention to his desires, even from women trained for the purpose. Her hands are peerless, shameless, yet delicate. He feels dizzy merely to think of her lips.

He knows what she loves to put inside her mouth. She likes everything exalted with sugar. She drinks her coffee, tea and chocolate sweetened dramatically. She likes all kinds of sugared and honeyed things, and even insists on fruited sauces for meat and fish dishes. The only person he knows with such a surrendering weakness for sweet things and a capacity for the consumption of confectionery is of course his ward, Pevenche, who is sorely afflicted with worms. But he mislikes comparing the two women.

The love of Mimosina Dolcezza is a continuous revelation, a daily peeling of flakes from his eyes. He did not know it could be like this. He did not begin to suspect it, and he is never replete with the sensations of it.

Now he has unwrapped the actress to her natal state, and he has made love to her in all the ways his fantasy can permit, and has been amazed at the additional postures permitted by hers. He averts his mind from how she knows what she does in the way of generating pleasure. Indeed, such pleasure is generated that he becomes mindless and numb with it, so much so that there is mercifully soon no need to think of its provenance. He spends whole nights with her, whole days too, neglecting his businesses apart from cursory visits to the depository when Mimosina Dolcezza must run some mysterious feminine errands or perform at the theatre.

Dizzom eyes him strangely, but says nothing. He presents the inventories of the nostrums, makes a rapid précis of the incomings at the depository and asks for instructions on specific matters, slowly, as if he understands that his master now hears everything filtered through the muffling gauze of love.

Of course Dizzom understands more after he first beholds Mimosina Dolcezza, not in the theatre but in her own rooms, in a tender deshabillé. When Valentine hears his man announced, he calls him in directly, forgetting where he is, and with whom. Perhaps he wants Dizzom to share this – not merely the public woman, but the flushed, tousled angel he alone knows. And despite the impropriety, she seems to understand that with Dizzom nothing is to be hidden, for she smiles at him enchantingly from between the sheets, with no reproofs for the intrusion.

Valentine is oddly satisfied that Dizzom has now seen his treasure: he neglects at first to ask what confidential matters could have sent him in search of his master at the actress's rooms. He watches his old friend with intense interest. On seeing the actress for the first time, Dizzom is visibly moved. He looks at her with glistening eyes. His expression suggests fear and abject devotion, all at once.

Dizzom too is almost distracted from the matter in hand, but after a moment he pulls his wits together and apologetically draws his master aside. He has matters to discuss that he judges unsuitable for the ears of such a lovely lady.

In whispers, Valentine is made to understand that Tom's body has encountered troubles in Paris. Coffins have become so commonplace a vehicle for smugglers that – the greatest of ironies – Tom's has been confiscated and opened up by the officers of the law. Now it reclines on a bench in a Parisian mortuary, awaiting fresh documents of release. Valentine shivers and turns away, his mind immediately filled with the sight of Mimosina Dolcezza, mercifully blotting out the image of Tom's corpse peered at by Frenchy customs officers with no great show of compassion.

Dizzom leaves and Valentine stumbles back into the arms of the actress.

He shudders to think that only the merest chance has put her in a production bound for London, that only the frail thread of her theatrical ambitions, thrown randomly across Europe, has now tethered her here, for him to love her.

Her English has improved amazingly, though she still minces her participles in the most endearing fashion. In fact, it turns out that she already possessed much more than a rudimentary grasp, though she has never been in England before. When he asks her about it, she casts a veil over how she came to acquire her relative fluency.

'I met English people, you know, before you, *caro*,' she says. 'You are not a rare breed in this world, you Englishmen.'

It is just another miracle, he thinks, that she was able to restrain herself from talking so much at the beginning of their relationship, as if she guessed that in his sad state he had need of simple physical comforts. For by now of course he has told her, sketchily, about Tom. He has spared her the details of the murder naturally; has implied a sad rather than a violent end. He has been baptised with the sweetly salt tears of her commiserations. She has held him while he cries, she has knelt over him, stroking the blistered ridges of his back that he has never allowed another woman to touch. She has rubbed aloes and oils into its dry excrescences and laid her cheek upon its old puckerings without any disgust and only with tenderness.

But tonight she will give him a moment of the purest horror.

This night, he undresses only her hair, laying the tresses about her shoulders. The mustard light of the candle has spiced her eyes so he can look nowhere else until she leaves the room, some time towards dawn. Then he lets down his shoulders, lassitude blooming like a branch of red blossom down his spine, and he's dropping on the sag to crush the vivid tiredness out of his back.

It's then that it impales him and he's leaping up, too much winded by shock to scream.

'Eecch,' he wheezes, scraping its talons from his skin: a bat is hunched in the bed she's just vacated and it's lying there quivering in a crook of the linen, misshapen, evil, with a taste for his flesh. He brandishes a candle, but the thing's impervious to light, afraid of nothing. Now it flattens its fluttering, feigns death, to draw him closer, so it can fly at him and dip its mandibles in his neck. Why, even now it's cultivating the throbs for a richer feed, he's read of such things. He feels more naked than the moon. He's never been so naked and never needed his clothes so much.

What's that smell?

Do bats smell? He perceives atoms of the inimitable perfume – white musk and apples – of Mimosina Dolcezza rising almost visibly from the disturbed sheets, a sweetness bursting out of the faint sweat of mildew.

Where is she?

In his panic it seems to him that his mistress has been transformed into this bat.

And his eyes do not once leave the brute as he backsteps to the too-close wall, where, espaliered, he prays for her to come back, and he prays for her not to come back and find him jellied by a bat, though surely of a rare and spiteful species, and the minutes pass and the decades of minutes and still the thing plays dead, garnering its venom, and still he's stricken to a standstill, only his heart skittering like a nutmeg grater, the guttering candle gouting down his wrists, binding his hairs to the skin that fear has plucked to goose. Then she sweeps back into the room, luminous, fresh, dressed for the world.

And picks up her black feathered hairpin and pushes it back into her soft, feathery hair.

And Valentine promptly puts his conscience upon the rack: how has he contrived to think so badly of this divine woman? The brutality of Tom's death has infected his ability to enjoy innocence. No, his whole life has contaminated the way he has lived until now.

This moment is the turning point, this woman the pivot. He wants to renovate his life so that she fits inside it. He loves this life of his – it's just that he now wants more than he has had before.

· 8 ·

Analeptic Electuary

Take powder'd Chocolate 2 ounces; juice of ground Kermes strain'd half an ounce; Ambergris (ground with a little loaf Sugar) 8 grains; Oil of Cinnamon 1 drop; Oil of Nutmeg 2 drops; Syrup of Balsam 2 ounce; or as much as needs to give it a due consistency, mix.

It nourishes and strengthens, repairs the wasted Flesh, recruits lost Spirits, and brings assistance in pining Consumptions. But I have sometimes observ'd it sit too heavy upon weak Stomachs.

Let half an ounce be taken at 8 in the Morning, and at 4 in the Afternoon, drinking after it Asses' Milk.

'Why do you leave me now?'

'I have promised my ward an outing.'

'Your ward? What is this thing?'

'The daughter of my friend.'

'Why must you do this thing then?'

'She is the daughter of my friend. My friend who died.'

Mimosina Dolcezza looks chastened and holds his hand tight, murmuring endearments. 'I had no conception,' she says again and again. After a while she looks up and asks, 'But where is the mother?'

'I don't know.'

'You don't know the mother of this child? The wife of your best friend in the world?'

'He never said.'

She stares at him and he clearly reads her thoughts: *Englishmen! Barbarians!*

And who can blame her?

Yet nor can he bring himself to blame Tom, who had simply arrived one day with the babe in his arms. 'Look what I got myself!' he said, and that was all his explanation. The red-haired baby looked like a jointed doll, dressed in an extravagant costume, and with Tom's face so bemused as to be foolish, he himself looked like an overgrown child. He was trailed by a little Blackfriars nurse, but it was Tom who inserted the feeding horn when the child started fussing, first checking the tiny sponge at its tip and testing the temperature of the milk with an expert finger. The child drained the horn in a scant second and was soon squalling for more.

All Tom would say in explanation of the infant was that he had begot her in 'Doctor' Graham's Temple of Health and Hymen in Adelphi Terrace, and had done so indeed upon Graham's Grand Magnetico-Electric Celestial Bed. At this Valentine had laughed heartily. Graham is a prince among quacks and his bed promises to guarantee both stupendous pleasure and fertility. Graham charges a five-shilling entrance fee merely to see the Celestial Bed, which measures twelve feet by nine feet and is surrounded by twenty-eight pillars of 'crystal'. It is claimed that this masterpiece is modelled on the bed of the favourite Sultana in the Seraglio of the Grand Turk. According to handbills distributed by Graham, the bed's 'super-celestial dome' contains 'oderiferous, balmy and aetherial spices, odours and essences', and is 'coated on the under-side with mirrors so disposed as to reflect the various charms and attitudes of the happy couple . . .' Their exertions bring forth music in a sympathetic rhythm and volume. The bed's mattress is stuffed with the tails of English stallions ('renowned for their sexual vigour') and below it are fifteen hundredweight of magnets 'con-tinually pouring forth in an ever-flowing circle powerful tides of the magnetic effluvium'; all this to stimulate the ovum in the act of generation.

Tom wasn't saying any more, having obtained the belly-laugh he wanted. Valentine Greatrakes had refrained from further inquiries. There were no shortages of willing females with a soft spot for Tom.

Making hard love to ladies all over the place he was, and always saying, 'It's a mean mouse that has but one hole to go to.'

The romance that had generated the baby must have ended badly. Tom's affairs often concluded in sore ways. While he had always to have a woman in mind, and at his disposal, Tom never desired a settled life. The women took it hard. Tom had no patience with tears and feminine laments. A weeping female inspired less compassion in him than an arthritic pickpocket. Valentine had several times occasion to reproach his friend with instances of heartlessness. Whatever had produced this child there was no doubt some of Tom's usual devilment in it. Tom's pleasures were inclined to cost someone else dearly.

But in the way of these things between them, Valentine refrained from asking more about the child, though Tom occasionally recounted, with a chuckle, precocious words reported by her nurse and later by the mistress of the highly respectable boarding school where he had placed her, and also, with guffaws, prodigious feats of appetite by the little girl. Tom never thought to ask the child to live with him, and his contact with her dwindled sharply as she grew portlier and less pretty. But the child was tenacious: Tom could not altogether shrug her off. He was summoned to the boarding school on various pretexts, always returning with a defiant expression, similar to the one he wore after a final confrontation with a staled mistress. It was clear that he wished he had never claimed the child; it was also clear that he did not hide this fact from her.

Another girl would have been crushed, but, far from shrinking, young Pevenche transformed her hurt into an outward display of supreme self-confidence. Just like her father, she learned to show no vulnerability, except tactically. On rare occasions Tom had brought little Pevenche – well, large Pevenche to tell the truth – to the depository, where she astounded all with her voluminous chatter and discomforted everyone with her shameless curiosity. Dizzom was plainly terrified by the huge child, who peered at him and repeatedly asked him to unscrew his back teeth and show her his treasures concealed in there. If he demurred there was a rare flash of temper from Tom, a side of him seldom displayed at the depository though it was sent out to work on the streets, of course, as necessary.

99

Once Pevenche tore the gauze top from a jar of living butterflies and stuffed one inside her mouth, biting it in half.

'Why did you do that, dear heart?' Valentine asked, shocked to his core.

'It's so pretty,' she said, 'but nasty, I'm afraid.'

She spat the rejected wing on the floor and demanded something quick and sweet to take the taste away. Tom joked, 'What an oesophagus! That girl will swallow anything. She'd eat a rat whole if it had cinnamon and sugar on it.' He tapped her large head, and not gently: 'Few intellectual symptoms in our Baby P. But full of big-girl appetites. Cunning with them, too.' The girl flinched away from her father, but said nothing.

The blistering, shameful thought had even crossed Valentine's mind that Tom had intended to raise the girl and set her up in a bawdy-house, that this motive lay dark and dormant beneath his taking up a female bastard, not a male one, to nurture. (He certainly must have had a choice of offspring.) Too often for comfort, Tom joked about moving the business of the depository in the direction of the Venus Sports, always stressing that the pleasurable company must be of known provenance and juvenility. Valentine had firmly discouraged Tom from such thoughts, but they continued to cross his own mind whenever he saw Pevenche, for Tom cruelly incited the child to dress with a vulgar ostentation that ill befitted her ungainly shape. The nastier the colour combinations, the more lamentable Pevenche's outfits, the more Tom applauded them. And the larger she grew, the more he encouraged her in a ridiculous pretence of juvenility. If 'Baby P.' saw that the joke was against her, she still chose to play it for laughs. It sometimes seemed to Valentine that it would have been better for Pevenche if her father had not snatched her away from a mother whose influence she sadly and demonstrably lacked, and who must have surely been heartsore all these years for the loss of her baby.

Tom's fathering was no way at all to put the manners on the girl.

Now Valentine says aloud to Mimosina Dolcezza, 'We never knew where the child came from. My friend did not encourage us to inquire.'

'How strange are you English. So this ward is still just a child, then?'

'Yes,' says Valentine and the actress appears to lose interest in this scrap.

It is not strictly true. Pevenche might more properly be called a young lady these days. She must be at least twelve, is it? He cannot remember and he cannot guess from looking at her. He has no talent for placing an age on a woman. Moreover, his experience of girls has never brought him in contact with one so *well-nourished* as Pevenche. But he does not wish to talk about her age with Mimosina Dolcezza. Pevenche's maturity makes him feel old, and somewhat encumbered.

And he must admit to himself he likes it that the actress finds it hard to let him go, even when it is to see his ward. He enjoys her touching little repertoire of petulance and hurt: all these things show the force of her attachment. She performs all her pouts most charmingly and he is never bored by this show of his indispensability.

But the next time he says that he must leave her for a day's outing with Pevenche, the sky darkens around him as she glares and tells him that he need not bother to call on her tomorrow.

'Don't be selfish, dear heart,' he says. 'The child is an orphan. Surely you can spare some compassion for her.'

'For a very little girl she demands very greatly much.'

'Not nearly as much as you do,' he retorts, provoked by the *froideur* of her tone. 'You are a cold one, aren't you, not to feel for the girl?'

She recoils and hisses at him: 'And you are no gentleman, to talk to me in this way.'

He hopes that this dismaying comment is lightly meant, that nothing lies beneath it. But he cannot be certain.

Until now he has been sure that Mimosina Dolcezza, an innocent in London, knows nothing of the rigidity of the British classes, and in no way comprehends his ambiguous position in the society she entertains. He is positive that to her his elegant clothes, his abundant resources, and his apparently endless leisure betoken just one thing: that he is that object prized for its very uselessness:

a London gentleman. Her English lacks the discriminatory organ that might detect the little cracks in his accent, the south London vowels and the splashes of Irish that occasionally insinuate themselves into the loftiest sentence. All this time he has been congratulating himself that he has found a lover who can see only his nobility.

With this one sally – 'you are no gentleman' – she has struck his self-assurance at its rickety foundation.

He stares at her, in one second as full of suspicion as he had previously been of love. And she herself narrows her eyes and stares back at him, with no mediating tenderness whatsoever in her glance. She turns aside and he notices suddenly that she's been losing flesh.

It is not becoming for a woman of her age – whatever it is, I'm sure I've no idea – to wax stringy in the flank. It's that ridiculous food she serves. With all that money she lays out on pampering the gut, none of it seems to stick.

He thinks about it with resentment. By night, all these days, he's craved a slab of moist gammon ham, a prime loin of beef dressed in nothing but stout, something a body can ravage about cleanly to obtain swift satisfaction. Not these coy turrets of sauced morsels fringed with frivolous herbiage. He observes miserably that nothing on the actress's table lies flat and meek upon the plate: everything is to be flirted with, assailed and conquered. Wearily he's ascended lucent aspics that resemble jewelled high heels, and pushed his fork through savoury architectural jellies studded with unknown high-coloured meats. His gorge clamps rebelliously, even at the smell.

And the desserts! What an insult to honest food! Why, there was last week a stag made out of marzipan that bled claret when, at her urging, he removed a miniature arrow from its creamy flank. And the next day it was a mousse in the shape of a hedgehog, fragrant with sorrel, nutmeg and saffron, and finished with a full bristling of slivered and blanched almonds. It is not merely ridiculous, this food, it is a mockery, and in it he is quick to sense a lack of respect for him that her present grumblings about his ward only serve to underline.

All the while he has mused on the food, she has been glaring at him. She is not about to let go the subject of Pevenche or his behaviour in her regard. Her eyes are stiff as glass.

'I am learning about you Englishmen,' says she. 'That you have, what it is called, a stricket' (he thinks she means a 'streak') 'of mean, that is as deep as your canal' – and she points in the direction of the Thames with a Venetian's unerring instinct for the location of water.

'All this because I criticised you,' wonders Valentine, aloud. Yet he's breathing more easily with relief that it is not after all his wrongness of class she has derided but his waywardness of temper. He decides to keep his tone light and mocking, thinking that perhaps she will meet him halfway, because he hates this country they have entered, this cold and dangerous territory without softness and affection, a barbarous place where heartfelt wounds are exchanged in a moment.

But there's no answering levity in her. She responds in a quiet, ironclad voice, 'You are leaving me now.'

His lungs and bowels contract then dilate with fear and despair, as if she means it is for ever, when surely she is merely staging a little and temporary theatrical scene: the only way she knows to carry the day. Her weapons are so poorly developed that he almost feels sorry for her, no, he does pity her, such a helpless little creature, who knows only how to mimic anger in a fetching way upon the stage, but has no depths of interior emotion to feel it. Her talent is for amiability, for sweetness, for yielding. She cannot denature herself to the point of actual rage.

She'd rather drop a tooth than an unkind word from that mouth.

If he leaves now, she will suffer terribly for his absence, and perhaps this is a necessary punishment. Although this little scene has been illuminating, he would not like to have it happen again.

He pulls on the minimal number of clothes. He strides out of the room without looking back, but he feels her lying motionless amid the spill of sheets, counting his steps. He dawdles down to the street door, stopping a second on each step, waiting for her imploring voice. He is aware that he has left certain items of clothing as hostages in her bedroom.

103

It is almost more than he can do, to stop himself from turning and running back up to her. What points his feet on their downward path is the thought of the worm that has now entered the apple of their mutual satisfaction. This single argument has unparadised them.

He is shot through with misery.

At the slam of the door upstairs there is a stinging in his nose, as if she has struck it. He feels unbearably excluded, even though he has brought this exile upon himself. He turns on his heel and hurtles back up the stairs. She is waiting for him just inside the door, and silently enfolds him in her arms, before leading him back to bed.

'Damn it,' he says aloud, still thinking about the quarrel, hours later, when, all forgiven – or at least bravely seeming so – they are taking a restorative promenade in the park and the figure of Dizzom can be seen approaching. The apologetic contortion of his silhouette informs them both that he bears another message from Pevenche.

Tom's daughter has not been backward in realising that her guardian is far more tender-hearted than her father. It is a shame, he reflects, that the girl cannot understand that he would happily do things for her out of simple affection.

She has to keep testing me, to make sure I'll deliver on a continuous basis.

Her timing is impeccably bad just now. He thinks again, silently. 'Damn . . .'

The sutures are too fresh; the wound is not yet healed.

The actress knows his thoughts without further explanation, in that magical way of hers, and she responds aloud, 'So it is a damning thing then to love me? Suddenly? Because I ask for a little proof? I see my mistake. I was stupid. And perhaps you have already tired of me and found a new toy to play with? *Va bene.* So it is with women like me. We are used and thrown away. I understand. I shall not detain you further. I wish you every happiness, my dearest darling. And your poor little baby ward, of course.'

Her voice grows softer and softer, husky with poisonous sweetness. She gives him the full run of her tongue, and she finds deadly words in English that he could never have suspected in her vocabulary.

Dizzom has by now arrived and delivers his commission in the void between them, and leaves hastily. More words are spoken, and looks are exchanged, both with such a bitterness as to rive their love asunder again. This time, when they part, it is with the indelible imprint of stinging words that can never be erased and, worse, images of an ugliness between them that will not quickly fade.

He has called her self-absorbed, a cold fish. She has defamed him as obsessive and as the foolish gull of a little girl. She has accused him of lying to her, that he goes not to Pevenche but to a grown-up mistress, using his ward as a pretext. At this he flinches, because this reminds him of his half-involuntary lapse of honesty with his mistress, who, based on something he has said, thinks the girl a small child.

Who can bear to see themselves in such dim and nasty lights?

· 9 ·

An Antiloimick Decoction

Take Roots of Scorzonera 2 ounces; Zedoary half an ounce;
Contrayerva, Spanish Angelica, Shavings of Harts-horn and
Ivory, each 2 drams; Cochineal whole 4 scruples; boil these in
fine, clear Barley Water, from 2 pints and a half to 24 ounces;
throwing into it, towards the last, Saffron 1 scruple: To the
strain'd Liquor add Epidemial and Treacle Water, each 2 ounces;
Syrup of Gilly-flowers 4 ounces; Juice of Kermes strain'd half an
ounce; Leaves of Gold 4; mix all together.

When the Venom of a Malignant Fever assaulting the Spirits,
Stupefies, and almost strikes them Dead; these generous
Alexipharmacks (timely and frequently exhibited) inspire new
Vigour, shake off the deleterious Copula, and so sometimes
snatch the Sick out of the very Jaws of Death.

Now he has all the time he wants to spend with his red-headed
ward.

He takes Pevenche to see Mrs Salmon's Waxworks in Fleet
Street, but she grows peckish before viewing half the figures there.
At Don Saltero's Coffee House in Cheyne Walk, while she consumes hot chocolates and egg-flips, he finds his eyes prefer to
wander the room and its many curiosities. Don Saltero's boasts two
hundred and ninety-three unusual exhibits, ranging from a nun's
penitential whip to a whale's mummified pizzle. His ward is mercifully silent at the important act of consumption. Then he hears
her drain her final glass with audible satisfaction and ask to be
taken to the Chelsea Bun House in Jew's Row 'just for a taste'.

Three buns later, his ear bruised with her prattle, he invites her
to see the beasts in the zoo at Tower Bridge, where she shows little

interest in the tigers, wolves, eagles and Indian cats, but demands to remain until the four lions devour a dog who until the very moment of his despatch sits serenely in the cage with them, exchanging pleasantries. This grisly spectacle appears to give Pevenche a prodigious appetite for lamb cutlets. He is disconcerted when she asks him to cut them up for her.

'Baby P. don't dare touch sharp knives,' she informs him in a lisping whisper. 'And the cutlets are so very large for her little mouth.'

That mouth, slicked with grease, works fast and furious over the cutlets, paring them to Hansel-like bones in short order. And then she is ready for a pudding of apple and blackberry with sweetened cream.

Tom always laughed about her feeding so enormously. He encouraged her to great feats of consumption: he could make anecdotes of them later. The girl concurred, it seemed, partly to win her father's brief attention, but also because of a natural inclination to gluttony. While she was cunning, she did not seem to understand the trap into which she had fallen. If she refused the mountains and valleys of food, if she shed some of her bulk to become less of a grotesque – why, then she might even have been appealing. But Tom had cruelly, thoughtlessly decided on her course, and there was Tom's temper, hung on its hair-trigger, to be faced if she disappointed him. She did not have to be a coward to be passive.

Sickened by the death of the dog, Valentine touches nothing on his plate. He wonders if the actress has been to see the zoo. He thinks of how he would have covered her eyes with his own hands if she had witnessed the poor hound's demise. At the thought of her translucent eyelids he closes his own and departs mentally into memories of intensest pleasure.

Pevenche is tugging his sleeve. 'Where are we goin' now, Uncle Valentine?'

They see the dwarf Count Boruwlaski performing his diminutive prodigies at Carlisle House and the midget Corsican fairy in Cockspur Street. Later they stroll in Vauxhall Gardens for a study of the grand ladies' dresses but she's soon urging his elbow in the direction of the Ham Room for a slice of meat so airy that one can read a newspaper through it. It's said that the master carver is so skilled that he could cover the whole garden with the tenuous shavings from a single joint. Pevenche consumes enough of them to line a large carriage. He takes her to the more exclusive Ranelagh Rotunda where she is not at all interested in the gilded porticoes and rainbowed ceiling but only in the regale of bread and butter, and afterwards persuades him to divert to Knightsbridge so that she may yet again sample the sweet Asses' Milk purveyed by Madame Cornelys, the Venetian society hostess now fallen upon hard times. Valentine looks with interest upon the vivacious but withered hostess, wonders if she is personally known to Mimosina Dolcezza. The lady herself has eyes only for Pevenche, who has consumed a quart of the sweet white froth and claims, as usual, that it has utterly renovated her appetite. The professional wits of Valentine Greatrakes try to configure what strange powders have gone into thickening the brew, and how sick it will make his ward.

But Pevenche appears to have a cast-iron belly to go with her steely will.

For some reason he cannot rejoice in this sturdy constitution and finds himself wishing, shamefully, that Pevenche might be taken ill and put to bed for a good long time, and not just because it would thereby excuse his attendance upon her.

And in the meantime, he could perhaps send some of his quacks to her, and do something about that appalling carroty hair.

The next time he sees the actress it is on the arm of Gervase Gordon, Lord Stintleigh, the Member for Hearthford. The man is rumoured to be tangential to the circle closest to ultimate power. He's already served as Foreign Secretary and it is said that in his current nameless position his portfolio has been, if anything, enhanced.

Valentine has come across the dandified wormcase before: for the man has intervened on several occasions with petty bye-laws against the free-traders, in a manner that shows an intimate knowledge of their ways and means. They have also met across various polished tables: Lord Stintleigh serves on some of the same committees as Valentine does; they are both active members of the Society for the Reformation of Manners, the Repression of Mendacity and the Prosecution of Felons. These organisations supplement the efforts of those overworked parish constabularies whom in daily life Valentine spends a great deal of ingenuity in thwarting. He sees nothing strange in this dichotomy: for no one in London has as much to gain from protecting his property as Valentine Greatrakes. Except perhaps Lord Stintleigh, whose motives for serving are undoubtedly corrupt. These days the politician has risen above such petty committee work, and is no longer heard of in connection with certain scams and rackets. The man has sanitised his connections. It seems that power has proved more attractive than the short-term gains of smuggling.

He despises Stintleigh already. And now the pink-skinned sight of him, walking from the theatre with the smiling actress on his arm, strikes a cruel blow to all the softest parts of Valentine, so that he staggers away into the shadows and sinks to his knees on the begrimed footpath. The couple pass him, chattering, sniggering, never deigning to lower the line of their sight to where he hides his head mumbling like a gin-soaked beggar. He catches a few words of Stintleigh's highfalutin burble. The politician has an unnaturally high voice: he trills like a girl, only speaks from the teeth out. He is complimenting Mimosina Dolcezza on her performance and refers to another he once enjoyed in Vienna.

'Enormously,' he bleats, cocking his eyebrows in ironic exaggeration, like a comedic villain. There is something insinuating even in that single word.

Valentine's eyes swing to the face of the actress: he sees a pure complicity there, an intimate species of smile, a smile that he had thought reserved for himself. It takes a lump clean out of his heart.

So they have met before! The actress knew the politician in the shadowy life before the one she now shares with him. Valentine feels no inclination and certainly lacks the strength to rise from the gutter even as their shadows follow them around a corner and they disappear.

Self-pity wells up at the final glimpse of the impeccable cut of Stintleigh's greatcoat. No doubt the work of the family's tailor. No doubt the cost of it was not even discussed, merely billed discreetly in copperplate on manilla some months afterwards, for the rich always grow richer by trading on their credit.

It is a gift which comes along with their other blessings.

No riches have ever flowed upon Valentine with such insensibility. Can the actress have somehow divined this fact?

Occasionally, he knows, he lets slip a word of dubious provenance, a lapse into the Irish, or St Giles' Greek or Pedlar's French, the copious dialects of the criminal classes. He uses them without irony – unlike a true gentleman who might play at them – these strange words made classical to his ears by long use. She cannot discriminate so finely: they must seem to her, he thinks, some kind of blue-blood patois. She would not know – how could she? – the difference between his conversation and that of the weasellish Gervase Stintleigh.

Could she?

So now he is doubly thwarted of the comfort of his love, of his peace of mind, and this time the odious creature, Stintleigh, is to blame. The part of Valentine Greatrakes that calculates revenge like a scrupulous tax-collector is now raking through the tokens in his mind.

The hot red haze of ire eventually departs. Reason, the best friend of efficiency, cools his mind. At this point, too, his natural optimism also breaks through. Valentine Greatrakes will give happiness every last chance, even on a forced march to Hell. He tells himself that the possibility exists that this is a mere single occasion, that Stintleigh wants only to refresh his knowledge of the Venetian scene with the innocent chatter of the little actress, who might unconsciously let fall something of interest. After all, she would be easy to lure into trust, as he knows himself.

He tells himself that after a decorous supper in some public place, Mimosina Dolcezza will return to the bed he has widowed, and lie there in the dark, thinking of him, and wishing with all her heart to have spent her evening – and her night – very differently, and far more robustly.

He has her followed. He does not care to be seen at that employment himself and nor can he yet bear to see what it might reveal.

Instead he toys with business and busies himself with Pevenche, taking her to Sadler's Wells to see Scaglioni's troupe of performing dogs, led by a brave canine named Moustache, acting *The Deserter*. This entrances the girl, and on succeeding evenings, which he might otherwise have spent trailing Mimosina Dolcezza, he is yet again to be seen with his ward, this time watching bulldogs ascending in a Montgolfier balloon and a prodigy of a pig, 'well versed in all Languages, perfect Arithmetician & Composer of Musick'. After applauding the pig, who reads the minds of sundry ladies in the audience, Pevenche feeds so voraciously on pork and crackling that she breeds a temporary famine in Valentine's pockets.

Every night, when he finally returns to the depository, it is to find no letter of apology from the actress despite the fact that he feels one is virtually owed to him now for her harsh words and silence; she cannot know he is aware of her small leaning in the direction of betrayal with Stintleigh.

Silence, eh?

He can maintain a manly silence, too. He sends no note, no flowers, and no diamonds. Instead he takes his ward to Regent Street to see Signor Cappelli's cats. The *corps dramatique* consists of a mother cat, two sons and a daughter who beat upon a drum, turn a spit, grind knives, play music, strike upon an anvil, roast coffee, ring bells, and grind rice in the Italian manner. Then he must submit to Pevenche's command that they attend a lecture by the quack doctor Katterfelto, whose necromancing black cats flash and sparkle when electrical currents are passed through their coats. The doctor also projects images of enormous influenza-spreading insects on to a screen, offering the only possible remedy, at five shillings a bottle.

With difficulty, he persuades Pevenche that it's hardly suitable entertainment for a lady to attend the cock-fight at Hockley-in-the-Hole at Clerkenwell, and that the ghost of 'Scratching Fanny' in Cock Lane is certainly a fraud and not worth the night-time vigil she urges on him.

Instead he invites a woman friend, the pretty widow of one of his colleagues, to share their next outing, thinking to cheer both of them up with a fine tea-party at an excellent establishment in Bond Street. To his mind, the women have their bereavements in common, and may offer comfort to one another. Widow Grimpen is no dealer in cullies, but a respectable young mantua-maker. She is also a one-time amour of Tom's, and in the back of Valentine's mind lurks a desire to see his ward together with Sylvia Grimpen, in case some symphonic arrangement of features might confirm his old hunch about the girl's maternal parentage. He cannot remember the time of the liaison. And he never *can* put his finger on the exact age of his ward. Her great size indicates adolescence, but her behaviour is often that of a child considerably younger. Seeing the two of them together will perhaps settle the thing once and for all.

Pevenche confounds his sociable plans. With the expression of a wall upon her face, she refuses the hand of the widow. She positions herself at an angle that precludes conversation with the woman and also prevents a clear comparison of their features from his side of the table. At first, the girl sits in flinty silence, her shoulder aimed at Widow Grimpen. But every time the woman speaks, Pevenche snorts loudly or interrupts with a different tangent of conversation addressed exclusively to himself. Valentine feels himself dissolving in a smelt of embarrassment and pity for Widow Grimpen.

Having taken the measure of Pevenche, and of the weakness of the girl's guardian, the widow decides on her own course. Which is to charm Valentine Greatrakes, the object of almost any lady he encounters, though he himself is not aware of it, merely thinking the female sex a charming one altogether. He is always a little bemused at other men's tales of shrews and viragos.

Ignoring the girl, the widow chats brightly and generally, two crimson spots nippling her cheeks. All three swallow their tea and consume their pastries. They present a spectacle of utter misery. And when finally the widow leans over and touches his arm to thank him for the treat, Pevenche starts to scream, 'Go! Go! Go! Go!' at a pitch high enough to scald a dog's ear.

The widow, bestowing pitying rather than pitiable looks, stands up and backs away. The staff of the coffee shop and other customers avert their eyes at the din. Valentine follows the widow to the door and discreetly presses some coins into her hand.

'I'm sorry, Sylvia,' he whispers, but stops short. He sees cynicism in her face.

She will not meet his eye, turns and disappears into the Bond Street crowd. Only when the door has closed behind her does Pevenche desist from her screams. She posts a large confection into her still-open mouth. Lush petals of cream bloom around her lips and daub tendrils of hair caught up in her moving jaws. She chews stolidly, throwing baleful glances at the door. She does not look at Valentine as he returns to the table, and when he looks at her he finds himself mesmerised by the trembling of a large crumb on the busy pinkness of her wet lips. He would like to run after the widow, catch up with her and speak kindly to her – for, after all, she too is in need of comfort – but something about Pevenche's malevolent munching holds him trapped in his chair. When she has finished every cake on the platter, she puts her sticky hand in his and whispers confidentially: 'It's excellent that she has gone. She was putting us off our food. She didn't like me. I have no friends, you know.'

For the occasion Pevenche has drenched herself in some kind of perfume that stinks horribly of violets and he fears that the stench will never be rinsed from his wrist, not the way she is prodding it with her fingers now, demanding his agreement which he cannot withhold or she will never stop stubbing those fat digits against his flinching skin.

'Yes, dear heart,' he offers. She nods in a businesslike manner.

He does not repeat the experiment.

In the end, he has found that Pevenche does not provide a welcome distraction from thoughts of Mimosina Dolcezza. Instead, the missing of his mistress has provoked some unkind thoughts in the direction of his innocent ward. He knows poor little Pevenche does not deserve for him to hate her presence, and he decides that it is better to ease off in his attentions to her, for her own sake as much as anything, for what use is a grumpy old guardian to a nice young girl? Yes, less of Pevenche, for her own good, until his mind has reached a state of equilibrium, until he has caught up with his work, until he knows just what the actress is up to with the politician.

He refrains from asking any questions, and strains to wait passively for Dizzom to bring him any news that is of relevance. Every day that passes without news is a blessing to him. It means that there is nothing to report, that nothing has developed, that the actress is innocent.

But on the sixth day comes the blow. At the end of a long and tedious report, Dizzom stutters: 'And in the morning, our man saw him leave.'

In the morning he saw Lord Stintleigh leave.

The heart of Valentine Greatrakes breaks in two with a great crack. He marvels that Dizzom is not felled by the apocalyptic noise.

Dizzom is saying, 'Shall we deal with him?' His face is all distorted, as if seen through a magnifying glass. Valentine realises that his own tears are doing this to him. Angrily he slaps his eyelids and the shameful droplets are gone, slipping between his knuckles.

Dizzom, whey-faced, repeats, 'Shall we . . .?'

With a subtle twitch of his left shoulder, he indicates the trappings and detritus of his experiments in new-fangled methods for undetectable and mysterious sudden deaths. He casts a parental smile in the direction of his favourite protégés, his Fulminating Balls, glass globules the size of a pea, primely placed in a wool-wrapped jar among bottles of fast-acting poisons. These pretty marbles each contain half a grain of fulminating silver. If a candidate can be encouraged to alight upon a chair, under the feet of which four of these Balls have been secreted, the unfortunate will disappear in a mysterious explosion, the means of which are elegantly destroyed in their act of usefulness.

But Valentine cannot answer. His head is afire with painful images, battling for space with a torrent of guiltless explanations. Perhaps she has fed the detestable politician on those high-flavoured foods with which she first tempted Valentine himself: not every man boasts a constitution as strong as his own. That's it: Stintleigh was taken ill with the excesses of her table. Or he slipped out in the night, and returned in the morning with a gift, or some news: it was possible that Dizzom's man had dozed in the interval. They always do. It's a lonely job loitering on a street corner, with only a flask of gin to keep a man warm.

I'm sure the worm can never have dipped a finger in her. She's not been touched by him. I would need to see her in the act of it to believe it for the truth.

114

It is searingly easy to imagine her in the act.

He feels the bile rising in his throat, and it occurs to him that this kind of suspicion is like the nausea that precedes a needful vomit: it is the same dilemma: the bitter impurity of doubt and hope must be cast up and out, however painful the purging convulsions, however vile the taste of the truth.

He is in no condition yet to judge the actress on her continence. But he must acknowledge at least the bare facts. Lord Stintleigh has enjoyed an overnight intimacy of one kind or another with the actress and there is but one possible outcome of this outrage.

He thinks wildly of challenging Stintleigh to a duel at Leicester Fields or the Field of Forty Footsteps. But he's stopped in his tracks by the impudent truth: why should an aristocrat accept an invitation from one such as Valentine Greatrakes? The weazen bastard would laugh at such a challenge, fleer and toss his nose at it. Valentine cocks his eyes at bizarre angles to avoid thinking of this.

No, better to do things in the time-honoured, unwhisperable way.

· 10 ·

A Cataplasm in a Quinsy Sore Throat

Take Figs 4 ounces; Album Gaiacum half an ounce; Flower of
Sulphur, long Pepper, each 1 dram; Brandy 2 ounces; Chymical
oil of Wormwood 16 drops; Diacodium as much as will serve,
beat them all in a Mortar 'till well mixt. To these may be added
Swallows or Pigeons Dung, lay it to the Throat, from Ear to Ear,
and renew it as often as it drieth.

In the end, he decides to watch it done, to make sure it is so.

At the appointed hour, at the corner of Hyde Park, he sees
Stintleigh swinging his cane and whistling as he walks towards the
apartments of Mimosina Dolcezza. A sneer of a smile curls his
thin lips, just such a smile as had been imagined by Valentine
Greatrakes, and the politician hums a little refrain from the
actress's London role, *L'Italiana a Londra*'s final aria.

In this vile appropriation, he marks his territory, thinks Valentine, *like the
dog he is.*

As he passes Valentine, who is concealed behind a tree,
Stintleigh's hothouse lapel flower releases its perfume. Even this
delicate invasion of his nostrils enrages Valentine, who snorts and
champs until he is free of it. He has awoken this morning molested
by a husking cough, and the politician's sharp musk-rose has served
to scourge the painful muscles of his throat.

Well, I shall have my revenge for that, among other things.

Valentine watches the bunch of amusers close around the politician, the leader already dipping into his pocket for the snuff to
fling into the eyes of their victim. Stintleigh utters a high-pitched
squeal and covers his face with his hands. The amusers push him
through the gate into the park and suddenly they are alone with

116

him in another world, a tenebrous dangerous world a thousand ages from the elegant thoroughfare. No one can see them through the evergreen foliage and the pitiful demurrings of the politician are muffled by the trees.

They surround him in a tight circle, pushing him from hand to hand. They taunt him with mock begging, all the while rubbing their hands suggestively around his pockets.

'Gi's a farthing, *SIR*! – be so kind and 'umble as to bless us with a little something . . .'

Lord Stintleigh writhes in their midst like a piece of paper in the fire. The leader draws his blade: his is the glory of the kill. The others smile, waiting their chance to rifle his body, for what they find there shall be their payment.

Sitting on the park bench, as Dizzom has suggested, Valentine waits to see it through. He does not flinch, but he finds it hard not to utter the ticklish cough that lurks dangerously in his throat. He's gumming for a glass of beer to lubricate and refrigerate the parched linings of his gullet. While Stintleigh utters his thin screams, Valentine is gulping on the dry fibres at the rear of his tongue.

He releases the cough at last, spitting its feathers into the air, but only when the leader has prodded all Stintleigh's vital organs at least once with the glass dagger. Then he throws a branch thick with leaves over his victim, addressing the dying politician with exaggerated courtesy, 'Keep your guts warm, Lord Stintleigh, *SIR*! The devil loves hot tripes.'

Valentine explodes in a jerking chain of coughs. Too discreet to acknowledge the noise, the leader finally leans down and pushes the stiletto into Stintleigh's groin and twists it slightly. Valentine is so close he can hear the pretty, musical crack as the hilt separates from the glass blade.

Only then does he rise to leave, coughing freely. There is no hope of salvation now for Stintleigh and in any case two of the gang will stay with him in case anyone stumbles upon the dying man to hear his incriminating last gasps, or lest the man himself writes some inconvenient message on his white linen with his own blood. Valentine hurries away, suddenly fearing to hear the name of Mimosina Dolcezza bubbling from those dying lips.

And of course it has become harder to watch these necessary executions since Tom died.

He knows that she must be aware of the murder, for every headline has screamed of it for days. Not just because of the importance of the man, but because of the final detail of his despatch. Finding his anger not quite absolved by the mere extinction of the politician, Valentine has decided to refresh a colourful old tradition of London Bridge. Though it is a hundred years since the last decapitated head was displayed on a pike there, he has ordered the surprised face of Lord Stintleigh, impaled on his own elegant cane, erected in one of the neat and cosy stone alcoves that recently replaced the leaning riot of old shops and houses on the bridge.

Of course the constabulary have promptly removed it and it now rests in close proximity with the body in the family crypt, but not before its ghastly likeness has graced several handbills, for the London hacks like nothing more than a bit of horror. They have wasted no time in finding a graphic portent that might, if but noted in time, have saved poor Lord Stintleigh. One of the lions in the Tower of London menagerie died the night before, always a sign of calamity to come. And even the satirists find humour in the grim discovery on London Bridge. Valentine sees a cartoon of two Irish thugs looking at the decapitated politician.

One says to the other, 'Didn't your old mother tell you that it's past joking when the head's off?'

Valentine flinches because this was one of Tom's favourite and most morbidly cruel jokes.

He can barely breathe without her and yet he is afraid to approach her now that he has cleared the way.

Cleansing it of Stintleigh should have restored order to the world, and erased the intolerable humiliation that he visited upon Valentine Greatrakes.

There is no longer a richer man, a better-spoken man, a man of impeccably blue blood, to call upon the actress.

But now this act, this impaling of Stintleigh, becomes his excuse for not seeing her. What if she reads it in his eyes? What if he reads grief for Stintleigh in hers?

She is become among the most fearsome objects in all creation. Just the thought of her twists and ties his tongue. Even internally, he cannot muster eloquence enough to face her. Can he merely blurt out the words she frames inside him, as if they were not the most important in the world? He's acting the maggot in not asking for the thing he most wants, making a bags of doing it, foostering about doing naught. Standing in the depository late at night, he touches his mouth to practise the necessary phrases, but the peccant part refuses to co-operate with his thoughts.

He cannot even ask her: *Would you ever think of coming back to me?* He cannot say the truth: *I'm heartscalded at the loss of you.*

He hates himself, not for the killing, but for his lack of following the matter through. The logical conclusion of the extinction of Stintleigh should have been the winning of the actress. The obstacle is removed. She is his, exclusively. Indeed, probably was so all along. Now that the deed is done, he grows hourly more confident that Stintleigh has been sacrificed to nothing more than a jealous suspicion. Not much of a sacrifice, true, but such a thing can haunt a man's night and disgust his conscience, on occasion, if he's lonely.

He realises that the humiliation of the nobleman's corpse was more poignant to him than the actual murder: he does not enjoy discovering this motivation in himself. It does not make him worthy of the love of an exquisite woman.

My nature is too coarse for her. She'll be fading and dying from my boorishness in a month. Now isn't that the cruel duality of it all in one? She's sweet enough to make a man throw stones at his own grandmother – and commit other acts of a brutal nature – and yet it's kindness herself the woman entirely.

That's the irony. He has connived this sinful act for her, who would faint from horror to know of it.

But he has done it because he wants her. Because, to admit the truth a moment, he sorely needs her. Now is the time to speak.

Yet look at him skulking on the edge of life! He has stopped at the last hurdle, refused like a sick horse. And, for all the coin stashed under the floorboards in Stoney Street, has he ever done any better? Does this crisis with the actress not insinuate what's amiss with his whole life? Valentine assesses himself with a grim eye. Always a here-and-thereian, never settled in any one business, always sniffing after something new, leaving Dizzom to pick up the pieces of each discarded enthusiasm.

What would I be without Dizzom? A mouthful of moonshine, nothing!

Confronted with – yes, he must admit it – love, he has failed at the first post, He has made a holy show of himself. Just one taste of love and he's caught in its seductions like a spotty poet, unable to do anything about it except wallow in its mires, condemned to suffer the craving for ever after blundering through the blood like a large beetle.

How pathetic is that? asks Valentine Greatrakes.

He is less than nothing. He is less than Dizzom. He is less than Dizzom's dog, Foible.

If Foible can survive a good drenching mouthful of one of Dizzom's nostrums, then it's fit enough for the denizens of Bankside. There have been more than several Foibles, none lasting more than a year.

That's me, Foible, thinks Valentine. *Just a dog on which a tender woman practises her sweet-seeming potions, with no life of my own but that which I am allowed by her grace, goodness or skill.*

And he's had just a dog's portion of the actress too, just a lick and a smell of her, and she's gone, yet taking the most sentient parts of him with her, it seems.

How dare she be doing that!

He will not go to seek the actress.

If she must have him, she must come and find him, and prove to him that she is worth all this devastation.

In the meantime Tom's body has at last arrived in London, and there is a funeral to arrange.

· 11 ·

A Traumatic Decoction

Take Roots of Burdock 3 ounces; Madder 6 drams; Rhubarb 2 drams; Herbs of Dittany of Creet, St Johns Wort, Sanicle, Bugle, each 1 handful; boil in Water 2 pints, and white Wine (added towards the last) 1 pint to 28 ounces; when strain'd dissolve in it Venice Treacle 2 drams; Honey 3 ounces; Oxymel simple 1 ounce, mix.

It dissolves concretions of the Cruor, wheresoever extravasated, and returns it again into the circulating Channel.

It is a symptom of love to want love.

So Valentine thinks when he looks down from the gallery to see – *of all people* – Mimosina Dolcezza in the reception room below his office. She stands there pale and rigid against the freshly painted purple of the walls. The public rooms of the depository have gone into mourning for the viewing of Tom's corpse two days before the funeral.

He marvels at her persistence and her intelligence. How has she found him here? He tells himself he feels not a flicker of shame that she should see him at his business, in his place of work. He has not lied to her about it; it's just that there are certain items he did not mention. The depository is enormous as any Venetian *palazzo* and run tightly as a battleship. There is nothing shabby here, and all his employees are well fed. And yet he finds himself coughing and swallowing hard to irrigate his dry throat.

She is distinctive among the shabby multitudes who are crammed down there, awaiting their turn to pay their respects to Tom. Still, he turns on his heel and pretends not to have seen her. This occasion is dedicated to Tom, not Mimosina Dolcezza. Even if she has innocently stumbled upon the day of mourning, she should have had the tact and discretion to leave at once. What right has she to be standing there, beautiful as a lake, demanding attention that today of all days belongs exclusively to Tom – and poor Pevenche, who has silently viewed the body alone with him this morning and is now safely back at the Academy?

Below him, Tom lies in his purple-fringed coffin, recognisable instantly. Valentine tries to forget how Tom's vascular organisation has been injected with oil of turpentine and camphorated spirit of wine, his viscera drained away and the cavity of his abdomen packed with powdered nitrate and more camphor. A carminative solution gives his skin that lifelike rosy hue. Yet all the orifices are plugged, his lips are invisibly stitched together and wadding of cotton has been slipped under his eyelids as the balls of his eyes have long since collapsed inside his skull. Dizzom's solutions, relayed via their couriers to Italy, have worked almost perfectly. Yet still there are touches of violet about the skin of the hands which have been rubbed with white lead to disguise the blackening. Tom died before the gangrene could fur his tongue and distort his mouth. And thanks be to God, thinks Valentine, the murderers did not much mark Tom's face, a sure sign in their world that they wanted his identity known. Just a cut to the lip, little damage upon his features. Otherwise Tom's body might never have come home to London to be wept over; it would have ended up in a poor's pit in Venice, unidentified and unmourned.

As it is, they have come in their hundreds for Tom. They have come from their stalls, lock-ups, inns, digs and garrets in Paris Garden, Bear Gardens and Rose Alley to see him and weep their tears over his body. Valentine nods to each familiar face. His own tears form to replicate theirs as he acknowledges the pain of soft-hearted thieves, quacks, whores and many other notables of Bankside.

Even the fugitives who inhabit the concealed stairwells of the Anchor have exposed themselves to danger today. In Tom's honour, they have staggered on their cramped legs round Bank End into Clink Street and processed unsteadily up Stoney Street to the depository, draped with purple silk banners at each window.

122

The preceding group is ushered out of the receiving chamber. The double doors at the end of the purple room swing open to allow the new swarm of grievers to enter. Mimosina Dolcezza is borne in by the crowd. A gallant gentleman of the lock-picking persuasion has even seized her elbow, and is valiantly clearing a path for her all the way to the coffin, little knowing this must be the last thing she desires. Her face is a picture of miserable confusion and helplessness.

Looking down from above, Valentine tells himself that he does not even feel sorry for her: her timing's bad; by some strange fatality she has arrived at an awkward moment. It is not his fault, and nor can he be held responsible if she's never seen a corpse before. Will he rush to help her if she faints?

Not likely.

It will do her good to see a real tragedy, instead of those picturesque dramas she likes to confect, built of nothing but hysterics and jealousy and fanned by her petty obsessions, culminating in the petulant act of allowing Gervase Stintleigh indoors. Still, Valentine keeps an eye on the lock-picker, making sure his attentions remain in the realm of decency. He would not like a coarse act to defile Tom's day, he reminds himself.

I want Tom buried in all manner of pride and splendour.

In the surge of the crowd, Mimosina Dolcezza is brought ever closer to Tom's coffin. Valentine sees her grow suddenly even paler. Her eyes widen. All around her, people are gently lifting Tom's hand to kiss it, taking away white powder on their lips. Men are thumping the coffin with emotion and women are throwing rose petals and carefully folded notes inside it. Mimosina Dolcezza alone stands still, staring at Tom's face, her own features immobilised by shock. Her white face glistens with perspiration.

No, it must be tears.

It is pity she's feeling for the poor unknown creature, lying there on the purple satin. She must have realised who he is and who he was to me.

Or it could even be that she weeps for Valentine Greatrakes himself, witnessing the grim reality of his great loss and finding it hard to bear on his behalf.

Unlike the weeping actress, he himself has not been able truly to look at the corpse, not to meet its closed eyes or touch it. He has dealt with it as if it were a precious possession of Tom's to be honoured and looked after. When Tom arrived, and Valentine went slowly down to greet the coffin, he had tried, though without success, to stop himself sniffing for the putrid signature of the violating fish. Smelling nothing but Dizzom's medicinal desiccants, he had simply nodded, accepting this box of flesh as Tom's. He had not even shed a tear.

And look now.

Even though this man can mean nothing at all to Mimosina Dolcezza, she is showing more emotion than Valentine has displayed in the entire span of the last weeks. She trembles visibly; she wavers on her feet.

Then she inclines her head upwards and meets the eyes of Valentine Greatrakes. She holds them. He reads terrifying pain in her pupils, and in a moment she distils a new tear from each lid. Now he is sure of it. The sweet lady is grieving for this stranger because the man who is now this corpse was once beloved by Valentine Greatrakes.

A sudden scream breaks their silent communion. A woman is shrieking and pointing to the corpse. Now men are shouting and pointing too. Through the glass their distress is muffled, as if underwater. Valentine cranes his neck to see what has caused such outrage.

Tom's white-wrapped chest is flowering with blood. The red stain spreads so fast that it is as if the life-force is still pumping the fluid from his body. Valentine turns to shout for Dizzom but sees his assistant already scuttling down the stairs. In the mourning room, his men are pushing the grievers away with the unnecessary force summoned by their own fear. Men and women are weeping, and one voice above them all howls the words everyone is thinking: 'The murderer must be in this room!'

Someone has locked the doors and all are pressed against the four walls, panting and pawing at the floor. Everyone is looking at everyone else with narrowed eyes.

Until this moment Valentine has easily dismissed as a fairy tale the belief that the corpse of a murdered man would bleed again if his killer drew near. Too picturesque, too fanciful to be true. In the real world of murder, nothing so fair or clean as cruentation ever really happens, except onstage in the theatre. There must be a real reason for the eruption of blood from Tom's corpse, and he is hot to deal severely with Dizzom who should have plugged all such possibilities, and who has clearly been negligent with the chemicals on this of all days.

He looks down on his assistant, even now bending desperately over the corpse below, tenderly sopping the blood with his own handkerchief and searching its face as if Tom's plugged eyes and sewn-up lips might suddenly burst open with some eloquent explanation of their own. Dizzom's shoulders are shaking: his tears drop into the pool of blood in the hollow of Tom's chest.

Valentine cannot stop himself from looking around the room at all the distorted faces to see if there is a relic of guilt written upon any of them. Yes, he sees three weeping Venetians of their business acquaintance but they are old friends of the enterprise, men he has trusted with all manner of opportunities, whose children he knows. They loved Tom as a brother and could not possibly dissemble at this unrestrained grief. Valentine knows that the Venetians are the most superstitious race on earth, and surely these men would not have attended if they had been responsible for the outrage in their midst. No, none of these men is capable of killing Tom and none has ever been furnished with a motive. Valentine's eyes rove around the room, looking for strangers.

He has momentarily forgotten Mimosina Dolcezza but suddenly he sees her cowering in a corner and is overcome with shame and pity for her; alone, in a strange city, a woman of acute feelings, she has been forced to witness a complete stranger's corpse perform a gory miracle. Now she is trapped in a room with a hundred vengeful strangers, and indeed they are eyeing her now, full of venom, for everything about her features and dress indicates that she is a foreigner. A foreigner killed Tom. There is no doubt in their minds. What is she doing here, if not gloating? Valentine feels his belly contract with fear: what if they should turn on this poor, innocent woman? Those who have come to mourn Tom are mostly of their own ilk: violence, though regrettable, is a necessary tool. If they believe her the author of Tom's murder, by act or even by commission, then there is nothing he shall be able to do to save her. The men have killing in their eyes: he sees it. He knows it. Several of them are edging in her direction; one has snatched up a pole from the curtains.

Then he notices something else: behind her stands the one man in the room upon whom Valentine has never laid eyes before. It is not the actress drawing the glares of the Banksiders: it is this man. He's an Italian, Moorish in colouring, but somehow refined. *Curiously over-refined*, if anything, thinks Valentine. His nose and lips are but barely in relief. It is as if the modelling of his face has been executed so obsessively that his features have been almost smoothed away.

With a face like that he'll not be needing a conscience. He'll be available for any crime, a complete creature of his masters, whoever they are. Such a man has no will of his own: this makes him more efficacious at the worst work.

The man stands too close to the actress and it seems as if he is breathing into the very tendrils of hair at the back of her neck. He barely glances at the corpse; when he does, it is with a faintly amused expression. He has eyes only for the woman.

Only a murderer, the thought suddenly strikes Valentine, *could be so callously lewd in the face of his cruel work. That look's so dirty that if you threw it at a wall, it'd stick.*

Perhaps this man has arrived in London with a mission to torment Valentine Greatrakes himself! He has taken Tom from him and now he plans to murder the woman who has stolen his heart? Perhaps those fixed looks at the back of Mimosina Dolcezza are serving to set her firmly in his memory, so that when he comes upon her silhouette in some darkened street he may know to rush at it with a knife . . .

Valentine crashes down the stairs and into the reception room only to find its weeping population surging out into the street. They have pushed aside his men and burst open the double doors. The murderous Italian has melted away with them. Only Dizzom remains, bent over the corpse, and Mimosina Dolcezza, who is rooted to the spot, staring at a point somewhere above the lid of the coffin.

He's burning hot. The crush of people has raised the temperature of the depository to that of a summer day. Behind the doors the spurned refreshments are already raising a questionable odour. The fine native Melton oysters and hogshead ordered to give Tom's lying-in-state some substance – all seem to wish to join Tom in grim putrefaction.

As he enters the room, the actress is already murmuring feverish apologies – she cannot ever forgive herself for intruding, she had not the least idea, how could she have done this to him? And he is interrupting her every phrase with inapposite exclamations,

'Sure, you've no call to be sorry. Sure, you're more than welcome,' he responds, ridiculously. They continue to speak together at the same time for many seconds, both drawing to a sudden stop at the same moment.

He crushes her into his arms, kissing her eyes, her hair, her ears, no matter who sees him at this soft work, and he calls his carriage, never taking his eyes off the sobbing woman. His antique Irish namesake, the famous healer Valentine Greatrakes, was said to be able to cure scrofula with his bare hands; now Valentine Greatrakes of Bankside uses his fingers to stroke away the fear and trembling of Mimosina Dolcezza.

He takes her home, holding her fast against him the whole way. He thinks he can erase the thought of her betrayal with the desperate quantity of his own feelings for her. But there's a cruel reminder on the stairs: they brush past a pile of discarded newspapers shrieking Stintleigh's death, his portrait uppermost on the front pages. An example of every newspaper printed in London is here, it seems, all obsessed with the same crime. He hurries her past, hating the rustle of newsprint raised by her trailing skirt.

Back in her sullied room, when she excuses herself a moment, he can't stop looking in her gilded Venetian mirror and regretting mirrors don't keep diaries that a man can get his hands on and consult for interest. Now the straining – not to do himself the damage of a whiff of something male – lies heavy on his ribs. He's singeing hair-roots with a bargain: the act itself he'll almost live with on condition she's not kissed or said or gazed or, worst of all, admired when – *O Lord here she comes herself* – swimming up behind him, and she ought to touch him now and she ought to kill the thought but no, she stands still and lets him drown gold-rimmed in the lens of petrified water.

He doesn't turn his fizzling head, instead he meets her smoky look in glass. The mirror's blear-eyed, nazy on fermented mould, a little piece of Venice she's brought here with her to distort everything with mystery. He hates that mirror.

Is it bilious with the witnessings laid up?

He cannot keep the question down. So he by-the-ways as if he doesn't care: 'D'you know at all that fellow, the politician, the dead one?'

The words jangle bitter as small change in his mouth and he's struggling to keep down the truer definition: *that humming man, that smug man, that nobler man than me.*

In the mirror, her face is blank.

'Did you not read about it? Are they not your newspapers we passed just now out there, out there on the stairs?'

'What stairs?' she asks.

'Your stairs,' he says, 'the stairs into your house.'

And she says absolutely not, why should she? She shakes her head in vigorous agreement with everything she says. She enumerates. She lays down as obvious.

He feels the individual fronds of hair curling and uncurling on his head, when, his belly stuck to his back, he tows Stintleigh's shadow to the bedroom. They lie down and make dizzy the mirror's pocked and perished silver.

Pleasantly occupied, he's not quite deaf to his heart's howling its bereftness and his head's aching dread that something fine has fallen off and rolled away, underneath this very bed.

Nevertheless he holds her all afternoon and night, never once closing his own eyes, lest there should blossom under their dark lids the vision of Tom bleeding to death when already dead, or the pallid face of Stintleigh grimacing at the end of his stick.

Valentine makes no more mention of the politician or of his murder. He'll not ask for any more lies, whether it's the little one, that she never saw the man, or the greater one, that she has not lain with him. There are of course a million and six reasons why

128

she would utter the smaller, almost harmless one: she would be afraid of his jealousy, not wish to hurt him, be embarrassed at the connection.

She says nothing about it either, merely gazing at him with an illuminated and tearless face. She clings to him. She submits to his lust meekly. She has need of forbearance for in the last Mimosina-less days he has not been able to find relief elsewhere.

She must take responsibility for what she has pent up.

So thinks Valentine, as he kisses her reddened eyelids, trying not to see the head of Lord Stintleigh as she caresses the back of his neck, or the drench of blood on Tom's breast.

He has hated her, and he loves her again, and the sweets of possession amply compensate for the bitters.

And how she inspires him!

For lying in her arms, Valentine Greatrakes comes up with the very best idea of his business life. Perhaps it is the joy she has distilled in him, perhaps it is a galvanising relief at their reunion, but he awakes with a plan of crystalline perfection. Mimosina Dolcezza has brought such clarity to his private life that its illumination leaks on to the business ledger. He will market not just Venetian liquids, Venetian doctors and their doses, but Venice herself.

He will patent a Venetian cure, allowing him to 'import' whole bottles of liquid from the little Republic. Naturally these liquids shall first arrive in his depository to be scrupulously controlled for the mould and taints of their long journey. So scrupulously that they shall be upended into other bottles, bottles more honestly labelled 'rum' and 'brandy'. Meanwhile the Venetian glass vessels themselves will receive replenishment – with a delectable and efficacious nostrum, no more Venetian than Valentine Greatrakes himself.

But it shall be all the rage in London in an instant. For what Valentine Greatrakes shall be selling is the very essence and perfume of Venice, the mystery of the Orient in which she veils her charms, the fragrant darkness of her apothecary's studios, the whispered reputations of her great true doctors, the condescension of her noblemen whose names shall unwittingly endorse his products, the mysterious depths of her dark jade waters, and the whole thousand years of her glorious history, golden, serene, imperial, all encapsulated in his little bottles, just as Mimosina Dolcezza now lies in his arms, soft and sweet as milk.

Sleeping, he thinks.

· 12 ·

Wafers of Tamarinds

Take Tamarinds 1 ounce; grind them in a Mortar with thin Mucilage of Gum Dragant, pass them thro' a pulping Sieve, dissolve also Spanish juice of Liquorice in the same sort of Mucilage 2 drams; mix, and make Troches as thin as Wafers to seal Letters; which dry in an Oven, according to art.

These are very pretty, desirable and useful things to hold in the Mouth, to alleviate Thirst, and take away an ill Taste in Fevers.

'You will take me as your wife,' she says, the next morning when she wakes up. 'It will be the greatest pleasure for you.'

'Ah now, wait a little there,' splutters Valentine.

'Yes, I shall leave the troupe and slip into your arms and we shall live together in your great house and none shall find me there.'

She smiles generously, like a mother who has pressed a comfit on an undeserving child. She is already ringing the bell for her maid Tabby Runt. An instantaneous sniffing by the door announces what Valentine has always suspected: the girl listens regularly at the keyhole, and that she does not find him satisfactory company for her mistress.

Valentine stammers, 'It's not so simple as that.'

He strokes her cheek in a mediating way.

She's having none of it. At his unkind cavilling, this tiny interruption to the romance she is spinning, her eyes glitter and she drops her chin so her face is entirely pivoted on huge tear-filled eyes. Tabby Runt enters the room bearing a large silver tray of her coffee, takes one look at her mistress, and backs out again, all the while bestowing upon Valentine Greatrakes a stare as bleak as a northerly voyage.

'So you do not love me after all, is it?' the actress whispers.

'Of course I–I–I . . .'

'It is just a small thing for you, not the great love that comes only once in a lifetime, as it is for me? I have thought, all this time, that our hearts were married already.'

And damn it, thinks Valentine, *it's true, they are. I love you. I love you. I love you. Damn it.*

But he thinks to himself. She is already leaping from the bed and dressing with demented speed. He hangs his head, his ears lacerated by the sharp swish of lace.

This time he lets her go. Just now he has no resources to refashion the peace between them. When she sweeps away to the dressing room, he quietly puts on his clothes and lets himself out of the apartments, walking slowly down the stairs from which the newspapers shrilling Stintleigh's demise have not yet been cleared.

Valentine forces himself to take the hand of Pevenche, emerging white and strong from her gaudy mourning cloak. She has fattened on tragedy and it suits her ill, he thinks. Together they have thrown the first clod of earth into the cavity that will swallow her father. He has watched her tearless face with concern: better for her to cry, really, like the other veiled women in the second and third tiers of onlookers around the grave. Anonymous under their black swathes, they howl and sniff, these brief loves of Tom's. He sees Pevenche opening her mouth at the sight of these ladies and quickly distracts her before she can make more scandal than a whole coffee house. 'Throw your little posy now, dear heart.'

And she unfastens it from her capacious sash and throws it into the grave, saying, 'Bye bye, Pa, I *hope* you are going to Heaven.'

People within earshot are shocked by the girl's equivocation and a chafe of whispers sprints her words to the back of the crowd in a moment. Valentine pulls Pevenche to him and speaks softly into the aperture of her bonnet, 'Of course he is, little one. Where else would he go?'

He sees that she is fully prepared to answer this question and desperately forfends her response by starting up an impromptu hymn in his easy baritone. The confused mourners are thankful to join him in this godly display. Meanwhile Pevenche observes the sly bottles handed round with thumps on the back and exhortations to 'have a little bit o' that, my lover, don't let the tears run dry'.

'They'll be drunker'n roaches,' she huffs above the doleful singing. 'They won't be able to taste the eatables at the party. And we've gone to such trouble over 'em!'

When the hymn is sung through, the mourners nod as if satisfied and gradually steal away in silence, leaving Valentine and the girl at the grave's edge, staring at the fresh earth for many minutes in silence. A moist wind brawls half-heartedly with the few trees not yet fallen to progress on Bankside. A smell of clay drags at their noses but no tears fall from the girl's small eyes.

Pevenche then announces, 'Well, that's him done for, then.' And Valentine flinches with pain, and feels more alone than he has ever done. Just now, with Tom gone, and Mimosina Dolcezza a questionable quantity after their quarrel, he feels bathed in self-pity. Dizzom and Pevenche are all his family now: what kind of life is this?

At the repast, he stands apart from the others, watching them stare suspiciously at the calves' ears and duck tongues forced, the puptoon of lobsters and veal sweetbreads carbonaded, the triple toasts, the bisques that Pevenche has specifically required and indeed supervised at the cookshop in Deadman's Place. After all the humiliation her father visited upon her with regard to food – yet still she has tried to make his funeral a feast fit for a gourmandising duke.

But Tom's friends do not want these jellied and parsleyed creations. After long moments of silence, one of the Bankside bakers rushes outside and returns with a vast tray of tall pies. The crowd swoops on them with unabashed glee. And Valentine too finally succumbs to the greasy delight of the pastry washed down by a motherly tankard of ale.

Pevenche, meanwhile, is mercifully nowhere to be seen. Later he finds her in the kitchen, happily confecting a monstrous pie from the spurned sweetmeats, and humming tunelessly under her breath, while a large bun smiling yellow custard hangs from her jaw.

He is moved to ask her: 'Do they not give you proper feeding at school, Pevenche?'

Far from it, she tells him. At the school there is merely roast beef on Mondays, roast shoulder of mutton on Tuesdays and Fridays, a round of beef on Wednesday, boiled leg of mutton on Thursday and on Saturdays stewed beef with pickled walnuts. But fibrous chops are sometimes substituted, she hisses, when there are fees unpaid, and then the undersubscribed pupil is made to sit at the head of the table and watch while her comrades gnaw the bones.

His mind wanders as Pevenche now recounts the whole pudding menu to him in even more lavish detail, lingering on the 'choke dogs', apparently a currant-studded dumpling, that would 'go blah' if overcooked.

Privileged girls are allowed to linger in the dining room and have a glass of port after supper, she informs him with a significant stare, and he reminds himself to make such an arrangement for her.

On delivering Pevenche back to the Academy for Young Ladies, she torments him with one more little scene. She greets Mistress Haggardoon with the loud words: 'Here I am back, he doesn't want me aroun', you see, he's got better things to do, I don't feel welcome any more.'

Pevenche runs through the hallway snorting sobs and thunders up the stairs. Both her headmistress and guardian flinch at the slamming of the door. They stand in agonised silence.

Why doesn't she say something mitigating? The atmosphere's so thick you could eat it with a fork.

At last the headmistress whispers carefully: 'She wishes you to think . . .' But her words are interrupted by the tarnished glint of the guinea he's tugging from his pocket.

'Yes,' she says wearily, 'I'll buy the girl something nice.'

'And the port after supper?'

She nods sadly, sacrificing the pleasantness of future evenings.

Marriage! The word tangs and needles all over his body as he jerks over the cobbles towards the theatre. Where else is there to go?

Tom is buried. It is time to make sense of Mimosina Dolcezza, and if that cannot be achieved at least to hold her while she rants. He must feel her in his arms again, even if it is just the once. The day has sucked him dry. He must have his fill of her before he renounces her, if that is what he is destined to do.

And first he must make her his lover again. This morning's skirmish is of the kind that can only be remedied with tenderness, and she, the doting girl, could never deny him that, not if she sees the hollows of his eyes and the funeral's tearstains on his shirt, both of which he has observed in the same mirror and not corrected before coming out to intercept her at the theatre.

Twelve hours apart, in a state of war, have been unbearable. When he sees her face he knows it has been so for her too. They fall gratefully into one another's arms in the hall outside her dressing room, the very site of their first encounter.

It makes a body ooze with desire all over again just to remember that.

He does not mention the matrimonial issue that rent their reunion apart, and nor does she.

· 13 ·

An Alexipharmac Draught

Take Alexiterial Milk Water 3 ounces; Epidemial, Compound Piony Water, Syrup of Gilly-flowers, Syrup of Saffron, each 2 drams; Diascordium, 2 scruples; Goa Stone 1 scruple, mix.

In suspicious, ill condition'd Fevers, it raises and supports the drooping Spirits, resists Malignity, and drives it out from the Centre to the Circumference.

Icebound London turns magical. The Thames freezes over, as if to demonstrate the solidity of their love. The usual frost fair enlivens the stilled river under London Bridge. Together they go there – the actress like a flame in her new rust-red redingote and black hat trimmed with matching ribbon. They drink hot wine in the refreshment tents, watch the skaters, and visit a printer who has set up a stall upon the ice. They have identical sheets set and printed, and fold them against their hearts where they crackle at every embrace.

Valentine Greatrakes & Mimosina Dolcezza,
London, December 15th 1785,
Printed on ICE.

Most nights are spent in her rooms, and after her performance they rarely go out, not wanting to leave the enchanted circle of their intimacy. Tabby Runt supplies all their needs without making her presence obvious. Every evening Valentine goes to watch his lover perform on the stage. Feeling the desires of the men in the audience sharpens his own later. And he finds messages specific to himself when he observes her now. Little sighs, significant looks, the style of uttering certain phrases: all these are private ways she communicates with him in public. He is sure of it. He delights in isolating new instances with each show, and later she blushingly confesses him right each time.

Then there are the romantic suppers, where he eats one-handed so that he may caress her throughout. These meals are not without their usual drawbacks, however, chiefly of a culinary nature. He still cannot, without grievous loss of face, refuse to eat the unnatural liaisons of fruit and meat she places before him. More than once he has barely arrived home at Bankside before spewing abundantly into a gutter and recovering himself at the Anchor with a cup of plain tea strong enough to trot a mouse across it.

He loves her apartments but sometimes their relentless femininity oppresses him. When he feels a cabin-fever descend, Valentine hires some rooms he knows near Bond Street, a comfortable building done out like the home of a gentleman of the first rank and fortune. He has Dizzom go there in advance of them, to spread some personal belongings about and to muss the chill perfection of the décor with a few morsels of bachelor squalor.

Mimosina Dolcezza is pleased with the accommodations and wrapping her naked body inside the curtains one night, she teases him for the luxury of their marquisite silk.

'No expense is spared!'

He fastens the curtain round her so that only her head emerges, a pale bud forming on a green stalk.

'For you yourself, nothing is too good.' And he puts his arms around the tube of silk and walks in circles, over and over again, until she can no longer bear the shimmying and hissing of the fabric against her naked skin, and begs him to release her. Then she steps naked into the room and she is so beautiful that he must douse the glim of the candle in order to bear it.

Christmas comes and he puts her first, instead of Pevenche who breaks a great many things in the drawing room at the Academy for Young Ladies. (Nevertheless, he increases the girl's allowance, on top of paying for the damage.)

He is neglecting his business, thinking of nothing but her. Dizzom is told to keep everything ticking over, but this cannot go on for ever without damage, and without dangerous talk. There are always upstarts in Bankside ready to surge into any vacuum of concentration. Valentine is dimly aware of the risk, but he tells himself that this cannot last. He is sure that he will satisfy himself with her soon, and that he shall be able to let her go. This love affair is like the ice that now holds the Thames unnaturally in check. It cannot stay so for ever, and its rare beauty is like a heart-beat stolen from time and displayed in a glass bottle. Such fraud shall have its detection and the bliss shall soon dissolve in his hands. And he will accept it as a natural thing, even if a hurting one.

Yet he cannot evade daydreams of a different nature entirely, and has begun to understand that these caressing manners of hers promise domestic pleasures above the sensual ones he already enjoys. How sweet a thing would it be to bring this woman a cut finger to wrap in linens! And how kind a homecoming with a lady like that to fuss him with such little objects of minor spleen that had grizzled her tame day. When she lowers her eyes there is a tinge of the Madonna about her. Yet, cruelly, her profession has not allowed her the joy of motherhood.

Not yet, he tells himself, and blushes at the thought.

And that's another thing, by God, we're not fecundating, despite doing the bold thing innumerably and without any precautions against it.

She's birdmouthed on that subject, doesn't raise it, never offers him a birthday bonnet for the bald fella, nor asks him to furnish one himself. And she seems so delicate that no one could bring home a child from her.

Or is it an unnaturality on her side?

And how can he tell if her winning ways are born into her, or if she merely enacts them? Can she love without a script? In the short rapture allowed to them, Mimosina Dolcezza has given him some few specimens of her oddities. She has not even managed to behave immaculately, viz her ungenerous attitude to his little ward, not to mention the sickening incident of Lord Stintleigh. She speaks languages he knows not; she has lived lives he knows noth-ing of: what would he be taking on in her? One woman, or a continent of them?

Another thing: she seems strangely distracted these days. He speaks more softly to her, so she is forced to concentrate on his voice. Even then it seems that she merely follows the faint tracks of his words, rather than really listening to him.

The painful thought strikes him down that a woman so exquisite, so much in demand, must be listening to his declarations with old ears. She cannot know how dewy is this vocabulary for him, who has never before had recourse to it. He imagines his loving words leaping fresh from his lips yet already staled, bent over and smelling slightly of mould by the time they are in her possession. He is driven mad by the thought of those other voices in her ears, uttering more powerful and more elaborate phrases than he can coin, in her own language even.

But I'll have her anyway. I'll take my turn. Just to be with her, that's the thing.

Finally, he brushes even that thought aside. The point is – he's a great one for the music and the dancing and the women, but he's not one of those men who are preciously self-deceitful.

The truth of it is just that Valentine Greatrakes has never calculated for a matrimonial sort of life. There have been too many women offered for him to think of settling for one.

But he has never calculated for Mimosina Dolcezza either. He's got the greens to clap a diamond on that finger, only the little finger, mind. It doesn't mean he has to marry her. He just loves her hands, and that a man may do in complete safety, it would be a stinting and ungrateful thing not to love those hands of hers.

What's the harm in that?

He spends a night apart from her, to see what it feels like, to gauge the pain of the prospect of many more such.

Valentine lies sleepless in a room at the depository. It is not a bedroom, but a room with a bed in it. Mimosina Dolcezza has taught him the difference. Rising in the early hours, he holds a candle up to the mirror and looks at himself, looks at what she must see when he is naked and prayerful in front of her. He notes that the hairs along his right side have worn away, for it is this way that he lies when he holds her in the night.

Lilies that fester, and all that.

Valentine Greatrakes knows very little about – *it*. He flinches from the tolling word 'marriage'. He does not believe his own mother knew the honour. He tries to think of any married people he knows, by way of encouragement. It fails to tempt. He thinks of the flower-girl at the Seven Dials, anyone's ten-minute bride, and all the sweeter for it.

He thinks that he will ask – just ask, mind, the price for the free-hold of the Bond Street rooms he now dissembles as his own.

It can only be a few hundred tiny little pounds.

It's not that he craves luxury, but for the first time he aches for a house, over the threshold of which he could carry her.

If it should come to that.

He's more or less abandoned his profession, and all his old entertainments too. It's weeks since he's been seen inside the Anchor. His silver season token to the St James's Cockpit languishes unused on his dusty bedside table at the depository.

Instead the lovers haunt the still-frozen Thames together, learning to skate, like newborns learning to walk. The significance of this mutual education is not lost on them. Nor is the melodious trickle of water flowing every day a little faster beneath the ice.

Valentine Greatrakes has meanwhile reinvented his wardrobe in a tribute to his lover. He commissions a cream waistcoat embroidered with goosegreen and yellow flowers, shoes braided with yellow cord like a string of mimosa flowers. He wears only the colours of spring in this bitterest of weather. She answers him mutely but eloquently, appearing in a dress of yellow silk and tulle with two hundred real butterflies pinned among the gauzy petticoats.

They are inside the City of Moscow tent one afternoon when a jagged sound is heard and the ice trembles beneath their feet. They peer out of the tent to see that they are now aboard a glassy island that bobs gently away from the thick white crust of the river-banks. Valentine's instincts impel him to action before conscious thought. He swings Mimosina Dolcezza into his arms and into one of the wherries that was previously frozen into the iced river but is now divesting itself of its encumbrance. He throws himself in afterwards but then leaps back out again to gather three toddling children who still stand on the edge of the City of Moscow with their mouths wide open but too frightened to scream. These he tosses one after another into the fragile arms of the actress while he rushes into the tent and picks up the remaining stallholders, the rest already following his example and scrambling into nearby boats. When he returns to the wherry the children, the actress and the other victims of the ice's shipwreck have all recovered themselves enough to be bawling lustily and he calms them on the instant with a huge smile.

'Is this not prodigious fun?' he laughs, tickling one of the children until the boy perforce begins to chuckle. 'Isn't this a hooting thing?'

One by one he catches the eye of all his terrified human salvage and works his eyebrows until they cannot help but burst into merriment.

And then he grabs an oar and commences to row the hilarious party back to shore, where the children are greeted with smothering parental caresses, the adults with warm brandies and Valentine Greatrakes with a great roar of hot love.

Back in her rooms the actress strokes his hair again and again. Each time she raises it to start again at the crown of his head; she shows him her hand in a gesture that he could not describe, except that it makes him know it's naked of a ring. She eels it slightly, indicating the vacant cleft, and it's hurting hard thigh-deep in his lapidary heart to remember that between those fingers he's known pleasures to make him mad or, if not mad, at least to visit the extreme peninsula of sanity.

She repeats it for hours, that turn of the wrist, that makes him blissfully believe her hand newborn from that sleeve, that it's never touched another man.

It is then, on the first night of the thaw, that she says to him: 'The show is finishing and I am going back to Venice, of course.'

· 14 ·

Diuretic Ale

Take whole Mustard seed 4 ounces; put it into a quart of Ale; after 3 or 4 days begin it; and ever as you pour out a glass keep it filled up with fresh Ale; thus do as long as the seed has any strength in it.

It attenuates pituitose, fizzy blood; dissolves its close contexture, and renders it fit to shed off its serum. Also it detergeth the urinary pipes, irritateth the papillae and pelvis of the reins, provoketh them to stir and squeeze, and perform the work of percolation. Thus it moves urine powerfully beyond expectation, and is convenient in the dropsy, gravel, scurvy, palsy.

It's cut and dried, says Valentine Greatrakes, swathing his sore throat in beer at the dear old Anchor, he'll simply let Mimosina Dolcezza go back whence she came. This little *storia*, as she calls it, has already been all the more piquant for its brevity, every savoury moment velvet-sauced with wistfulness, every nerve fresh-strung each day.

There can be no doubt about it – the closer looms the date of her departure, the more beautiful she becomes.

But of course it could never be: Valentine Greatrakes – *another of the same please!* – not now nor ever has been in the business of settling down to fatten and slacken with any one woman; true, his eye has not yet gone a-wandering from this lady but how long can it be before it falls cheerily on some alluringly brackish riverside doxy or yet a bored great lady with the greens for a bit of –

He could drink the cross off a steeple today.

It has been amusing to fancy himself 'in love', no, *really* – caressing the glass – it forks a warm frisson through a body to think this

142

may be the one he'll remember when he's in his decrepitudes, oh yes, porter that faraway look to his eyes when they've grown milky under stiff hoods; indeed, this one will be inventoried in large letters in his stock of stories.

It will be flourished like the plume of my aunt's cap, in fact.

Down all the years, down all my days, I'll be thinking on her, of how she was the measure of all my dreams, how she left my heart shaken.

Indeed, he thinks, dragging on another tankard, *the letting go of her may well be the sweetest part of all.*

And it shall be so for both parties.

For of course he'll let her feel she's forsaking him and confect some trinketish feminine triumph from the notion that she's the one doing the leaving; that she leaves a man near expiring from the cleft she's wrought in his heart: so he'll go through the motions of that – acting most finely, every drink a toast to her.

Best pass her on, while she's yet fresh.

For no one man could get the viewing of all of her beauty.

And to this end, delicately, on their last day, the soon-to-be-uncoupled pair eschew the Bond Street house and tousled bedchamber of Valentine Greatrakes, and nor does he follow her into the perfumed twilight of her own fainting rooms. Instead, they take a turn in frost-crisped Hyde Park, where even the squirting cupids are frozen midstream and the pigeons hunch in moaning clusters like droplets of black dew.

Both she who leaves and he who stays are elegantly attired, as befits the occasion. The ruffles at his wrist are so strongly starched they froth upwards like wave-spume. The butterflies swish drily in the hem of her skirts. They perform decorous farewells in perfect synchronicity, from the twinned crystal tears sidling down each wan nose, the soothsaying looks into their julep glasses, to the few, brave words and the last lingering kiss during which both feel their lips wasting away, and, in deference to the sadness of the occasion, the masculine organ of Valentine Greatrakes gallantly fails to rise.

He is surprised to find that he staggers slightly as they leave the park. He had thought himself merely bemused in the beer, but now he's wall-falling drunk, scuttered with the drink, it must be that which has put the heart crossways inside him. He is drunk as

143

a lord, no, drunk as an emperor, which is ten times as drunk as a lord. Fortunately, he knows how to hide it. Why, the actress can have no idea, he's done his hiding oh-so-well.

And he hands her into the post-carriage that will bear her to Dover and refrains from running after it, finds it in himself not to call another to the chase; draining one more glass of beer in the park's diamond-latticed refreshment stall, he reflects that he has not tucked a love-letter in her glove, or spoken in the future tense, or presented her with a basket of sweetmeats for the journey: it's as if she will not exist any more and therefore needs no sustenance.

As her coach lurches a blinding corner, and his swilling groin jolts in the same direction, he swears he'll never go whimpering runtishly after her to Venice, not Valentine Greatrakes, *no sir, vehemently not, no tears, it's over* – instead, unbuttoning urgently by the shadowed railings, easing his sluices – *ah, yesss it'll melt away like this snow.*

Valentine Greatrakes, boarding the next day's carriage for Dover, stumbles on the step.

Part Three

The Bitter Febrifuge Decoction

Take Camomile-flowers dried 2 ounces; Cochineal 16 grains; boil in Water 3 pints to 1 quart; in the strained liquid dissolve Salt of Wormwood 2 drams; mix.

It's justly esteemed a Specific in Intermitting Fevers, and a Remedy inferior to none, but the Peruvian Bark, nay sometimes it hath succeeded when that hath fail'd. I use to order 4 ounces of it every three Hours, between Fits.

At Christmas he left me alone, can you imagine it?

At Christmas, when the other girls were pushing their hands into special-made muffs and dining on goose with prunes and apple in the best places, I ate at the Academy alone, that is, with only Mistress Haggardoon for company. She'd been weak enough to give the servants a holiday, so we ate *cold cuts*. When it turned out there was no hot pudding for lack of a fire in the kitchen – well, then I had a little turn of my own.

Uncle Valentine came to see me the next day. He had to walk beside the carriage because it was so full of gifts. I received him graciously in my bedroom. I had not left my bed since the little turn, and I intended to stay there for a while, nursing an upstart disorder of the belly that could be soothed only with nonsenses curdled of truffles and cream.

Said I to him, sweet as syllabub, 'I hope you enjoyed your Christmas, Uncle Valentine.'

I asked him to unwrap the gifts as I was feeling a little weak. While he went in search of a knife for the ribbons, I hastened out of bed to search his pockets, which is always worth my while.

I secreted sundry coins of which he had no need in the sleeve of my nightdress, and then I found something much more interesting: a large piece of paper on which was printed the words:

What kind of name was that, Mimosina Dolcezza?

Poor foolish man! Knee-deep in romance, and no doubt the inflamed form of the thing too.

I was back languishing in my bed by the time I heard his foot on the stair.

I could see from his face that Mistress Haggardoon had intercepted him below and that he knew of the damage in the parlour.

I worked up a good head of tears in just a few seconds, and before he left my allowance was doubled. And the bedroom was draped with the dresses and hats he's gifted me, all most killingly modish.

He was off to see 'Mimosina Dolcezza' no doubt.

Who had cost me my Christmas dinner.

Even my Pa would not have denied me that.

Venice, 1769

A Warm Cardiac Electuary

Take Conserve of Gilly flowers, Conserve of the Yellow Peel of Lemons, each 1 ounce; candy'd Citron peel, Green Ginger, Electuary of Sassaphras, Juice of Kermes strained, each half an ounce; Oil of Nutmeg 2 drops; Oil of Cinnamon and Cloves, each 1 drop, mix.

It operates primarily and properly upon the Stomach, comforting it, by being Aromatic and Warm, and from thence raising up the Spirits into a kind of Ovation, refreshes the languishing Heart, and recruits wasted Strength.

It was bizarre how well their plans for me fitted with those I had devised for myself. Mine, however, were simple compared to theirs, which had rooms and annexes remote from my own childish design.

It appeared that my talent for histrionics had not passed unnoticed or unreported at San Zaccaria and indeed was known beyond its walls. Nor had my personal appearance, the effect of which had noticeable effects on the men who surrounded me. Some could not look at me; others could not tear their eyes away. I lay rigidly in the bath, looking at the dwindling fire in the grate, wondering if I should freeze to death in this observant company.

One remarked, 'Her skin has a good lustre.' His companion replied, 'She's altogether well-formed for what we have in mind.'

It seemed that they planned to leave me immersed in the aromatic water until I had heard them out, and until I had agreed to perform their will not just grudgingly but with enthusiasm. And if I did not – I had no doubt that they would not scruple to push

151

my head under the water and hold it there until I submitted, or died. I was already dead, as far as my parents knew. My eyes groped around the room for a sympathetic face. I found none; not a particle of compassion for my plight, respect for my nakedness, concern for my physical welfare or the state of my mind. I saw instead a refrigerated kind of curiosity and a patrician impatience.

My interlocutor murmured, 'Gentlemen, let us begin.'

First, they tested the purity of my Italian. Without resorting to Venetian dialect once I was able to answer them fluently, despite my chattering teeth. I was handed a warm drink, fragrant with citrus and cinnamon. Then they tried my French: it had rusted for there was little use for it in the convent and, in any case, my tongue had grown sluggish in the months during which I had been solitarily confined. They appeared satisfied by my answers, halting though they were. They had me sing a few bars. My interlocutor turned to his companions: 'The nuns were right: it is an attractive voice. It could be trained.'

In the cold water, all my sensations were leaching away to the point where I was almost incurious as to where this interrogation was leading. I answered mechanically. But at the back of my mind a filament of hope remained aglow: if they intended merely to murder me then they would not be troubling themselves with my linguistic abilities.

They asked me about my crime; they inquired into any pangs of conscience. I did not know any better than to be honest; I said I was certainly sorry that it had come to this pass, but that I had simply done what must needs be done to save my own life. I felt myself dying under my imprisonment, I told them, adding bitterly, 'And the *conversa* is suffering, like a good martyr. If she dies, she will no doubt go to Heaven, which is, after all, her ultimate desire. She can have her bridal night with God all the sooner. I assure you, she was one who was looking forward to it.'

I heard one of the men whisper then, 'She has a barbarity the devil would shudder at.'

Another answered, 'Well then, it is all to our purpose, is it not?'

152

Finally they told me what they wanted, and it was not anything like my expectations. In exchange for my life, which might otherwise be extinguished as easily as a candle in this secret room, they wished for me to become an actress! A place had been reserved for me in the troupe that was attached to the theatre at San Luca. This troupe was shortly to depart on a tour of European cities, and I was to go with it.

My original interlocutor explained all these matters in a dry voice, concluding: 'We are of the opinion that the stage is exactly the right place for a female of your somewhat surcharged character.'

I lowered my eyes as he added, 'And with one child clandestinely gotten already, we have little need to instruct you in your supermural duties, or indeed relieve you of that perishable commodity treasured by all *decent* young women.'

For my change of vocation did not end with mere actressing. I was not merely to act the parts written by the playwrights. I was to act at being an actress. My real purpose was far more subtle. In each city, I was to accept invitations from the princes, lords, politicians and men of quality who wished to make my acquaintance. I was to charm and fascinate them, seduce them and bed them, and in their arms I was to ask certain innocent-sounding questions, and when they left I was to write certain letters that would be collected by a private courier and brought back to this unidentified *palazzo* for my interrogators to examine.

And it was not in my own Golden Book name that I was to perform these tasks. That name was to be extinguished for ever. For the purposes of my new life – and in delivering this news my interrogator smiled beneficently – I would be rechristened Mimosina Dolcezza.

· 2 ·

A Golden Julep

Take Canary Wine 1 pint; Cloves bruised half a dram; Saffron clipped small half a scruple; digest close in Balneo overnight; to the strained liquid add Spirit of Clary (ennobled with Essence of Ambergrise) half an ounce; Spirit of Lavender compound 1 dram; Syrup of Gilliflowers 1 ounce and a half; Juice of Kermes strained half an ounce; Leaves of Gold 3, mix.

This is a very rich, comfortable Cordial.

The morning hour has gold in its mouth. A Prussian minister once told me that, hurrying from my bed, stripped of his secrets.

In the years that followed my escape from the convent, I was always busy in the morning, earning gold, writing the letters that paid for what it pleased my employers to call my freedom.

By evening I acted the actress; by night I acted the whore. Only by morning did I act the truth of what I was: a spy for the Council of Ten and the Inquisitors of Venice.

The day after my interview in the bath I was released from the unknown *palazzo* into the custody of one Giacomo Mazziolini, toad of state. If I had known that this reptile was to be my sole constant companion for the next sixteen years, I would have screamed that the bargain was too hard, and I'd rather be put to the rope instantly than die by degrees in his pitiless grip.

I was confined in a suite of rooms and never saw the outside world, except through a shuttered window, until I had perfected the arts required of me by my new employment. I was given tutors in French, German, Russian and English. I worked with them from dawn until the midday hour and met with them again in the evenings, one each night, to eat and drink in their respective languages. The conversation of the intimate dinner table requires a specialised vocabulary of flirtation, insinuation and flattery, and this was what I learned. I also studied the foods and wines of seduction, and which combinations are most efficacious. Within four months I was sufficiently fluent in all four tongues to perform what was required of me both on the stage and in private with important men.

During the same period, two old actresses had taken charge of me during the afternoons, teaching me all they knew. By the time they finished with me I knew how to conjure up a duplicitous ghost of every human emotion. The fits of melodrama that had finally provoked my parents to reject me now gave me an advantage in my new trade. With my lover, I had already taught my eyes to cry and my mouth to kiss strategically. Now, with the help of these tough painted ladies, I was taught to utter the screams of satisfaction that every man longs to hear. When I performed well, the actresses did not applaud. They closed their wrinkled eyes and chuckled like wizened parrots.

I learned to dance, not the simpering steps of the noble ballroom, but the desperate footwork of the boards. I learned to respond to the greasy tide of the orchestra as it soaked up through the stage, staining my tapping slippers until I waded though the overture to centre stage where the beat gripped my ankles.

This was now my life: a graceless dance from which I could not escape.

When I had mastered all there was to teach me, they released me into the company of actors.

They let me take small parts at first, to see how I managed. It was soon decided that I did best in the style known as *'dramma giocoso per musica'*: two-act plays as light as a breath of air. I played the *'seconda buffa'* in *Il Bon Ton*, as my first role, and triumphed.

During rehearsals for *I viaggiatori felici* my employers told me to seduce the actor who played Pancranzio. Eusebio Pellicioni was an easy target: he was mine in an afternoon. I felt nothing for him; I knew also that he felt nothing for me except a thin glaze of physical coveting. I participated in the same external intimacies with him that I had shared with my lover, the first time I had been with another man. I did not die of it. I did not like or dislike it. I possibly liked it more than dancing.

After that, all men seemed the same to me.

Whether I was on the stage or in the bedchamber of a count, the performance of love, too, was all the same to me. I performed my raptures with a fidelity scarce surpassed by Nature. I was skilled, thorough and absolutely cold-hearted. I was creative and shameless. I never worried about conceiving another child. I guessed too well that the cranioclast had ruined that possibility. When I saw other women with their sons I looked away.

Later I came to realise that there were seducers of both sexes planted in our troupe. We Venetians make such good love-spies. Merely knowing that we are from Venice prompts shy confessionals and boasters. Our victims are inspired to describe what special qualifications might render them our equal, give them pretensions to an amorous relation with us. And it so often fell out that it was exactly that special piece of knowledge that we were sent to get.

I even liked the work sometimes. With my lover, I had grown happily accustomed to satisfying meals of manhood, and I gradually took to that side of my work with relish. And it suited me to hunt scalps for my belt. My lover's rejection cooled its burn with each new lover and his declarations. Even when a man was personally irksome to me, I forced myself on, reminding myself that in his eyes I was an angel of beauty and wonder: after the abuse I had suffered from my lover, I was greedily absorbent of unqualified admiration.

I always arranged three fine chairs facing the bed in whatsoever chamber I performed my ultimate sacrifice. This was to remind me, lest I be swept away by the painted *putti*, the silk drapes or the candlelight, into the false conception that I had entered a romance and not an enforced transaction. Three chairs for three Venetian Inquisitors, for them to witness what sordidness they generated in pursuit of the information that kept them potent in the world outside their little city.

And such reports I despatched, such indiscretions I gathered unto me! How blithely I moved from place to place, too quickly for my deceptions to catch up with me. By the time that Prussian minister was found, his throat slit by a stiletto, I was already in St Petersburg, tickling the belly of a huge white whale of a general, and learning all about the secret trade in skins that financed his army.

All these things I scribbled down, sealed and sent back to Venice. I was industrious, obedient, and highly successful.

I served sixteen years, a model employee. Had I been imprisoned for my attack on the nun, I might now have been released, my sentence served, my fate my own again.

It irked me, therefore, that the Council still distrusted me so that I was constantly attended by their own spy, Mazziolini, who shadowed me from city to city, and no doubt despatched his own reports by the same courier as mine. None of the other actor-spies had a custodian enforced upon them. I resented the implication bitterly.

If it were not for the unshakeable Mazziolini I might have fancied myself almost content. I might have contrived to picture myself in an exciting enterprise on my own account. I might have imagined myself more free than I would have been had I pursued my Golden Book life in Venice. But over the years Mazziolini's presence came to resemble, in my mind, the grille of the convent doors. It reminded me that I had no more choices open to me than a nun, not of where I lived, or how, or with whom I passed my time. He also made sure that my disgust in myself was constantly refreshed. He always had some choice barb ready at my employers' choice of a new lover. And it was unfailingly apt and memorable, despoiling any satisfaction I might feel when my professional romances ran smoothly. Mazziolini despised everyone – Russians, French, Spaniards, almost alike. Above all he hated Englishmen, and when I was embedded with one of them, I felt not just his scorn but, even less bearably, his pity.

I felt increasingly trapped, despite my manifest liberties and luxuries. I soon learned that I might request any item of attire that I coveted and it would be supplied. Without question, with a speed that seemed almost contemptuous, my employers indulged my every proposed extravagance in food and drink.

But I was poor, despite all my finery and fine accommodations. I was given only discretionary sums of actual cash at the onset of each assignment. In every new city, Mazziolini went ahead and set me up in an excellent house, obtained staff from the intelligence office, paid these servants till they gasped, and so bought their rapacious little souls. As an extra precaution, none was permitted to stay with me more than a few months, so that no one might become bonded in affection with me and so conspire in an escape. I was never allowed my own carriage, or any documentation that gave me a separate identity from that which I had assumed when I first stepped on to the stage as Mimosina Dolcezza.

When the letter arrived from Mazziolini, telling me that in three days' time I must leave for London, at first I bridled at the arrogant tone. He had recently left me in peace for a few days, in the loose stranglehold of my latest Venetian maid, and I had known that this absence meant only one thing: that he was away setting up a new appointment for me. The maid proving a drunkard, I had profited from his absence to steal a few flavoursome freedoms for myself and it was not pleasant news to hear that I would soon be back under Mazziolini's taut rein, with none but his faceless face to look at in my leisure hours.

Yet the appointment to London could not have come at a more provident time for me. I had been treading the boards and warming political beds in Paris and Salzburg in one dreary assignment after another for six months, and, even though I had only briefly returned to Venice between missions, I was chafing to be away from the city again, for many reasons of my own.

Then I also laughed out loud to remember that Mazziolini loathed the bread-and-butter English, how, for some reason, they revolted him above all races. *Anglosassone* was his foulest epithet for anything to eat or look at. The fact that Mazziolini would abhor the London assignment served to sweeten its prospect for me.

The play they chose for London was *L'Italiana a Londra*, in which Domenico Cimarosa's music perfumed a dull text. It seemed perfect fare for a London audience. My English was by now excellent. My looks demonstrably appealed to Englishmen: politicians and noblemen of that race had been among my proudest trophies, much to Mazziolini's contempt. Yet I had never actually been to England: my conquests had been made among the peregrinatory tribes of adventurous Englishmen who frequented the courts of Europe, seeking advantages for their countries and preferment for themselves. In view of this, I had often wondered why my employers never sent me to London, the font of all Englishmen, and I had answered myself thus: *They do not want me to seek out my first lover. They fear the consequences; they mistrust my lack of control.*

They did not know that I no longer desired his love. I was not even curious to know what lay before him, be it Heaven or Hell. I was well cured of his tortures.

· 3 ·

A Gargle with Myrrh

Take red Astringent Wine 1 pint; powder'd Myrrh 2 drams, mix.
It Detergeth, Astringeth, Repelleth, Drieth, Healeth. Is a most excellent Wash for swell'd, fungous, flaccid, bleeding, eroded and putrid Gums; cleanseth and freeth the Mouth from foulness and ill scents; Healeth (even Venereal) Ulcers of the Jaws and Throat. Moreover it may be injected or snuffed up into the Nose, to good Purpose in an Ozena, where putrid Matter lodg'd in the little Caverns of the spongy Bones, sends forth abominably stinking Effluvia.

London seemed to offer more than I could have hoped for. When I saw that an elegant Englishman of evident means was violently smitten by my stage persona, I was only too happy to let him think that he might take advantage of what passed for my true self.

As for me, he roused a strange and sudden ambition in my soul: a very specific one – to be his wife. As the wife of an English aristocrat, I saw myself beyond the grasp of my Venetian employers, who could never reveal their hand in a public altercation. Relations between Venice and London must be seen to run smoothly. They would sacrifice their hold on me rather than their discretion.

So I chose him, after overhearing that one conversation with my nominal *padrone* Massimo Tosi, liking his face, even liking his name. For who could not enjoy the flavour of those syllables, *Valentine Greatrakes*, upon the tongue and the ear?

I must confess, as well, he was easy on the eye, drew it to him, even. Exceptionally so. That evening I first saw him he was attired as if specifically to please me and my over-petted weakness for fine clothes. His greatcoat was expensively tailored and buckrammed to an infallible crispness of line. His double-breasted waistcoat was of a coming style, as was his fantail tricorn. He wore a plain linen shirt with an immaculate stock of stiffened cambric fastened at the back. His black solitaire ribbon was tied close with a perfect bow. His breeches were fitted with the latest in silver fixings for catching up his stockings. And I caught my breath when I noticed that his shoes featured what could only be an Artois buckle of Sheffield plate: such a thing I had heard of but not yet seen.

I was determined to be pleased by him. He was my selected destiny. Even so, he took a little getting used to. Accustomed to the ceremony of European courts, I was surprised by the brusque informality of his preliminaries in seduction. But then England was known to be a coarse country, I told myself. I should not have expected to find it overloaded with civilities. And therefore I supposed that his approach via Massimo Tosi, unintroduced, marked the zenith of the polite arts of romance insofar as they were developed in London.

In contrast, my own preparations for him were thorough, both practically and mentally, though all in a spirit of cheerfulness. I reminded myself constantly that I actually *liked* the look of this man.

I was not lacking in self-confidence. When I made an assault upon a man's heart, he had need of all his faculties to defend it. I was not often successless. But this was different: my life was riding upon it, not merely the gainful employment of a few heady months.

I reviewed my stratagems. I groomed myself to behave as I must. Better to let him speak, I must say little myself: this was one of the first tricks of seduction I had learned from the old actresses. Yet I would frequently lean so close, listening to him, that he would smell the sweet myrrh on my breath. To make him bold, I would be meek. And for the first evening we would spend together – for that I would contrive such a feast as to blind him to anything but lust.

I put it about the theatre that I was in need of the best French chef in London and that expense was no object for one night of his services. Borne on the wings of rumour, there came to my dressing room two or three cringing dwarfs, ejected from the kitchens of noble houses, their palates and their skills already ruined by servitude to English tastes. I tasted the sample sweet-meats they had brought in grimy covered baskets, and despaired. They could not answer my questions about certain foods, and I dismissed them.

Finally there arrived a trim Frenchman who interrupted me to say, 'So you want a man to eat so that he must spend? Why did you not say so?' At the word 'spend' he moved his hips slightly, so that I was in no doubt that I had found the right man. I handed him all the coins in my purse and he widened his eyes. The fact that this money was supposed to be spent on another lover entirely, a politician in the sights of my employers, struck my mind most pleasurably, as did the fact that I had conducted all this business under the pretext of rehearsal, and so Mazziolini knew nothing of it.

No doubt he watched me leave that first night on the arm of Valentine Greatrakes but by then it was too late for him to inter-vene discreetly. For the first time, I had managed to surprise my custodian. I exulted in my success.

That night I fed Valentine Greatrakes anchovies, artichokes and asparagus, ruinous to buy in London, but known to porter heat to the genitals. And the sea-course was of Barbel fish, infal-lible in rescuing men from incipient effemininity, and French eels. Instead of water there was an infusion of the Cubeb pepper berry, alternating with a muscadel cloudy with the powder of bruised acorns. The kidneys were served in cream. To accom-pany the desserts (spiced plentifully with candied ginger) there was angel water, made of the essence of orange blossom, rose and myrtle, plus distilled spirit of musk and a dash of ambergris. And finally a glass of brandy with an egg yolk beaten into it.

I rose from my chair two or three times on the pretext of serving him and performed complete circles as if it were the most undesigned thing in the world, so that he might admire me in the round. Then I sat down again, as though restlessly, like a cat afflicted with a seasonal imperative for love-making but lack-ing an understanding of her own condition.

162

Meanwhile, *his* hands shook so that he sputtered the sauces over the damask cloth I had hired so expensively. After the third such incident I renounced hope of that tablecloth and looked upon it as mine, for I should most certainly be required to pay its full value now.

And then I sang for him. To steady my nerves, and to remind myself what I was about, I selected a cynical little refrain from a Venetian *opera buffa*, but I sang it as if it were the tenderest love song, all the while gazing deeply at him. He drank it up, little guessing what the words meant.

> They say beware
>   of love, of love –
> It melts your heart
>   in waxen pools.
> They say beware
>   of love, of love –
> They say love hardens
>   as it cools
> They say beware
>   of love, of love.
> But not with us
>   of course, of course.
>   Not with us.
>   Of course not.
>   Fool.

He was touchingly nervous, a state of mind that infected me too. Something was afoot, something different. It seemed that instead of the usual bloodless spasm, he too wished to make this coupling finer. It must be done, certainly, or the evening would end unsatisfactorily. But it was not the whole object. It was as if the love-making must be got over for the deeper intimacies to begin.

I saw that tears came to his eyes. I asked him in sign language, 'But why do you weep? The song is not sad.' And I smiled, encouraging him to feel pleasure in the midst of the bittersweet pain. I was feeling it myself and thought I must have taken too much wine.

163

He answered simply, 'I do not understand it. It is as if you have possession of my eyes now. You have commanded tears, and so they come.'

This was so satisfactory a response that I sang the same song again but, as I sang, I found myself despising the brittle words. I wished I had chosen a sweeter song. This Valentine Greatrakes was worthy of better. He was worthy of kindness. I liked this idea. I saw more than convenient lust on his face, and I own that I was pleased to see it. I was more than pleased, and not in my habitual way, for in my professional seductions such a sign of weakness meant profitable information. I liked his enthusiasm because – strangely – it met my own.

On his face I saw speculation, and anticipation, and I saw something rarer: hope. I felt it myself: at least that is how I identified the liquefying of all my calculations as I looked at him. Yes, I wanted to put myself outside him, get a bellyful of him. But I wanted more. The wine seemed to be headier than usual. That was the only way I could account for my tooth-numbing, eye-widening sense of anticipation.

I excused myself briefly and in the corridor I seized my pocket sprunking glass and checked the freshening effect of singing upon my complexion. I dropped into my mouth another *pastillo di bocca*, a perfumed lozenge to sweeten my breath, I loosened my clothes with practised speed. I did not wish to be seamed with their imprints when he saw me naked. I wanted to look new as a child. A part of me longed not to part with my clothes at all, though I wanted above all things to be intimate with him. But a greater part was not yet ready for the naked confession of the secrets of my person with *this* man, those same secrets that I bartered so cheaply for information with men selected for me by my employers.

For the first time, I did not arrange the three Inquisitional chairs at the foot of my bed.

Something about this English nobleman had contrived to do what I had thought impossible. There was about him a quality of humanity that served to rub the rust off my heart.

· 4 ·

An Hysteric Electuary

Take conserve of stinking Orrach 4 ounce; Oil of Amber 48
drops; mix. The Dose is the quantity of a Chestnut.
Every 6 or 8 hours, according as the Case shall require.

The overtures being played out swiftly, we were united. And I
was lost.

I knew this because I was sad; a tender elegiac melancholy
evoked in me the sensation of slow music. Instead of the usual
hard bud of professional triumph or the acrid tingle of mere
animal satisfaction, I felt a melting sense of renunciation. From
a woman who had no heart, I had been transformed into one
who had found hers and lost it in the same moment.

I felt certain that he actually loved me too. His stammers and
his silence declared his sincerity. Mechanically, I filtered his
behaviour through my specially adapted wits, monitoring flattering symptoms in his mode of address or the lingering of his
eyes. Not in his gifts. All men offer gifts. And he was not to
know that I have never cared for the cold glare of diamonds, not
since a trifling incident in my adolescence.

Initially, I had exalted his drinks with certain ready-bought
English preparations, to calm him and dispose him for seduction,
but I soon desisted, for I found that I wanted to spend time with
the whole man, not just a shadowy edition of him. I was no
longer capable of stage-managing an operatic romance; I myself
was the music being played.

Sometimes I regretted dimly that to transmit my honest rapture I had only the ways of an actress, the face and hands of an
actress. The motions were the same as those I had gone through

so many times. Now they were the truth, and yet I did not know how to renovate them, how to uncounterfeit myself.

From time to time I roused myself from my abstracted state and gloated over my unexpected good fortune. Here, finger-tame in my hand, was a man who would be desired not just for his position and wealth but for his innate attractiveness. I felt a twitch of anger at the unfairness of my work, that in the course of my duties it had never sent me any man half as appetising as this one. I had been given to dozens of men. Yet for myself I had to find – and illicitly too – the only one who truly pleased *me*.

It was of little matter to me that he could easily afford the cost of my entire maintenance. In my whole life I had never met anyone who was actually poor, except the despised *converse* nuns at San Zaccaria. I had grown up in a luxurious *palazzo* and my adult work had been among powerful voluptuaries. If they were possessed with the gambling vice or desired women as expensive as myself, these men could afford it all, from the deeps of their ancestral coffers. Money was nothing to such men as they never earned it, and yet Valentine Greatrakes – for all his wealth – seemed to intuit my lack of it, unlike any man before. My new lover automatically seized any little bills of account that he saw upon my bureau, and instantly paid off a number of trifling sums that had been bothering me. This meant that I had a little ready money at my disposal for once, and I squirrelled it away in my glove case. Until now my way of accumulating cash was to save on the normal articles of femininity such as perfume. Instead I had used my craft and *acted* the part of a perfumed woman to great effect.

Every word he spoke of himself was a cordial to me. He talked with the utmost naturalness of his 'manor', which I took to be his country house in Ireland, his horses, which I under-stood to be thoroughbreds, and his stables, which I assumed to be situated in the parks of his ancestral home.

Yes, I liked him extremely. I liked his looks, his style, even his careless accent, something affected – so I had been told – by many English aristocrats. I liked his luxurious rooms in Bond Street. I liked the untouched copies of the *Gentleman's Magazine* scattered carelessly on the table, even old issues. I liked the fact that he had so much time to give me, and thought with gratitude on how many fashionable assemblies at fine London houses he must have renounced in order to stay sequestered with me. I was exceedingly sensible of the fact that a man such as he must daily receive crisp snowstorms of invitations to other nobles' houses, and I appreciated the delicacy with which he kept them discreetly tucked away so I should not even have to see them.

One simply couldn't help liking him. In fact, I soon developed an unrestrainable greed for his company. I loved talking with him. He had a by no means contemptible supply of brains. And yet it was easy to frighten him. That ridiculous incident with my hair feather that he thought was a bat! Even that episode nourished my tenderness for him, however, and my anxiety.

It is so very easy to put a man off his pursuit. The tiniest thing can make the sex falter.

At first it seemed that I was playing on velvet with my new lover, that I could do nothing wrong in his eyes, nor he in mine.

Then came a surprising irritant from an unexpected quarter. At first I thought it a trivial interruption to our happiness, but in that I was most grievously mistaken. A poisoned pinprick can make a nasty wound.

The problem was with his ward, the daughter of a close friend and employee who had recently died in circumstances he did not properly explain to me. I gathered that a business rivalry had gone fatally wrong, but I saw that the subject gave him pain so I did not press him on the details.

I never saw the daughter, but I assumed that she resembled her parent enough to keep the sentimental dolour liquid in his heart whenever my lover beheld her.

And that chit of a girl kept him wrapped around her small finger, no doubt perfectly aware that he suffered under a delusion of responsibility for the death of her father. About this cunning little she-goat, my lover was fawning and stupid with indulgence, and I did not like to see him so debased.

Young as she was – it seemed from what he said that the child's years most likely numbered about eight – she appeared to think that she had an inalienable right to be cared for by my lover; it was all one to her whether he performed his duties with pleasure or pain, so long as she received what she wanted. I could not but draw bitter comparisons. Since my parents had consigned me to San Zaccaria, *I* had never enjoyed that luxury. I had always needed to earn any favours I was given, often in ways that were expensive to my self-respect.

From visits to his ward he always returned miserably tense. What a job of work she gave me, to soothe and comfort him! What distresses I smoothed out; what dark unspoken fears I assuaged. It was exhausting. I soon grew to hate the little girl, the more so for the allowances he infallibly made for her.

A sore punishment it clearly was for him to be in her company.

For I felt that he did not like her, despite her parentage. She did not seem to give him any pleasure in return for all his efforts.

I heard him instructing his grey little butler Dizzom (for whom, with characteristic simplicity, he dispensed with livery): 'And she has told me that she dislikes her French teacher. The woman has reprimanded her in front of others for something or other. That teacher is to be dismissed, understand? – not just from teaching Pevenche but from the school.

'And another thing. It seems that they are feeding her some articles she does not care for. I've written down this list of things she has dictated and they are to be kept out of the kitchen. And replaced with these.'

Other ragged lists were brought forth from his pocket, and once a snippet of some ribbon that another girl owned and she grieved not to have. Dizzom was to find it and have three yards cut and delivered in the instant.

What a monster, this Pevenche! I thought, listening to her demands. Aloud, I inquired tenderly, 'And in what subjects do they instruct the poor girl in this school of hers?'

Inwardly I was thinking: *I observe that she has learned some useful lessons already in how to get what she wants.*

He did not even know the answer to my question, poor man. Pevenche's education plainly failed to interest the girl herself, so it was not a subject on which she permitted discussion, apparently. He dared not ask more, and nor did he truly preoccupy himself with the matter. The grim determination with which he satisfied her whims showed me not that he loved her but that he had given up on making a sweeter person out of her. He merely chose the easier path of denying her nothing. Giving her what she wanted, immediately, also obviated the need for prolonged contact, and I suspected that having discovered this advantage, he subconsciously acted upon it.

Other times he returned from visits to his ward looking furtive, and I wondered, *What did she sell him this time? What piece of finesse did he suffer today?*

And when he did not see her on an almost daily basis, he was obliged to submit to letters from her in laborious, large handwriting with a superfluity of capital letters and misspellings in even very simple words. These missives were usually signed 'Baby P.,' no doubt her father's pet name for her. Obviously the girl had seen the utility in prolonging her infancy, and certainly it was the notes signed in this way which received the most feverish attention from her guardian.

He always answered them, never mind other commitments or pleasures that called him. 'I am sure you are taking the right course.' Or 'I admire the way you handle such obstacles. You are definitely in the right.' And once, 'Yes, the other girl is a species of pig, you are quite justified in this course of action.' When I interrupted him at such work, he slid the letter under his sleeve, even at the expense of the resultant black blots on his cuffs. Then I thought it a good thing that he was embarrassed, because at least it proved that he was not an utter imbecile in her regard. At least he *knew* that he was making a fool of himself.

The thing he wrote most often was, 'Of course, dear Pevenche. Have the account sent to me.'

She had one further talent. I observed the sequence played out several times. (I always glanced at those severely misspelled letters when my lover was out of the room.) In one note she requested, for example, a 'cheap' pair of gloves made from pink kidskin. Of course my lover was instantly stumbling in his haste

169

to have them located and supplied to her. But the very next day a noble little letter arrived, reeking of self-sacrifice, saying that of course the gloves didn't matter and that she could very well live without them if they presented even the slightest problem. She had some old black ones which would do just as well once she had contrived to mend them, which she could surely do as soon as she was feeling a little better. Valentine Greatrakes was soon scribbling back to her, begging her not to reduce herself to such circumstances, that ten pairs of the pink gloves would soon be found. She replied begging him not to trouble himself, really, she was absolutely suited to her old black gloves. Anyway, she never went anywhere elegant – why had she need of such fashionable trifles? Reading this note, he grew agitated: there seemed to be a real possibility that she would deny him the possibility of performing this service for her. Of course it always ended with the girl receiving multiples of her original request and yet also retaining the appearance of martyrdom.

In a moment of weakness he told me that when Pevenche did not get what she wanted she would go to a corner of the room, pick up her ukulele and pluck the strings, making an abominable noise and mewing little snatches of self-pity distantly out of tune with her dreadful chords.

'When I hear her do that, my heart goes out to her,' he confesses. 'Her father gave her that ukulele. She makes such a horrible noise with it, and she looks so pathetic, that it reminds me of her orphaned state. She is not so – mentally developed – as to realise its effect on me.'

Do not depend upon it, I riposted, but silently. *If she made a noise like that I would turn up her posteriors and flog her with rods.*

Aloud I exclaimed, 'Poor little thing. But you mustn't take on this guilt. She is acting as if you somehow made a human sacrifice of her father. You were nothing but the dearest friend to him, you must remember that. And your devotion to the father is witnessed in your great generosity to her. No one could be a more generous guardian.'

'You think I am too indulgent?' he asked.

And I ventured a smile: 'A little, perhaps.'

'You are too clever for everything,' he lifted me up in his arms.

But later, when I criticised her – a light matter, for her lack of manners in phrasing a demand for cash – the embarrassment fled away and all his anger was funnelled up and flung at me, bitter words hurtling like an arrowhead of black, migrating birds.

I knew from the hard things he said to me just how mean-spirited, just how selfish, just how demanding was this girl Pevenche, because I understood very early on that whatever insults he used on me were the ones she merited and which he longed to hurl at her, but which guilt about her father forbade him to use in her direction. Pent up inside him, they had curdled and were ejected at moments when he was undone, at me.

It was not anything like the dark assassinations delivered by my first lover, for it was both inept and regretful, but it was far from pleasant. After that, I had no opportunity of undeceiving my lover as to the motives and methods of his little ward. I was not permitted to mention her name without his feelings hardening against me.

I learned to feel fear every time a discreet knock on the door announced the arrival of a message from Pevenche. Too often it happened that we heard the timorous tap of Dizzom late at night and he entered the room, lowering his eyes at my deshabillé – he was always a neat and tactful little personage – for an urgent and discreet conference with his master in a far corner. His hunted expression announced that Dizzom bore a fresh demand from the girl. I had begun to suspect that Pevenche had divined a new attachment for her guardian and that having discovered a rival, she had immediately gone into battle.

'She is always so . . . attentive?' I asked once, out of breath, after a particularly untimely interruption.

'No, not always,' he had panted, letting loose the clothes that were kept upon him solely by the clutch of his fingers and throwing himself back upon me. He was eager to forget her, and soon did.

I did everything I could not to set myself up in rivalry with the little girl, which was incredibly difficult given the fact that she

171

had declared war on me, and that, worse, he himself had most unfortunately subscribed to the opinion that I wished to duel with her for his attention.

Meanwhile the girl was busy with her precocious manipulations. A parcel arrived one afternoon from Mr Lackington's Temple of the Muses, the vast book emporium in Finsbury Square. Mystified, my lover tore open the paper and a shabby novel fell into his lap. I had a glimpse of the title: *The Adopted Lover*. When he was at his ablutions later, I flicked through the well-worn pages. It was the story of a dashing guardian who, little by little, falls in love with the adorable young girl who has grown up as his ward.

I shuddered. Even I had not been so scheming at the age of eight. Compared to Pevenche, I had been an innocent child. Truly! Then I noticed the inscription in her childish hand: 'To my guardian, sorry I had to get a second-hand copy: my allowance would not stretch to new. With kisses from poor little Baby P.'

'I'll not be waiting for you to grow up and snatch him out of my hands,' I promised the girl, under my breath. But I was aware that my breathing had quickened, and that I felt myself threatened by her far-fetched plans, as if she were already a potential rival for my lover's romantic affections, and not just an infantile pretender to his time.

One day it came most painfully to a head.

We were again walking on the ice, enjoying the beauty of the frozen river, when Dizzom came panting with a new commission, the greasy shine of apprehension on his face.

I had been so happy; my hand in my lover's, his cheek against the top of my head, his tall body protecting me from the wind. And here was Pevenche's newest demand come to fluster and take him away from me.

I couldn't help myself. I tore my hand from his. I asked him: 'Are you not humiliated by these manipulations? I myself am humiliated merely to witness them.'

He shivered then, and his lips drew into a straight, thin line.

Dizzom flushed and turned aside sharply.

'Have you no feelings,' my lover asked coldly, 'for a poor little girl without a father?'

The thought traversed my mind that he would never address his ward in that brutal tone of voice; that the worse she behaved towards him the more craven he would be with her. He would never humiliate Pevenche in this way in front of Dizzom.

With this man I wished not to act a role but to be my own self. Now I chanced it.

'Yes, I have feelings,' I answered seriously. 'I feel that she uses you to the point where you are ridiculous. I shall think very little of you if you do not begin to use your intelligence in dealing with her as you deal with everyone else.'

He turned his back on me then and walked away.

I had lost my gamble with the truth. The truth did not keep him at my side. Tears pricked my eyelids as I watched him leave, but I knew I could not retrieve the situation with a simple apology. I myself had sent him rushing to her.

My instinct was to run after him, to beg his pardon and be enfolded in his arms. But my instinct to show my hand and express my honest feelings had led to this rupture. With regret, I resorted to strategy.

For a few days I would let him miss me, I resolved. That was the subtler path. Let him contrast the gratifications of my company against those of Pevenche's. Let him draw his own conclusions. If they seemed like his own productions, they would be all the more valuable to him.

And when he was used up, miserable and lonely, full of resentment against the vile little girl, then I would go to him. And perhaps we could begin again, with one more truth established between us, however painfully.

· 5 ·

A Cordial Epithem

Take Queen of Hungary's Water 6 drams; compound Spirits of
Lavender, Spirit of Saffron, each 2 drams; Apopletic Balsam 1
scruple; Oil of Cloves 10 drops; mix.

It's a proper Prescription against swooning Fits and
palpitation of the Heart. But it is not agreeable to Hysteric
Women, because of its perfume, which few of them can bear.

Meanwhile, I had other duties.

Mazziolini made it known to me that my employers were
grievously put out with my choice of lover, not to mention the
fact that I had presumed to elect one at all without their first
instructing it. It emerged that I had been sent to London to
decoy a different kind of man, a politician, an aristocrat called
Gervase Stintleigh. I had met him the previous year in Paris, and
made the running with the preliminaries – a smile, an exchange
of certain smoky looks across a dinner table – though at that
time I was principally at work upon a French nobleman for his
knowledge of some trade routes to the Indies.

My employers never forgot a smile, even though so many hun-
dred miles away. Sometimes I longed to read the reports that
Mazziolini made of me: did he describe the exact moment I caught
Stintleigh's small eye across the opulent table in the Place des
Vosges? Did he follow this with an account of his own researches,
which would have shown that this Englishman was at present
intriguing with two French colleagues on the matter of some
Oriental drugs? It must have been so, for my instructions in
London were clear as light: I must re-establish contact with
Stintleigh and follow through on that single smile, and make it talk.

It was abhorrent to me to drag my attentions back to the politician, when Valentine Greatrakes had filled them so capaciously. But I did, for it was necessary to throw my employers off the scent of my plans. Gervase Stintleigh was just starting to sing like the wizened canary he so much resembled when he was most vilely murdered in Hyde Park, while on his way to my apartments. And his head – what a barbarity! – was found piked on London Bridge.

Mazziolini, who almost never spoke to me, made an exception in this case. He came beating at my door with the news. Perhaps even this was his duty: to observe and record my reactions. I managed some screaming and some tears, and even swooned, which seemed to please him – at least he enjoyed slapping my face and administering a stinking epithem he had spitefully brought along with him. But it did not shake him. He was without a compassionate fibre: he cared not whether my shock was genuine, but he found it good meat for my employers.

Whatever had happened to the politician, it was my own dire misfortune. If Stintleigh had remained alive, I would have been permitted to stay in London. As it was, I had no doubt that I would soon be ordered on to a new assignment. I assumed that had my relationship with him been allowed to flourish, I would have found out not only what my masters wished to know, but also what it was that made him a worthy candidate for murder.

A single night with him had resulted only in one laboured and manual manipulation in the ignominious domains of his anatomy and no verbal emission that would clear up the mystery for me or my employers. He had rehearsed upon me a few times without coming to the point. I had not been able to force myself to perform an entire act with him, although my instructions were clear. When I could not make myself yield to the clammy pleas of Gervase Stintleigh, my refusals drove him to such a peak of frustration that I was at last able to evacuate him with a few deft prods of my hand. He was not dolefully disappointed, no doubt assuming that night was just a preliminary skirmish, the first step in some heartless minuet he foresaw as cynically as my employers did, though for different motives.

But there was a grisly surprise in store for both of us. I imagined that the arrogant little string had run foul of the dignity of some rival in politics, commerce or love. At that last thought I smiled, for of course Valentine Greatrakes could have no knowledge of that solitary and inconclusive tryst, being safely ensconced with Pevenche on the relevant evening. I had exiled him to that condition myself by virtue of offending him in her regard.

A prideful, savage part of me fantasised that my lover *had* killed him in a duel. Indeed I could picture it: the solemn ceremony in an appointed field, both men immaculately attired, cocking their pistols over cascading lace at their wrists. I found it strangely pleasing, this vision of my kind lover brandishing the gun, his handsome face intent and serious, of the deferential black-coated seconds, of the ritual questions being posed and answered in elegant accents.

But no, Stintleigh had not died like that: the tale soon emerged that he had been shabbily despatched by a low-life gang in some aggravated robbery. My lover was probably as shocked by the death as I had been myself: the nobles of England were doubtless bonded together by more than their castes, at least as clubbish as their Venetian counterparts. No doubt he had read about it in the broadsheets; perhaps he attended the elegant funeral.

Naturally I shared none of these thoughts with Mazziolini. More urgent matters were afoot. My fears proved correct. On receiving the news of Stintleigh's death, my employers ordered me back to Venice, with immediate effect.

It was time to erase my quarrel with my lover. In spite of the bizarre behaviour with his ward, I could not tolerate the thought of leaving him, of returning to Venice, and after that Paris or Amsterdam or Rome.

I balked at the idea of another mission, of launching my body into yet another commercial adventure. I could not bear the vision of myself growing old in harness, scribbling my reports at elegant desks in foreign rooms. I could not endure the thought that there was no resting place on earth for me, until my employers thought me all used up, and discarded me, in all probability back at the convent of San Zaccaria. For them, there would be a certain tidiness in such an end. And what sort of existence would I endure, interred alive there for the remainder of my days? Nuns have small lives and therefore large memories, and of all breeds of women they are the greatest lovers of revenge. They would not have forgotten me or my crime. I shuddered at the thought of poisons cooked in almond biscuits, or plague-sheets left on my bed, not to mention the thousand subtle insults and feminine barbs that would discolour my existence. They would certainly shave my head, none too carefully, and sell the hair. And no one would lift a finger to help me.

I had given grave offence, and hurt my lover in a tender place.

Still he did not come to see me, and I knew that I must go to seek him out. Only that tribute would convince him of my sincerity.

Unfortunately nothing would now shake Mazziolini from my trail when I needed to essay out of doors. Instead of trying to contrive a secret flight, and provoking him to extreme actions, I simply informed him of my intention and suffered his ridicule with lowered eyes.

Chasing after a man? An *Englishman*? His arched eyebrows sneered. *How very quaint.*

And so when I went to find Valentine Greatrakes at his place of work, there was Mazziolini in the carriage beside me, his smooth face vicious with contempt.

It was the first time either of us had been south of the river, and neither of us, two fastidious Venetians, could possibly be pleased by it. Valentine Greatrakes had talked with pride of this industrious part of London, but he had never described the squalor or its stink.

Mazziolini had done his research beforehand. He took pleasure in taunting me about it, and explaining the provenance of all those smells: the tanners using the droppings and pissings of dogs, the soap boilers their noisome fats, the glue-makers their bones. Meanwhile, he told me, the poor girls of the Borough frequently lost their minds pulling rabbit fur for aristocratic hats because of the daily contact with the mercury and nitrates used to gloss the pelts. And the prostitutes were drowsy with stinking contraceptive potions administered by quacks who were in turn supplied by local purveyors of counterfeit medicines. The taverns of Southwark swarmed with smugglers, declared Mazziolini, and the streets were the haunt of thieves. The 'businessmen' of Bankside were nothing but underworld entrepreneurs and coarse brewers, according to him. I held my head up high and refused to allow his lies to ruffle my proud composure.

'This is the kind of man you think to be with,' Mazziolini sneered at me. 'Who conducts a shady business among these stews.' He mashed the assorted stinks with a resentful wrist.

'I do not believe that there is anything shady about Valentine Greatrakes. He is a merchant. Naturally not all of his transactions are picturesque,' I said, with dignity. 'And how many Venetian merchants of noble families profit from filthy camel processions in the East?'

'You understand nothing!' laughed Mazziolini. 'This is an *Englishman*, not a Venetian. Of all the people you might choose, you have chosen that one. Your masters have been kind to you, compared with what you have chosen for yourself!'

He spat.

I fell silent. I could think of nothing but seeing my lover again, and of the terrifying joy of our reunion. I was nervous, fearing rejection. Yet I also thrilled with sweet anticipation merely at the thought of seeing his face, and I allowed myself to fall into a pleasant trance, imagining his eyes and hands gently upon me again. Mazziolini, seeing my rapt expression, snorted with disbelief.

When we trotted across London Bridge he insisted on pointing out to me the stone alcove where the head of Stintleigh had been found, impaled, he informed me, on the politician's own cane.

'Spare me the details,' I snarled at him.

He smiled, mockingly, triumphant at succeeding in rousing my temper. My fingers twitched to claw his face, but I forced them to rest demurely in my lap.

And so we entered the depository at Bankside, in an armed state against one another, and confronted the horror within.

· 6 ·

A Cephalic Julep

Take Waters of Black Cherries 4 ounces; of Rue 3 ounces; Peony compound 2 ounces; Bryony compound 1 ounce; Tincture of Castor, Spirit of Lavender compound, each 2 drams; Oil of Nutmeg 4 drops; Syrup of Peony compound, 1 ounce and a half; Powder called de Gutteta, 4 scruples, mix.

It's used with Benefit, against the Epilepsie, all kinds of Convulsive and Soporose Affections, the Head-ache, Giddiness and Palsey.

Five spoonfuls may be given, before, in, or immediately after a Paroxysm; but for Prevention, near the Lunary Periods; for about these Times the Brain suffers wonderful Alterations; insomuch, that at the Full-Moon, it groweth so turgid (which appears by Wounds of the Head) as to fill up the whole Capacity of the Skull; yea, hath often been seen thrust out through a Wound.

From one side of the river to the world on its opposite bank.

From the image I could not quite bed down, of Gervase Stintleigh's severed head, to the real sight of an embalmed man freshly bleeding in his coffin, the first thing I saw in the depository of Valentine Greatrakes at Bankside.

You cannot imagine my feelings when I saw the corpse. Nor reckon how many sharp pieces of information suddenly came crashing through the oblivion I had drawn around myself in the cocoon of Valentine Greatrakes' love. My paroxysms were genuine.

The giddiness gave only a temporary relief.

From the storm of revelation on my waking only one clear thought emerged. I must be with this man, Valentine Greatrakes, because I had need of his protection from the violent world and more because I urgently desired his love, that I could not ever again live without it, having known its balsam.

But I failed. Even our tender reunion failed. I did not make him marry me. A depression fell upon me: it seemed that none of my lovers were bound to me in any way that might do me good. I thought of my first lover, cursed his soul, and of Valentine Greatrakes, tender as a dove, yet nevertheless fully prepared to lose me now that he had truly possessed me.

Even then I kept trying, kept hoping that he would declare himself. I played for time, telling my employers that there were other things in London worth investigating, hinting wildly at certain items of interest in depositories on the south side of the Thames. They did not believe me. A second order came, more imperious than the first. My proposed researches were deemed worthless, but, more to the point, I had no choice in the matter. So I was informed.

There was worse. Sweet as our reunion was, I was haunted by the rank smell of cheap violet perfume on the clothes of my lover. It racked me to see that he had taken comfort with another woman in my absence. I tried to close my mind to what I had done with Stintleigh or at least what I had set out to do.

'We are even,' I said to myself, grimly. 'I shall not make trouble over it, though he should have been more subtle.' I comforted myself with the vulgarity of the scent: at least he had sought relief with a whore and not some lady of quality who might have inspired his admiration. So I told myself, but my unconscious mind tortured me with my rival. That night I suffered a dream in which Valentine Greatrakes was dancing an intimate eye-strung minuet with Angelina, the nun whom I had blinded. Her features were not only undamaged but transformed into an incandescent beauty, and his face, gazing down on her, was illuminated with all the passion I had thought reserved for myself. In the dream, he caught my eye while his chin rested softly on her curls. An angry guilt ravaged his features for a moment, but he did not follow me as I fled. As I ran down dark dream corridors, scraps of paper

181

pursued me like malevolent snowflakes. I grasped at a handful. They all bore the same words, in my lover's fine handwriting, 'Lovely little Angelina, Lovely little Angelina, come away with me.'

The dream shipwrecked the night. For the rest of it I lay by his side sad and still as a leaf frozen on the surface of a pond. I did not dare turn to him for comfort, for fear of all that I would then need to explain.

And anyway, by this time, my mind acknowledged what my body had known since our first night together: that I felt for him the kind of affection that transcends misuse, even in dreams. I loved those things about him that a mother loves – the tousle of his hair, the dip of his neck where his queue was ribboned, the single eye opened to greet the morning. His poor blistered back inspired not disgust but a tender, eager desire to soothe it. I loved him like a lover for all the rest, of course.

And I was comforted by the unselfconscious grandeur of his giving – even the repulsive Chelsea Porcelain figures, which I consigned to a cupboard whenever I could, barely remembering to restore them to view when I knew he was coming. The expense of these creations was enormous. This I knew because when Mazziolini rented my rooms, the inclusion of our own Chelsea china had almost doubled the price.

'A merchant must lay out her wares in attractive packaging,' Mazziolini had jeered, no doubt imagining all the dinners I would be serving Lord Stintleigh on these bilious creations, pimpled all about with roses, snickering with gold at the edges, and wherever there was an area of blessed plain white, well then the tireless craftsman had embossed it with some busyness quite at odds with the rest of the decoration.

My lover, with typical sensitivity, must have detected my lack of enthusiasm for Chelsea work because suddenly I was showered with the busts of ancient Roman matrons. All slightly chipped and expertly repaired, but still genuine objects of antiquity. Then I received trays of pinned butterflies, always bestowed with significant looks, or so I fervently hoped. I had them sewn into a dress to please him, but he did not seem to notice.

With my lover I now tried to make up lost ground in every possible way, even with his ward. When I spoke of her, there was always sugar on my tongue. I even suggested some mutual excursions, but he appeared undelighted by these propositions, so I did not press him. But when, one day, he admired a bonnet of mine, I went straight to my milliner and commissioned a perfect miniature of it for the child, telling the woman that I estimated her age at about eight. The resultant confection, small as a doll's, I presented with a flourish a few days later. But my lover merely mumbled an embarrassed thank-you and distractedly crushed the delicate little masterpiece into his large hand. He never mentioned how my extravagant gift was received and I dared not ask. It seemed that the situation was irretrievable. There was no act of generosity on my part which would remove the stigma of ogress he had bestowed on me in her regard.

Like the icebound Thames, I allowed myself to grow numb. In that calmer state I hoped that some clear thoughts might emerge. But all the time I was aware that our sweet meetings and partings were merely tiny rehearsals for truly being severed. Those separations of a few hours were survivable only because we would soon be together again. How would I manage an indefinite rupture?

As the end approached, I let Valentine Greatrakes make a great sentimental fool of himself, mooning over my departure, drinking himself to a slush, such as I had not seen in him before, yet never quite bringing himself to ask me to stay, when at one word from him I would have fallen into his arms.

On the last day I suggested a walk in Hyde Park. I gently guided him to the place where Gervase Stintleigh had met his death, at least according to the journalists. My lover had been suspicious of my interest in that story when he unfortunately saw my collection of newspaper reports. But now he walked heedlessly over ground recently soaked with the vital fluids of Lord Stintleigh. Then I reflected that perhaps the papers were wrong, anyway. Maybe the politician died on London Bridge and the murderers brought his lower body back to Hyde Park. These gore-drenched thoughts drew my mind involuntarily to something that I had once heard said in Venice: that Englishmen were three times more afraid of getting married than they were of the sight of blood.

So I had not conjured a consuming jealousy in my lover: true passion was not what he felt for me. He could countenance my loss, even though it hurt him sorely. I was not indispensable to him. I felt so much used up in failure, so piteously lacking in whatever gains the hearts of men, that I grew dim and silent. I lost conviction to plead my case. I did not flaunt my charms any longer because I no longer believed in them. I simply sank in the wash of my own misery. On that final afternoon, I let him hand me into the post-chaise and never once uttered a complaint at his ill usage, or appealed to his mercy.

But to the last I flattered him, made him think that it was love for him and not disappointment in his weakness that paled my cheek and stole my voice.

'Shall I sing for you?' I asked, listless as mud, as we strolled in the park in that dying light.

He took his punishment like a man. He whispered, 'Yes, darling, sing.'

I sang in English, a tinkling volley of notes cold as the frosty branches of the trees above us.

> I bought myself a red rose at Rialto
> The vase in which I put it left a ring
> (a ring you did not give me)
> On the love letter you did not write me,
> In front of the mirror which showed me
> The face you did not love any more.

He blushed and turned away, hiding his face.

I asked: 'Did it not please you? Shall I sing you another verse?'

He shook his head mutely, and took my hand in his.

I held fast to his wrist, thinking, *You have a pulse, so you must have a heart.*

But I let it go, when that was what he wanted.

184

· 7 ·

A Litus for the Face

Take Ox Galls 3, rectify'd Spirit of Wine 3 pints; having
extracted a Tincture, and exhaled to the consistence of Honey;
dissolve it in Juice of Lemons 2 ounces; and add powder'd
Calomel 3 drams; Salt of Vitriol 2 drams; Venetian Borace 1
dram; Faeculae of Cuckow 1 dram and a half, digest in the Sun 4
days, strain and evaporate to a mellaginous Consistence.

For Sun-burning, Freckles, Spots, Pushes, Pimples, Redness,
Gutta Rosacea, and all blemishes in the Face whatsoever. Strike
it over the part thrice a day.

After that frozen leave-taking, I remained almost comatose for
the whole journey back to Venice. Mazziolini, who, as always,
magically joined me at the first changing post, observed my passivity with evident satisfaction. It was only when the gondola left
Mestre, and the towers of Venice bloomed in front of me, that I
at last woke up from my stupor.

I sensed that I was coming to danger: what mercy would my
employers show me? I had not failed them in a mission before
and so never had cause to wonder. But Stintleigh was a notable
lapse. Worse, in the grimy glass of the last inn of my journey, I
held my curls away from my forehead and confronted the truth.
My skin was tired; my eyes bore a tracery of fine wrinkles. There
were blemishes on my nose and chin. My mouth was losing its
fullness. An awareness stole over me that in the last months my
beauty had taken on a variable quality: I still had my beautiful
days, but there were also days when it was better to hide away
until I was in face again. I was losing my looks, my free passage,
my key to unlock my fate and keep me out of the convent.

185

When I was called to the interview with my employers, they would read my face with cold eyes, and my future would be decided.

As the gondolier poled towards Venice, the salt wind snarled around my cheeks and filled my eyes with tears. The towers and churches of my native city were distorted and magnified in the teardrops that hung on my lashes. I clutched a velvet cushion against my breasts and sniffed its mustiness, compounded of the perfumes of dozens of women who must have reclined upon it while borne from one man's house to another: daughter, bride, mother or widow. The smell and the images it conjured repulsed me. I threw the cushion against the curtains of the *felze* and it disappeared through the parting at their centre. I lifted the velvet aside and was astonished to see that the cushion did not sink, but floated away, its tassels glinting gaily in the sun. The gondolier, fortunately, faced the other direction, and did not observe the liberation of his expensive accessory.

I came to several swift epiphanies. I did not need to allow myself to be handed, passively, from one man to another. I need not allow Valentine Greatrakes to surrender me as a victim because he lacked the backbone to demonstrate his love.

None of these thoughts were visible upon my face or Mazziolini would not have acted as he now did, in a rare instance of carelessness.

Thinking me all but delivered, and lulled by my sleepwalking state, Mazziolini had pushed my gondola from the shore, but he had not accompanied me. For the sake of discretion, in Venice he seldom travelled in the same conveyance as I did, but always followed me closely. Now, I saw him distracted by an acquaintance at the shoreline. Mazziolini was from *terraferma* himself, not a Venetian of the floating city. I saw him motion to his own gondolier to wait while he exchanged a few pleasantries. It occurred to me dimly, *Yes, he too has a life.* From time to time he turned his head to make sure of my progress. I saw his eye skim to the shining cushion now floating towards the shore, and dismiss it.

A larger vessel, a fishing boat, now hove into sight, heading back to *terraferma*. I calculated that in about five minutes, at our

186

present progress, our paths should cross. Seeing the danger, my gondolier escalated his speed, and soon the fishermen were between us and the shore, blocking Mazziolini's view of me.

Swiftly I crawled out of the *felze* and stood up, rocking the boat dangerously. I clutched at my belly. At the same time I cried out at the top of my voice in the direction of the fishermen, 'Help me, I am taken ill!' I turned to the astonished gondolier, and whispered, 'Pray continue your journey without me.'

I tossed him a large coin which he caught dextrously. He had no idea that I had just paid for his certain discomfort at the hands of the Inquisitors. I selected just one valise, and told him that he might make a gift to his wife of all the others and their contents. Whatever mystery he thought to have stumbled on, the sight of the elegant luggage soothed any worries. He made me a happy salute and hoisted me up to the arms of the anxious fishermen.

In moments I was lying on my back in the dank cabin beneath the deck of the fishing vessel. Begging my pardon all the while, one of the fishermen felt my belly for the signs of a pregnancy. Finding none, his fingers rested on my neck glands and my wrists. I told him that I was feeling better now: the nausea had passed.

'Perhaps you would like to go on deck, my lady? It's close in here.'

He did not exaggerate: the boat's cargo raised up abominable fetid belchings with each new wave.

'The sight of the horizon would do me good,' I agreed, 'but I am afraid to sit up there among all the men. Let me just climb the ladder till only my head is above the deck, and I may take some breaths of fresh air.'

And so I hid and yet allowed myself the gladdest of views: that of Mazziolini poling swiftly towards Venice in his gondola, and, if I turned my head, the shore of Mestre, fast approaching me in the other direction.

On landing, I told my rescuers that I was now fully recovered and that I required only their help in directing me to a coach that might take me to Naples.

187

'Naples, how I long to be there!' I sighed. For extra emphasis, I added, 'It's the only place in the world where I feel safe,' lest any of them forget what I had said during the interrogation which they would shortly undergo when my pursuers caught up with them. I tried not to think of them being used hardly, and hoped it would not be so: they had thwarted the Council of Ten inadvertently and with only gallant motives.

I permitted them to help me with the single valise I had selected from the gondola, and to put me in a coach, which, with the greatest of good fortune, was due to leave within the half-hour.

At the first pausing place, I climbed down from the carriage, and joined another going in the opposite direction. For two days my progress scribbled a criss-cross of feints and doublings-back so dense as to lose any pursuer.

At last, when I felt dizzy myself with all these manoeuvres, I made my first honest move, and joined a coach that headed north and west. At Torino I found a stationer who, for a ludicrous fee, prepared me some unimpeachable identity documents.

In two weeks I was travel-soiled, exhausted, barely able to speak. But at least I was back in London.

Part Four

A Cardiac Infusion

Take conserve of red Roses 1 ounce; conserve of Borage flowers 2 ounces; candy'd Citron peel, beat to a Mash 6 drams; pour on them Borage water 9 ounces; Meadow sweet water 3 ounces; Damask Rose water 2 ounces; having mix'd all very well in a marble Mortar, and let them stand cold an hour, strain out the Liquor and add to it juice of Kermes half an ounce; juice of Lemon 1 ounce; Syrup of Raspberries half an ounce; and pass it all through Hippocrates's sleeve, till it be pretty clear and fine.

It restrains the Fervour, and allays the impetuosity of the too inflammable Blood at the same time, it also clarifies and rouses up the Spirits, darkened and depress'd with atrabilarious Vapours. 'Tis a very grateful and comfortable thing in a burning Fever, especially if the Patient be inclinable to Hypochondriacism and Melancholy. You may give a large Wine glass full thrice a day.

Off he went to Venice without a word of goodbye.

As if I deserved that. As if I had not done everything to keep him charmed almost to convulsions these last weeks since my Pa died.

I was more than a little disgruntled.

All I got was a hasty letter with a quite nugatory quantity of apology in it. He scribbled that he was going to make some personal inquiries into the 'tragedy', and that he was meantime researching some vastly exciting new opportunity of a commercial kind. And that, moreover, he might well be bringing me a wonderful surprise when he returned, something that would make me a happier girl, and improve my life in oh-so-many ways.

'I'll not be hinting more, dear Pevenche, on account of otherwise you'll be second-guessing me, perspicacious as you are,' he added. He loves a four-syllabled word, does my Uncle Valentine. And when he finds a new one, he carries on with it as if he had discovered hot water! Yet it's impossible not to be fond of the fellow. Even my Pa loved him. My Pa, who didn't have any love to spare, who'd fight with the nails of his own toes, and was always ready to use the heel of his fist on anyone at all, even young innocent persons, just for asking a little favour of him.

While Uncle Valentine went a-gallivanting, I was to content myself with Dizzom for my requisites. Risible little Dizzom, with his pantaloons forked so low it seemed like he had four equal limbs. It was an embarrassment to me when he came to the Academy. I gave him dog's abuse when he did so, only to discourage him, not to be personally hurtful.

If I needed him, I would go to surprise him at the depository, a thing I loved to do. I always hoped to happen upon Dizzom in the act of smelting the Venetian glass daggers out of the tallow candles in which they arrive at the warehouse, and to beg one from him. The pretty little things are never delivered to the ultimate clients still embedded in the wax because the secret mode of their smuggling serves to increase their price. Like every good scam, it is head-smackingly obvious once explained, but delectably arcane when not. My Pa would never let me have one and got quite irate when I asked.

Deprived of my treats and excursions on the arm of Uncle Valentine, every day passed slow as a wet week inside the Academy. I was not happy about any of this, and I intended to make my displeasure felt in all the ways open to me, chiefly of a melancholic and hypochondriac nature. Abandonment will certainly ruffle a delicate girl's constitution, sometimes dangerously. And this behaviour had galled, piqued and hurt me until my every feeling was perforated with a thousand tiny rips.

Uncle Valentine would be hearing of my afflictions, my fevers, my weaknesses and my depression, and they would rend his heart with guilt, and bring him back to London all the sooner.

I had my suspicions about his 'wonderful surprise'.

Venice, January 1786

· 1 ·

A Cephalic Electuary

Take powder'd Male Peony root half an ounce; Human Cranium, Cinnabar of Antimony (or rather Native) each 2 drams, candy'd Nutmeg 1 ounce; Syrup of Peony compound 2 ounces; or as much as is requir'd, Oil of Rosemary and Sage, each 4 drops, mix.

It cheers and roborates the Brain, depurates the soul, and fixes the too Volatile Spirits.

All the way to Venice, Valentine tells himself that the woman comes second. Or even third.

No, he's *not* whimpering after her. No, he's going to find out what happened to Tom, and to avenge his death. Forthwith. In fact, he is amazed that he has not thought to do so before now. How could he even hope to resolve matters remotely, from London? Tom's death has festered unavenged too long for anyone's animative well-being. A body should always have a just, swift revenge and not merely a gesture towards it.

Otherwise the insulted heart will continue in its aching.

And, to sweeten the dolours of this expedition (something *perfectly* possible without the company of the actress) Valentine is going to research the idea that was, by purest coincidence, born as he lay in her arms. Once he has dealt with Tom himself, then he will proceed as Tom would have wished, to business. He is going to orchestrate a symphony of hard goods and sweet relationships that will in the end bring forth his quintessential Venetian nostrum, which the denizens of Bankside will be lining up to buy.

He is eaten from the inside with ambition on both fronts. He sees himself in Venice, busy about the town, attending to both matters with scrupulous attention and flair. If he happens to fall upon Mimosina Dolcezza while striding up an artisans' *calle* near the San Luca theatre, well, that will be a pleasant surprise, of course. He might see if he can catch a performance of hers. If he has time, naturally. Which is doubtful.

Why, he has to source the bottles and make sure they are of appropriate splendour (the whole true worth of the package reposing in them, in fact, as the nostrum itself will be a masterpiece of nothings) and he must find the brandy distillery that will be prepared to bottle its wares in such unusual containers. He has already contrived the scam to pay for these expensive items.

English wool, whose export is outlawed on pain of death, is the most prized of all raw fabrics among the Venetian clothsmiths. Surely one can be found who will take free-traded English sheepskins, paying not Valentine himself – the ways and means must as ever be carefully blurred – but the local Venetian distillery in cash or kind, all the while preserving the utmost secrecy about the whole procedure.

The intricacies of this plan, and the text of his new handbill, keep Valentine occupied as the coach pounds down the icebound road to Dover, and during the lonely hours while he waits in his inn for the next packet to Calais, a high wind preventing today's crossing, meanwhile negotiating the stages of his outbound journey with various agents. By morning, Dizzom has arrived, having followed on the next post-chaise with trunks, wool samples, waybills, coins, not to mention a snowy mound of clean linen for Valentine.

He brings one more thing: an offer to accompany his master, although Dizzom is a highly domesticated creature and hates to travel, and he moreover feels a fearful antipathy to foreigners. Tom's murder in Venice has merely served to confirm Dizzom's suspicions of all Italians as vile assassins. He loved Tom, albeit warily: he cannot bear to lose his adored master in the same way. If only Valentine were going somewhere other than Venice! Worse, he knows the man is deranged lately by romantic love, an unruly emotion that has never touched his own plain heart. And having beheld the object of desire, he tremblingly knows her worth all manner of wild acts. Dizzom fears that in this condition Valentine is far too vulnerable to set sail for that fatal city, where the mystery of whoever killed Tom remains unpenetrated, and where therefore the same violent danger quite possibly awaits his master. Although Dizzom has never met his Venetian counterpart, Smerghetto, he has always thought ill of the man, an opinion embittered by undeniable jealousy.

Dizzom needs to say none of these things. His own shabby grey valise and his fierce expression of bravery say it all to Valentine, who, in his weakened state, is touched almost to tears. Or perhaps the tears are just seeking pretexts for showing themselves. But he will not hear of Dizzom coming with him: he needs him back at the depository, to take care of business. With both of them gone, there are elements of their fraternity who might become a little frisky, a little reckless of authority. And there is much work to do at home regarding the proposed Venetian nostrum. Dizzom must busy himself at his *bain marie*, his powders, his bruised seeds and his dried herbs. He must also consult with the metal-workers and chymists of Bankside, for it has already been decided between them that this nostrum shall contain, as far as the consumers are concerned, a vast number of – apparent – flakes of gold, which is widely known not only to prolong life but also to retard the unsavoury symptoms of old age.

Yes, while Valentine makes his journey Dizzom must perform some credible counterfeits of alchemy, so that a preparation is ready on his return that does not kill the patients before the blame for their death can be diffused over any number of circumstances. A nostrum that produces fatal grimaces and kills at a single mouthful, no matter how lucent its golden depth, will be no good to man, beast or business. Whereas great expense is no object: in fact the monstrously high price of the Venetian nostrum will only serve to increase its desirability.

Dizzom and his master shake their heads, discussing the finer details over a large English steak pie studded with oysters, the like of which will not be seen by Valentine Greatrakes for many a week. He lays in store a plentiful amount, washed down with beer. Valentine has long since learned to regard every foreign table with suspicion and depression, arising from the impossibility of a plain chop. He tries to encourage Dizzom, who nibbles sadly, and takes no beer at all. 'Look now, eat up, you've got a face on you as long as today and tomorrow.'

Neither of them speaks of Mimosina Dolcezza, and so they pass the time in manful, hearty ways before the Calais packet is announced.

Valentine, waving to Dizzom from the departing boat, calls out to him unheard above the moiling of the waves . . . 'Take care of Pevenche. Just give her any little thing she asks for.'

And Dizzom, scampering up and down the jetty, calls back to him, in a sentence that likewise perishes in the wind, 'I shall visit Pevenche every week, and take her for outings! And any little thing she needs . . .'

As Dizzom disappears from view, Valentine jerkily paces the wind-scoured deck until his damp hair whips his face. It feels good to be travelling south across the water. He feels fractionally less helpless; he has found his direction.

Yet his cheeks burn bright with the humiliation of it all. All the way across the guffawing water, he thinks that he should have waited for a letter from her imploring him to come.

· 2 ·

An Icteric Decoction

Take Roots of Turmerick, Madder, each 1 ounce; Celandine roots
and leaves 2 handfuls; Earth worms (slit open and washed clean)
20; boil in Water and Rhenish Wine (added towards the last)
each 1½ pints to 28 ounces; to the strained Liquor, add Tincture of
Saffron (with Treacle Water) 1 ounce; Syrup of the 5 opening
Roots 3 ounces; mix.

It inspires the Mass of Blood with a fresh, yet mild Ferment;
searcheth the Hepatic Glands, and specifically cleanseth and
cleareth the bilious Passages.

Venice flutters in a light wind that pleats the water and tousles his
hair in an insinuating manner as he passes under the bleached
sternum of the Rialto bridge.

The winking fanlights, the flapping curtains, the beckoning
aroma of coffee, too much seems to be trying to attract his attention at once. Everything is arranged to entice: shop windows, cages
of exotic birds and silk hangings. He feels faintly bilious, too much
sought after. Yet he feels the charm of it all stealing over him. And
what strikes most of all at the affections of tired, travel-soiled
Valentine Greatrakes are those guileful Venetian faces and those
sweet, beseeching looks bestowed on ladies of even mild attractions. Even now, in the working hours of the afternoon, there is
time for each Venetian to be made pleasantly aware of the partic-
ularities of his or her gender.

It is two years since he was last in Venice. For some time Tom
has handled the Venetian business with such a flourish that
Valentine has had no need to be there. So he's forgotten how
women here practise the art of being watched, and of making it

worth the watcher's while. In London the women hold their necks up as if nailed to the sky; they keep their hands rigidly to their sides. Venetian women are infinitely flexible and always in movement, be it a graceful inclination of the head or a subtle flaring of the fingertips. It's all finely nuanced so as to be above any reproach of unladylike attention-seeking. Yet it's impossible to take one's eyes off these fluid women, even those who bear no resemblance whatsoever to Mimosina Dolcezza.

When he's not watching the women, his eyes keep falling on gavotting liquid light: his spirits dance too, despite his exhaustion. Observed from the gondola, every coralline, banner-streaming *palazzo* is lengthened by a good six feet or so – and, by God, what this adds of grace to the spectacle! And of course there is always something offered to fascinate the gondola-borne eye: tiered rolls of wainscoting, as he calls it, at the foot of each building, all grimacing with lions and gargoyles, glimpses through water-gates into paradisical, rampant gardens, the striped poles of the noble houses standing sentry, but in fancy dress, for no serious threat can be made against a city as beautiful as this.

The Venetians think themselves unsinkable, he reflects with a smile, for the city proves that they are. It is infectious. He bounds ashore from his gondola, convinced that all things will stay afloat for him here.

Hoarse voices salute him; hands reach out for his.

'*Bentornato! Ti vedo in forma splendida,*' he hears from all sides. '*Signore Greet Raikes! Che piacere!*' He does not know the words, but he feels their warmth, and feels the better for it. He has forgotten the flattering effect Venice always has on the spirits, washing the blears from the eyes in an instant.

He nods and ducks his head, murmuring, 'Sure you're more than welcome,' and the boatmen take these incomprehensible words with evident delight, pointing at him, announcing excitedly, '*Eccolo quà!*' to one another, 'Here he is!' – as if the presence of Valentine Greatrakes was the very thing required to perfect their day.

He is well known in Venice, for he has done a little business with everyone here. He has his Venetian Dizzom and his own Venetian depository. Smerghetto, part interpreter, part lawyer, part chemist and part pimp, lives in some unknown part of Cannaregio and materialises at Valentine's side like an inescapable thought every time he goes abroad by day. Somehow, Smerghetto is waiting at the exact point and time when the gondola brings him ashore at San Silvestro, and together they walk down the Campiello de la Pasina to the apartments that Valentine rents there on a permanent basis.

The Venetian headquarters of Valentine Greatrakes boasts a garden, something that is beyond the realms of possibility in crowded, smoot-sprinkled Bankside. Every time he comes back to this city, he must force himself to accommodate not just the aqueous sensations of her arterial traffic but the scarcely less distracting ones of being in the country. On opening the secretive gate to the Venetian depository, Valentine always feels that he enters a separate world, not in Venice but perhaps in Tuscany. Closing the door, Venice is excluded.

At the other end of the garden is the depository, with convenient access to water-doors on the Grand Canal. The street façades of the building are eaten into by various professions and their needful ingresses. Valentine Greatrakes has the store space, the garden and the second-floor apartments it overlooks at the back. A tavern with a separate entrance in the street occupies the ground floor and lets rooms on the first. A little shoemakers is etched into an alcove of the west *pianoterra*; a pie shop dedicated to the appetites of the wharfmen occupies its twin to the east.

Another workshop, this time connected to Valentine's own business, is let in through a discreet street-side hole to the garden: here he employs skilled craftsmen to damage rare antiquities from Rome. They must do so in a way that is easy to repair, but the missing noses and lopped ears facilitate the export licences that will allow them to reach London. This studio conducts a thriving double life as a Knickknackatorium, selling historical trinkets of fresh manufacture, *ex-voto* paintings of a cunning naïveté, and lifelike effigies of their deceased friends, on moderate terms, to Grand Tourists. For the Italian pilgrims, who have a taste for the morbid, his craftsmen toil on *memento mori* of all kinds, but particularly miniature ebony coffins with ivory skeletons inside, the smaller the better, and holy-water bottles exquisitely painted with the like-nesses of saints. The studio is of course conveniently situated to fill these bottles with small measures from the Grand Canal, a liquid which in no way other than visually resembles the pure spring waters from consecrated streams eulogised upon their labels.

And in a light-flooded room on the third floor, several lady artists blessed with tiny fingers bend their heads over freckled cowrie shells that have been fixed with secret hinges. On the pearly inner curves the ladies paint tiny tableaux of bishops unlocking the chastity belts of otherwise naked nuns and similarly instructive scenes. None of these ladies, of course, is directly employed by Valentine Greatrakes. In Venice, as in London, he makes sundry genuflections towards the rules, regulations and shibboleths of the law.

Innumerable trackless staircases obfuscate the entrances from one part to another of Valentine's enterprises in Venice. This is as it should be, lest Smerghetto or any of his employees need to deny knowledge of any part that might come under suspicion.

Meanwhile the great canal-side rooms of the *piani nobili* are still occupied by the elderly nobleman who inherited them, and who yet maintains a show of dignity, not to mention nonchalance, at even the most disastrous gaming table, while living off these diverse and shabby rents, which are in no way charitable. So frag-ile is his dignity that the diminutive nobleman cannot afford to acknowledge any of his tenants in the street, maintaining a taut, faraway expression on his powdered face, should he unfortunately cross their paths. This expression bespeaks, or so he believes, the delicate sensibilities of his class.

But should any tenant lapse, even by a matter of hours, in paying the rent, the shrill bark he emits through his tiny rouged mouth can be heard from the arches of the first *piano nobile*, and the nobleman himself is soon beating at the unpaid door, demanding restitution in a tight, pained voice that trembles between falsetto and tenor, the paint of his face peeling away in mange-like flakes.

Following his usual habit of discretion, Smerghetto has made sure that this never happens in the case of any premises linked to Valentine Greatrakes.

Tom of course used the place more than he did, and standing at the door to the second-floor apartment, Valentine faces down the pain of seeing the rooms where his friend last slept and woke. On entering, he sees with relief that Smerghetto has tactfully cleared Tom's clothes and personal effects from view, and that the only evidence of the dead man is the goatskin pouch he used for papers. The pouch lies closed upon the table. Valentine already knows that it was recovered with Tom's body. He wants to see what papers Tom was carrying, in case they can point to an explanation for the murder. They have yielded no secrets to Smerghetto's examination. Perhaps Valentine can do better. He knows everything about Tom, after all.

But not just yet.

He has just seen one corner of the pouch is discoloured with what can only be Tom's blood. And although he has already beheld Tom's body in London, somehow this crusted splash of dark brown is more hurtful, more terrifying to behold, fresher and more violent.

He sits heavily on the bench, with his back to the pouch, and asks Smerghetto, 'Did you find anything else in here? Anything which might explain . . .?'

He already knows that no weapon was found, and that Tom's own stiletto had been discovered here, in his trunk. This is another mystery. If he was out on the Venetian streets by night, Tom should have been armed. He knew the dangers better than anyone. Yet he'd had nothing in his hand but his fist when the time came to defend himself.

Smerghetto grunts and reaches inside a cupboard. He pulls out a froth of lace and shakes it open, spraying delicate petals of silk. It is a woman's chemise. 'It was on the floor,' he says simply.

So Tom had been with a woman before he died. Well, that is hardly unexpected. Tom's nights were always as busy as his days in Venice. He had a known weakness for Venetian girls. Valentine Greatrakes spreads the chemise over the table.

He raises it to his nose for a moment, in case the perfume can tell him something of its owner. But the one sense, which, for the sake of greater felicity in Bankside, Valentine Greatrakes has learned to keep blunt, is that of smell. Smerghetto tells him: 'We gave it to a dog, of course, but it seems to have been too late to catch a scent.' The chemise is of expensive silk, but this scarcely narrows the field. The great whores and great ladies of Venice alike are clad in garments of equal luxury. And it is hardly one of them who has murdered Tom with such savagery.

Tom is tucked up by a spade, not by a woman any longer.

The answer must lie in the pouch.

He forces himself to turn and pull the thing towards him, though he recoils at the soft *human* texture of it, so like his own skin, so like Tom's. There is no help for it – he must now open it, and there is relief in that, for with the flap spread the bloodstain is no longer visible. He fans out the papers. They supply no very special set of explanations.

There are lists of prices from a distillery they use regularly, the very one he hopes shall now provide for his plans with the Venetian nostrum. There are sketches of hollow candles from a waxworks. There is an address near the fish market, which is where Tom's body was found. But Valentine already knows that there is no such house. Whoever sent Tom there had given him a wrong steer and perhaps meant to lure him to his death. There is the faint possibility that Tom made a mistake in writing it down, too. He was sometimes careless of detail, and it had got him into trouble before.

There is nothing in the pouch that spells a reason for Tom's murder.

His mind goes back to the refined, evil face he saw behind the sweet visage of poor Mimosina Dolcezza, struck with horror at the sight of Tom's body in the depository. He is again consumed with a visceral sureness that Tom's murderer had come all the way to London to behold his handiwork one last time. 'His face raped with fish' – the phrase reasserts its horrible thrall over Valentine. A man who could murder so sadistically was also capable of such perverted voyeurism, and would enjoy the view of the grief he had caused and would travel many sore miles to see it.

Without doubt he could.

He could kill a man stone dead in a scant second, that dog.

Valentine Greatrakes tries to picture every feature of that face, but finds it fast dissolving. It is replaced by the lovely features of Mimosina Dolcezza, fainting to the ground, her mouth open in a mute appeal, which, in the end, he had ignored.

When Valentine at last looks up from the impenetrable papers, Smerghetto is lighting candles, deferential and correct even in this small duty.

The ruins of the afternoon have long since sent slim shadows into the room where he sits. It is winter, after all, even in Venice. The brave light is already compromised by three in the afternoon, definitively breached by four and vanquished an hour later.

A crowd of heavy footfalls can be heard approaching the apartment. Valentine starts and shudders, his eyes fixed on Tom's leather satchel. His first instinct, now he is so close to the scene of his friend's destruction, is to feel himself threatened. His hand reaches for the dagger in his pocket.

But hearing a quick tangle of curses and laughter, he relaxes and stands up, smiling.

By evening Smerghetto supplements his meagre presence with that of two large half-idiot boys from *terraferma*. Tofolo and Momolo trot into the room, bounding up to him affectionately, overspilling with delight to serve their master again. In the two years since he has seen them, the *signorettini truncheoni* as Tom christened them, being unable to differentiate between the two, have added a foot of solid flesh to their mid-sections. When Valentine pokes at their bellies in a playful interrogation, they tell him, through Smerghetto, that they have married wonderful cooks! Not to mention their new mothers-in-law! With relishing gestures, the young men add that these grand old ladies can slaughter pigs with the finesse of a *bravo* slicing up a foreigner in the middle of the night.

The faces of the *truncheoni* suddenly fall as they realise, too late, their catastrophe of tact. In unison and harmony they compound their offence, moaning, '*Poveretto! Povero Signore Tommaso! Mondaccio! Che tragedia.*'

Valentine's face has already darkened because these two were supposed to have guarded Tom, just as they now guard him. The streets of Venice, so amiable by day, bristle with footpads by night.

When the boys commence to snivel and weep, he stills them with an upraised hand. How is he to explain to them that he cannot bear this operatic display of emotion? Not in the room where Tom spent his last night. Not at this time, so many weeks after the deed, when his feelings are worn out at the elbow, and his own eyes become so quickly sodden every time they light upon Tom's satchel.

'Peace,' he mimes at them, 'I want only an explanation. Not your blood' (he draws an imaginary *stiletto* across his own throat and points at them, shaking his head vigorously).

'Tom sent word that he did not need us for two nights,' the men explain, partly through Smerghetto and partly with gestures. 'We guessed, naturally, a romance. His message said that for what he was doing, we were not needed.'

Each of the *truncheoni* cradles an imaginary woman in his hands and kisses her passionately. Then they stare mournfully at Valentine, knowing that he has several times given the same instruction himself when a spell of feminine company has been arranged for him.

'You did well,' he tells them, forcing himself to smile. 'I do not blame you for what happened. Now we are going to find out who did it and give them some very special treatment of their own.'

His gestures are unmistakable.

And Momolo and Tofolo contort their every fibre to assure him of their enthusiasm for the work, never mind how grim. So long as Valentine Greatrakes is here to perform the intellectual feat of solving the crime, they are ready to execute the punishment.

· 3 ·

An Electuary of Mustard

Take powder'd Mustard seed half an ounce; conserve of Rue 2 ounces; Syrup of Stechas 1 ounce and a half; Oil of Rosemary, Lavender, each 4 drops, mix.

It penetrates into the Nerves, opens their Obstructions, and puts a new spriteliness into the clog'd Spirits.

By day, he works. By night, he hunts.

Calling up a nonchalant air, he goes looking for her in the theatres. While pretending not to look for Mimosina Dolcezza, he endures *Armida Abandoned* at the San Benedetto, *The Woman Mute from Love* at the San Samuele, *The Deceptive Wedding* at the San Cassiano, and more of the same at the San Salvador, the SS Giovanni e Paolo, the San Angelo, the San Giovanni Grisostomo, the SS Apostoli, the San Luca, the Sant'Angelo, the San Moisè and the San Fantin.

One night after another he hears what all the giants and the pigmies of the Venetian Parnassus have to offer, and what warbles – *amabile*, *strepitoso* or *arcistrepitoso*. Unable to pose the questions he needs to ask, he spends a wretched evening in each theatre, scanning the stage for Mimosina Dolcezza, felled by disappointment when she fails to materialise, slumping back into his box, his spirit clogged with loneliness, but not quite able to call for a theatre-girl and draw his shutters.

How discouraging, he thinks, for the performers, to see that more than half the boxes are shuttered, or that they frame aristocratic couples in the latter stages of foreplay, in animated conversation or busy at cards. Worse still must it be when the shutters burst apart to reveal tableaux of flushed satiety.

Valentine scans the boxes over and over, waiting for another to pop open. Between rounds of the boxes, he leans over to the *parterre*, where a turbulence of common people makes open demands on the actors, roaring at them to revive the corpses of popular performers killed off too early in the piece, flinging themselves to their knees in front of peerless examples of beauty and virtue. Baked apples and pears, sold at stalls outside the theatres, are the preferred missiles slung at actors who fail to please: the exploding fruit makes such a satisfying squelch. The other foods, sold by brave girls roaming the *parterre* in the *entr'acte*, are too delicious to waste on poor talent. Instead, the audience whistles and yells thickly through their mouths full of *fritelle* and roast chestnuts, inadvertently spraying fragments on their neighbours in moments of irrepressible passion. Some sit on wooden benches, but more mill around angrily waving their arms or enthusiastically kissing their hands to lovely actresses, both sides miming all kinds of proffered services. The only thing that stops the self-described geniuses of love from running on to the stage and seizing their brides is the empty space just in front of it, clearly labelled both with a sign and by its redolence as the area for relief of women suffering from an incontinence of urine.

Even there the eyes of Valentine Greatrakes seek out Mimosina Dolcezza, and down among the trampled crowds, upon whose loused heads rains the picturesque refuse from the boxes: orange peels, petulantly discarded bouquets, even, sometimes, rejected bracelets and items of intimate apparel.

The last night at the week's last theatre, and Mimosina Dolcezza has not yet made an appearance, not on the stage, not in the boxes, and most definitely not in the pit. His hopeful eyes have painted her on every backdrop, have seated her in every piece of cloud machinery, descended her from cardboard stairways and risen her from dusty graves, yet the woman in her own flesh has still not appeared. Valentine is losing heart, and it seems that the audience lacks the bowels for the latest revival of Goldoni, too. The theatre is half-full: under this circumstance the gondoliers are permitted to enter. But few of them do so: the reputation of this play is dismal, and rightfully so, as far as he can tell.

Valentine sits in his box, too dispirited even to work on the script for his Venetian nostrum, too tired to call out for the *truncheoni* to come up from the pit where they sit dozing. He can recognise their snores, twenty feet up. The pit audience is eating even more heartily than usual to compensate for the lack of meat on the stage, and are starting to look greenish with the variety and sequence of foodstuffs they have consumed in fast order. Unable to stop himself watching the relentless passage of food into hundreds of crumb-haloed mouths, Valentine starts to feel himself awake inside a nightmare. Thousands of teeth crunch down in time to the music. Hundreds of greased fingers reach out for more paper-wrapped cutlets still shaggy with rust-coloured flesh. He envisages ugly scenes when they start to pour more wine into their queasy stomachs, and decides to leave alone and quickly.

Padding the silent streets he feels a loneliness descend of a kind he has known only since he met Mimosina Dolcezza, for it is a sensation that is particular to her absence. No other human company would satisfy it. Not even Tom's, and yet it is compounded of Tom's absence too, for did he not misguidedly choose the actress for himself as a consolation for Tom's loss? If Tom had not died, he would not have been made so permeable by grief that a simple actress could reach into his breast and pull out his heart.

As he walks he examines his memories, turning them over in his mind, his heart panging like church bells at certain vignettes etched in flesh tones by candlelight.

At each crossroads he stops a moment, imagining that he hears her light step.

He carries his love for her in front of him. In Venice, in the absence of his lover, he has no need to protect himself from the truth. He loves her. He is in love with her. He has let her go. She is gone.

It is my own fault entirely.

And now that it seems impossible to have her, it is painfully obvious that the only thing that would entirely repair everything out of order in his life is the return to it of Mimosina Dolcezza.

209

In this moment he even thinks how her presence would surely help him to solve the problem of Pevenche. What the girl needs more than anything is someone upon whom to model herself, from whom to take subtle instruction in the ways of a lady. Grace is what the girl lacks and what the actress has in superabundance.

He realises now that the ill-fated London tea party with the Widow Grimpen was something of a rehearsal in his mind. He admired the young woman's reticence and quiet ways. He had thought her well-fitted to take Pevenche in hand, cultivate her a little, perhaps teach her something of the feminine arts. Had the meeting gone according to plan, he might have made Sylvia Grimpen an offer to install her as a companion to Pevenche, some kind of gentle and constant influence.

God knows a little timely instruction is needed on how to charm a fellow or two.

Of course something about Sylvia Grimpen rankled with Pevenche – *what?* – but perhaps the girl was right, thinking herself destined for better. For what is the humble mantua-maker, Widow Grimpen, in comparison with Mimosina Dolcezza? And what is a paid *companion* compared to . . .? He shrinks back from the direction of that last thought.

Mimosina Dolcezza: how he loves those words on his tongue.

They are a poem in themselves, he thinks, and rehearses their recital in a dozen different expressions.

Sometimes he asks himself, what if the love *she* offered had been smutted with a little gamey venality? What of it? He knows in his heart that he would still have wanted her. And indeed there was nothing of the fortune-hunter about her: remember how she had refused all those diamonds! In fact it is a little frightening, the fervency and purity of her love. He almost wishes for it to be fissured with a minor fault to make its perfections less intimidating. In truth, he has always welcomed the slight tawdriness of her profession. It makes her seem less impossibly high.

Valentine Greatrakes is only an ordinary man, accustomed to pleasant but ordinary and light-footed loves.

When a great love came his way, he did not even know how to recognise it. He let it slip from his grasp like a clumsy child. He quite possibly does not even deserve a woman as arrantly wonderful as Mimosina Dolcezza.

And yet, and yet, his heart is aching for the want of her.

For his sleeping quarters Valentine has chosen not Tom's last room directly overlooking the garden but one that glimpses it and also surveys the Campiello de la Pasina. In the early hours of the morning he lies abed, listening to the chuckle of light carts and the rasp of laden trolleys over the stones, and the voices of the Venetians, gruff, emphatic and ironic.

On the night of the Goldoni *opera buffa* he is awoken by a different noise, less urban and more earthy. Rising, he walks naked to the window. A few yards away from him, and clearly visible through their bare window in the first-floor apartment of the *sotoportego*, a couple are making love by candlelight. It is tender, thorough, and takes a long time, and he stands there, watching them, until they not so much stop as slow their motions to a somnambulant languor. He realises that they have fallen asleep while still engaged and that their unconscious bodies still move drowsily in their habitual ways.

In the spacious days of their love, it was just so with himself and Mimosina Dolcezza.

Valentine backs away from the window and drops on to his empty bed. From there he regards the wisps of tree-tops from the garden. The garden is large, all nuzzled about by fragrant bushes and softly pricked by cypresses.

By day, the mustiness of dead rosebuds tickles his nose. And the sounds are of summer in the countryside. Even now, in the depths of winter, a swarm of pre-dawn birdsong nibbles his ears. And the usual noisy litigation can be heard from the derelict pavilion in a far corner that Smerghetto has wryly christened the Temple of Feline Amore.

Butterflies haunt this garden even in the cold months, the dark tops of trees smudged by a pale flutter of wings. Valentine thinks now of netting a roomful of them: when he finds Mimosina Dolcezza he will lead her there and let a million wings caress her before he touches her with a single finger or his lips. He shrugs away such thoughts immediately. He is here to avenge Tom, and

211

further the business of the nostrum. Somehow he lets loose of consciousness, weaving plans for the bottled liquor.

Seconds later he is roused by a dangerous pounding. He is in the instant on his feet, dagger in hand and running to face his attacker. The hammering continues, and he flings open the door, to find no one waiting for him. Still bleared with sleep, still naked, he runs down to the garden. The vicious knocking seems to be coming from outside.

When he bursts into the garden, he sees the ground inexplicably glittering with stones like the diamonds he rained upon Mimosina Dolcezza.

He lunges all around himself with the sword, which strikes small hard objects but no human assailant.

Someone is attacking him with small, sharp missiles. They are landing on his goose-pimpled arms and neck where they commence immediately to melt.

His eyes adjust to the darkness. And then the revelation comes. There is no enemy here. It is yet another of Venice's mystical phenomena: a hailstorm of a kind he has never seen before.

For the hailstones are not the crumbled pearls of his normal experience but large pointed shards of ice. They resemble nothing more than arrowheads or small daggers.

He glances up to see if he has been observed. It seems no one has woken in his own building. He spins around to look up at the window of the lovers. It, too, is blank.

Now that the shock is lessening, the cold has begun to sting his skin. He creeps inside and up the stairs, praying that no one has seen him at his ignominious work.

It is only when he reaches the warmth of his room that he notices the two streaks of black flowing down his breast. Two of the hail shards have struck him so hard that they have drawn blood.

In the full light of morning he mourns the hailstorm's massacre of butterflies in the garden. Their corpses are everywhere, wetly smashed.

The couple in the Sotoportego de la Pasina haunts him.

During the day he comforts himself by denigrating their congress. He tells himself that he has witnessed yet another commercial transaction in this city where everything is for sale, and got up beautifully for a higher price. Her extravagant sighs and his Olympic postures are only what has been paid for, thinks Valentine, when he cannot avoid thinking about them.

But the next night he is pressing his nose against the window again, watching the same couple at their same sports, and he is forced to acknowledge a mutual passion, and yet more convincingly, a curiosity, that makes him conclude that they are real lovers. They are playful as otters and just as supple, but the looks they exchange are deep. Twice, he has witnessed the man weeping solely at the beauty of his mistress's proffered thighs, and once, feeling more of a voyeur than at any other moment, he has seen the woman kiss her lover's closed eyes.

From that night onwards he makes nightly trips to his window to watch over them. Yes, he is jealous, but he's also taking succour. The incredible optimism of Valentine Greatrakes has yet again burrowed to the surface of his mind, against all the odds that in this moment comprise the deafening silence and inexplicable absence of Mimosina Dolcezza. Each act he watches is a promise of what she and he shall some day share once more. He wishes the couple well. He thinks of them indulgently. When they finally sleep he watches over them, to make sure that no harm befalls them.

He even makes them a present, as he cannot offer one to Mimosina Dolcezza. He sets the bemused *truncheoni* to catching the surviving butterflies in the walled garden, and cannot stop chuckling when he sees the lumbering balletics of these human Alps armed with tiny nets. It's good to laugh; it unrolls the tightness of his belly. And when they have caught a dozen of the little beasts, he puts them in a large glass jar decorated with cupids, its lid pierced with holes.

The following dawn, he leaves the jar outside the door of the house where the lovers sport. He does not know if they will find his gift or not.

For him, it is enough to have made it.

· 4 ·

A Cataplasm of Herrings

Take white Bryony Root new digged up (or if it be dried, then the powder of it) 2 ounces; black Soap 3 ounces; Pickled Herrings (or Anchovies) 4 ounces; Salt 1 ounce and a half, mix.

It's to be bound to the soles of the Feet, and changed every 12 Hours, and is chiefly used where the Febrile Matter assaulting the Head, and oppressing the Spirits, causeth a Stupor or Sleepiness.

The lovers of the *sotoportego* are exceptionally active the next night, as if by way of acknowledging his gift. Valentine does not even pretend to sleep. Pressed against the window, he sees soft golden flickers swooping around their candle, and realises that they have released the butterflies in their room.

His night broken by the couple, he is fit for nothing the next day.

Valentine takes a morning walk to the square and settles sleepily at a table that gives a vantage all over the Piazza. He orders coffee and *fritelle*, and, as an afterthought, an ale. His feet are raw, swollen, distorted with blisters. Carriageless Venice always performs this assault upon his soles, and yet every time he forgets to take precautions. His nights standing at the window do nothing to relieve the damage. Fortunately Dizzom has inserted into his baggage a flask containing the efficacious Cataplasm of Herrings. Tonight he will bind up his feet with this paste, which has none of its boasted effects upon the brain but does in fact operate magnificently on sore feet.

Valentine aligns himself lizard-like in the winter sun, stretching out the afflicted parts. His feet may hurt but his cough has gone, the sore throat likewise vanished. He can feel all his hunched atoms stretching and opening out to the magnificent, imperious rays. In London he never thinks about the sun. Sometimes a rainbowed stripe of it passes across the newspaper he's reading. On rare days the sunstruck Thames hisses blinding sparklers at him as he walks over London Bridge. It soon passes. And even if the sun shines on London, the chances are that it will not fall upon Valentine Greatrakes. He lives his life in the depository, in the vaults of bonded warehouses, inside carriages, theatres and bedchambers. The sun rarely touches him there – but here in Venice he feels well handled by it. It is his companion wherever he goes and even when it sets, he knows that it has sealed a promise of its return inside his bones.

It's as well that there's sun, for nothing else offers to throw light on his dilemmas.

So far his inquiries about the actress have produced disquieting results. At the mention of her name, friends look searchingly into his face.

'*Ma caro, come mai chiedi?*' Why do you want to know?

When they read the eagerness in his eyes they grow sad, with that instant facility all Italians have for tragedy. They pat his hand with tender sympathy and say, 'Clearly, she's no longer here. We must find you another woman.'

This is universally judged the safest way to respond to Valentine Greatrakes, as if his partiality for this particular actress will now automatically shift to another object of a similar shape. No matter that he protests, 'But she just came back from London!' The reply is always the same, conclusive: 'However, my friend, apparently she is no longer here.'

And the way forward to other questions is thus also blocked, delicately and firmly. An actress who is not available to perform is easily replaced with another lax-fibred lady. The names of other actresses are offered. Valentine burns with a cruel embarrassment. How much has he betrayed himself with these questions? He has compromised himself for nothing: there remains an utter malnutrition of information about her.

The *truncheoni* are sympathetic. They bring him flower-girls, fish-girls, pastry-girls, pigeon-roasting girls, seam-sewing girls, and are bemused when he sends them all away. They knew him once as a most cheerful and vigorous fornicator but now he just wants to droop about moonishly, alone. In desperation they bring him a pouting little boy, for it is well known in Venice that Englishmen disappointed in the female gender do sometimes incline towards the more robust pleasures of their own. But Valentine shows every spitting sign of outrage when he understands what the boy is for, and is heard to utter a number of terms that even Englishmen (of the salubrious suburbs, that is) would fail to understand.

After four weeks he has lost faith in his ability to simply happen upon the actress in Venice, even here in the Piazza where there are women of her height and shape and colouring to be seen everywhere. Some of the whores are superbly dressed but look saucily. The noblewomen are little different.

Now, sitting in San Marco, Valentine realises that the parade of female flesh that passes him interests him less than the pigeons. He thinks that, unlike himself, the pigeons have a plan. From above, he is sure, the lacy trails of their droppings spell out messages for other, descending pigeons. There is something ineffably ironic in their curtseys. They follow certain humans with a clear satirical intention, mimicking important walks and snickering among themselves. At the edge of the Piazza, when their quarry mounts the shallow steps to depart, the pigeons turn and mince back to their compatriots, chortling, 'Hey! That was a good one, was it not? Did you see that?'

After three sharp ales, ill-advised at this time of the morning, Valentine is somewhat in his altitudes. He knows that if he rises he will be struggling like a newborn gazelle, good meat for the pigeon parodists. Better to stay here a while longer.

A body could sit himself down in a worse place than San Marco square, after all.

Valentine smiles to himself. The downward-slanting eyebrows leap upwards, his jaw draws skyward as a laugh breaks out of him. People turn around to look at the handsome Englishman. Some women look wistful, wishing to share the cream of his joke. But Valentine sees none of them. The fact is that the comic portraits painted by the pigeons have given him an idea.

It is the nature of Valentine Greatrakes that he cannot allow a door to close without the light of another beckoning at him. He has just remembered that after his last visit (the last visit but one, he reminds himself) Tom raved of a portrait painter in Venice, an artist able to capture the essence of love-making on the skin. This wonder is a young woman, and of a noble family, who has been a lover of Casanova's. She is in extreme request with all the nobility and beautiful women of the town.

Surely any woman in the flame of her youth would want a portrait to remind her of it? It seems a stroke of genius to Valentine, that he has recalled even the name of this Cecilia Cornaro, who must at this very moment keep in her studio sketches, if not – dare he hope? – an unfinished portrait, of Mimosina Dolcezza. The actress herself might even now be reclining on a *divano* while the painter takes her likeness at an easel. He leaps to his suffering feet, ready once more for work. All day, between his appointments and inspections in the cause of the Venetian nostrum, he muses on the idea of the portrait, and the more he thinks upon it the more he likes it.

An image surfaces in his mind, painful to recall. For he suddenly remembers how, so many weeks before, he and Mimosina Dolcezza had come upon an ambulant maker of portraits, who had set up his easel on the frozen Thames. Observing the man's skill and delicacy – and not insensitive to his blue hands and thin face – Valentine had begged the actress to have her likeness captured.

Laughing, she had refused, and had suggested that he donate a little something to the starving artist in any case. He thought nothing of it at the time, except that it was yet another manifestation of her modesty and generosity.

But now he recalls her words, and they clout him achingly.

She said: 'I would not leave you with a ghost of myself to console you.'

His duties with the Venetian nostrum occupy him until evening, when he makes another pilgrimage to the San Fantin theatre, just in case: the Venetian casts are liable to change at any moment.

All through another performance of *Armida Abandoned*, he muses on this morning's idea. Even as he leaves the fruitless theatre, his pace is quickening. When the show is over, with not a sight of Mimosina Dolcezza, he calls to a gondolier and asks to be rowed immediately to the studio of Cecilia Cornaro.

It is all he needs to say: Tom was right – she is known to the gondoliers and therefore to everyone. The gondolier raises his eyebrow, not at the request but at the late hour. Valentine chooses to find such punctiliousness trivial. A great artist, like a great businessman, surely keeps all hours, lest something unexpected be inadvertently lost.

And indeed, as they cross the water, the gondolier points out in the distance the milky splash of a chandelier aglow inside an upstairs window. Her studio turns out to be a magnificent *palazzo* on the Grand Canal, approached through three marble arches by the jetty.

The weather is mild. The air rustles against his cheek like a silk handkerchief. The moon dips in and out of clouds, foreshortening and lengthening the view. The studio of Cecilia Cornaro sometimes seems a breath away, sometimes a mile. All around them the night has flattened the façades of the *palazzi*, and the blackened arches of their water-gates seem like the flicked tongues of enormous sea monsters lurking just below the water's surface. A paunchy moon slaps clumsy brush-strokes of light across the canal.

The gondolier curses suddenly. The boat chops over a hidden obstacle, and is jostled from all sides with light nudges as if from large, hard-bodied fish. Blinded by the light from the artist's windows, Valentine cannot at first make out what has happened. His eyes adjust to the lesser glow of reflections in the water, and he beholds a most extraordinary sight.

Someone, perhaps as a joke, perhaps as a living kind of poem, has released upon the water a full tide of masks. All around him bob the half-faces and feathered head-dresses of *papier-mâché* people, all borne so swiftly on the current that it appears as if a strange aquatic tribe swims in formation down the Grand Canal, each on his or her back, empty eyes staring up at the moon.

Valentine chooses not to take this phenomenon as a warning, but an omen to the good. A hundred faces have forthrightly offered

218

themselves to him, he thinks, a picturesque and romantic gesture: surely he shall – now this minute – find the one face he wants.

Leaping to shore, Valentine gazes up at the candlelight dancing in the black window panes. Yes, it is all as he imagined! He is so close to finding his mistress that it is almost laughable. He hoots with mirth, and the departing gondolier turns back to look at him strangely. The man cannot possibly understand: she must be in there, even now, her head held delicately in classic three-quarter posture, her unringed hands demurely in her lap.

He finds the water-steps and hurtles up them, panting not just from exertion but with the emotion of this reunion. Should he gather her in his arms immediately? Should he simply stop at the door and give her a look that shoots through the heart? He is even thinking: *I shall have myself inserted into this magnificent portrait. Cecilia Cornaro shall paint us together, touching along every line of our bodies.*

At this vision, of a *matrimonial* sort of portrait, he suddenly pauses on the penultimate step of the jetty. It is an absence of such trappings that has driven his mistress away from him. He will not be given a second chance. If he offers such a thing now, then he must mean what it indicates.

Such a surge of joy constricts his heart, that he can feel the tracery of blood vessels rubefying. He takes another step upwards. The loneliness of the last forty days, of his whole life on earth, when Valentine thinks about it, is about to be terminated. So what does it matter if their lives are practically alien, one to the other? They have the rest of their allotted time to make up the discoveries.

Again he stops dead, stubbing a blistered toe against the last step.

Why not? It is exactly what he wants. In the last few seconds a sizzling marriage-fever has come upon him, and he knows it can be cured only by a nightly application of her skin against his, and the lullabying of her sleep-sighs, and the surety of her company in the morning, every morning, until the end of his days.

If he cannot live unmarried to Mimosina Dolcezza, then he must be married to her. In the silent archway, in front of the swift silent water, he can hear just two things: his own hurried heartbeat and a banknote in his pocket that is crackling with the involuntary jitter of his legs. *Crit! Snick!* With each move, it sizzles with crude venality against his thigh. How can he get to his knees with this infernal noise as his accompaniment? He whips out the banknote and throws it into the canal, only too late remembering that it is a large one.

In the *androne*, the lanterns are swinging as crazily as his heart, their facets spreading roving contagions of black and white spots over two grandiose statues of men larger than life and caught in mid-swagger. The first and second doors are firmly closed against him but the third opens smoothly at a touch of his finger.

In a moment he is halfway up the *palazzo* stairs, biting his tongue with the effort of remembering to breathe. His hands prickle and he would swear he can smell gunpowder. When he bursts into the room, he immediately goes down on his knees, closes his eyes the better to concentrate, and clasps his hands together, preparatory to asking the all-important question, to which the answer is surely a foregone and happy conclusion.

Will you have me, then?

When he looks up he finds he is in a room lined floor to ceiling with love-flushed painted faces. Dilating among them are two living visages, those of a large striped cat and a small brown-eyed girl of about seventeen years, with voluminous auburn hair. The cat regards him with polite interest, and the girl wipes her beautiful but colour-stained hands on a cloth, while looking at him with an avid and undisguised curiosity.

She is not Mimosina Dolcezza.

· 5 ·

A Consolatory Draught

Take Waters of black Cherries 2 ounces; of Mint, Damask Roses, Orange flowers Coelestis, each 1 dram; strong Cinnamon, and compound Peony Waters, each 2 drams; Confection of Alkermes, Gascoin powder, each 1 scruple; Oil of Cloves 1 drop; Syrup of Gilly flowers 3 drams, mix.

It notably succours the Spirits when sunk, and failing; and does eminent Service in Weakness, Faintings and Palpitation of the Heart.

Valentine Greatrakes, sipping *fragolino* from an earthen bowl, has not quite perished from embarrassment, though he thinks it a near thing.

He has by degrees risen from his knees, introduced and even explained himself to the girl, who turns out to be the artist herself, and to be quite expert and but lightly accented in his own tongue, no doubt as a result of long hours in the company of the many celebrated Englishmen she has painted.

Her soft voice is no less grateful on the ear, he must admit, than that of Mimosina Dolcezza and he is surprised that the accent is so similar, for Cecilia Cornaro is a Golden Book daughter, albeit a wayward one. He supposes that an actress of humble origins must learn to imitate the timbre of an aristocratic voice as a matter of course. It is a trick he regrets that he has never managed himself, of course, no matter how he distends his sentences with flourishing words. Only a foreigner like Mimosina Dolcezza would be deceived about his true social station, and he believes that Cecilia Cornaro has already seen through him and detected the truth.

She is much too kind to say so, of course, treating him with a graceful courtesy, somewhat underscored by what appears to be an irrepressible and playful spirit of irony.

Cecilia Cornaro, twinkling and smiling, is very sorry, but she cannot help him as he needs to be helped. She is not currently painting the portrait of any beautiful young woman just returned from London. She would like to help him more, she says, and he believes her. There is unmitigated sincerity in her humorous brown gaze. Moreover, she is alight with a happy curiosity.

'No one has come to me with such a story before!' she says enthusiastically, as if he has brought her a marvellous gift – and he has told her but the bare bones of it, leaving out the theatrical and free-trading connections, out of sheer shyness and confusion. She scents better gleaning. She cannot wait to strip off the pith of it and discover the fruit. Her very hair is electric with the excitement, and her curls appear, to his tired eyes, to have grown alarmingly in profusion while he has recounted his tale. She walks to and fro across the room, too excited to sit still. Her movements keep the medicinal aromas of her paints in constant circulation through the air. In a moment, in this most alien situation, Valentine feels completely at home. Cecilia Cornaro's studio, with its bottles and pestles of vivid powdered tint, reminds him of Dizzom's lair at the depository on Bankside.

Now that, surely, is a good omen, is it not?

But no, she believes that she has never painted anyone named Mimosina Dolcezza – she smiles widely at the name. She asks him if he possesses a miniature or some other sketch of the woman, which would recall her instantly to mind. He thinks of the undrawn portrait on the ice, and the warning that accompanied it, and shakes his head sadly.

She hands him another bowl of *fragolino*. While he drinks it, she walks around him. His skin prickles, feeling her eyes travelling all over it. She offers him chocolate cake from a platter she pulls unexpectedly out of a large bath-tub. When he refuses it a third time, she reluctantly puts it away, and observes in a slightly disparaging tone, 'Ah, so you don't like sweets, then.'

He shakes his head, watching her from over the rim of his *fragolino* cup.

222

'And your mistress, what's her real name?' asks Cecilia Cornaro, finally, now leaning forward to scan his face, and at the same time brushing a lock of hair that has fallen in his eye, so that she may behold him fully. She continues to stare at him with a consuming interest, and he finds himself blushing. But in a moment she has turned, and is lighting small candles on a hat made of stuffed leather, which she now places on her head. She ushers him to a stool, presses him down upon it and sits so close to him that his face is warmed by the heat of the tapers that cluster around her spiralling hair. She pulls a stick of charcoal from her pocket and taps it on her palm, then draws a small easel closer to her, all the while never taking her eyes from his face.

Valentine whispers: 'That is her real name. Mimosina Dolcezza.' He loves to say it, and repeats more loudly, 'Yes, Mimosina Dolcezza.'

She looks at him with transparent pity. 'Ah, *Signore*, I see you need some things explained to you. That name – is not a real one. It is the assumed name of a courtesan or a dancer, perhaps . . .'

'She is an actress.' His voice is breaking.

'Ah yes, indeed. And you say she is Venetian?'

'Yes.'

'But I have never seen or heard of a woman of that name.' She adds, not bothering to conceal her pride, 'I know everyone. I paint everyone.'

'She is frequently away on tour in foreign countries.'

'Well, yes, that could explain it perhaps. Some Venetian actresses live their lives almost entirely in exile. Venice treats them shabbily. They are cared for better outside of their own town. Still, it is strange that I have not come across her, if she is young and beautiful. The ones like that, they usually come to me. Or their lovers send them.'

The mention of 'lovers' is heartily unwelcome on the ears, I must say.

It would seem an act of extraordinary disloyalty for Valentine to utter the truth: while she is beautiful, actual youth is no longer among the fascinations of Mimosina Dolcezza. So he does not.

Cecilia Cornaro chivvies him, 'And what is she like? To look upon, I mean.'

'Why must you know?'

223

'So that we may play a game. I would like to have you paint her for me.'

Valentine Greatrakes recoils.

She is toying with me. I need not games but hope and hard facts now, preferably intertwined.

Valentine stammers, half-rising from his chair in his distress, 'You mock me. I cannot paint . . .'

'No, I want you to paint her with words.' She lifts her charcoal and turns the easel away from him, simply confounding his disarray with a businesslike demeanour. 'First, the shape of her face – is it an oval, a strawberry or perhaps an apple? And her neck . . . is it long, or short?'

The happy tongue of Valentine Greatrakes, so long kept silent on this most delectable of subjects, needs no third inquiry. It bursts forth into a most refulgent description of Mimosina Dolcezza, not neglecting any detail which has given him pleasure, and there are so many that he talks for a great length of time. He closes his eyes the better to see her.

All the while Cecilia Cornaro is making rapid movements at the easel, and asking yet more questions.

So many and such intricate questions that Valentine falls into a trance and lets his mouth frame answers without reference to his brain. For how is a man consciously to know if the eyebrows of his mistress are natural or tweezed? Or remember the distance between eye and brow? He sees her as one single vision, as everything he desires fused in one, not as her separate parts.

Women probably think differently, he muses, and for the first time he wonders how Mimosina Dolcezza sees *him*. This does not quite bear thinking about, not in view of the last time she laid eyes on him, guttered with drink at the door of her departing coach.

Still, he trusts this young woman with the blackened fingers. Perhaps it is the *fragolino*, perhaps it is exhaustion. But he has every confidence that a most perfect and living portrait of Mimosina Dolcezza will shortly be presented to him. To help her, he talks without drawing breath until his lips are numb and he can think of not one more image, simile or exclamation. Cecilia Cornaro nods, smiles sometimes, and at other times looks quite grave.

'You're sure?' she asks after some answers. 'You're really certain? That she is fine and plump? You know the heart can put a blindfold on the eyes, and you never know until it's far too late. The eye is a lens that magnifies the objects it likes, and magnification, of course, distorts.'

'I'm certain!' he exclaims, time after time, and so he is. He feels as if he's extemporising a love poem, a paean to the attractions of Mimosina Dolcezza, a sadly overdue tribute, one he is ashamed not to have delivered before. He wishes she could hear him. She would not feel unappreciated now.

He is growing excited. This is the closest he has been to her for days. Lacking her substantial presence, he's hungry for her image.

But when Cecilia Cornaro finally drops her charcoal and turns the easel to face him he sees a face that bears only a glancing resemblance to that of Mimosina Dolcezza.

The face still strikes him as familiar, though. For there is some glancing resemblance in it to Tom. Then again, the girlish softness of the lips to make it look – fleetingly – and with the utmost flattering – a little like Pevenche too.

'I suppose I've made her too young and too plump,' says Cecilia Cornaro regretfully. 'That's what usually happens when I have to do it this way.'

She dabs a disfiguring shadow under one eye in a way that is not infused with kindness.

'Either that or you were not telling me the entire truth about her,' she accuses.

He does not trust himself to speak. It seems that his earlier words have betrayed not just his love for the actress, but also his other preoccupations, Tom and Tom's daughter. He should do her the honour of an explanation, but his tongue is tied.

The artist must have her dollop of praise or blame, and Cecilia Cornaro is growing impatient.

'So I have monstered her then?' she asks waspishly.

Valentine recovers himself enough to make noises of protest.

'Shall you take it with you? I thought not.'

The girl is angry. He sees the colour in her cheeks and remembers that Tom had told him one more thing about her: that Cecilia

Cornaro is endowed with what the Venetians call the *lingua bifor-cuta*, a famously sharp tongue. He quails now, thinking of all the lacerating things she might say to him in his weakness and confusion.

She's not the kind to whom I'll be singing all my sorrows.

She says succinctly: 'If you must know, if *this* is your mistress, then she has deceived you. She has only pretended to be a Venetian actress. Perhaps it is not the only thing she has pretended, eh, *Signore*?'

Valentine flinches and bows his head.

Cecilia Cornaro seems a little ashamed of her sharpness. More kindly, she advises, 'Better go back to London, Signor Greatrakes. There's nothing for you here.'

The woman in the picture is not his lover, and the moment turns the tide for him. He scurries back to his rooms, orders his things packed up, bids farewell to the bemused *truncheoni*. He makes a final round of all those studios and workshops that shall be involved in the preparation of the Venetian nostrum, and shakes hands until his fingers ache. When he tells his colleagues of his imminent departure, he is roundly embraced, and the warmth of human skin closed around his own is almost too sweet to bear. One last time, he watches the lovers in the neighbouring building, his tears sliding down the window pane. He has never been so depleted in his spirits. He is bitten with desire for home.

He is not so much homesick for unlovely Bankside as wearied from being humbled by Venice's beauty. He is worn out by her incessant seductions, humiliated that she takes him so cheaply, even in the midst of his preoccupations. A lithe curve of the Grand Canal, the rich mew of a violin behind a shutter, the sun embla-zoning the *ferro* of a gondola – and his heart turns over, helpless and flabby as any Grand Tourist's. He is denatured here. He cannot think properly. In London, his brain will be restored, and perhaps his heart will gradually mend.

He is floundering. As he makes his farewell rounds, clouds are strewn like dirty bandages around a feverish bruised sky. The air is gross and thickening for a shower. The stone pillars are already sweating droplets, not waiting for the rain to come. And in the canals the water quivers and spasms rather than flows, as if someone had prepared and poured into them a gelatinous sauce of squid ink.

And surely all the belfries in Venice have been tuned to furious, sawing tragedy by the red priest Vivaldi – how else could the bells play on his spirits as they do?

In disappearing, Mimosina Dolcezza has burst not just the delicate structure of their romance but has revealed him to himself as a man who knows not how to love or be loved, an accomplished side-stepper, a flim-flam man. How exquisite is her revenge on him for his neglect – had she but the wit to know it. His happiness has melted like foam, as he now realises, being just so insubstantial. He threw his whole heart into her lap. But she could not know it: that doll's face, that doll's heart, a little mechanical device that knows nothing of the dark side of passion, and whose ticking can be quickened only at the sight of simple love in a man's face, of lovely gowns, at the glitter of ice on the Thames and snowdrops in Hyde Park.

Time to go home.

There is one duty he must perform before he leaves.

To conclude and make an end of this.

For the first time Valentine forces himself to walk through the fish market to the place where Tom died. Until this moment, he could not bear to do so. Now he has fallen so low in that the sense of loss cannot be made worse. It is a needful part of the so-far botched investigation to examine the scene of the crime. He has been absurdly neglectful in not doing so before. To make it more bearable he chooses to go there not in the dead of night, as Tom did, but in the bustling hours of the morning.

The promised storm has not delivered its relief.

Instead it is another azure day, pleasant and charming in inverse proportion to his spirits. The sky is dotted with just enough clouds to charge the heart of a landscape painter with delight. Gondolas are furrowing the grass-green water, on which the sunlight crackles like toffee.

He is not walking for his recreation, he reminds himself. To help him concentrate, he has hung Tom's satchel over his shoulder, a light but painful weight. At the last minute he had rifled the cupboard for the silk chemise and pushed it inside the satchel.

He sets off across Campo San Silvestro, turns left down Calle del Stivaleto, and right, left again. Before he even sees the market, the sudden reek of fish makes him blink, not just for its own salty pungency but because of the phrase he cannot forget.

Valentine has reached the glistening trays of the market. It is an unbearable thought, but it flickers in his mind at the sight of each different fish, each cod, each barbel, each crab, each eel.

Was it this one?

His back is rigid with the misery of it all. He walks stiffly to the bridge at the Riva de l'Ogio and leans over its parapet to the concealed corner beneath where he knows Tom's body was found.

And he recoils, for there lies below him just one limp mackerel, its belly unseamed and its viscera taken by a gull. His eyes skitter away from the fish. He forces himself to examine the pale stone on which it lies, all the while afraid to see anything that might remind him too accurately of Tom.

But he cannot face it. His whole body cries out for flight.

And he's breathing fish, slipping on fish scales, tormented by the dead mackerel. The shouts of the fishermen make him tremble. They are loud and, it seems, violent. Even the screaming colours of the fruit are hurting his feelings. He feels his heels pursued by the wheels of the fishermen's carts. The satchel slaps against his hip and a foam of lace spills out of a corner of it.

The reflections in the water have stolen a fierce red from a wall at one side. It looks as if blood is still pulsing into the canal.

It's more than a body can bear.

Yet he cannot help gazing at the stone pavement by the canal, and it's impossible not to see Tom's form there, especially now that he has a real Bankside memory of that coffined corpse, flowering with blood at the heart, to superimpose over the damp, blank stone he sees now. Dimly, and for the first time, he recalls that there were no wounds to the front of the chest.

So why should Tom bleed from his heart?

It is too much for him. Valentine stumbles away, unilluminated. He almost runs back to his apartments, where he approaches the window and fixes his nose, hoping to see the lovers. They have vanished and their room is, for the first time, ruffled and untouched, as if they had never existed.

He is on his way back to London within the day.

Valentine Greatrakes, on the gondola to Mestre, turns his head back for a moment to see the towers of Venice rising behind him, sharp and black against the boiling colours of the sunset. The next moment evening wraps the town conclusively in mist, as if hiding a malign surprise. In this tricksy light he feels unsafe, and stubs his fingers against his windpipe. He senses that the city is truly empty of Mimosina Dolcezza, but he cannot renounce the idea that she is something of it. In London he has the means for more detailed inquiries, both about her and about Tom.

Anyway, he has left Pevenche alone for far too long.

'Small notice of poor me', her usual phrase for neglect, is one that now rings in his ears. Strange, surpassingly strange, that he has not heard from her these past weeks. Only one communication, that arrived in Venice just the day after he did, and that a poignant little note of just seven words. They are easy to remember, like any matter inscribed on a flinching conscience. Pevenche had written just this, and not even signed it:

'No inquiring after poor me at all.'

Part Five

An Hysteric Julep

Take Waters of Black Cherries, Mugwort, Pennyroyal, each 3 ounces; of Bryony compound 1 ounce and a half; Tincture of Castor half an ounce; Oil of Amber (ground very well together with white Sugar, 1 ounce) 24 drops, mix.

This and other fetid Medicines, take off Hysteric Fits, by handling the Spirits roughly, and driving and dispersing 'em ... the best Course is, to send such a stern Remedy among them, as may use severe Discipline, and lash and scourge them till they are glad to leave their Disorders, and run to their proper Posts, and fall to their Charge again. But this Medicine is not equally agreeable to all, for we meet with some, in whom Oil of Amber raises such abominable fetid Belching, and makes them so sick, that they cannot possibly put it away.

I knew without a doubt that he was with his 'Mimosina Dolcezza' all this time. I was as solid on this point as a graven image. What else would have kept him in Italy so long?

I was careful not to mention her name if I asked Dizzom when Uncle Valentine would be returning. I let him bore me to conniptions with some fairy tale about a nostrum that needed a great deal of research in Venice. As if the stupid bottle were not going to be filled with the usual farrago of herbs, chocolate and intoxicating spirits all bound together with some impudence and a spot of Uncle Valentine's ticklesome puffery.

Oh indeed? I drawled, feeling twenty miles meaner than a yellow dog, for poor little Dizzom flinched and ducked his head, the way he used to when he spoke with my Pa; the way most people did when they spoke with my Pa.

Twice a week Dizzom came to the Academy with a little carpet-bag of remedies for my moody bowel and imperative bladder. Some were delicious. Others had unladylike effects, a bit of hard luck for the girls who shared the after-dinner port in Mistress

Haggardoon's parlour. I noticed that attendance of this previously coveted occasion was dropping down at a great rate.

Observed I to Mistress Haggardoon, 'The smaller, the more select, y'know.'

London and Venice, January 1786

· 1 ·

A Solid Errhine

Take Confectio Hamech, powder'd Scammony, each 2 drams;
Euphorbium 16 grains, make it into a Mass like Paste, out of
which form longish Pellets to be thrust up the Nose, and to be
kept an hour with a Muffler.

I was still pondering what to do when I arrived in London.

I had to resist all longings to fling myself straight into my
lover's arms. For Valentine Greatrakes would unwittingly lead
my pursuers straight to me. They knew of our liaison: his bed
would be the first place they would look for me, with dire consequences for us both. No, it was essential to let my trail cool a
while, allow Mazziolini to get to London, scour it, pronounce it
empty of me, and leave again. Only then could I claim Valentine
Greatrakes for my own.

The journey back to London had sponged my purse almost
dry. My employers always kept me short of cash, in order to prevent just such a flight as I had made. Now I must live upon the
dew, unless I could contrive a way of earning money.

How was I to earn enough to support myself while I waited?
Theatrical roles were not safe, not with Mazziolini on his ram-
pages. I could not cook or wash or sew: I had neither the skill
nor inclination to live upon such paltry labours. I did not wish to
contaminate myself with their humbleness: a woman who has
slaved at low work always shows it in her face.

I decided to lie low south of the river, where everything was
cheaper. In an obscure way, it comforted me to be close to the
place where Valentine Greatrakes operated his business. None
of his colleagues, save old Dizzom, would remember my face.

Dizzom rarely left the depository. I might safely walk those streets, fearing only to meet my lover himself. I was alert enough to see him first and hide myself, while he had no idea of the need to be vigilant, thinking me in Venice.

To this end I befriended the coachman with every kind of flattery and the alluring appearance of helplessness. He directed me to a clean house in a back street near London Bridge where a cousin of his kept a boarding house. I gave out that I was an Italian woman tragically widowed on a recent trip abroad, and that I awaited the remittance of the not inconsiderable sums due to me from my English husband's estate. In the meantime, I told the coachman, and soon after his cousin, I planned to live with exceeding modesty and in virtual retirement.

I concluded, 'Finding my affairs temporarily a little embarrassed, I think it unseemly to live large.'

My wily landlady looked at my elegant clothes with satisfaction. I could see her calculation: even if my story turned out to be bunkum, my dress would fetch a good sum.

I sank into a bed with sheets that stank of nothing worse than cheap soap and slept for some hours. When I awoke, the landlady served me some greyish pap she thought suitable for recent widows. Clearly, she planned to use my bereavement as an excuse to feed me as inexpensively as possible.

I forced down a decorous quantity of food under her watchful eye. I declared myself replete and told her that I had a great longing to take a walk.

'After many days and nights enclosed in my husband's sickroom, behind dark curtains, it seems months since I have breathed and smelled fresh air.'

Her lip curled, and I realised why. The air of Bankside was far from fresh. It was better to arrive there with perfumed pellets in the nose, and wrapped in a muffler. Bankside stank of urine from the tanneries, belchings from the brewery, and the sky was flecked with smoots from the glassworks. The coachman had warned me that there were no elegant places of refreshment here, like Morandi's Chocolate House in Playhouse Yard: such places were to be found only on the salubrious northerly shores of the river.

238

Feigning nervousness, I asked my landlady: 'Is it safe for a lady of quality to go about unaccompanied in this place?'

She was not taken in, but she preferred to play my game with me: 'No one will hurt you, madame,' she told me briskly.

I drew on a hat with a veil, just in case, and walked with an unerring Venetian instinct towards the noisome flow of the River Thames. Down there the air was thick with the clatter and stink of every kind of small trader. And the English, who are known to love their fruits, were gathered around stalls, handing over pennies and grazing like goats on apples and pears.

I walked fast, as if I had a purpose. I was hoping to clear my travel-worn brain that had begun to run in interminable circles like the wheels of the carriages that had borne me across Europe. In those lonely, crowded moments, jostled by strangers, my mind frequently taunted me with images of the face of Valentine Greatrakes, candid as a lighted window at dusk. I could not resist walking down Stoney Street and past his depository, though I kept my eyes firmly lowered. How easy it would be to walk straight through those gates and claim my rightful refuge; and how dangerous too.

At the end of Stoney Street I turned left through an archway into Clink Street, and walked past the gabled houses, tenements and the ruins of an old prison. I continued down towards the vast grounds of what my nose infallibly informed me to be a brewery. My ears rang with a great thumping of sacks that split to spill malt and hay in mouldy heaps in my way. On my right, the grey swell of the water appeared through a gap in the houses. Steps and a jetty tottered straight into the Thames. I passed by the establishments of discreet ivory merchants and pulverous coal merchants. Children in rags skittered past me, marching barefoot through puddles of mustard-coloured effluvia, their squeals rich and deep with tubercular infections. It was a far cry from the quiet luxury of my former London lodgings at Soho Square. But I was not repulsed by it: on the contrary. It had a vivacity about it that reminded me not a little of the humble quarters of Venice.

For one heart-stabbing second, I thought I had caught sight of my lover, or perhaps my desirous eyes conjured up what they most wished to see. My body was convulsed as if suddenly struck by a hundred pinpoints at once. I flattened myself against a wall and averted my face. But I had been deceived by a man of his enviable height, dressed in a waistcoat embroidered with green and yellow flowers.

And there was the Anchor Tavern, that sanctuary of which I had heard a great many pleasant things! Valentine Greatrakes, gagging over one of my rich *veloutés*, had once declared that the Anchor prepared the finest mutton chop in the whole of Christendom and that its cupboards contained the finest and most useful concealed stairwells in all Bankside. Seeing me mystified at the latter, he returned to his laudation of the Anchor's mutton.

'Simply done,' he had said, looking ruefully at the next item of culinary artistry I had placed in front of him. 'Nothing but the meat, seared and turned.'

Indeed, the smell of overcooked and greasy flesh was churning out of the tavern and through an open door I saw that the inn did a busy trade. The tables were laid with wooden platters and green earthenware pots into which (or at which) the gnawed bones were thrown with varying degrees of accuracy. The tablecloths looked as if a cat had recently kittened upon them. None of this raised any dismay in the customers, many clearly members of starving trades, who had come to drink their pittances and look with dripping jaws at those who were eating such horrors as pigeon barely transmogrified and wrapped in pastry or larks on a skewer.

I was surprised to see what kinds of men were being served. Not gentlemen, like Valentine Greatrakes, but working men, in shabby clothes, with shabby manners if any at all, from the way they grabbed at the condiments and wiped their slick chins with their sleeves. They yelled in coarse accents, laughed with their mouths full, and brawled with the harassed waiters. The door swung shut on an infernal scene, like a dining room in the hindquarters of Hell. I stood still a moment, telling myself that there must be another dining room reserved for the aristocrats and men of quality like Valentine Greatrakes, probably with its own entrance to avoid promiscuous social mingling.

But I did not see it. For it was then that my eye fell on another spectacle, and I found my means of subsisting in London.

· 2 ·

A Cordial Julep

Take Waters of Baulm, Black Cherries, each 3 ounces; of Barley
Cinnamon 2 ounces; Epidemial 1 ounce and a half; of Peony
compound, Syrup of Gillyflowers, each 1 ounce; Syrup of
Lemons half an ounce; Confection of kermes 4 scruples, mix.

As soon as these sorts of Spiritous Cordials come to touch
upon the Stomach; yea sometimes as soon as ever tasted in the
Mouth, they exert their Virtues; for by a grateful appulse they
refresh and restore the Spirits waiting in the first Rooms, or
Porch, as 'twere of the Body. And then these Spirits affecting
others contiguous to them, and they likewise others successively
onward, the pleasing Ovation undulates, in a trice, through the
whole System of the Sensitive Soul: And so the Brain and
Praecordia being recruited and irradiated with a full Influx of
exulting Spirits, perform their Business of Vital Functions, with
a new Briskness, and fresh Alacrity; and the Pulse, that lay
before weak and wavering, rouseth up, falls a vibrating lustily,
and drives round the Wheel of Life vigorously.

A quack doctor had trundled his wheeled rostrum into the cobbled lane outside the Anchor. The horse was quickly
unharnessed and tethered at a small distance. Ingenious levers
and pulleys transformed the rig into a small stage under which a
knot of spectators assembled: a restive mixture of shopkeepers
and labourers. A snowstorm of handbills was distributed by the
doctor's jester. I heard someone say, 'Look at the Zany!' Eager
hands reached out for the handbills. The semi-literate set themselves up reading aloud in pompous tones to those who could not
guess at their inventions.

The Zany, got up in an extravagant confection of multi-coloured rags, now hurtled up on to the stage and began to warm the mood of the audience with his capers and jokes. Hearing laughter, more people drew near until at least fifty souls, baying and helpless with mirth, were the Zany's to do with as he wished.

I felt homesick suddenly: such a sight was to be enjoyed on the Riva degli Schiavoni any day in Venice. This stage even boasted the familiar effigies in wood of Cosma and Damiano, patron saints of medicine. Nor were the services of such a clown disdained by the most pompous of Venetian quacks. The Zanies were useful to draw the crowds and unlock their ears, all the better to steal a passage to their pockets. Sometimes the arrant silliness of the Zany served to underline the seriousness of his master.

My mind travelled back sixteen years to those nights when I had crept out of San Zaccaria to the Riva degli Schiavoni, pretending to be with my first lover, and watched the mountebank doctors at their work. I had not seen such a thing since.

All Zanies have their particular talents, acrobatic, theatrical or musical. This one was a singing Zany and most tunefully he treated us to song as he scattered his creamy largesse of printed handbills advertising the services of the Great, the Unparalleled, the Most Rever'd Dottore Velena, the wonder lately come to London direct from Venice – (*Indeed!* I smiled) – with his Universal Cure that had lately saved many thousands of Venetians in mortal danger from the Itching Flux. I glanced behind the threadbare velvet curtain to see the said Doctor Velena, whom I had previously thought the horseman, applying his make-up. He was no more Venetian than I was an Englishwoman.

The Zany scampered about warbling:

> See Sirs, See here
> A Doctor rare
> Who travels much at home,
> Here, take his bills,

He cures all Ills,
Past, Present and to come;
The *Cramp*, the *Stitch*,
The *Squirt*, the *Itch*,
The *Gout*, the *Stone*, the *Pox*;
The *Mulligrubs*,
The *Bonny Scrubs*
And all *Pandora's* Box.
Thousands he's Dissected
And such cures effected
As none e'er can tell.

When the Zany had finished the last of five such verses, he backed away deferentially, making many respectful bows towards the curtain at the back of the stage, from which the quack now strode forth in a dramatic manner.

Strikingly swarthy in his paint, impressively wigged but quite simply dressed, he stood silent for a moment, glaring at the rabble, and then addressed them in an accent that but crudely pretended at Italian. However, he had a talent for rolling his 'r's, which he used to great effect.

Ignoring their rags, stinks and low accents, he began, 'Most noble and illustrious Signorrrrri and egregious beautiful and virtuous Madonnas, and the rrrrrest of my honoured friends and scrupulous Auditors . . .'

His customers, marinating in this flattery, drew closer, shrugging their shoulders and smiling shyly at one another.

'May I present myself, Dottore Conte Marchese Paracelsus Theophrastus Velena, lately arrived from the most ancient and stately city of Venice where I was wont to fix my bench in the face of the great Piazza.'

Full half an hour he intoned. He introduced himself as a friend to the ill and weak. A mere Mortal himself, he said modestly, casting down his eyes, just a man whose tender heart was easily riven in two by the sight of needless suffering.

'Little children . . .' he moaned, '. . . wasting away. Young women, ripped from their adoring husbands' arms. How shall I

244

bear it? How shall *you* bear it when it comes to you, gentle people?'

And from somewhere the quack conjured up a true tear, which he wiped away with a gesture of desperate bravery, before it could smear his paint.

Suddenly he drew himself up to his full height. He gyrated his features into a rictus of righteous indignation and stamped his foot. His boot was apparently tipped with iron, for the noise echoed like a shot. People in the crowd jumped. Women clutched their babies.

Good, good, I thought. *A nice touch. Bravo.*

'You see here no boastful, upstart, bum-peeping apothecary,' he thundered. 'No rumbling quack, no piss-prophet, no greedy physician rambling tamely among you with some mouldy tales out of Boccaccio and discoursing of my exotic travels. Not I.

'No no no no no. Neverrrrrr!'

To a man, the crowd hastily shook their heads, banishing such a possibility.

Such despicable men went about the country, he told us, robbing honest citizens not just of their wealth but their corporeal health, prescribing the same deceitful cure for every illness, and inventing illnesses to suit their wares, active not in the Hippocratic arts but in the crass pursuit of the hard-earned pittances of foolish people.

'Behold at last an honest man!' he cried, pointing to his modest garb. 'Too honest to be rich! You will not hear me talking of the Moon-Palls or the Strong-Fives nor the Hockogrocles, nor the Marthambles, all spurious maladies genesised for his own profit by that arrant quack, Doctor Tufts, who has recently passed through this fair town, spreading misery! Nor even the Dogmatical Incurables of Nathanial Merry, so named because of his rejoicing in his profits earned at the cost of a dozen young lives! How often have I been called – too late, alas, and so futilely to the victims of the hoax quacksters, such as the notorious Doctor Trigg of Tower Wharf, Spawner of the dreaded Golden Vatican Pills! And, though it pains me to say so, of mine own countrymen, no better are the so-called Dottore Salvador

Winter and his deadly Elixir Vitae, and Giovanni Francesco Borri, with his false Sovereign Julep! Doctors? No! Thieves? Yes. These men would steal the eyes out of your head and come back for the eyelashes.'

There is the competition destroyed, I thought. *Well done.*

Dottore Velena described himself as a mere Enthusiast in Physic, a scholar who had stumbled on a great benediction while engaged only in the search for knowledge – what this benediction was, well, he humbly asked our patience, but he would return to that subject shortly.

This was his genius, *not* to mention his wares at all, until he had built up a pitch of fervour for them. In the meantime he spoke with great passion of his many and esoteric studies, interlarding each sentence with Latin phrases of a faintly familiar yet not quite comprehensible provenance: this, I soon realised, was because they were nonsense, a mere concoction of learned sounds without substance. And into each sentence he inserted a morsel of Pseudo-Physics or Chemistry, drawing down upon us the Science of a thousand years, and the secrets of a dozen great but extinct cultures.

I lost concentration for a while, amused myself looking on the rapt faces of the crowd. When I re-entered his sphere, he was rolling on about how, as a learned Antiquary, he had recovered out of some Ruin of Asia the formula for a certain precious balm, which not only kept the ancient races immortal but also beautified them beyond belief. He recounted how the members of the College of Physicians had embraced him and wept for joy when presented with the results of his life's work.

Men and women in the audience nodded sagely at his references to the great Dr Chamberlen, the inventor of the Anodyne Necklace that had lately saved upwards of twelve thousand London children from 'dying of their teeth'. And they smiled approvingly at his casual mention of 'just a mere few' of his esteemed patients, not solicited by him but who had sought him out, despite his begging to be left to his scholarly retirement.

'But my Lord Hathaway would have none of it when I told him I sought just a simple life, away from court!' the quack cried. 'Nor Prince Eugene of Russia, who begged for my help, and whom I had not the heart to turn away when I beheld his suffering, knowing that in my possession I held the instant cure to the painful malady that ravaged his entire family on account of their overindulgence in the Venus Sports. Only when I had seen them all sound and well did I leave the court at St Petersburg and make my way to Paris where the Queen herself did await me, all other surgeons having forsaken her as a Case Beyond Hope. And when I left her again blooming in health, and freshly with child, I returned to my native Venice' (here he allowed his eyes to show the rheum of nostalgia, and wiped away another tear) 'where the Doge, growing blind, required my services to remove the cataracts on his eyes. It is he who awarded me the title I so rarely use, for motives of modesty, but in this case I shall share it with you: High Venetian Physician Empirickal.'

There was a smattering of applause at this. Dottore Velena bowed deeply.

'And what,' he asked us, rising up pridefully, 'has led to the conferment of such honours?'

Only now, and without a word, he produced a single blue glass bottle from a cavern in his breeches. He fondled the little bottle as tenderly as if it were a kitten, allowing a moment's silence for all eyes to fall on the affectioned object.

'This Physic,' he cried, now holding it up so it caught the light and glistened like a sliver of the ocean, 'does cure all the diseases that God ever entailed upon the race of Adam.

'Behold this tiny bottle, so fragile, so delicate. Yet it contains inside it a moiety of that greatness that the whole Universe could not afford to purchase, were it to offer the just sum. This miraculous Elixir contains not just the purest distilled gold, but all the very heart of a Mandrake, the liver of an African Phoenix and the Tongue of a Nile Mermaid, Anise, Mastich, Ginger, Cardamoms, Cinnamon, Zedoary, Manna, Senna, Mirabolams, Scordium, Bayberries, Catmint, Balsam of Peru . . .'

The list of ingredients ran on and on, interrupted by explanations of the processes used to fuse them together. These included the contracted and pulled rays of the sun, boiling over a cedar-wood fire, and the blessing of a noble Cardinal.

Breathlessly, he assured us: 'And lastly, this golden juice is divested of any crudities by a true separation of the pure from the impure, and impregnated with Beams of Dawn Light and tartaragraphated through an Alembic of Crystalline Transfluency.'

There were moments when the audience seemed to be losing the thread, starting to shuffle or eat apples. When this happened, a curious thing occurred, which I had never seen before, even in Venice. The back wall of the rostrum was perforated with a number of small doors. At somnolent intervals, one of these little doors would pop open, to reveal the grinning head of the Zany, who waved a cautionary finger at the crowd and then disappeared behind the door he had slammed shut loudly. His timing was immaculate: he was clearly adept at earning his snack in the profits. At the clack of the shutter, everyone dozing in the audience would wake up, smile, and address their full attention to the quack again.

The pharmaceutical part of his discourse completed, the quack suddenly fixed his eye on a tripe-woman, glaring at her sternly. 'Yes, YOU!' he thundered. 'You know only too well of the lapsus of which I speak.'

All eyes fell on the fainting tripe-woman, who could only weep and moan, 'Yes sir, you have discovered me. How was I to know what pocky kind of present he had brought for me in his breeches? I beg your kindness. Oh Sir, do help me.'

'PRRRRESENTLY,' thundered the quack, holding the medicine away from her outreached hand, rendering it infinitely more valuable in the eyes of all watching.

The question was, would he allow the poor tripe-woman to perish before he finished his speech? How soon would he relieve her misery by allowing her to purchase the bottle of salvation?

Some time, it seemed, for now the quack had reached the very climax of his speech, in which he described the ongoing symptoms of the disease which at present showed but feeble signs among them.

'Those who suffer from the light cough, or the mild itch,' he warned, 'are already in the grip of the Scurbattical Humour which even now sucks on their vitals and enfeebles them. These distempers are but the first steps to a Worse Fate.'

The audience drooped visibly, running solicitous hands over various parts of their bodies. The tripe-woman was by this time lying on the ground, her legs twitching.

At this moment, the quack uttered a sharp whistle, and the Zany gambolled on to the stage, holding a miniature theatre with shabby red curtains.

'Behold!' announced the quack. 'Avert your eyes, if you are female, juvenile or delicate. For I am about to show you your Futurrrrre!'

The Zany held the little theatre up so all might behold it, and with a grand flourish the quack flung open the curtains.

A deep groan coursed through the audience. Several men staggered where they stood. Women, none of whom had averted their eyes, were openly weeping, and two pickpockets working the crowd froze with their hands in the breeches of their victims.

For revealed on the tiny stage was a most appalling waxwork, showing a man and a woman, naked, and in the final stages of a foul disease that had empurpled their skin, caused their hair to drop out, and reduced their fingers and toes to bloodied stumps. Their faces were scarred with striated tissue and worst of all, where the eye should detect the organs of generation were mere blackened holes, from which small waxen worms were seen to emerge.

Dottore Velena closed the curtains with a weighty sigh. He seemed to have lost all his former vigour and proceeded in a weak voice: 'All my life I have slaved to counteract the mischiefs that are bred in our blood. Now I am old' – here the Zany plucked at a grey curl of his wig – 'and I am weary from my travails' – here he sagged to a stool that the Zany placed beneath him, and he continued in a rasping whisper, 'and I shall no more make this curative of mine, despite the entreaties and earnest prayers of several Lords, Earls, Dukes and Honourable Personages. What you see here are the last drops I shall ever produce on this earth.' He winked back a tear. 'Of course I shall continue with their manufacture in Heaven.'

The silence of the crowd was palpable. The audience strained on his every breath.

'Because I value the living soul of every creature on this earth, I have examined my conscience and found it commands me to sell this Infallible Preparation at so small a price as one shilling, even though I rob my own pocket in so doing and condemn myself to a lingering death in abject poverrrty.'

Now the Zany stepped forth with a very small tray of bottles. The crowd surged forward, demanding their share of the precious dwindling stock. While butchers loaded their aprons, housewives their baskets, the quack held himself aloof from the sordid commerce at his side, and continued with a soothing litany, never desisting from his recital of curable symptoms until the last bottle had been snatched from the tray that the Zany repeatedly replenished from a trunk behind the stage. His gambols had lessened: his harlequin tunic was weighed down with coin. Sometimes he teased the crowd, pretending to find the trunk empty, but they soon set up such a howl that he contrived to find some more bottles secreted in a back corner of it.

All through the sales Dottore Velena was murmuring, 'If you deign to buy this humble preparation, then I can personally guarantee that it shall save you from the Shrinking of the Sinews, the Scurvy, the Rupture, the Consumption, the Falling-Sickness, Wens on the Neck, Agues of all kinds, the Tertian, Quartan and Quotidian, Retired and Shrunken Nerves, Excrementitious Blood, Colt Evil, Scabs in the Head, Catarrhs, the Humid Flux, Gouty pains, Hare-Lips, Dwindling of the Guts, Green or Canker'd Wounds, Polipus up the Nose, Disruption of the Fundament, Swimmings in the Head, Stoppage of the Spleen, Looseness of the Teeth, Nocturnal Inquietudes, Vertiginous Vapours, Perdition of the Huckle-bone and Dolour of the *Os Sacrum*, not to mention Hydiocephalus Dissenteries, Odontalgick or Podagrical Inflammations, Palpitations of the Pericardium, the Hen-Pox, the Hog-Pox, the Whore's Pox, and the entire Legion of Lethiferous Distempers.'

He uttered these words with a mechanical perfection, and while he intoned them his eyes were busy counting the number of bottles being dealt out by his Zany.

'Drink but sparingly of this little bottle, it serves best when you allow but fifty or sixty drops (more or less as you please) and they are to be taken in a glass of spring water, beer, ale, Mum or Canary. It works just as well without sugar and a drrram of brrrandy may make it more palatable too, of course. It may be taken by sea and land, in any season too.'

Even as the last few customers were reaching out for their bottles, Dottore Velena was till chanting his instructions. 'Don't forget, 'tis most excellent in coffee and chocolate too, and will perfume both beverages with the most fragrant spirit of goodness. It will wipe off (abstersively) those tenacious conglomerated sedimental Sordes that adhere to the Oesophagus and Viscera, and annihilate all Nosotrophical symptoms. It removes all Webs, Pearls, Spots, Sparks, Clouds and Films from the Eyes . . .'

Just before the last customer could be satisfied, he made a little motion of his head and the Zany made one final trip to the cupboard, returning with an empty tray and a tragical expression. The unsatisfied customer departed, weeping and bemoaning his fate, and the quack and the Zany quickly closed up their little stage with curtains and retired behind it.

Bravo! I thought to myself. *An almost faultless performance*.

I had rarely seen better, even in Venice.

But they lacked one thing, and in this lack I thought I might help them, and at the same time help myself.

I walked back to my lodgings, pausing only to buy some white chalk powder, an apron, and a simple grey dress that, I was assured, had only been worn twice, and that by a woman of quality.

· 3 ·

Pectoral Snail Water

Take Snails beaten to mash with their Shells 3 pound; Crumb of
white Bread new bak'd 12 ounces; Nutmeg 6 drams; Ground-Ivy
6 handfuls; Whey 3 quarts; distil it in a cold Still, without
burning.

　　This Water humects, dilutes, supples, tempers, nourishes,
comforts; and therefore is highly conducive in hectic
consumptive Emaciations.

The next day I was waiting in the same spot when the cart
arrived and the Zany tripped forth. Quacks invariably revisit
fertile grounds, for they can rely on one day's gulls to bring
friends and neighbours the next.

Again, I witnessed the singing and the capering, the declama-
tions and the horror stories. When the crowd had been roused
up to the previous day's pitch of desire, to the point where
Dottore Velena sought a victim, I pushed myself to the front.
Using the skills of my former trade, I had made up my face to a
deadly white with rosy spots of fever high on my cheeks.

At first Dottore Velena avoided me, for a truly sick person was
of course the last kind of patient any quack wants to treat. His eye
roamed the crowd, refusing to meet mine. When at last it did,
dragged there by the hoarse scream I uttered, I winked at him.

Not for nothing do quacks live on their wits. In an instant
Dottore Velena had the measure of me, had grasped my plan and
was prepared to give me a try.

I performed a graceful faint, falling heavily against a robust
butcher at my side. Through lowered lids I saw him kneeling
above me, gazing with concern.

'Help me,' I moaned softly. 'In God's name, save my life.'

Dottore Velena leaned over the stage. 'What's this then? A poor woman who lies a-dying? Shall we see if we can hasten a painless end? Fetch her up here.'

There was a warning implicit in his words, and I was determined not to fail him.

I lay limp as I was passed hand over shoulder to the stage, where the Zany propped me up against the doctor's stool. I allowed my eyes to open, blearily, and hung my head, the very picture of fast-fading life.

'Behold this tragical sight!' called out Dottore Velena, peering into my eyes, and feeling my pulse. 'A young girl undone by the Caledonian Cremona. A thing I have seen all too many times, a promising creature doomed to be snuffed out imminently by the dread disease.'

He leaned down to me tenderly. 'My dear, have you any last requests?'

In answer, I released one fat tear that rolled down my cheek.

Someone in the crowd yelled: 'Can you not cure her, Dottore?'

Dottore Velena looked amazed, 'But of course I can. It is the work of an instant! My softer sides were so overcome with the pity of this spectacle that the *scientist* in me lay dormant. Here, my dear, take a little of this.'

He lifted my chin and poured a few drops from his bottle, this time a green one, into my mouth.

This was the worst moment, for I knew not if I would be forced to drink some bitter decoction or whether I could stop myself from vomiting it up. Fortunately Dottore Velena had offered me succour from his own personal bottle, the one used for demonstrations, and I was relieved beyond measure to find that it contained nothing more unpalatable than watered Amsterdam gin.

Nevertheless I promptly screwed up my face with horror, for it is a known thing that the viler a medicine tastes the more potent its effects. Then I buried my face in my apron, and coughed violently for a few seconds, long enough to rub the

253

white powder from my skin and produce a heated glow in my cheeks.

Dottore Velena was explaining: 'This Physic contains, among its parts, the chiefest Antepudenda Specifick in *Venus* Regalia, which infallibly cures the French Pox, with all its Train of Gonorrhoeas, Bubo's and Shankers, Carnosities, Phymosis and Ragades, all without Baths and Stoves . . .'

Meanwhile the crowd had grown anxious. They began to deride the quack. There were cries of 'Look! You've killt her!' and 'Pore little lamb, she were only a young-un.'

At this I rose to my feet, tearing off my apron and balling it up to hide the white and red stains of my cosmetics. I stood proudly, letting them see my strong posture, my high Italian colour and my glittering eyes.

Then I threw myself at the feet of the quack, crying, 'I am cured! 'Tis a miracle! Thank you, kind sir, for my very life!' And I embraced his knees, wiping my grateful tears on the coarse fabric of his breeches, despite their musty odour.

All the while Dottore Velena was declaiming with his usual aplomb, 'And this is but a simple cure for this potent Physic. A mere sketch of what it may do. Why, if a man chance to have his Brains beat out, or his Head chop'd off, two drops, I say two drops, Ladies and Gentlemen, seasonably applied, will recall the fleeting Spirits, re-enthrone the deposed Life-force, cement the Discontinuity of the Parts and in six minutes restore the lifeless Trunk to all its pristine functions, as well, nay better, than before. For it shall cherish up any saddened spirits, and restore Virginity forthwith.'

I stood beaming and nodding. Presently, a roar arose from the crowd that had been stupefied by my recovery. They were in this moment absorbent of any claim that the doctor might make, and I feared that he would run to more extreme boasts, leading in the end to ridicule. But Dottore Velena had judged his victims to a nicety.

'Give me some o'that!' rasped the man with the tumoured throat.

'I'll have three bottles!' screamed a woman far gone with the scrofula.

'I must have it now!' yelled another woman, clearly nearing her time for parturition.

But Dottore Velena held up a sorrowful hand. He had a new strategy to increase desire for the green bottle, so that even those who had bought yesterday's blue one would feel themselves bereft without the newcomer.

'Stay, stay, good people, if only I could help you all. It breaks my heart to remind you that this particularrr preparation takes a good nine weeks in boiling to distil just one bottle . . .'

The Zany appeared with his tray of green bottles, which was emptied in a moment. Again and again he went back to his cupboard, so often that I began to fear that the supply might actually run dry.

Dottore Velena's list of curable ailments rolled on interminably, twice as long as the day before. This meant that I had done well for him. It would put up my price. I listened to the list, hoping to catch him out in a repetition and was astounded that I could not.

'. . . Which is why,' he intoned, 'it refreshes the Bowels and relieves the Spirits. After the good offices in the Ventricle, it deterges and opens the mouths of the Lacteals, that were almost baked up with slime; dilutes and refrigerates the blood, allays the fervent heat, and crispations of the Parboil'd Fibrillae, repairs all the wastes with Nutritious Chyle; cleanses the minutest passages and emunctories; and helps the whole mass to circulate freely, and duly, to nourish and cherish the parts; and to throw off its recrements by Urine, and (where there is an aptitude) by Sweat and Spittle.'

Only then did he pause to draw breath, and look with satisfaction on the crowd. But when his mantra ceased, so did the frenzied purchase of the drug. Men and women stopped with their coins held high in the air, waiting for him to go on.

He obliged: 'When the Fermentation of the blood is grown low and languishing, this rouses it up again afresh; concocts and incides crude, and pituitose Juices. It removes Atrabilarious Humours stagnating in the Viscera. It opens the obstructions, and discusses the Tumours of the Spleen, quiets and suppresses

255

convulsive corrugations of Fibres. A few drops applied, cures all curable wounds in twenty-four hours; and old Ulcers, Fistulas, Cancers, Wolf in the Breast, *noli-me-tangere*, in fifteen days, using it daily. It is also good against the Carbuncles, and extinguishes them in three hours . . .'

At this point he allowed his voice to weaken and trail away. He paused entirely to swig on a bottle himself, and then threw himself back into the fray, at a louder volume than before, his agonised whispers of the last few seconds replaced by a vigorous, loud tone.

'And I have known it do good service in Cutaneous Affections. By reason of its neurotick quality it comforts the Nerves, and restrains the raging Excandescence of the Spirits. It's endowed with a mucilaginous, soft, and friendly sweetness. By incrassating the blood disposed for Fluxion, and correcting it when acrid, it's also laudably used in Pleurisy, Rheumatism, Small Pox, Measles and Stone. It retrieves the failing Tone of the Intestines, corrects their slipperiness, and represseth their continual bearing downwards. It draws out watery and pituitous Humours, by irritating and vellicating the parts of the Mouth. It consenters Acrimony, appeaseth Gripes. It coats over the upper parts of the Throat and Larynx with a sort of Emplastic Slime, and so obtunds their exquisitely irritable sense. It also prohibits the extillation of too thin, sharp and fluxile Serum from the Glands; corrects nidorous Belching. It does edulcorate, stop up, stringe, and ronorate; give ease in the Lumbago. It is Stomachic, Anticolic, Anthelminthic, Antapoplectic, Febrisic; and good in the bite of a mad dog . . .'

The Zany now produced from his waistcoat a most frightful wax model of a rabid dog with his foaming mouth clamped to the foot of a bellowing child.

At this point, knowing the inevitable and profitable conclusion, I withdrew, catching the eye of the quack and pointing at the Anchor Tavern. He nodded.

I went inside and ordered myself a gin. I believed that I had earned it, having carried off my part most handsomely.

· 4 ·

A Quilt for a Cap

Take Male Peony root 2 drams; Spanish Angelica root 1 dram; Florentine Orris, Lavender flowers, each half a dram; Arabian Stechas flowers 1 dram; Cloves, Nutmeg, Mace, each 1 scruple; Storax calamite, Laudanum, Amber, Balsam of Tolu, each 1 dram; Oil of Rosemary 5 drops; reduce it to a gross Powder; which being mix'd into Cotton, is to be quilted in a silk Cap according to Art. Every Night at Bed-time, let this Cap be fumed and warm'd with the smoak of Amber, Olibanum, Balsam of Tolu, or the like, Sprinkled upon Coals.

It's of signal use in Humid, Pituitose Affections of the Head, in cold, customary, rheumatic Pains of the same. And it's believ'd to recreate the Spirits, and roborate the Brain.

The Zany bent over his food and flung large particles of it in the direction of his mouth.

'There's no need to gollop it like that, in front of a lady,' reproved Dottore Velena. With his handkerchief, he wiped the worst of the dirt off a chair close to his own and offered it to me with a flourish.

'Lie-dee? 'Er? She's nuffin but a hairy, she'd do it wiv anywan'.'

For emphasis, the Zany spat vehemently against the window-sill. He tore another mouthful of meat from the bone with his teeth and slammed the cutlet back on the plate. With a great spraying of masticated gristle in my direction, he snarled, 'Whar you staring at me lek I was a monument?'

I lowered my eyes. Not wanting to be unfriendly, I moved from my own chair to the seat of honour offered by the Dottore.

We were in the filthy dining room of the Anchor. I was still wondering where the elegant diners were to be found. Perhaps on the upper floor? I told myself it was better to be down in this room, despite its savoury wallpapering of grease, for the last person I wished to meet today was Valentine Greatrakes, who no doubt took his refreshments upstairs with the other aristocrats.

The Dottore raised his voice to a stage whisper and loomed over the Zany: 'No more of your snash, shut it, or you're in for a light bruising,' he hissed. 'I'm just about heart-roasted with you already.'

His Italian had dissolved in two pints of Russian stout. I believed that I knew his accent: I had once been engaged to extract information from a Scottish laird. Though more refined, there had been something in the Milord's warbling vowels that now reminded me of Dottore Velena, who continued to berate the Zany for his 'aggravatious' table manners, to no avail.

The Dottore smiled at me as he called over a sweat-stained waiter. 'You look proper famished, my dear. We must supply you with some brute necessities.' He ordered me what he termed 'a spitchcock of eels and a plate of buttered crabs'.

'And another gin,' I added.

When the food arrived, grim and greasy, he advised me, kindly but inexplicably, to put myself 'outside of that'.

I did my best to eat it while the men ate, belched, drank and gossiped in their impenetrable way.

At last the Zany announced conclusively, 'There was ructions and then the two of them got beasted into each other. 'Arry was mollocated.'

This meant very little to me. And now that the men were fed I thought it was time to talk about business. I leaned over and boldly pulled the bottle out of Dottore Velena's top pocket.

'What's in it?' I asked, holding the emerald glass to the light and jiggling the liquid. 'I mean the bottles you sell the clients?' I was sure they would not be deceived by gin.

'Now that would be telling, lassie,' said the quack, winking and thumbing his nose roguishly.

I added, 'And how ill shall it make them?'

The quack laughed heartily, 'Not at all. When I sell it in the country, the farmers buy it to exterminate their plaguey rats, and they find it does the beasts a favour, for they thrive noticeably upon it.'

'And where do *you* get it?' I asked, carelessly.

His reply teetered my world on its axis.

'We all round here get it from Dizzom at Bankside.'

'Dizzom, who works for Valentine Greatrakes?' I gasped.

''Ark at 'er, sitting lek a craw in da mist,' observed the Zany, highly diverted by my discomfort.

'The same,' said Dottore Velena approvingly. 'I see you know a thing or two, young lady. It's teeming with brains, you are: it's clear the education's been at you, dearie. Aye, it's Dizzom that fills our bottles and prints our handbills, and supplies our quilted caps and what-you-will, all on behalf of his master, naturally.'

'But . . . but, I thought Mr Greatrakes was a . . . gentleman.'

'Indeed, a very great gentleman, of his kind!' Both the Dottore and the Zany were smiling broadly. There was no disguising the mockery in the quack's voice. 'The very greatest patron of all quacks, whores, thieves and beating-boys. The very pinnacle of a gentleman, at least on this side of the river, the one who has an interest in every glassblowers in Bankside, for only he can replenish their bottles with free-traded liquors just as fast as they can blow 'em. Not bad for the bastard brat of a Corktown maid, brought up by the Angel-Makers, and who's served his time up chimneys and down drains mudlarking before coming to his present great estate.

'The said *gentleman*'s presently in *Venice*,' the doctor added confidentially, 'free-trading a little Venetian treacle our way.'

My lover? A smuggler? A fabricator of nostrums? A pimp? A printer of quacks' handbills? I felt faint. And what was he doing in Venice? The likeliest answer warmed my cheeks – *he had gone looking for me!*

But I had no time to examine my feelings. The quack was rising from his seat. Like me, he was anxious to settle terms. He had not noticed how I now trembled and struggled for breath, though the Zany still looked at me with contemptuous curiosity.

'I'll give you a shilling on each dozen bottles sold,' pronounced Dottore Velena, in a conclusive manner.

I had planned to negotiate: I had need of all my scattered wits now. I did not wish to be condemned to demonstrate only cures against love diseases. I hoped to change my illness to something more respectable, like the Bloody Flux. But first I must make sure of my employment, and survival.

'A shilling for each half-dozen, and a say in which disease is killing me,' I countered.

It was the Zany's turn to gasp. 'A shilling! For that minky girl!'

'Now, now,' temporised the Dottore, with his hand on his companion's wrist. 'Don't ye see that the good fairies have showered all their gifts on this lady and the bad fairies have been most sparing in their attentions? Did ye not hear the snapping of the heartstrings when they looked at her dying? We took twelve guineas today, and it wasn't *you* they paid to see. You wait; we'll be knee-deep in prosperity in no time with this one.'

'Knee-deep,' I repeated, staring hard at the Zany.

'You're a piece of work,' the Dottore laughed, now looking intently at me. With a slight menace in his voice, he added, 'But you do a good job, almost professional, I'd say.'

He narrowed his eyes and spoke harshly to me for the first time: 'Is it Doctor Trigg who taught you? Or that bastard Merry?'

Certain that he would never believe me, I was able to give my first honest answer: 'Oh no, I trained on the stage, in Venice. I am an actress.'

'Oh yes indeed! How could I not have guessed it,' he sneered, though in a jocular manner. 'Well, I'll not ask you more.'

I winked, and looked shifty. 'So I can teach you some Venetian words – or those that will pass for them, surely.'

I could see that this concept had caught his interest. While his nostrums were doubtless the purest effluent, he took a definite pride in his act. Any refinements I might bring to it would be gratefully received.

'So what do we call you, lassie?' he asked me.

'I am Mistress Giallofiore,' I said, thinking quickly.

'Missis Jallowfi-*whore*?' he chuckled, emphasising the 'whore'. He raised his glass: 'To Mistress Jallowfi-*whore*, our Venetian *actress*. Your blood's worth bottling, my dear.'

The Zany howled, 'It's nobbut a wheen of blathers the whole story. A shilling! Jallow-fi-whore, wha' kind of a name is that?'

'The first thing we shall work upon is your Venetian pronunciation,' I said as primly as I could manage.

'Where do you lodge?' the quack was asking.

I smiled cheekily. 'From today, wherever you lodge, master.'

The Zany choked on his beer. 'She'd skin a flea for half a penny, this one.'

I pointed to the valise at my feet. I had been so confident of my performance that I had taken leave of my landlady that morning, explaining that my fortune had come in with unexpected swiftness.

· 5 ·

An Expression of Millipedes

Take live Millipedes and white Sugar, each 3 ounces; when they are well beaten and mix'd together in a Mortar, add white Wine 1 pint; and strain and squeeze out the Liquor.

Millipedes abound in Volatile Salt (as all Insects do) they incide, and dissolve tough clammy Phlegm wheresoever it sticks, attenuate, exalt and depurate the Blood, penetrate into the Glands, Nerves, Fibres, smallest Pipes and Passages, piercing through Obstructions, deterging, cleansing and comforting, and are famous for their Diuretic quality. They are used in cases of Gravel, Sand, Dropsy, Jaundice, King's-Evil, Cough, Phthisic, Consumption at the beginning, Hypochondriac Affects; Scorbutic Joint Pains, dimness of Sight.

Dottore Velena's handbills advertised that he was to be found 'at home in his rooms' between the hours of ten and eleven 'to be spoke with'.

Like most quacks, he lodged above a tavern. His was the Feathers, in Winchester Square. A fine, corrupt, leaning old building it proved, on a par with the Anchor for its sordidness and noise.

When we returned there the light had already grown dim. Business done, I had permitted myself to sink into a dispirited state, cast low by the shocking discovery about my lover. A smell as frowsy as a dove's nest smacked my nose as Dottore Velena opened the door to his private apartment. The Zany, whose real name was never revealed to me, was put out that he must now share these limited digs with a third party, and that a female. He turned his back on me immediately, pulled down a kind of

262

hinged plank from the wall, threw a blanket on it and lay down to sleep, rather theatrically framed by a curtain of alligator skins with a canopy of dried poppy heads, all strung in rows from the ceiling above him.

The Dottore showed me the screened chamber-pot and the jug of stale water for washing, and finally a kind of large cat-basket, where I might sleep myself. He told me, with a sentimental tremor, that it had previously been used for several cats who had perished in experiments, and whose mummified remains dangled stiffly from a beam.

The Dottore himself seemed content with a minimal desha-billé. He donned a quilted bedcap over his wig and stretched himself out in a leather chair, a strange object that had suffered a large neat bite out of its seat and boasted two separate footrests that spread his legs wide apart. He was soon unconscious, snor-ing in an oatmealish kind of way, the satin ribbons of his bedcap ruffling in the gusts. I do not remember falling asleep, but drowsiness must have overtaken me fast, despite the lumpen pillow, leprous with stinking mould. My last clear memory of that night was starting up at the looming silhouette of an enor-mous bird, but that image too had the quality of a dream.

The next dawn I was amused to see the preparations made for patients. The Zany jumped up smartly at cockcrow and stalked out of the door without a backward look, presumably gone to his preferred cookshop to breakfast. The quack's cap and wig had tot-tered from their perch in the night, revealing a bald head above the collar of his undershirt. This, too, was removed and he performed thorough ablutions in his native state while I averted my eyes. Then he remounted his voluminous wig, which boasted not one but three beribboned tails, and he pulled on the decent black suit I had seen the day before, finally shrugging a plush jacket over it.

Thus arrayed, he proceeded to pull all manner of accou-trements into view that had been concealed on trays and drawers closed fast into walls and desks in the night. Within minutes he had transformed our sordid sleeping chamber into an Aladdin's cave of potions-in-the-making, all, he informed me proudly, according to the highest fashion of the trade.

Every surface glinted with mysterious bottles, some filled with swarthy tar-drippings, others with fair water, coloured, so he told me, with sandalwood and cochineal. The largest of them was boiling with live millipedes, though a grim, still sediment at the bottom of the jar showed unfortunate trampled multitudes. Laid open by the divan was Cornelius Agrippa's *Occult Philosophy* propped up on a pile of musty Greek and Latin tomes. Only the most observant visitor would notice that this pile was glued together and wheeled at the bottom, to allow for speedy stowing in a low cupboard. The morning light gradually revealed shelves stacked with small bags. I was told that these were much sought after to hang about the necks of children as an infallible prophylactic against rickets. Inside was the finest muscovado sugar imported from the West Indies. This, and the loose knot, ensured that children frequently consumed the contents, thereby providing a brisk trade in re-orders.

On the desk of Dottore Velena reposed a human skeleton, marked up with esoteric calculations. Behind him hung the stuffed corpse of a monkey, who, he informed me, had formerly performed the duty of Zany for him. He patted it affectionately and a cloud of dust rose and glowed about its mournful head like a halo. 'Used to drink a pint of ale like a Christian every night,' he reminisced. 'And he certainly drew the ladies.'

Next to the monkey a pure spermaceti candle was prepared for swift lighting at the sound of a client's foot on the stairs. Its luxurious glow would illuminate an artfully careless pile of gilt coinage, done up to look like guineas, an indication of rich fees already received that morning from grateful patients.

The chair in which the Dottore had slept now revealed its obstetric nature as he plumped up in it a large leather dummy of a woman in the throes of birth. And in a corner I discovered the truth of that nightmarish bird that had haunted my last moments of consciousness the evening before. It was an impressive duck-billed alembic where even now Dottore Velena hovered, stirring up some fragrant powder with his lotion spatula. The whole device trembled upon a crippled table, bandaged at the joints and yet extravagantly gilded with hieroglyphic decorations around its rim.

It was as elaborate as any stage set I'd trodden in my life as an actress, and there was something pleasingly familiar about it.

I pulled on my own costume, the respectable grey dress, after boldly demanding my turn at the ewer, and presented myself for work more cheerfully than I had ever done before.

Dottore Velena handed me a cup of hot chocolate that spouted from the beak of the alembic. With the other hand, he poured me my morning glass of gin.

For any actress there are moments of boredom on the stage, when she is not the centre of attention and is obliged to erase herself from the eyes of the spectators to allow some other actor to strut his grandeur or his pitifulness. There are slow buildings of character, and early deaths. Even the prima donna is sometimes backstage.

But with Dottore Velena, I performed nothing but climaxes: I was always either Expiring-in-Dolorous-Convulsions or Being-Born-Again-in-the-Very-Blossom-of-Health. I lived Life-after-Death-by-a-Regiment-of-Diseases. By the time I made my entrance, the crowd had already grown mobbish, and were satiated on the Zany: I was beautiful, I was haunting, and they loved me.

We developed the act to the highest pitch of quackery, rivalling anything to be seen on the Riva degli Schiavoni in Venice. Sometimes Dottore Velena relieved me of a worm as long as the Maypole in the Strand, using his *Vermifugus Pulvis*, or Anti-Vermatical Worm-Conquering Powder (made chiefly of flour). In this case I clutched my belly and crossed my eyes while Dottore Velena explained the grim battle taking place therein, as the complicated knots of the worm were broken up in my duodenum ('Aah,' I sighed), and its Phlegmatick Crudities were dissolved in my bowel ('Oooh,' I shrieked) . . . Presently he reached under my skirt and brought away a long white woollen skein slicked with grease that came and came and came, and which the Zany seized and wove around the stage like a

265

demented spider making a web. The Dottore all the while intoned his soothing explanations, and the audience hung on his every word, their faces fervent with belief.

The Dottore also had a vermifuge for those with carious teeth, popularly believed to be the work of the dread tooth-worm. For these demonstrations we sat up late the night before, trimming tiny curls of paper and dyeing them in beet-juice. These the Dottore inserted under his ample fingernails before our performance. In front of the crowd he dipped his fingers in the blue bottle, as reverently as if he baptised them in holy water, and then commenced some excavations inside my mouth. Fortunately, in this case, it was important to demonstrate the ease of use, so in a few moments he desisted, and I spat out into a bowl a large number of apparently bloody morsels, looking for all the world like worms in a state of rigor mortis brought on by our nostrum. As a sideline, Dottore Velena always accompanied the tooth-worm extraction with the offer of fine sets of agate teeth imported directly from Italy, ready-made to be worn in the manner of the famously attractive Lord Hervey of Bristol.

Other times Dottore Velena treated me to beauty-cures. I was obliged to make my entrance covered in hairy moles (of velvet, gummed) and horrid wens (painted) and wrinkles (pencilled with coal). Hauling me up on stage, Dottore Velena spoke of the smooth beauty of foreign women, compared to those in England, whose natural good looks were blighted by such disfigurements as mine.

'See this old lady, ruined in the visage by God alone knows what kind of life! Poor soul, how her sufferings are written on this wizened face!'

He bent down to me kindly. 'And are your grandchildren equally deformed?' he asked, 'or are you the grandmaternal brute of a lovely family?'

At this I burst into loud wailings and neighings, prompting him to add, nastily, 'In my native Venice, beauty is of course compulsory. How you would faint and fall to your knees to see the loveliness of even our humble womenfolk. And they all appear of one age – that of perfect ripeness, but here in England, look a horse in the mouth and a woman in the face, and you presently know their ages to a year. You, my dear, are easy to read at seventy-nine and three-quarters.'

I hung my head, protesting with thrashing arms.

'What do the Italian women have over their English sisters? A simple remedy, when all is told!'

And yet again the blue bottle was prepared, a napkin anointed with it, and my face turbaned up in that cloth for five minutes while Dottore Velena extemporised on the magic taking place within.

In this case the bottle contained a warm solution of soap and water, which dissolved all my blemishes forthwith.

When I was unwrapped, and my glowing, youthful complexion revealed, Dottore Velena would ask me softly, 'And may I be so bold as to inquire your true age, my dear?'

'I am fifty-five,' I answered sweetly, in the soft tones of a twenty-year-old, but loudly enough to make myself heard above the women clamouring for their bottles, and the soothing sound of Dottore Velena making his final pitch: 'And it will be of greatest help to those of you, like the Irishwomen, who are afflicted in the limbs, having received a dispensation from the Pope to wear the thick part of their legs on the downward end. A nipperkin of this and you'll be on the arm of the finest man at any party.'

I was busy, and I was never alone. These two things conspired to prevent me from fully absorbing the shock of the new information I had received about my lover.

It was a cruel blow and I could not resist thinking on it in all my free hours. Thinking only made it feel worse.

I had wanted to take him at face value. It had been so alluring to do so. I now felt nostalgic for my previous state of happy ignorance. I was angry with myself, too. I should have realised that he could not be true. Stupidly, I had thought him a gentleman like Stintleigh. I had believed his money aristocratically unearned. Now I was to understand that he laboured like a chimney-sweep when the occasion required. In my darkest moments, I imagined him spitting on crudely printed labels to stick them to the bottles of nostrums he peddled via quacks like Dottore Velena.

And all the time I was uncovering yet more horrors about Valentine Greatrakes and his business, for his was a household name around Bankside. This meant that I soon discovered one more thing: it was gossiped everywhere that his errand on the Continent was likely to keep him away for some time, being of a nature to cause all his cohorts to chuckle with secretive glee, though without breathing a word as to its style. We heard at the Anchor that nothing would prise a word from Greatrakes' men, not beer, not money, not the tickling of whores. There was not a man among them who would risk losing the favour of his chief.

So I felt secure, though I still averted my face when we jolted down Stoney Street to the Anchor. Who knew when Dizzom might appear from between those stalwart gates?

One day, as we passed the depository, Dottore Velena nudged my rib, saying: 'Lord knows what keeps the great man away. It's been weeks. Most unusual. Many's the Bankside maiden sighing for the empty bed of Valentine Greatrakes.'

Knowing now that 'maiden' meant prostitute in this part of town, I smouldered with outrage. So he was the kind of man who consorted with Southwark prostitutes then? I had seen them lined up along the streets like tawdry dolls on a shop shelf. I was learning, slowly and painfully, to tolerate the thought of his running a superior brothel, or better still, an empire of brothels, for the golden gain of it, but the thought of him actually engaged in sentimental rapports with the street-whores suffered to tatter still further my vision of him as a *kind* of gentleman, who, if he must, visited the discreet and luxurious bagnios in the exclusive parts of town. I discarded my notion of him as a man of pure habits whose great love for me had comprised some natural elements of lust. I now saw him as another kind of pig who romped disgustingly. I had moments of ludicrous indignation, thinking that not even my employers had sent me into the arms of a creature as low as Valentine Greatrakes. Dukes, princes, politicians, great ladies of unusual persuasions even, but not dubious businessmen from the wrong side of the river! A lowly maggot who had ripened into a notable criminal! This was abundantly worse than a gentleman who had fallen on hard times.

'Come now, lassie, don't be blushing like that!' teased Dottore Velena. 'What are you remembering?' Today my face was unfortunately naked of paint, for I had elected to be a Madwoman-Afflicted-with-the-Tremens-and-Possession-by-Devils-and-All-Their-Kin. I was to impersonate one of the poor mad rabbit-pullers of the Bankside furriers. These girls frequently lost their wits to the corrosive chemicals of their trade. The Dottore himself had thoughtfully sewn a little rabbit scut to the back of my dress, to remind the customers of my supposed profession.

Another thought occurred to me. 'You mean he *sleeps* there! In that warehouse?' I asked.

'Valentine Greatrakes, my dear? He sleeps above the shop, like any good trader.'

I thought of the vileness of Stoney Street by night, lit with globe lamps that burned on stinking whale oil. These humble half-timbered shops were the view from his bedroom window! I thought of the sumptuous rooms where he had taken me, in Bond Street, furnished to the highest taste, looking over white stucco and a miniature park, all kempt and elegant. I had believed it to be his ancestral town house! The Turkey carpets and immaculate wainscoting, the marquisite curtains, the down bed with soft blankets and fine linen, all these must have been bought for a guinea a time.

Of course, at the time I had never asked, and I had never even thought to search the drawers or check the wardrobes, so busy was I swooning with foolish calf-love for this arrant trickster. So he had hired those echoing halls by the night, and it was not lost on me that he had more frequently insisted on conducting our romance in *my* rooms, which had cost him nothing.

I exposed myself to the possibility of one more horrible revelation.

'So are you acquainted with Greatrakes, then?' I asked my colleague. 'I mean on a personal basis?'

'Well, I wouldn't say that. It's not completely *safe* to be so acquainted with him. Things have happened. Never ye mind what. But yes, I've been introduced on a scant few occasions. Not that his Greatrakeship'd remember, him being so very occupied on so many things.'

'And how does he speak?' I asked.

'My and aren't you the little cat who is asking for a drowning today? He's a man to charm you into tomorrow. If ye lost all your family in the morning and met him in the afternoon, ye'd be laughing by teatime.'

'But his *accent*?' I persisted. 'Is it that of a gentleman?'

Dottore Velena laughed uproariously. 'She wants to know if he's a gentleman, does she? Valentine Greatrakes? I would say that he talks like the sarf Lunnun crook he is, my dear girl. With a great many fancy words thrown in, for the show of them. But one of us'd know him anywhere. And the real toffs would have nothing to do with him.'

I had not so much need to call on my acting skills when it came to throwing a violent tantrum on the stage a few minutes later.

· 6 ·

A Paste for Aphthae

Take new Butter, just out of the Churn, unsalted (and washed in
Rosewater) 1 ounce and a half; Liquorice powder 1 dram and a
half; white Sugar candy powdered, and passed through a Searce,
as much as serves to make it up like a Paste, mix.

Let a little Pellet of this be put into the Mouth to dissolve by
degrees; it's good against the Thrush, parchedness, Heat, and
roughness of the Tongue, foulness in the Mouth and Throat,
wheezing and painful Breathing. It may also be put up the Nose
when stopped and sore.

Soon I had changed so much that I doubted if a returning
Valentine Greatrakes would know me, even had he stood in my
immediate proximity. Scorning the scorched roasts of the
Anchor, and saving hard, I grew lean on a diet of over-stewed
herbs in thin, heartless broths that the Zany stirred up in the
grate at our digs.

'You're a woman. Why can't you cook?' he mumbled indig-
nantly. 'What sort of broughting up did *you* have?'

Again the truth protected me. I answered: 'I am a noblewoman, reared delicately. I have never been inside a kitchen.
Except in a convent and then just to look.'

And the Zany was obliged to lie on the floor and hold his
belly till his violent pangs of mirth subsided. Between his howls
of merriment I distinguished odd phrases: 'Reared on the hind
teat of a donkey, more like' and 'Fell orf the back of a tinker's
cart and weren't missed'.

But after this exchange I would have to own that he showed
me less stinging acrimony. So long as I put on no 'lawdydaw'

271

airs, and refrained from 'moping around like a duck in thunder', he accepted me. I had proved myself a distinguished liar, and that made me a worthy colleague in his eyes.

I blended with my new peers, quickly becoming unobtrusive. My adopted profession called on me to resemble a woman of the streets, not a goddess of the stage. I was working nearly all the time, and soon I came to dress without a second thought in my costume of a grey dress and white apron.

Very occasionally I opened my trunk and looked at the black silk dress of my escape, now laundered and carefully folded with lavender sprigs between its layers, and the one cerise satin, the butterfly dress, and sundry other pretty garments that I had lifted in and out of carriages all the way across Europe. When I gazed at this finery I felt that it belonged to someone else, to some great lady who would shortly arrive in a flounce of white mares and bear it away.

I never sought more eligible accommodation. I decided that I found our eccentric rooms picturesque; I rose above the dirt by not looking at it, and learned to squeeze my nose as I passed the necessary vault at the bottom of the staircase. I even appreciated that primitive luxury, for having descended the social scale at a plummeting rate, I was surprised to find that I was nowhere near the bottom of it. Within a few weeks I knew that I was one of the lucky ones in London, where twenty thousand souls awoke each morning, leaving verminous twopenny beds cluttered like larvae on garret floors, not knowing if they would eat that day or where they would lay their heads at the end of it. This whole class of unfortunates had bypassed me in Venice. Here in Bankside I rubbed shoulders with them daily, saw the little, doomed, scald-headed men and women shuffling about the business of mere subsistence.

I came to know every cranny of Bankside, all its glassworks, its breweries and gin shops. The latter made up fully one-sixth of the local businesses. I was shocked by the degree of drunkenness in this part of town, something I had never glimpsed in salubrious Soho Square. Men, women and even tiny children were to be found stretched out unconscious on bales of straw inside and outside the London Bridge gin shops. Dottore Velena liked to pull up near them, for those in the early stages of intoxication, or those waking with all the parched ills of over-imbibing, were our best and most gullible customers, particularly for Aphthae pastes.

At first I wondered why the people of Bankside spent their hard-won pennies on Dottore Velena's spurious potions rather than go to Guy's and St Thomas's Hospitals, so conveniently situated on their doorsteps. Men who earned fifteen shillings a week were prepared to lay out a guinea on our liquid nonsense. Laundresses and rabbit-pullers spent their pittances on our cheats.

Once I would have disdained their idiocy, just as I had mocked the *contadini* who fell for the blandishments of the charlatans on the Riva degli Schiavoni in Venice. Now I looked on them with pity, on the braziers gone deaf and gibbous from their crooked working posture, the coppersmiths stained green from poisonous steams, the mirror-makers grown cadaverous from the mercury, hairdressers and chimney-sweeps crippled with pulmonic diseases, the confectioners dropsical from too much strong heat.

Surely, I asked my companions, the St Thomas Apothecary would answer better to their needs?

The Zany tersely explained: 'They won't go there. If they goes into tha 'ospital, then tha have to give up a deposit for their burial first. And it's pretty much a sure thing that tha'll come out in the box they's already paid for. Anatomised to boot, if tha're not careful.'

The poor people had a terror of being dissected by the surgeons, who required a steady supply of corpses for their paying medical students. If a person died in hospital, no one trusted the orderlies not to sell the body.

The Zany added, 'And it's much the same crock o' fock they'll be served up in tha 'ospital anyway. The St Thomas Apothecary swears by Dr Mead's recipe for snail water and peacock dung too. The only difference is he bothers with real snails and real dung. Oh and to be sure he separates the white shite from the brown, as only the white is supposed to do yer any good at all, or so tha'll be having it in the manuals.'

273

With this, he heaved a gobbet of saliva at the Dottore's copy of the *Pharmacopoeia Extemporanea*, which lay open on a lectern to give confidence to visiting patients. Many of its pages were puddled with similar outbursts from the Zany. This time the Dottore rose from his chair with dignity, lifted the heavy tome, and smashed it down on the Zany's head. The Zany accepted his punishment without demur.

Always in a state of near war, the Dottore and his Zany were nevertheless inseparable, as if each mistrusted the other, unsupervised, to find some illicit font of pleasure and gain. Nightly, we infected the less salubrious taverns of the Borough with the temper of our irascible party. I remember one evening when Dottore Velena was moved to push the Zany over the balcony of the George into its courtyard, and another when the two men simultaneously spat in one another's left eye at The Old Pick-my-Toe.

Squabbling amicably all the way, we went to Peele's Coffee House in Fetter Lane to read our rivals' notices in *The Gazette*, *The Times*, *Morning Chronicle*, *Morning Post*, *Morning Herald* and *Morning Advertiser*. I eavesdropped on the conversations of the coffee-drinkers whom Dottore Velena mysteriously called 'men of exceptional parts'. Amidst their braying I never detected one morsel of piquancy in these supposed wits and scholars. And not a soul among them looked up at me, which was exactly what I wanted.

Sometimes, late at night, the Thames called me down to its banks. In front of the Anchor I several times beheld the sport of the porpoises that occasionally made their way under London Bridge. Seeing them, I felt a sharp pang of nostalgia, for they resembled nothing so much as bucking gondolas in a sharp wind on the Grand Canal.

In the interval during which I had travelled to Venice and back the thaw had dissolved the platform of ice where I had played out such scenes of pain and pleasure with my lover. On those blessed nights everything had been darkly oystered in gentle moonlit mother-of-pearl. Now the moon's reflection was smashed to pieces and roughly jostled on the hard chop of the liquid river.

I would return to my friends, hungry for the company, and with an honest appetite for the first time in my life. I loved the nights when we bought little dabs of meat in the Borough Market and roasted them on packthread strings dangling over the fire, turning them with Dottore Velena's obstetrical forceps and cutting them up into bite-sized portions with his tiny metacarpal bow-frame amputation saw. I do not believe he had ever used these instruments for their intended purposes but they were good props for the consultation room.

With my two friends, I became an adept at candlelit games of whist, cribbage, putt and all-fours, sometimes staking my whole week's earnings on a single game, finding the excitement well covered any losses. When the wind blew from the east, I awoke in the morning to hear the roaring of the lions in the Tower menagerie and smell their gamey scent borne on the same breeze. From under my warm blanket I heard the parish scavengers on their rounds collecting what people had discarded, in order to sell it to such as might find these pickings their heart's desire.

In Venice I had been solitary, even in the company of my family or the nuns. Here, I had companions, of a sort. In front of these men I lived shamelessly, undressing down to my shift to sleep or wash myself, eating, picking my teeth. And they behaved likewise with me. I knew all their rituals. Before sleeping, for example, the Zany emptied his pocket of many mysterious objects including a grubby letter which turned out to be his official document to forfend the press-gangers. When I reached out to touch it, he slapped my hand away: 'That cost three sterling, you little hoor, more than you're worth for a week of hard treatment.'

It was a revelation to exist in such intimate proximity with other human beings. I had no need to dissemble, or pretend my looks were anything but what they were. I was as never before stripped to my personal merits. I had no appearance to keep up with these men. I did not hesitate to apply a Vizard cloth to my tired face in the cosy fug of their tobacco, after we had dined *in famiglia*.

'It'll do you a power o' good, dearie,' said the Doctor, sniffing at its medicinal perfume of wax, gum benzoin and oil. 'Shall I rub your feet the meanwhile?'

Dottore Velena was no sort of doctor, but as a massager of feet I would name him prince of the profession. When I lay under the Vizard, and he rubbed my toes and ankles all over with gin, I found my feelings dissolving. I did not trouble to hide my lassitude but wept openly and refreshingly, allowing my softened mind to stray lightly over the dreadful scenes from my past life.

The Zany looked on indulgently, grumbling, 'Not enough brains to give 'erself a headache, but she'd drown us if she could.'

'Aye, there's a sweet gurrlie,' purred Dottore Velena. 'Have a guid greet. Don't ye sprauchle to hould it all back. Wash it all awa'.'

And so I did. After he had finished with me, I was purely content, as a child is, all the wicked memories having flowed out of me. I lay down and slept more soundly than I had done in my life, despite the unmelodious snores of my companions and the noisy bad dreams of the Zany, whose unconscious hours were beset by 'gipes', 'sleekit weans' and 'a great black bitch of a devil' who caused him to be 'clarried in gar, man', a phrase he keened, repeatedly, on nights of heavy liquid consumption. On the rare occasions when he woke me I crawled over to his plank and took his hand in mine. He never woke, but commenced to tremble, and whisper that he would be quiet and good now, if the beastie would only promise not to come back and 'mange' him up. He shivered so that I would sometimes cover him with my own scrap of blanket. He would remain silent for the rest of the night after that.

And I too slept, enmeshed in the preferable dreams of my companions' past lives, instead of the nightmares of my own. I had a passion for their memoirs, for their voices smoking out of dim corners of the room when the sun had set. I, who had only ever known the luxury of pure spermaceti candles, now came to live by the cheap glow of rushlights. A pound of rushes for a shilling and the daily scummings of the bacon pot could keep an illiterate London household in light for a year. The Dottore and I, of course, knew our letters, but there was no incentive to read books, and there were no books to read, except medical texts, and so we talked, he of his past, and the Zany sometimes weighed in with teary reminiscences of his old Ma and of a certain Sukey who had used him ill and bled his heart 'dry as a monk's bum'. The more I knew of them, the less willing I was to lie to them, but the truth was inconceivable, so I stayed mostly silent, or encouraged them by asking questions.

On these nights, the retrospective affections between the two men warmed the room, and there were times when they leapt to their feet and collided in embrace at the thought of some previous triumph. Whenever the Dottore uttered what the Zany described as 'ne'er sich a true word', there was always a peculiar ritual by which the Zany rose and lifted his leg like a urinating dog, at a right-angle to his body, as if this triumphant display marked the territory gained. Then the Zany would declare himself 'drier'n a nun's nasty' and lope downstairs for a jug of gin which he shared out in scrupulous portions.

And the Dottore's affection spread in my direction. 'Dear heart', he often called me, rocking my own with the memory of another man who had used that term of endearment.

I did not cook but I loved to shop. I had never known it. A Golden Book daughter or a nun in Venice would never experience the pleasures of running to the chandler's shop in Foul Lane for an hour's inconsequent pleasantries with the proprietors over the purchase of half a peck of coal and sundry provisions; even more sundry advice was ladled out for free. In Venice, I would have been ashamed to be seen at such humble pursuits but in London I was declassed, and happy to be that way. Sometimes I chuckled to myself about what my new friends Mr Crumblestalk and Mr Gibbons would say if I told them that I was a high-born Venetian lady with thousand-year-old blue blood. I suspected it would be, 'Well, of course you are, my sweet, and here's an apple for you, darling. You tell that Dottore Velena you're looking a spot peaky and should have a bit of a lie-in tomorrow. And take a drop of gin.'

As I passed around the streets I was saluted by my new name and with affection by wholesale haberdashers, hair merchants, rope- and twine-makers and all the cheerful parties of St Giles' Blackbirds, as London's plentiful blackamoors were called, at work on their various free enterprises: all such men as would never dare to lift their eyes in my presence in Venice. Nor did I feel demeaned by their familiarity. On the contrary I was warmed by it. I had found no comforts in superiority. What a crew of gelid hellhounds seemed the noble nuns of San Zaccaria in comparison to my new comrades!

I even made female friends for the first time in my life, and happily passed hours listening to the grumblings of Mrs C. who sold pease porridge, soused pigs' ears and sheeps' heads, three delicacies much beloved by the Zany, at her shop in Borough High Street. I made another friend in Sarah Mince, a sewer of books, who took in lodgers because her husband, a watch-motion-maker, was afflicted with the gin and could no longer pursue his profession. I was on smiling, nodding terms with the young widow Mistress Grimpen who worked as a mantua-maker and fitted me up with a few of my costumes. I took pleasure in the feel of her delicate hands on my skin, and the way she spun me lightly around to view her work from all angles. I was sorry to hear the gossip that her business did not thrive, and that times were hard for her. Perhaps the physical intimacy of her contact precluded actual friendship, but the possibility was there to be cultivated, I fancied.

Not that I gave up my male companions. In fact, I was becoming more and more like them. The sophistication of the West End coffee houses soon palled on me. We took our leisure north of the river less and less. I grew to like the maltish comforts of the George, the Bell in Clink Street, and of course, our own Feathers in Winchester Square. I liked the Dog and Duck, the Shepherd and Shepherdess and the Temple of Flora, all safe houses for highwaymen's spoils and effervescing at all times with a resultant edgy humour. Some boasted camouflaged cesspits below stairs: these offered a surprise all-over embrace to curious customs officers, several of whom were said to have perished in their unfragrant stews. My favourite, surprisingly, was now the Anchor. To me it was a country inn, kept for sailors. The reflections of the Thames pulsed on the ceilings and the whole interior was washed with a sea-light. I had entirely renounced my former poor opinion of it and now found it a heart-warming place. Moreover, it seemed that my lover had not entirely misled me about it. Although there were no elegant quarters concealed upstairs, the Anchor had seen its share of great men. Dr Johnson himself had frequented it: indeed, his great friends the Thrales were until recently the owners of the vast brewery, the only totally legal business in the whole of Bankside. In its shadow, smaller, more discreet businesses were happy to prosper.

Like my fellow Londoners I had developed a taste for gin. It was cleaner than the water. The Thames was visibly poisoned by the effluent of three-quarters of a million inhabitants. I had heard my lover describe it as 'monster soup', referring to the innumerable pestilences that churned inside it. What came out of the wells here was too brackish to be palatable: it was only good to wash with. I wondered that more Londoners did not think to use it for that. I swore by their fumes that some of them had not known a drop of water on their bodies since the priest sprinkled them at the baptismal font. I had what the Zany called 'good legs' for gin, and was able to slake my thirst without addling my brain, or so I thought at the time. In retrospect I think it was probably a mild but never-broken inebriation that allowed me to suffer all the other privations of my life on Bankside without dying of disgust.

The gin helped me swallow the food that tasted so insipidly, if it tasted at all. It was principally of a fibrous texture, and not spiced but merely aggravated with pepper. And a most unchristian stink arose from it, mysteriously disproportionate to the weak, pallid taste. Yet it seemed rude to cavil when Dottore Velena and the Zany smacked their lips at the prospect of indulging me with hot furmety from the Fleet Bridge Tavern, or eel pie in Baldwin's Gardens.

My nose was given a thorough education in all sordid matters.

In the taverns of Bankside I learned to recognise my drinking companions by their stenches, be they the tripe-dressers and catgut spinners of Field Lane, the singed glassblowers of Stoney Street, or the salty sea porters from St Mary Overie steps. I learned like all the other denizens to pick myself up and throw myself towards the door if anyone came running in: such an event was likely to be the announcement of a press-ganging or a cockfight or another flimsy building falling down. Any house with seven windows or more was taxed, so the tenements loomed dark, like prison hulks decrepitating into the mud.

It was a squalid area, this demesne of my lover. But as my acquaintance with it became more intimate, somehow I forgot to be shocked. To those of us who inhabited it there was a certain fraternity, camaraderie, and code of honour, but let a fashionable carriage from north of the river venture to pass a night in Naked Boy Yard and it would be stripped like a carcass under the desert sun.

I came to recognise the bulky silhouettes of the smugglers and the Heavy Horsemen, dockers whose loose clothes concealed pockets and bags for pilferings from the cargoes of sugar, coffee, cocoa, ginger and pimento. I became familiar with the swagger of the dippers, come to fence their rich pickings from among the mercers' stalls at Ludgate. I came to know professions I had not dreamed of, such as that of the wretch who stockpiled dead dogs and rotten fish for flinging at the black-mailers and the sodomites pilloried at Smithfield; even he had his story and a smile for Dottore Velena's Zany, with whom he shared a passion for the adamantine Sukey.

Too late, of course, I learned to distinguish the various accents of London, from the truly aristocratic (to be heard shooing us low-lifers away from their carriages) to the genteel, dirty-genteel, genteelish and right down to the snipes of the gutter. Somewhere among this rabble floated the remembered tones of Valentine Greatrakes, and they did not bear any resemblance to those of the crème de la crème. But this discovery no longer angered me. As I grew fonder of the Banksiders, so I became more indulgent of their prince. And it seemed to me that to be princess of this vivid realm would be no bad thing.

· 7 ·

A Sweetening Scorbutick Ale

Take Pine (or Fir) tops, cut 4 handfuls; boil them in 5 gallons of very strong Wort to 3 gallons and a half; when its tunned up, pour into it the juices of Brooklime, Water-cresses, Dandelion, Cleavers, each 1 pint; also hang into it the following bag of ingredients, and work all together. Take roots of sharp pointed Dock 4 ounces; Sarsa, China, Juniper-berries, each 2 ounces; Shavings of Sanders yellow and red, Harts-horn, Ivory, Liquorice, Sweet fennel-seed, each 1 ounce; Harts-tongue, Liverwort, Agrimony, Ground-Ivy, each 2 handfuls; Crude Antimony 1 pound: Prepare all rightly.

It brings adult, fervid blood to a temper; quieteth it when in a furious ferment.

After two months of this existence I felt as if I had lived in Bankside all my life. I had got away with my little swindle, and I was even well in purse from it, for Dottore Velena was exceedingly generous with the takings I had swelled. Now there was no danger left, at least while Valentine Greatrakes stayed away.

My audacious plan had worked, but the perfection of it served not to gratify me but to reveal the paltry dimensions of my ambition. It was no great thing I had achieved: why, any smart young woman might have got where I stood now, with a modicum of good looks and a few atoms of wit. What was so clever about existing in a slum, making a living swindling poor people with fake medicines? Living in company with the dry squeal of mice behind the wainscoting all night, a quack doctor who addressed me as his 'wee sweetie creatur' and a coarse flunkey who usually denominated me in terms I would not care to repeat.

Familiarity was beginning to breed not contempt but boredom. This fermented a more dangerous new emotion: anger. My old arrogance made a reappearance. Why was I confined here, living like a street-woman? Was I not a Golden Book heiress, a noblewoman of Venice? How had it come to this pass?

When I answered this question to myself I refused to hear certain essential elements of the response, those that cited the nun I had blinded, the dangerous ways of my former employers, the lies I had told and implied to my lover.

The only thought that came into my head and was allowed a hearing was this: Valentine Greatrakes was the author of my predicament. He had scammed his way into my heart by pretending to be a gentleman, and pretending to love me. He had failed to honour the love I had given him, and now, when I was ready to make him happy – he was obstinately absent. Why did he not return? Moreover he was lacking in guile, despite all the fear he inspired at Bankside. How was it that he had not discovered me yet? For surely he had sent spies to find me? Were they not, every man of them, as incompetent as their master?

It seemed to me a shoddy turn of fate that I still languished in poverty in London, when I might at least have been revealed, brought to him, abjectly apologised to, and persuaded to resume the romance that had been so cruelly interrupted. My fantasies in those days were centred on the depository in Stoney Street and the secret comforts of the bedchamber there that I – another sore issue – had never seen.

These were the images poisoning my thoughts one morning when we drove down Stoney Street, this time heading for Borough High Street. The doors of the depository were open for once, and I glimpsed Dizzom in conversation with an expensively dressed but grotesquely overgrown young woman. The toes of her enormous shoes were acutely pointed and adorned with silk roses. I could see only a snatch of her profile, partly hidden by the violent gush of velvet peonies swarming over her hat. These framed a short column of hair, which was of a colour that the English in their sprightly moments call 'strawberry blond' but in reality better merits the appellation 'boiled shrimp'.

From the nervous way Dizzom looked up at her, I guessed she was finding fault. How did she dare? In the absence of my lover, Dizzom was king-regent of Bankside.

I had never seen her before: not in the crowds I worked, nor on the streets, nor yet in the shops or taverns.

Of course not! She was not the type to live around here.

I have no idea *how* I came to the realisation, but in one swift moment it fell upon me. There was something about her that made this unprepossessing stranger instantly familiar to me. I calculated rapidly. Even though the girl was at least a dozen years older than my lover had led me to understand, I had the clearest inkling of who she was. The gigantic and arrogant young woman was no other than the so-called Baby P.! No wonder my lover had fingered the miniature bonnet I bought her with such embarrassment. It would barely cover her brawny fist!

My mind sped. As we rounded the corner to Clink Street I cried out to Dottore Velena: 'Stop! We must go back to the depository. I sense a superabundant day's work ahead of us. We must refresh our supplies.'

Eyes gleaming, for he knew that I was capable of delivering what I said, Dottore Velena swiftly turned the cart and we trotted back down Stoney Street. The Zany grumbled cynically in his gizzard.

The young woman was still there, hectoring Dizzom, who had his back to us, and her eye passed coldly over our rig. It paused a moment on me, and then swiftly dismissed me as an older and shabbier woman than herself.

From under lowered eyelids, I studied her in brief glances, while seeming to stare vacantly at Dottore Velena and the Zany loading bottles into the back of our cart. Over her shoulder, I caught a glimpse of a vast, ordered storeroom lined with shelves crammed with ranks of bottles. Each shelf bore a large, clear label . . . Canada Maidenhair Syrop, Geneva Cordial Water of Lemon. There were several signs I recognised – they were Venetian! Of course, Dottore Velena had told me that my lover sourced his supplies from the infamous Black Bat in Santa Croce and the discreet Fir-Cone in Castello, but it was another thing to see the actual objects here at Bankside. I was amazed at the precision of the storage and labelling. The Black Bat's products were announced by a perfect replica of the original Venetian shop sign, wooden wings prettily paired like a browsing butterfly. It turned my heart over to see its familiar shape again. But the door was soon slammed shut and bolted. There was a moment of danger as Dizzom glanced back at us, but his eyes were glazed; his attentions were fully occupied by the girl.

'I shall be telling my guardian about this!' The words, laden with menace, turned my head back to the girl berating Dizzom. 'He's on his way back, you know. Or, perhaps you don't?' she sneered.

My heart turned over again with this news, but I forced myself to look at the girl and gather information.

Apart from her age and size, she was everything I had suspected: lumpish, spoiled and plain as a pike. Her coarse pale red hair was fashionably dressed but lustreless. Her voice was like iron filings being scraped. And yet this lardish, charmless creature was loved by Valentine Greatrakes, treated by him as a lady and not as a whore to be used and let go. I supposed he had not told me her true age, which I reckoned at around twenty, for fear that I would find his tenderness towards her a threat.

My poor lover, always so considerate of my feelings, and so misguided! I did not blame him but myself. I should have guessed, from the quality of her manipulations, that she was more mature than the 'little girl' he described. There was nothing little about Pevenche. She was a hefty piece of nastiness. There was nothing vulnerable about her to my eye. She was all too well defended.

It would have been easy for me to hate Pevenche from that first moment but she did not raise any strong emotion in me, and this enabled me to see her not as a person but as an object of use.

· 8 ·

A Decoction of the Woods

Take Guaiacum 4 ounces; Sassaphras 2 ounces; Sanders both red
and yellow, each 1 ounce; Ivory, Harts-horn, each half an ounce;
infuse and boil according to Art in Water 6 quarts to 3 quarts;
then strain, and sweeten with Sugar so as to make it grateful.

It warmeth, drieth, attenuateth and procureth Sweat: it's
suitable to such as are of a cold, shabby Temperament.

It was an easy matter to seize the girl.

Fortunately I remembered the name of the school, seen so
often on the outside of letters sent to her: 'The Marylebone
Academy for Young Ladies'. Two days after glimpsing her at the
depository I was there, requesting an interview with the headmistress. Modestly dressed in grey, my hair newly tinted a
mouse-brown, I introduced myself as a chaperone appointed by
her guardian Valentine Greatrakes to convey his ward to Paris
where he awaited her arrival with some impatience.

The mention of his name cast fear upon the countenance of
Mistress Haggardoon, but an expression of relief flitted covertly
across her face at the same time. Her greying eyebrows shot up
as I explained myself further and she looked at me suspiciously,
while ushering me into her office and indicating a chair opposite
her desk. She was thin and tense, appallingly dressed.
Englishwomen! I thought. What withered objects they are, all
several hundred years old, even the young ones. It amazed me
that the race continued to propagate. Yet even this one was once
married, I saw from the ring on her knotty finger . . . a painful
reminder that the one Englishman I myself truly loved had been
numb to the opportunity of marrying me.

285

Well, I thought now, not a little triumphantly, *he can be jolted to it.*

'Madame,' I said, modulating my voice to express surprise. 'Did you not receive his letter?' I rustled in my pocket and produced a neat packet addressed to 'Mme Jaune-Fleur Kindness' in an unmistakably masculine hand, something I had perfected in an afternoon's practice. She looked blank.

'Ah, the unreliability of couriers,' I sighed. 'That it should reach me in Mayfair and yet pass you by in Marylebone!'

The headmistress nodded vigorously. The mention of Mayfair was soothing and the vagaries of couriers were well known to her, I suspected. How often were her fees mislaid or delayed by reason of their mishaps? Now she smiled at me. 'Pray explain what has been requested by Pevenche's guardian. I hope he finds himself well? I have not seen him for some time. I know he is abroad, of course.'

'Indeed,' I smiled. 'He prospers greatly, and wishes to share some of his good fortune with his poor ward. He has decided that it would be advantageous for the girl to undertake a species of Grand Tour. He himself shall accompany her, for he has business matters to progress in Vienna, Prague, St Petersburg and of course Venice. I myself shall attend, instructing her in the Italian tongue. I believe that she is already fluent in French and German.'

By the headmistress's stammers and blushes, I understood that Pevenche had bullied her way to ignorance in these subjects and all others.

'When should we have the girl ready?' she asked eagerly.

'I thought to take her immediately,' I explained, 'having expected to find her ready to travel, of course,' I reminded her, reviving the idea of the undelivered letter in her head.

I did not know when Dizzom might next come calling, and I did not want to take the risk of his intervention.

Her eyebrows rose again, and I saw a flicker of concern cross her face.

I explained quickly: 'A complete new set of outfits awaits her in Paris, already ordered by her guardian. Her London clothes

286

are hardly suitable for the life she will pursue in the foreign courts.'

At the word 'courts' the headmistress looked stunned and she offered me no more resistance. She excused herself to go and find the girl.

When she left the room I immediately leapt to my feet. Trained as an actress, I usually performed my scripted emotions from a standing position. It had been unexpectedly hard to interpret the role of governess from the depth of an armchair.

I heard Pevenche before I saw her. Outside the door, she was berating the headmistress in a language that was coarse and offensive. I noted that she used the faux-common accent of one who in fact pretends to a very high class.

'Who *is* this female?' she was asking. 'Why did not my guardian write to me personally with this plan? Not that I'm against it – I ain't – but this method of delivering shows me a lack of respect.'

She slammed open the door and paused dramatically on the threshold, the headmistress trailing behind, murmuring ineffectually about lost letters.

She was preceded into the room by a stink of violet perfume. The unsubtle odour swept me into thought. I realised that I had smelled it before, on Valentine Greatrakes, when we were reunited in London after our quarrel. Then I thought he had been taking consolation with another woman, but he had not betrayed me after all: he had only been with Pevenche. I smiled with relief.

Pevenche took my smile as a greeting, but it did not meet with her approval.

'Why did he not write to me?' she fairly screamed, and I could not help admiring how she conjured up a tantrum. Tears squirted from her eyes, and once they arrived she was soon encouraging them with shudders to gather into a proper convulsion. She made a masterpiece of a fit of the vapours, a distemper that rarely fails to kill, I reflected, except perhaps onlookers afflicted with strong sensibilities. I myself stood impassively, which enraged her more. A tender application of

287

hartshorn and water, sweetened with the trilling of the head-mistress and two maidservants, combined to restore her somewhat.

It was only when the storm was over that Pevenche looked at me directly, full of scorn, taking in my simple dress and coiffure. 'What is it about *you* that inspired my guardian's confidence?' she asked rudely, without preliminary courtesies of any kind.

I curtsied slightly, a show of deference that brought a grin to her moonish face. It was a master-stroke, establishing her supe-riority exactly to her satisfaction, and being conveyed in a gesture of my whole body rather than in words, it seemed more sincere than any humble phrases I might have summoned up.

Then I murmured, 'I hope you will find me acceptable as a temporary companion, Miss Pevenche. Your guardian has sub-jected me to the most rigorous interview before entrusting you to my care. And now he is so very anxious to see you again. I trust that you will be kind enough to accede to his wishes.'

She stared at me insolently, defying me to prove my claim. It was a moment of supreme delicacy. In front of the headmistress, I was losing ground.

I forced myself, from gritted teeth, to say, 'Your Uncle Valentine has told me he cannot manage any longer without his Baby P. close to him.'

At the mention of her own pet name for herself Pevenche smiled, almost prettily. I had shown my credentials to be impec-cable.

Yet she did not deign to answer me directly. She cast one more brief look in my direction and marched out of the room muttering, 'Well, at last he's seen sense. And he must have got rid of *her*.'

Over her shoulder she flung at the headmistress: 'Get my things. Didn't you hear the woman?'

I watched Pevenche's back, noting its girth, and her spacious rear quarters.

The girl was clever with a rag of silk and flower, I observed. She had dressed herself in what was possibly the one colour that flattered her: *soupir étouffé*, stifled sigh, a wan kind of lilac.

But nothing could disguise what she was lacking of character in her features.

Even though she was too tightly packed in her dress, she had learned the art of walking as if she were gossamer light and it was the uninformed beholder who might think himself wrong if he observed the thickness about her midriff. She was not professionally trained, so she must have spent a great deal of time watching herself in the glass.

I could see that she had a vile temper upon her, and that crossing her would be an unpleasant business. This was proved to me when I followed her to her bedchamber, as if in proper attendance. She was not aware of my presence and walked in her natural way. Then she was heavy as a veal calf, bumbling into the corner of a credenza which the maid had pulled away from the wall so as to dust behind it. That maid had the benefit of a stream of the bluest language I heard in London, not excepting the Dottore and the Zany in their cups, but worse was the shrill and insistent tone of it. Pevenche shrieked at the maid like a crazed ape, like a monkey to whom someone had administered an over-stimulating nostrum.

I watched with interest.

Her self-centredness and laziness, combined with that temper, were the very ropes that would bind her to my plot. With Pevenche at my side, my lover could not long stay far from me.

And I liked the poetic nature of the justice of the thing: Pevenche had tried to kill our love and had almost succeeded. I had not wanted to see her as a rival. But as she had thrust herself forward as such, well, then, I would bury her.

Bury her alive, that is, in a place that swallowed young girls like sweetmeats.

· 9 ·

A Temperate Pearl Cordial Julep

Take waters of Borage, Woodsorrel, each 4 ounces; Damask
Rose, and Barley Cinnamon water, each 2 ounces; Pearl prepared
1 dram; white Sugar candy 3 drams; Oil of Nutmeg 1 drop, mix.

It brings an exceeding grateful and present Relief to those
that are troubled with sick Fits, and Anxieties in Fevers; for it
neither exagitates nor rarifies the Blood; neither doth it
promote or increase its effervescence; and yet nevertheless,
succours the Ventricle, labouring and almost sinking under the
oppression of sharp Feculencies, and adult Humours flowing
from the Blood, endeavouring Despumation, and excocted by
preternatural Fermentation: And all this it does, by imbuing
the Stomach with a sweetly pleasing Gust and Flavour,
whereby it being recreated and rejoiced, the Spirits (both
indwelling and inflowing) through the whole Machine, are
inspired with fresh Vigour, at an instant recruited, and mightily
supported.

I had told Dottore Velena that I needed to attend to family matters in Venice.

And he tried to believe every word, unlike the Zany who listened in silence and rolled up his eyes, as he had done when he
noticed the new dulled colour of my hair. Nevertheless I kissed
the Zany fondly on the cheek, and though he rubbed at the spot,
he did not recoil from me, nor did he expostulate when I promised to rejoin them both if I ever returned to London. At this
Dottore Velena waxed a little Italian, and became sentimental,
and called for a bottle of port to lubricate our valedictory coddle
of sausage and onions. Needing my wits, I only pretended to

drink it. After a roistering final evening at the Anchor, the Bell, the George and the Feathers, I negotiated the purchase of one of my costumes: the padded apron that gave me the silhouette of middle pregnancy, which was used to illustrate the goodness of our nostrum for painless childbirth. The Zany did not for one moment let up from his disputatiousness with the Dottore or express regret at my imminent departure, but, for the first time, he stood me a small gin.

Before settling into sleep in his parturition chair, Dottore Velena delivered a speech that meandered into romantic decla-rations, and he even tottered over to my basket to make a hazy approximation of an attempt upon my virtue. I clipped his ankle with a candle-snuffer and he fell headlong into the fireplace, smiting his forehead with a smart clap. He fell asleep there, shuf-fling in the ashes, muttering about the tragic impossibility of 'sewing up a broken heart without the aid of fairies'.

We parted in good, if subdued, spirits, the next morning. The Zany had already slunk out before dawn, perhaps in search of 'combustibles' but also, perhaps, to avoid the final embarrass-ment of a farewell. I had expected nothing more, so I tucked a small eel pie, wrapped in a beautiful silk handkerchief, into the angle of the plank where he slept.

Then I walked out into the dawn of the Bankside morning, holding a valise that I had forced to accommodate sundry items plucked from the quack's surgery as well as my old grand clothes. As I listened to the pigeons croodling in the privet hedge of St Saviours, I stopped a moment, looking back up at the Feathers and the grimy window behind which the Dottore was shuffling about his toilette. As if he felt my gaze, his face appeared at the window and he saluted me with a silent bliz-zard of blown kisses. I kissed my fingers back to him, unexpected tears on my lashes. A tender part of me was sorry, and also a little afraid, to leave the scene of so much rollicking amity, but I knew that it was time to move on, and to bring my lover to me.

I didn't have much time: he'd be back in London within days.

I turned my back on Bankside and set off for Mistress Haggardoon's Academy for Young Ladies in salubrious Marylebone.

Pevenche had decided that it was beneath her dignity to talk to me, so the first part of our journey to Dover passed blessedly in silence, apart from her disbelieving snort at the inelegance of the equipage. She herself had dressed in a lilac silk gown and sported a white hat lined with dusky pink underneath, causing her oblong pale head to resemble the pitted stalk of an over-grown toadstool.

'Only two postilions!' she muttered, jangling the steel-sprung carriage with her weight as she lumbered aboard. Although there was space for four passengers, we were fortunately alone, so I had no need to fear her indiscretions. I passed the entire distance fret-ting at the cost, which would run high at threepence a mile. I was already afraid of the furious sums of money that it would take to transport my spoilt hostage across Europe. My plan, more vis-cerally than intellectually made, seemed insane even to me then. But it was too late. I was committed to it, however thin its logic and however fragile its framework. And I had no other.

At an inn on the way to Dover Pevenche and I consumed the first of several cheerless deaf-and-dumb dinners together. I sus-pected that she also feared to enter into conversation with me, for such talk would expose the shameful truth of her capacities in French and German. I had a hint of her deficiency already. If she was forced to address me, it was as 'Madame Joanfloor', her crude approximation of 'Jaune-Fleur'.

I was speechless when she pushed her plate of cutlets in front of me and thrust her knife and fork into my hand.

'Cut them up,' she ordered.

Why not? I asked myself fiercely. *Anything to keep her quiet, to let her think that she rules.*

I obeyed her, though I could not resist saying lightly, 'I'm not quite old enough to be your mother, my dear.'

From the look I received I saw that she considered me decrepit enough to be her grandmother. But she was soon deep in the consumption of the cutlets and speculating on the manner of their flavouring. It seemed a point of intense interest to her whether thyme or bay predominated in the marinade. This girl was the stuff of nightmares. Why had I done this senseless, dangerous thing of stealing her?

The answer was always the same: *she is bait, like any worm or maggot*.

When we resumed our journey, she pretended to doze. I pretended to read – a guidebook for the Grand Tour – and so had an opportunity to watch her covertly.

While not quite formed yet, hers was a face that did not make any rash promises to deliver ecstasy. It was, I thought sourly, a typical English rose, sodden and parboiled in complexion. Even its freshness was not unimpeachable. Her small features were strictly consonant with the limits of her personality.

Yet she was extraordinarily adept in the artifice of juvenility. She contrived to display her mouth perpetually open, revealing a natural gap between her two small front teeth. Her upper lip did indeed overhang in a childish manner. The two pretended milk teeth above rested on the lower lip like a doll's. She cultivated a fixed, averted gaze, that seemed to be full of delight sacred to the private world of childhood, and then sometimes her eyes were full of wist as if she listened to a faraway nursery rhyme.

Eventually, we were forced to talk a little. Carefully, in the manner of a respectful governess, I asked her about her accomplishments, avoiding the subjects of French and German. It appeared she had no talents, and no energy even to develop such skills. She did not busy herself with embroidery, and certainly not with charitable acts, which would be natural to one of her ambiguous station, being a way to establish her superiority. She had a strange, obsessive and unseemly interest in food, and could take on that bootless subject with surprising eloquence. Music was not her delight at all, despite the dreaded ukulele. I noticed that she had brought it with her, clearly thinking that she would soon be using it on her guardian.

Out of curiosity, I asked her to play for me. She sniffed petulantly. 'I only play for my Uncle Valentine. He would not like me playin' to *you*.'

I was in a condition to slap her face, and would have taken a bare delight in doing so. But that was not to my purpose. The tindery aspect of my character was not to be provoked by so poor an adversary. With caution, I changed the subject, groped for one that would please her. I soon found it. Pevenche was full of grievances for the way she was treated by the other girls in her school. Her complaints were as the tides of the sea, but sadly none so subtle. She recounted triumphs of humiliation she had visited upon girls who offended her, and of mistresses dismissed and servants demoted: all the amusements naturally dear to a young woman who was no prodigy of wit but a genius of spitefulness. In talking of these tiny wars and her victories, she grew flushed and happy. English boarding schools, like Venetian convents, were evidently prime breeding grounds for monstrous bullies.

And so we whiled away the remainder of the journey to Dover, and the wait in the customs house, where we were but lightly examined. The weather was fair and we entered our vessel with ease, the journey running to less than six hours. Neither of us was taken with the seasickness. I fully expected the girl to part with her copious breakfast. She turned out to be fitted with a surprising pair of sea-legs, though as far as I knew she had never been upon the water before. At Calais we were disgorged with facility on the quay where the usual porters seized our baggage and conducted us to the municipality to obtain our *passe-avant* and show our own documents: mine hastily aged to look much-travelled and that of Pevenche, white and crisp. I had commissioned them hastily from an amiable forger I'd met in the Anchor. I had stood over him anxiously in his discreet cubicle, giving her description, trying to find neutral words for her appearance.

'And her age?' asked my accomplice, busy at his calligraphy.

I realised that I knew it not, but instructed him to write 'twenty', my original guess on first seeing her.

I had the document drawn up in French, trusting that she would not interest herself in anything so impenetrable.

Now Pevenche's face was frozen, listening to and pretending to understand my fluent French. My explanations, similar to those I had given Mistress Haggardoon, were accepted and we were gallantly waved away by the officers and set free upon our road almost instantly.

I decided not to stay the night in Calais but to leave immediately for a town more obscure. I did not believe that we had been followed, but I could not afford to be complacent.

By now my hostage had begun to fascinate me. I had never come across such a grotesque creature. Nature had justly denied her charm, having endowed her richly with conceit. In every carriage she behaved like the reigning beauty at a ball, condescending to meet the admiring glances she imagined by turning her head from one fellow passenger to another, as if to linger too long on one might utterly ruin him. Her artillery of giggles, winks and lash-fluttering was unleashed on both men and women. I am sure they thought her deprived of her senses by some accident.

The only accident that has befallen her, I wanted to say, *is a surfeit of tolerance regarding her monstrous vanity.*

My lover, and evidently also her father before him, had fondled all her fantasies about being an invincibly charming young woman of heroic intelligence.

When she saw our companions looking at her curiously, she whispered to me: 'You see! Do I not intrigue them? Do they not all think that I am a foreign lady? A foreign lady, bred abroad? Do I not have fascinating graces and airs that mark me out from other English misses?'

She fully believed that no male could behold her squab charms with impunity. If a man's glance strayed involuntarily in her direction, she would squeal in a whisper, 'Oh no! He's looking goats and monkeys at me! I dare not meet his eyes! I'm so shy!'

At the end of one meal I watched in astonishment as she carefully wrapped the well-gnawed bones of her fowl in a napkin.

When I asked her why she did so she told me in stiff terms that these delicacies were for the coachman's horse. My heart was too cold to disabuse her and I admit that I enjoyed the spectacle the next morning when she, simpering, presented the bones, and the incredulous coachman looked over her head to his friend the ostler, who was making a pretty pantomime of her bizarre ignorance.

Myself she regarded with exaggerated pity. The fact that she condemned *me* as dowdy was so ridiculous that I should have been able to dismiss it. But the poor opinion of anyone, no matter how contemptible, is wearing, and I found my self-confidence mysteriously wilting under the power of her scorn.

She would ask with mock concern, 'Oh dear! Have you sore eyes today? They are so very small and red!' or 'Have you dyed your hair freshly this morning? It looks dreadfully darker again, but I *think* all the grey is gone.' And my hand, all involuntary, would dart to the insulted part of me, while I blushed. It was true, my homespun efforts at hiding the gold of my hair were clumsy, the tincture I'd bought at Bankside no doubt too cheap to be efficacious.

If a man glanced at me with admiration she regarded him with pity too, as if he had been shockingly swindled in the gift of discrimination. And it happened that every time I looked up I was confronted by her small but vivid eyes, the blue pupils taking up the entire cavity and seeming like opals sinking in the cream of her fat cheeks. When she was caught out by me like this, she lazily swung her glance away, as insolently as possible, as if to convey that I presented not the slightest object of interest to her.

Nor was she concerned with the towns and landscapes we passed through, rarely glancing out of the window, and always rejecting my suggestions of making a visit to a famed church or view. She was entirely resourced from within, and passed her time in happy speculations about what awaited her when we finally caught up with her guardian. She shared her thoughts with whichever companions were in our carriage, entirely without self-consciousness, or perhaps so utterly racked with it that the close little chamber seemed a kind of theatre to her in which she must perform.

She invariably introduced me as 'my spinster companion' to travellers who kindly lowered their eyes with embarrassment. With the rejection of Valentine Greatrakes so painfully on my mind, the discouragement of that fatal denomination struck me most cruelly.

It was a theme Pevenche mined richly.

'I imagine that you shall soon be returnin' to London, to some garret where you may live cheap and retired, until some man takes you up. But do you know,' she added, 'your prospects are dim, for there is a vast superabundance of women against men there.'

She then stared at me in silence, as if to say that with the market so hard against our sex, someone of my feeble attributes was not likely to prevail.

'But where is my guardian?' she asked continually.

'An urgent matter came up. He has gone on to Nice,' I told her. Or to Lucerne, or to Freiburg. Each place where we arrived, I pretended to receive a letter from him, explaining that he awaited us in the very next town. I gave the letters to her. I had written them in the same masculine hand, full of love and concern for his little ward, late the night before, while she snored.

'I hope that my Baby P. does not find the journey too hard,' I scribbled. 'I cannot wait to see her again.'

Like a fish pulled on a gentle and sweet-baited hook, she swam voluntarily in the direction I hoped. Of course she behaved mutinously at times, particularly in regard to her dresses. She had kicked up a considerable storm in Paris, refusing to leave until every last promised chemise was delivered.

'And there should have been fittings. Lots of fittings, with lots of little girls fussin' around me!' she wept, genuine tears spurting on to the fatty slabs of her cheeks.

When we stopped in towns, I was obliged to stay with her every moment. Otherwise she was capable of tripping into the establishments of milliners and mantua-makers and bludgeoning them into some costly service, despite her lack of language. An account would be delivered forthwith to our rooms, along with some fashionable garment, like a caraco jacket *à la polonaise*, pleated and flared at the back and cut away at the front, or a pink silk mantle figured in hideous red spots, always too tight for her and frequently discarded after one breathless wearing. When questioned by me, she riposted: 'You told me Uncle Valentine wants me to lack for nothing. I ask the bare minimum, y'know.'

Or she would ask me for 'a little loan until Uncle Valentine can take care of it'. For obvious reasons, I dared not refuse her. Looking into her cold blue eyes at moments like that, I thought she must see through me, and that she mocked me with these requests, and it seemed that this monster stayed with me only because this journey, in some bizarre way, suited her own purposes. I trembled then, and wondered if she would denounce me at the next town, or in front of a carriage full of strangers.

It took a little gin, but I always soothed my fears. The same thought came to rescue me on the balmy wings of the drink: Pevenche was malicious as the devil on his throne, but she was not burdened with his wits. She lacked the native cunning to play me for a fool. What I saw of her was what she was: a fat, dull girl who thought of nothing whatsoever beyond her next dress or dinner.

A new problem was bearing down on me. I was running out of money, despite my generous cut of the nostrum profits. I plainly could not afford to keep indulging Pevenche.

So she simply helped herself. One evening, returning to my room at the inn after a blessedly solitary stroll in the garden, I found her sitting on the floor, raking through the contents of my valise. When I entered the room her eyes flickered over me but swiftly returned to the pile of clothes.

My first throat-tightening thought was that she was spying on me, and I was too frightened to speak. I tried to remember if

298

there was anything incriminating among my personal effects. Nothing came to mind.

Meanwhile she continued to paw through my possessions, discarding most items with exaggerated disdain. But two or three items she laid on one side, as if they alone were worthy of consideration. She did not look at me, and I stood silently regarding her.

Eventually, with a sigh, she gathered the chosen garments – some ribbons, a shawl, a spotted jacket that would never stretch to her girth – and rose gracelessly to her feet. Then she walked out of the room without saying a word.

Stupefied, I remained looking at my pillaged valise for many minutes. Then it came to me – the manner of her thinking. She saw nothing wrong in this behaviour. To her I was merely the employee of her guardian. I was his creature – and he, he was *her* creature. My possessions, by this construction, were her possessions. I shook my head, unable to feel anything but wonder.

I was not inconsolably distressed by her thievery of my clothes. It kept her quiet a while. But when the spotted jacket, ripped across the shoulder, was flung back at me, I hit upon the happy idea of setting small mousetraps in the pockets of my favourite things. After one encounter with a jacket that bit back, Pevenche desisted from rifling my valise, and instead adorned her injured finger with a sensational bandage of red silk.

Such a sturdy creature as she was, Pevenche was still born to act the martyr and it was a constant struggle for her to maintain her victimhood without any ill-treatment to support it. She had a wonderful power for making people feel that they had done her a great wrong. I ceased to wonder why Valentine Greatrakes had felt himself so obliged to make everything up to her. Poor tender-hearted man, what hope had he against such assaults? As we travelled in our carriages, she often stared vacantly straight ahead, uttering a long and eloquent sigh. When asked what troubled her, she would wave away the question with a resigned hand.

She complained of everything. Her vocabulary was pulvilled with schoolgirl words. To be rid of the sniffing lady to her left

299

would be 'killing fine'. She herself was 'up to the ears in love' with the pink satin slippers worn by another. And nor could she live without the 'darlingest' parrot-feather muffetees sported by a woman of fashion we glimpsed at an inn outside Nice. For days afterwards she stared pointedly at her naked wrists every time she caught me looking at her. In the end I found her some, but they were made of swan feathers and she professed herself heartily dissatisfied with them.

I was lonely, missing those evenings with Dottore Velena when we sat up late gilding pills by rolling them in coconut shells lined with powdered metals. I missed the company, I missed the sordid comforts, that close little room at the Feathers, and it behoves me to admit that I missed the gin. At this realisation I sternly resolved to divest myself of the pernicious habit of taking most of my fluid in that form. It was sorely difficult: every time I looked at the girl, my bile rose and I craved a glass of something warming to wash away its bitter taste. But I could not afford to be overtaken with the gin in her company, nor to be seen engaged at the bottle.

There were times, when looking at Pevenche, that the Zany's voice struggled to burst out of my own mouth. Such as now, when he bellowed in my inner ear at her, 'Never mind the pelted lip, you sulky cow. I won't be taking you any kind of shopping with *that* face tripping you up.'

When her manoeuvres drove me to a pitch of distraction, I started to dose her with various condiments I had taken from Doctor Velena's surgery, just spoonfuls here and there, nothing seriously damaging to her health.

'You poor child,' I would say, 'you look a little peaky. Your guardian would never forgive me if you arrived in his presence sporting such a pallor.'

She laced herself so tight that I feared for her viscera and it was all to no use anyway, for the confined flesh merely migrated to rolls under her shoulders and below her hips.

Of course the drugs made her hungry. To keep her subdued, I did not give her quite enough to eat – enough to satisfy a

300

normal creature of her age but not her sweet tooth. My purse was running to speedy decay in trying to support her appetite. The hours she was sleeping, as I saw it, were hours in which she was not eating.

After the second day on the road I had put on my pregnancy apron. It felt in an odd way comforting on my belly. I remembered my own true pregnancy sixteen years before: this one was definitely more comfortable. I was curious to see how Pevenche would react to it, but she appeared not to notice it at all.

When, however, men started to offer me extra attentions such as handing me in and out of carriages, and when women started to stroke my cheek sentimentally, and ask coy little questions, then Pevenche was forced to mark the difference in my shape. I caught her looking at me with a superior smile. With amazement I realised that she did not understand the implication of my enlarged belly. Despite her great age she had not the least idea of the facts of life. She merely thought me grown fat like herself and this diminishing of my attractiveness gave her no little pleasure.

· 10 ·

A Pacific Mixture

Take Liquid Laudanum tartarised 2 drams; Oil of Nutmeg and Cinnamon each 4 drops, mix.

It has the common Virtues of Laudanum, but in a more especial manner, respects Vomiting and Looseness; besides which, it's a good blind for Laudanum, to hide it from the knowledge of Patients and By-standers; which Trick is sometimes exceeding necessary, when they are curiously impertinent and meddling, or have taken up a foolish aversion to Opium.

The closer we came to Venice the more genial grew the climate, and the more nervous I became. Undermined by Pevenche's thick-spread contempt, I was losing belief in my flimsy plan.

How was I going to drag this great blouzed lump of a girl, taller than myself and far wider, through Venice and have her shut up in a convent without attracting attention? The last rumour I wanted spread around the city was one of a foreign girl imprisoned in Sant'Alvise, the convent I had decided upon for her.

And in the middle of my worries Pevenche appeared to do something that chilled my blood.

I had always known her for a girl who made a solid treasure of her infancy; I had seen for myself the miniature ukulele, so ridiculous in her fat arms, the nursery vocabulary. In general, alone with me she did not make a feature of her juvenility, but whenever there were other people around, she fell into the performance of it. She also cultivated a fondness for fairy tales and one of her affectations was to refer to the characters in them as if they were historical personages. I reflected sourly that she would have evinced a belief in fairies if they could make good strawberry pies.

One day, as the carriage jolted interminably through a mountain pass, she was put out by the crying of a small child whose voice lifted in lament above the fug of the little chamber we shared with four other travellers. The mother was too motion-sick to pay attention to her little boy. She wilted against the window while he howled. Our other companions were a fiftyish, elegant man and a sharp-eyed widow, possibly a Frenchwoman, of some forty cruel winters and apparently rather fewer renewing springs. If they were together, it was in some kind of decayed clandestine rapport, for their eyes never met. There was something about them that made me uneasy. I tried to reassure myself that everyone aroused my suspicions in my fugitive state, and that there was nothing of worrisome note about these middle-aged travellers. As the little boy wailed, both of them stared out of the windows, clearly wishing themselves a thousand miles away, but too unversed in child matters to take things into their own hands, and full of distaste at the thought of addressing themselves to the squirming boy, who probably numbered about four years.

Suddenly Pevenche's voice rang out above the child's wails, the clattering carriage wheels and the wind's whine outside. It was not a pretty voice but, like her ukulele, it penetrated the brain and claimed attention, without hope of escape.

Here, in the middle of the fabled forest, she had decided to make a great flourish of her own babyish nature – clearly reading competition for that status in the cries of the little boy. She had chosen to tell her unwilling audience the tale of Hansel and Gretel.

The child stopped crying and was listening. I have no idea if he spoke English but he most certainly knew from her tone of voice that she was telling a fairy story. I did not know if the mother understood either. She smiled wearily as her child snuffled into a rapt silence and took the opportunity to stuff the bead of his anodyne necklace into his mouth. This he sucked contentedly as Pevenche carried on relentlessly in her high, artificial, storytelling voice, reserving a hissing stage whisper for every appearance by the monstrous stepmother. I could not guess if the older man and woman were able to understand her, but in my paranoid state I imagined that I saw the twinkle of comprehension in his eyes, anyway. Hers remained opaque.

Pevenche concluded triumphantly, 'And the stepmother had already expired in convulsions.'

I hated every word of this story and I hated her way of telling it, in her childish affected lisp. As ever, she was representing herself as a splay-legged little faun instead of the thumping heifer she was.

Meanwhile, caught in the story's thrall, the small boy had soiled his wraps. The close air snagged on the salty rottenness of his effluvia. I sniffed loudly to alert the mother to her duties.

At this, Pevenche turned to me and smiled. 'How well do you smell, Madame Joanfloor! Remember *witches* have very poor sight but a monstrous good sense of smell.'

It was only then – how had I been so blind until now? – that I noticed that the silent couple were not French but bore a Venetian crest on their luggage. They were Golden Book, but a far-flung branch, to be travelling in relative humbleness like this. I tried to contain an involuntary shudder, for on that dark night, with the coils of the fairy tale tightening round me, it was hard not to fantasise that here were two more spies in the pay of my employers, set to follow me and report on my movements. Having failed to track me down, Mazziolini had handed over the baton to this unlikely couple, more discreet and more dangerous even than he.

The wheels rolled on ceaselessly and I had never felt so trapped, not even in San Zaccaria. I thought of Valentine Greatrakes, and how much I would have enjoyed this journey if I'd had his hand to hold as we hurtled over the stones, and his sweet shoulder on which to rest my head. I mused on, uncomforted, with painful thoughts pricking me like knife blades. Without realising it, I had opened the flask in which I kept my emergency supply of gin, and drained it. Pevenche leaned over

304

to our companions, indicating me with a turn of her head. She told them confidentially: 'Poor Miss Joanfloor. The consolations of her antiquity should include a natural softening of the temper. But she needs the gin, you know.'

The horrible little polecat had made sure that no one would forget this journey! Through the medium of the fairy tale, she was telling them that she, a young innocent girl, was travelling in the thrall of a hard-drinking older and duplicitous woman. Like a wicked stepmother! A perverted kind of mother-figure who meant her no good! It followed that she had been kidnapped, surely. Whether she knew it or not Pevenche was laying a trail by telling this story, just as Hansel left his little white pebbles. I must watch her like a falcon: make sure that she left no actual scribbled notes to this effect in that false childish script of hers.

I hated to admit that the poisonous chit could have an effect on me, but I did not like to be painted like that. It spoke to all the weakness in me that had made me so sad and passive when my first lover abused me. I was furious, helpless, out of breath. I sat brooding on my revenge and how to take control of the situation again, while Pevenche, inspired by the success of her story, talked continually in her wood-scratching voice, pronouncing, with a very important face, a number of banalities.

That night, in my only moment of laxity, I did her a small violence.

She had been complaining of the smallness of the signet ring I had presented to her over dinner, pretending it was a gift sent from her guardian.

After the usual 'poor me's' and sundry accustomed laments, her voice suddenly changed to a steely tone and she fixed a superior, reproving look upon me.

'Admit it,' she said. 'You chose this trifle. He would never have insulted me with something so light. You bought this cheap ring and you have kept most of the money for yourself.'

'You are wrong,' I lied evenly. 'The ring arrived from your Uncle Valentine. I had no say in the transaction.'

She snorted.

Then it became too much for me. The fact that I had gone without gin so that she might have this ring. The fact that she was fortunate to be given any gift at all, that she insulted me so relentlessly, that Valentine Greatrakes had refused *me* a ring at last.

I reached over and pulled the ring off the tip of her littlest finger where she had placed it to show her contempt.

'I agree,' I said, holding it up in front of her face. 'It is a poor morsel of a thing. Much too delicate for you to *wear*.'

And with that I pushed it deep into her mouth which snapped shut with surprise, and before she knew it, Pevenche had swallowed the ring.

She was shocked into silence, and then I saw a peculiar smile of satisfaction illuminate the liverish fat of her cheeks. I had made a grievous error. I had finally given her some ammunition against me. She had known from the first that I did not admire her, but she had made herself very easy about that. She had been waiting for me to put a foot wrong. I had just obliged her most handsomely. She could now, to her mind, denounce me to her guardian, and have me banished, like everyone else who had stood in her way.

Quickly, I decided to say nothing, not to corroborate the fact of what I had done. If I apologised, it would acknowledge my crime. Then at some point later it would be her word against mine.

She was so full of her victory that she had no need of confirmation from me. She hugged her happy prospects to herself and retired to her bedroom without any further word. It was contiguous to mine, and I ascended shortly afterwards. I heard her draining another bottle of the Drops, and soon after her familiar snores that throughout the journey had forced me to shrink my head under my bedclothes.

I sat at my table, thinking hard and fast. I was amazed that she had perforated my self-control, as no one else had ever done, except my first lover. I could not allow it to happen again. But how was I to prevent it?

Finally the answer came to me.

If her greatest subconscious fear was being eaten alive like Hansel and Gretel then I would work on that! If she wanted to paint me as a witch – I a professed nun – and a wicked stepmother – I who was no one's mother! – then she would have witches and wicked stepmothers by the spadeful.

It was an old actor's trick, but new to her, as was everything of course, the booby. I had stripped to just a black shift, and prepared one ounce of oil of almonds, with half a dram of phosphorus and two grains of the flour of sulphur in a thick bottle. I held the mixture in a candle flame for a moment to dissolve it, then I shook the bottle and drew the cork . . . a fine glow-worm of light shimmered inside. When I was ready I rubbed a line of this mixture along the edge of my arms, the outline of my cheek and nose . . . and I entered her room mildly aflame.

I saw her eyelids snap up as I slammed the door open. I spoke through the haze of her sleep: 'If you betray me or even behave badly, I shall eat you.'

She was too drugged to scream but I saw her eyes widen, and the helpless small convulsions of her fingertips. I stopped in my threats only when I thought she might die of a seizure brought on by her inexpressible fear. She closed her eyes, hoping to eliminate the vision I presented, and rolled upon her left side, away from me. As she turned I had a glimpse of her breasts sliding from the lace-daubed mouth of her chemise; they were mismatched and already swagging southwards, I noticed.

I placed a little chicken bone in her hand so that she had something to wake up with to remind her of what had happened, a tangible souvenir of her dreadful dream.

After that, she was mine. She was mute all the way, eating what she was given, including the drugs.

· 11 ·

A Cataplasm of Bitters

*Take Venice Treacle, Lupine Meal, each 3 drams; Wormseed 1 dram
and a half; Species of Hiera picra half a dram; Chymical oil of
Wormwood 16 drops; Juice of Tansey, enough to embody it, mix.
Apply it to the Navel, against Worms in Children.*

When we arrived at Mestre, it was early evening. The colour
drained from the sky seemed to have come back in the form of
piquant aromas. Pevenche emerged from the carriage blinking
and sniffing at the stink of seaweed and the rasping odour of hot
stone suddenly cooling as night descended.

I hurried her into a gondola.

'Sant'Alvise,' I said, in as calm a voice as I could muster.
Distressed women rushing to nunneries were always good
fodder for gossip in Venice. I was glad of Sant'Alvise's solitary
situation at the north-west extremity of the town, perched on the
very edge of the lagoon and so remote from the fashionable
hustle of San Marco and the crowds of Rialto.

When Pevenche saw the gondola she started spluttering and
carrying on in a good simulation of a hysterical fit, till I was
obliged to dose her with a swig of one of her Specificks.

'She suffers from the seasickness,' I told the gondolier, who
nodded sympathetically, saying, 'Imagine, *una Veneziana* who
cannot bear water, *poveretta*!'

I was relieved that he had called her *'una Veneziana'*.

He asked me no questions as we boarded and the boat slid
into the slate-grey water pointed towards Venice. The waves
hastened to embrace the prow, like the eager and thorough touch
of a blind man.

Pevenche arrived in my city semi-conscious, and lay back on the cushions of the *felze*, looking out of the window with slackened eyes. As the bell towers arose before us, she burbled in a simple-minded kind of way, 'I don't believe this. I don't believe this.'

That was more or less all she said until, a merciful half-hour later, we were grinding into the upper steps of the water-gate at Sant'Alvise.

Of course the city stunned her. She had arrived almost entirely ignorant of its appearance. She had read nothing and showed no interest in the guidebooks I pressed on her, and yawned widely at the snippets I read to her unless they were of a retail or culinary nature. I think that before seeing it she must have perceived Venice dimly as an inconvenient city without carriages and with many shops of cunning glass beads which she had swiftly and conclusively disdained in advance, saying, 'My guardian insists I wear only real precious stones.' And of course she saw no benefit in covering her face with a mask, *Carnevale* or no *Carnevale*.

It was clear that my explanation of the gondolas, the canals and the *Carnevale* still in progress had passed her by. As we entered Cannaregio, she roused herself somewhat from her stupor. She looked fearfully at the boats and the masked figures hurrying along the *rive* as if they inhabited a demented dream. It was too much for her. By the time we reached Sant'Alvise she was in what I suspected to be the first genuine swoon of her life. Her Gothic hauteur had slumped into the dumbfoundedness of a country bumpkin.

And she had not even seen the glories of the Grand Canal, a glimpse of which I craved like cake but which I dared not permit myself. I contented myself with breathing great gulps of the sweet sea air and let my eyes devour the dentillations and ancient reliefs on the façades of sundry small *palazzi* that we passed. It gave me inexpressible satisfaction to think that I had returned to Venice, from which my employers had so long banished me, as a free woman.

Apart from its convenient remoteness, I had chosen Sant'Alvise from the kindest motives – it had a reputation as the best bakery in Venice, and for a motherly regime that regarded a weakness for the pleasures of the table as the very least of sins.

At least Pevenche would be able to indulge her sweet tooth while she awaited her fate. I had a fondness for the place myself, with its companionable little *campo* spilling on to the canal of Sant'Alvise and the sweet lineaments of the brick convent placed at comfortable right-angles to the church. It was closer to the salty haunts of the fishermen than the perfumed offices of the Inquisition. And there was something precious here that almost all of Venice lacked – a high sky and a far horizon, speckled with hazy islands. The quietness was palpable, broken only by the lap of waves and the subdued cries of the seagulls: even they seemed to respect the peace of Sant'Alvise. The church had always been my favourite, simply for the delectable cobalt blues of its ceiling. How different it was from the stern chessboard blacks of San Zaccaria! Even the grilles that separated the nuns from the congregation, so rigid and prison-like at San Zaccaria, were airy and light-heartedly curlicued at Sant'Alvise, seeming more an expression of pleasure than enclosure.

When I handed Pevenche over to the nuns, I did have a moment of feeling sorry. I knew what she was about to go through, after all. But I comforted myself that her blood now ran with an equal proportion of opium to vital fluid, and that she was lost in her own world, awash in the scum of trivia that enslaved her brain. She would be scarcely conscious of her privations. I had left enough of the nostrum – 'without it she's a dead woman in a day' – with her new guardians to last until my plan came to fruition.

'She also suffers horribly from worms,' I told the abbess and her colleagues, whose round faces creased immediately with a tender concern for Pevenche's infested belly, 'and needs this cataplasm three times a day, laid on the navel in a bag.'

I put a jar of paste into the hands of the nearest nun. I was embarrassed about the grossness of her appetite, and that I tried to excuse it with this tale of vermin.

Sant'Alvise was far more humble than San Zaccaria. The

nuns were grateful even for the small sum I now offered for her care. 'It is just until her guardian arrives,' I told them. 'A matter of a week or two at the most.' This short time made my ducats look larger and they thanked me with seriousness.

'She's a sweet child,' I told them. 'You'll find her quite tractable. In spite of an aristocratic education in London, it seems that they have neglected to teach her Italian, but she will respond to whatever way you communicate with her. She is an extraordinary girl.'

I fused every stage skill I'd ever possessed in a gesture that conveyed and *transferred* to them a heavy wonder at her magnificence.

The nuns looked gratified that I had brought them such a pearl, as I hoped they would. By stressing her particularity, I hoped to persuade them to find her strangeness becoming and even attractive. Novelty appeals to all Venetians, and most particularly to the city's enclosed nuns. My parting words brought smiles to their kind faces: 'She shows an extreme partiality to sweet foods.'

All the while I was thinking to myself: *This Pevenche, she is indeed extraordinary. She is a girl one cannot love. Every attempt I have made to befriend her has been quickly decayed by her contempt. Anything I have taught her – that for her own curious motives she did not disdain to retain – it is like a diamond set in lead. I hope she does not abuse these kind women.*

Pevenche tottered from my arm to that of the abbess, a plump and homely nun, so unlike the hard-eyed anatomies at San Zaccaria. The abbess looked kindly on my fake belly, without any insinuations against the respectability of my incipient offspring.

'We'll take good care of this one,' she smiled, 'and you, my dear, must take care of the new little one. These blessed months of gestation are not to be taken lightly.'

'You will be safe here,' I told Pevenche in English. She flinched away at the sound of my voice. Even though she was awake, she was still afraid of me. But whether it was her memories of my 'ghost' or the knowledge that I was cold-hearted

311

enough to torture her with its appearance, I would never know and I did not preoccupy myself with the question. It was nothing like as evil as the deceptions that had tricked me into San Zaccaria without a fight.

'I don't believe this,' she said one more time, and that was the last I saw of her: the abbess with a gentle arm about her shoulders, leading her down one of the innumerable corridors of cells radiating from the reception room on the first floor.

· 12 ·

A Comforting Glyster

Take Canary Wine 1 pint; Diascordium half an ounce; Yolks of
Eggs 2, mix.

What Cordial Juleps are to the Stomach, the same this
Glyster is to the Guts. For it so refreshes them, as to raise an
universal Exultation of the whole Systasis of the Spirits,
whereby they are roused up, and enabled to perform their
Business briskly; and throw out whatsoever is offensive to
Nature, and noxious, vigorously.

The last anyone here had knowingly seen of me was my back
firmly turned from Venice. Even if they had discovered the true
trail of all my perverse routes around the north of Italy, even if
they had followed me through France, it seemed obvious that
they had not tracked me to London.

Or, if they had, my shabby life as a quack's assistant had given
me sufficient cover from their vigilant eyes. Perhaps they never
looked for me, a Golden Book daughter, south of the river, among
the breweries and the glassworks and the humid parlours of the
Blackfriars laundresses. They were probably still scouring
Mayfair for a woman of my style and quality, being kept by the
kind of man who could afford me. Perhaps they were touring the
theatres and the high-class brothels, thinking that the stage and its
related profession were the only way I might feed myself. Or
having found that trail quite cold and dead, then they might have
given up on London, and were perhaps even now looking up my
old haunts and my former lovers in Paris, Vienna or St Petersburg.

I imagined Mazziolini, his energy fed by fury, arriving in yet
another city. For him, too, it would be a point of honour to find

me, and to administer a little homely chastisement of his own before he handed me back to my employers. My escape would have disgraced him in their eyes, and only my recapture would restore him to their favour. He would be after me like a bloodhound, eyes splayed, fingers avid, that soft insinuating voice asking the same questions in language after language, in city after city, proffering a miniature of me: 'Have you seen her? Was it recently? Where exactly? Do you know where she is now?'

I dreamt of Mazziolini's eyes. Eyes so pale a green that in certain lights and at certain angles they looked like tiny pools of milk, and the apertures too small in any case to give any access to a reading of his soul. I knew he would not stop looking until he found me.

After consigning Pevenche to Sant'Alvise I hurried to a quiet parish in Santa Croce, where for the second time I rented a room by posing as a recent widow who awaited her inheritance. The story fitted with my naturalistic air of desperation and apparently swollen belly.

I did not leave the house for several days. When I did so, my preparations were elaborate. I was masked and kept my cloak around me. I bulked myself up like a bear with concentric layers of clothes and on top of them all, beneath the ultimate dress, I tied the pregnancy apron from my quack days in London. To make me waddle, I wore a rolled chemise strung between my legs.

After my first anonymous costumed circuit, I flung off all the dresses and petticoats. Dressed only in my chemise, I lay on the bed, panting.

I had done it! I had arrived in Venice, and I had delivered Pevenche into a safe house. No one had detected me, and no one knew my true identity. I was safe. All I had to do was write my letter to Valentine Greatrakes, keep my head down, and wait. I knew that there was a risk that he might call my bluff, but I preferred not to think about that. I saw only sweet hope in that direction of thought. What I must fear lay all around me in the silent streets of Venice: the eyes and ears of Venetians who might betray me.

The sooner I wrote the letter, the sooner I would be delivered from this danger. But something in me stopped me from writing it. My plan had worked perfectly until now, but I still lacked the confidence to use my own words to ask for what I wanted. And so I prevaricated, never even setting pen to paper. Each day for a fortnight I sat at my little desk, dipped the quill in the ink and turned to stone. Eventually, when the darkness made the streets less perilous, I stole out and foraged for some food.

I walked to Zattere, and listened to the water chanting. For hours, I stood there, sniffing the salt and watching the lights extinguish on Giudecca, until the island lay nakedly dark, crooked as a gibbon's arm flung round the promontory of Dorsoduro.

Then I went back to my desk, and did not write the letter.

I drank a little gin, and then a little more.

· 13 ·

A Cordial Caudle

Take sweet Almonds beaten in a Mortar 12; Yolks of Eggs 2;
Conserve of red Roses and Gilly Flowers, each 1 ounce; Aqua
Coelestis half an ounce; Canary Wine, Damask Rose Water, each
half a pint; work them about well together, then strain and add
confection of Alkerms 2 drams; Oil of Cinnamon 2 drops.
It greatly Nourisheth, Recruiteth and Reviveth the Spirits.

Meanwhile the strangest thing was happening with Pevenche.

Instead of screaming and fighting, instead of sulking, instead
of threatening, she settled calmly into life at the convent.

I did not at first go to visit her. I wished neither to witness the
histrionics nor to hear her lamentations. I had endured enough of
her voice and her dull repertoire of self-pity on our journey. I
hoped that the nuns would be generous with the bottles I had left,
for their own sakes. Dottore Velena's opiate was sweet enough to
please Pevenche and I knew that the nuns would have no trouble
administering it. In fact, they would probably have to ration it.

But I received reports from the nuns, and they were good.

After a scant hour of repinings and tears she had asked to be
let out of her cell so that she might dine with her companions.
The next day she made a hearty breakfast and later a substantial
luncheon. In the afternoon she had remarked on the beautiful
smell of almond cakes and asked to see the kitchens where they
were made. There she had been fascinated by the sight of nuns
measuring flour and butter, and stirring powdered almonds into
marzipan paste.

The following morning she asked if she might be able to try
making the marzipan herself, and within three days she was

working with the most accomplished bakers in the kitchen. She proved to have a good touch with all sugared dishes, and her productions were of high quality, her only fault being a tendency to over-sweeten.

Despite her lack of Italian, the other nuns found her a very acceptable companion, and in her way, she was popular among them. They even admired her. The appalling red of her hair, universally despised in London as a fashion item, was optimistically seen as approaching the gorgeous tint of Titian's painted tresses in Venice. Her foreignness and the expensive cut of her clothes meant that she was not classified as a Venetian girl would have been. No one knew her bloodline: Golden Book, *borghese* or peasant. No one countenanced the idea that society might be organised differently outside of Venice. They took her as they found her. She appeared to think very highly of herself, so they did too. Her interest in cooking was viewed as charmingly and cunningly faux-naïve. Her productions were exquisite, and much appreciated. And when she sat at the supper table it was among Cornaros and Mocenigos, the highest-born girls in the convent and those who were most arrant in their pride. The *converse* jostled to wash her sheets.

She did not ask when she would be released. She occasionally asked for more cream and sugar, because she wished to experiment with recipes of her own. And she was soon hosting cake festivals in the convent laundry, with the noble choir-nuns as guests and the *converse* serving. In honour of their new sister, the nuns commissioned a ukulele-shaped baking tray for the kitchen, and in it Pevenche produced the most exquisite *panpepato* flavoured not just with ginger and saffron but also with powdered red sandalwood. She even went down to the orchard with the other nuns to decorate the trees with sugared almonds and candied fruits on the days when young girls were due to come and see the convent. Stupid young girls, such as I had been! Pevenche was already a part of the conspiracy, from the powerful end of the operation.

One more extraordinary thing: Pevenche, tone-deaf to French and German, had begun to chatter in Italian and even Venetian.

I had not bestirred myself to instruct her in Italian. I had assumed it a hopeless task. But the nuns reported that she was proving an able pupil.

Now I heard that she was a veritable queen bee among her set, and that she had begun to rule the social order with an iron hand. The little world of the nunnery, its febrile politics and coiled-up emotions, clearly suited her. While her Italian was still basic, the lack of nuance was an advantage to her, as she was able to press home her superiority in ways that were adapted to her own special kind of bullying. She had taken under her wing one younger noble girl, spurned by the rest on account of her ill-looks, and had taught this child some ideas about dress. The girl was pathetically grateful, and served Pevenche as if she were a duchess.

Now I had no fears for her being seen or reported to the three magistrates of the *provveditori sopra monasteri*. No one outside the Order would actually lay eyes on her. Three times a day she lumbered to the suspended choir-stalls and sang lustily with the other nuns – just 'la-la-la' to their words of devotion, and she had begun to take her ukulele along with her. I wondered at the effect on the congregation of Sant'Alvise of her harsh voice and the squawking of the disembodied strings floating above their heads.

She even lined up with the other nuns to receive communion through a slit in the curtain over a grille beside the altar.

When I went to visit her at the end of the second week, the first thing I noticed was that she had gained a visible amount of flesh. She came into the room warily, and on seeing me did not stoop to a greeting but quickly assumed her usual attitude of disdain. She left it for me to greet her and try to begin a conversation.

I asked how she did, and she looked out of the window. Humiliated, I repeated the question with the servile formality that she preferred in me: 'Your guardian has asked me to inquire as to your condition.' She nodded to acknowledge the question but clearly felt it beneath her to answer such a lowly messenger.

At this point two young nuns burst into the room and Pevenche's face changed completely. It flowered into a smile, and she even took one of the girls by the hand. Then she pointed to me, and scowled. The little nuns erupted into knowing giggles, and I felt myself aged to ninety years by their cheerful disrespect. With a series of hand gestures, Pevenche indicated that she would not occupy herself long with such a paltry object as myself and the girls tripped out of the room.

Left alone with me, Pevenche seemed less sure of herself. She did not meet my eye, but looked at the floor. I saw that she was waiting to hear what I had to say. I noticed she was clutching her ukulele against her belly like a ridiculous toy shield.

It seemed too feeble to explain that I had come merely to see how she was. She would mock me for that pathetic weakness. I envisioned her laughing about it with her new friends. So I said merely, with as much menace as I could convey: 'Now I have seen you are alive, you may go.'

She left without a word, moving faster than I had ever seen her, ducking her fat neck down in a poor approximation of humility. In her rush she dropped the ukulele on the floor, where it issued a more musical complaint than her fingers had ever sent forth from it. She started at the noise but did not stop to retrieve the instrument as she fled. Thoughtfully, I picked it up, thinking it might be useful, marvelling at her panic.

I suddenly realised that what she feared was that I would take her away from there. The irony had not escaped me that the girl was insensible of every service I had done for her except this one – to leave her at Sant'Alvise, the single action of mine that, in my own opinion, fully amounted to a crime against her.

Pevenche seemed altered, not just by her extra weight and evident felicity. She seemed somehow more handsome, or at least less wholly unprepossessing. You could almost see a shadow of beauty in her when she smiled at her young companions.

This gentle thought was immediately electrified by a wild conjecture that came bustling into my tired brain and which I was helpless to repel: that Valentine Greatrakes' devotion to

Pevenche could be explained by the fact that *he* was truly her father. The improvement in Pevenche seemed to make her resemble the person I thought most attractive in this world.

Surely he would still come to me, if only to fetch his child back.

· 14 ·

An Hysteric Nodule

Take Asafoetida half a dram; Castor, Camphire, each 1 scruple;
Oil of Amber half a scruple; mix, and tie up in a rag or piece of
Silk.

   Being often held to the Nose, it helps Vapours and Fits, for it
represses the raging Spirits, drives them back from their wild
excursions and exorbitancies; forces them into order, and hinders
'em from running into Tumults and Convulsive Explosions.

In the end, the letter, so long stopped up inside me, poured out
in a rush. I had meant to draft it point by point, explaining as
briefly as possible why he must meet with me and a priest and
marry me immediately. I had meant to be cool. I had meant to
spell out the fact that this was a marriage of convenience only, to
rid me of certain encumbrances in Venice, and that while I
regretted causing him worry over Pevenche, it had been necessary to achieve my ends. I had meant to preserve a delicate
balance: a stiffened tone of injury underlaid with inescapable
tenderness. My ultimate aim was to make him feel guilty for
forcing me to such lengths, not having the greatness of heart
simply to take me to himself and marry me all those weeks ago,
when the time was ripe and our love perfect.

   I wrote no such thing. I wrote of how I had suffered for his
absence, about how I longed to be in his arms again. I reminisced about our brief time in London, deliberately using words
that had been currency between us then: terms of endearment,
jokes, phrases that still gave off a faint perfume of certain unfor-
gettable moments. I candidly admitted to feelings for him that I
had never experienced before. I told him how I had returned to

London and sought him out, though incognita. I explained, as delicately as I could, that I knew all about his business now, and that I forgave him his deception – as he would surely forgive mine – because everything each of us had done was to one end, which was to find one another again. Subtly, I reminded him of his heroism at the frost fair. Now, I explained, I had dire need of a heroic rescue, for I faced perils too dangerous to explain in a letter.

When the letter was done, I folded it quickly. I did not want to re-read it. I wanted to trust my instincts, not treat them to a surgical examination. I hoped the letter would have the same effect upon the instincts of Valentine Greatrakes.

But how to deliver the letter? There was no one I trusted here, except perhaps the nuns at Sant'Alvise, and they had no reason to be sending couriers to London. If I sent it via a Venetian messenger, he would be questioned at every customs house and how long before the letter was opened and its contents fed back to the wrong people in Venice?

It was Pevenche's new profession as *pasticciera* that gave me my idea. The convent of Sant'Alvise was famous for its marzipan cakes, so famous that even well-informed foreign tourists in Venice sent orders to the bakery. For many years the nuns had produced their own paper boxes decorated with a woodcut of their convent and a smiling angel rising above it. In these boxes they placed twenty-four of their little cakes between delicate sheaves of scented rice paper, cakes so delicious that people were known to consume the entire contents in a single sitting.

Now I asked myself – would it be so strange that an English gentleman, a frequent visitor to Venice, might conceive a craving for those unparalleled delicacies he had tasted in the city, particularly when back in London and forced to wean himself back to the unfortunate local cuisine? Might he then not send for a box of his favourite sweetmeats to console his saddened palate?

So on one of my visits to Pevenche, I begged a box of cakes from the nuns and took it back to my rooms. They had been happy to give it to me, patting my pregnancy apron, 'for the little one, too, of course'. They also pressed on me a can of creamy milk. I carefully lifted the cakes and lined the lower part of the box with my letter. The cakes smelled so good that it was hard to put them all back. Too hard for me. I had eaten four before I knew it. They made me thirsty. I drained the can of milk. Then, disliking its maternal taste, I took a little gin.

I restacked the sheets of lining paper interleaved with cakes and sealed the box. I then packed it in a stout pouch of parchment loosely tied with twine and labelled with the address of Valentine Greatrakes at the depository in Bankside. What a tug of nostalgia I felt, merely writing that name, not just for my lover and our happy time together but even for my eccentric adventure with Dottore Velena and the snug company of that room at the Feathers. I sipped a little more gin, raising my glass in a silent toast to my old colleagues.

In my mind, eye and ear, the Zany lifted a tankard, saying 'Here's to a Glimmering of our Gizzards' as I had seen him do so many times before. I smiled fondly at the memory.

I surveyed my work. There was nothing exceptional about this packet. People despatched such gifts from Venice all the time. The parcel begged: 'Open me, if you must! I am, however, innocent.'

In the sending, the normality of the package was proclaimed by the fact that everyone in Venice knew the boxes from Sant'Alvise. But in receipt the situation would be different. Valentine Greatrakes had no great sweet tooth. He had balked at my jellies and compotes and egg creams, preferring a haunch of beef boiled till the flesh dripped off the bone. He drank beer to my chocolate. His Venetian trade was in stronger substances than little marzipan cakes – he would not have come across the Sant'Alvise delicacies. Or so I hoped.

In my hopeful imaginings the parcel arrived at Bankside and was opened by Dizzom, who would be alert to the mystery of its provision and understand the importance of the contents. He would find the letter and pass it on to his employer, and soon my lover would come to Venice and all would be resolved and made happy again.

I had only to keep myself safe and discreet in the meantime.

And to somehow survive. After paying off the nuns at Sant'Alvise, I was down to my last fifty *lire*. Thinking fifty days the maximum time before my rescue I mentally divided the sum into fifty parts. One *lira* being twenty Venetian *soldi*, I now put myself on a regime of almost poetic frugality. I had already renounced every luxury. I had, of course, long since learned to live without perfume. (I had economised even on the ink, buying an anonymous bottle of powder to mix from a stationer's in Cannaregio, instead of expensive liquid ink. Perhaps I diluted it too much, for it wrote palely, and dried paler, but I told myself it would endure its short journey without further impairment.)

I had eight *soldi* each day to spend on my bed – a tiny room above a tavern, five for a cup of coffee each morning, and seven to eat. I lived on bread and black olives which made me thirsty enough to drink the brackish water instead of craving something more expensive. I rationed myself to one small glass of gin per day, and not merely for economic motives.

On this meagre diet, my stomach was constantly fermenting acid glandular juices and ironically I suffered as if with the early symptoms of pregnancy, including a severe wind colic that distended my belly and pushed out the profile of my pregnancy apron. On my retrenched expenses I could not afford any palliative drugs, but only an extra ration of gin, to soothe the pain.

And there was only gin to warm me against the bora wind that now hauled all the bitter cold of the Russias down to Venice. When you are poor and ill-fed, I realised now, the wind hunts you down alleys and disrespectfully lifts your too-light skirts in ways in which it never victimises the rich in their heavy velvets.

It was fortunate that the *Carnevale* still raged in the city. I was able to walk about in my mask without anyone looking at me curiously. Even pregnant women went masked in this season. I did not draw attention to myself. My apparent state even ensured me indulgent extra titbits on my plate. It was thanks to these that I survived.

Despite the dangers of it, I had need to leave my lodgings every day and go to the place appointed for my rendezvous with my lover. I did not know when he would receive my letter and when he would respond to it. For obvious reasons I had not given him an address at which to write to me directly.

There was always the risk that the letter might have fallen into the wrong hands, and for this reason I could not even be specific about the place of our meeting. I had embodied it in a subtle riddle, a reference to something that only he would decipher. I had decided to make use of his memory of the night when he believed he had found a bat in my bed, a feathered bat that was only my hairpin.

'I shall be waiting for you,' I had written, 'at the place that takes its name from the thing that so falsely frightened you. I shall attend it each day at four, until you come to me.'

Thinking of my dulled hair and the pregnant disguise, I added: 'You will find me changed, except in the part that loves you.' I hoped he would understand the hint.

I had reason to think that he would easily remember the apothecary known as the Black Bat in Santa Croce. I knew that it was the source of some of the most expensive Venetian nostrums. The day I saw the doors yawn open at the Bankside depository, I had glimpsed the shelves devoted to preparations from the Black Bat, and even a replica of the shop sign. I told myself it was not possible that my lover should fail to make the connections.

It was only a question of time now, until the letter reached him and until he came to me. Until then, all I had to do was shelter from the cold and snow, and from Mazziolini and my employers.

But they found me anyway.

One night, crossing the snow-muffled Piazza, I felt myself shadowed.

They have come for me, I thought. *I'll not make it easy for them.*

I walked swiftly into the middle of the square, where the crowd was densest, knowing that if they wanted to take me, they would need to do so discreetly. But my captors were thick among the costumed crowds. A feathered Indian was soon jostling me north across the Piazza, and I found two tall white birds at my shoulders, each with a claw gripping my upper arm. When I turned my head, I saw a Queen of Diamonds, implacably masked, blocking any rear exit.

In my cordon of outlandish creatures I was borne out of the Piazza and into the narrow streets behind. To my horror, I realised that I was being taken towards San Zaccaria. Then I began to scream.

They were too quick for me: a bitter liquid was thrown against my open mouth and, to rid my palate of its vile smack, I had swallowed it before I could stop myself. In a few moments my lips were numb and I was sagging to the ground. I have a dim memory of being carried through the gates of San Zaccaria but the drug had paralysed me. I could not fight. I looked up into the face of the old abbess, horribly aged by the last sixteen years. She said, grimly, 'Yes, it is her.' Then all went dark in a blaze of nausea. I thought I heard the Zany's voice cry out, 'Purr wee gurlie, she's wrackt orf to the lees, now!'

When I woke up again it was because someone was holding a nodule to my nose that stank fulsomely of amber oil and asafoetida. I was no longer in San Zaccaria. Sixteen years had dissolved and I was again in the chamber of the dark *palazzo* where I had lain in the bath and received my original commission.

My old interlocutor again appeared, his head greyer, his eyes harder.

'You have become inconvenient for us,' he said. And once more the other men filed into the room. No one was interested in putting me in the bath. I lay on a vast table, a bitter crust of vomit on my unwiped lips.

'We have some questions to ask you,' he stated, with icy formality, when all were seated.

The first one was: 'Catarina Venier, why did you kidnap your own daughter?'

Part Six

Poterius's Electuary

Take Poterius's Antihectic half an ounce; Haly's powder fresh made 1 ounce and a half; Syrup of Jujubes as much as suffices, mix.

It destroys all manner of exotic, corruptive Sharpness and Asperities of the Blood and Juices; and induces a Balsamic, Soft and Oleose disposition. It's second to none in an Hectic Fever, and may be taken to two or three drams twice a day, with a draught of Asses' Milk.

She did not strike me as a governess. But it so happened that her plans for me fell in with my own.

I never intended to squander my youth and prettiness incarcerated at Mistress Haggardoon's. I knew that the only way out of there was on someone's arm. I had always assumed that arm would be Uncle Valentine's, so it seemed to me that one of his minions would serve just as well.

Said I to myself, 'I must fulfil the divine franchise of this opportunity.'

The journey was tedious – with the poor foolish woman staring at me so fearfully all the way. I could have denounced her at any point: she did not seem to understand that I desired the journey as much as she did. When her nerves fretted her almost to convulsions I tried to calm her with gentle conversation on tranquil subjects. But as the gin sank, so her wits began to swim. Once or twice she lost command of herself and tried to frighten me with bizarre tricks. It was piteous, really. The rest of the time I myself felt strangely drowsy, and the time passed as if in a dream.

When she stopped coming to see me at Sant'Alvise it was a relief. The wretch looked so unbecoming, trussed up like a roasting fowl in those shabby clothes, that I was embarrassed to receive her as my guest. Low blood gives off a certain smell: Venetians can always tell, so I hoped that none of the Mocenigo girls would see her and associate me with this portionless person who had degraded herself to the extent that you could smell the gin on her breath, and see her need for it written all over her face.

And the shame lay not merely in her offences against elegance. One of the nuns explained to me the nature of that swollen belly, and another *wicked* girl, supplementing her giggles with diagrammatic hand motions, made me aware of the squeamish details of the ghastly belly-swelling activity that I intend to avoid all my days.

I believe the poor deluded Jaune-Fleur is irretrievably in love with my guardian. No doubt Uncle Valentine was the begetter of the belly, a horrid thought. And clearly Jaune-Fleur has no idea that he is up to his ears in another lady, the Mimosina Dolcezza of the ICE certificate.

Said I to myself: 'She'd weep a headful of tears if she did!'

I'm sorry for her. Mimosina Dolcezza, whoever she may be, is nothing to me, except that she once stole my Christmas dinner. And Madame Jaune-Fleur is to be thanked for my present, delightful existence at Sant'Alvise, a far superior establishment to Mistress Haggardoon's in every respect.

I feel vastly at home, not just in the convent but on the streets of Venice, where now I go whenever errands to the sugar and spice merchants bring me forth from the beloved portal of the convent. No one but myself can be trusted to evaluate the quality of the merchandise or to haggle a nun's bargain for it. And none but me can tell true Asses' Milk from counterfeit.

I love to walk around this city, which seems strangely familiar. The sight of it soothes every asperity in my blood. The canals run pure sugar syrup in the light of the morning, burnished chocolate in the afternoon, crème de menthe in the evenings. There's always something in the air, sweet and sanative as the breath of a pastry shop and the quality of light, even when the snow falls or evening presses against the window, comforts my eyes. I am ravished with contentment to be here. Of course, for all these excursions I veil myself carefully for I don't want to be happened upon by Madame Jaune-Fleur. It would put her in a dreadful pucker to find me out and about enjoying the liberty of the town.

Uncle Valentine would shortly come to visit me, poor Jaune-Fleur kept babbling.

I rather hope he won't. I have found what I wanted, though a supplemental allowance might sweeten my way a little. This is not one of those sackcloth convents. One may *dress* a little here.

I imagine I'll be hearing that quick step of his on the threshold any day now.

Then I will give him the little gold ring, which I have carefully wrapped in a handkerchief to preserve, shall we say, *all* the evidence. I mean it as a tangible warning, to show him that the woman is capable of violence and he should keep his wits about him if he intends to make a life with her instead of, or as well as, with Mimosina Dolcezza. You know how men are.

There is something about Madame Jaune-Fleur that makes me a little uneasy. I cannot put my finger on it. I am not impatient. I'll work it out at my leisure. Sometimes the truth comes upon one like crime in the night; sometimes it is there smiling when one wakes up in the morning.

London . . . and Venice, February 1786

· 1 ·

An Hemoptoic Draught

Take Plantain water 4 ounces; Wine Vinegar, Syrup of Comfrey, each half an ounce; the white of one Egg beat up, mix.

This is in truth, a Noble, Experimented, and easily parable Remedy. It mightily Refrigerates, Incrassates and puts a restraint on the vehement hot, bubbling, leaping Blood; constringes, purses up, closes and consolidates the apertures of the Vessels.

Back in London, of course his first thought is for Pevenche, safe and bedfast at Mistress Haggardoon's but no doubt morose with neglect.

Dizzom, unusually, is away from the depository when Valentine returns and no one can tell him where the man is. His staff jitter like sparrows and, for some reason that he cannot fathom, not one of them will meet his eye. They do not even seem pleased to see him. They look afraid. He assumes that there has been a little unpleasantness in the borough during his absence – Dizzom is probably off somewhere sorting it out.

This is what happens when a man neglects his business.

Meanwhile, Valentine can use this time to catch up with his ward. He strips, washes and dresses in fresh clothes, happy to feel his skin reunited with the unmistakable fragrance of the Blackfriars laundresses' soap.

He hurries along Marylebone High Street on foot, having despatched the coachman at Oxford Street to buy flowers and comfits for the girl.

At the Academy he fidgets on the doorstep, waiting an unconscionably long time for the maid to answer the bell. Eyes wide, she ushers him into the empty study of the headmistress where he

335

faces another unacceptable hiatus. Twice he moves towards the door, with the object of going to find the girl himself. But something stops him, and he closes his eyelids, and thinks he hears the clatter of carriage wheels and even feels the ground rolling beneath him again. Hastily he reopens his eyes. No, he has really finished his arduous journey. He is truly back in London. Awaiting a headmistress who has no business, given his generosity, to discommode him for the merest second with her tardiness.

You may be sure she'll be hearing about this fact, after I've seen Pevenche.

And when Mistress Haggardoon bustles forth, blinking at him as if to exorcise the vision, what news does he hear? He can scarcely take it in.

'. . . and Paris, and St Petersburg. And Venice,' the headmistress is warbling, through fast-welling tears, as if this mantra will hold off his rage. Clearly, she has guessed from the first news of his arrival at the premises that she is the author of a grave error.

Venice.

What was her name again?

'I wrote it down. Look. Oh, not there. Here. Perhaps not, after all. I can find it in an instant. I always put important things in this drawer, and of course anything to do with dearest Pevenche is *most* important,' the headmistress gabbles with terror; her hands tremble so violently that she cannot insert a finger in the hollow of its tiny handle. Three times she drops the key, dipping her head and shoulders like a manic bird to pick it up from the carpet. The refined odour of her civet perfume is cut through with unladylike sweat.

Valentine strides across the room and rips the drawer out of her desk, scattering its contents in a wide arc and throwing the drawer itself at the mantelpiece. It crashes down into the fire and commences to burn.

Then the headmistress is on her knees, raking through the ruins of gewgaws and trinkets confiscated from various girls over the decades, love-letters to past students, and even an anonymous pornographic *billet-doux* to herself (which she would hardly have kept if she had known that it was sent by the coalman on a dare some fifteen years back). She pauses over it for a heartbeat, wishing her life had turned out otherwise, and that it had not brought her to this moment.

As she scrabbles on the floor, Valentine stands over her, his arms folded, barely holding back the lava of the anger seething in his breast. He does not trust himself to say anything. Once he starts, he will break her in half with the savagery of his words. But meanwhile, he needs the name.

At last she finds it, holds up a blouzy sheet of simpering pink paper on which she herself has written 'Madame Jaune-Fleur Kindness'. Valentine stands stupefied. What does this doggerel mean? 'Fleur', he knows is flower. 'Jaune?' Does it mean 'young'?

It's a nidget I am with foreign lingos. I never can fix 'em in my head.

The headmistress is whittering, 'I *did* observe to the maids that it was a most unusual name, particularly in a governess. "Yellow-Flower". Very whimsical, no? But then of course the lady was a foreigner, and they are apt to be picturesque sometimes in their namings, don't you think? Why, I have a young lady student here, from Portugal even, and she is called . . .'

Valentine silences her with a look. He crumples the paper in his hand, smearing his fingers with ink. The headmistress edges forward with a dabbing handkerchief and an abject expression, but he throws the ball of paper at her, not with force but with contempt. It strikes her perspiring cheekbone and then her left breast before it lands on the floor. Both of them watch it roll towards the grate. Valentine assists its passage with a dextrous kick into the inferno raging round the corpse of the drawer. He knows he should apologise to the headmistress, make amends for the damage, but his tiredness and his humiliation send him trudging out of the room and into the street, head down in ignominy.

His own coach stands in front of him and the coachman is jumping down with a velvet box of comfits in one hand and in the other a plump bouquet of hothouse blooms.

'For the young lady,' he says jovially. 'I hope she likes 'em, sir. They smell so sweet. And the colour!'

But Valentine is ripping the bouquet apart, discarding the roses and the carnations and the baby-breath, until all that is left is a core

337

of little yellow tufts nodding on dark wood. He stares at them for a moment and flings them into the path of an oncoming carriage.

He feels stupid as a brute, his tongue dozed to slurry. A mew of outrage spills from between his clenched teeth. From the corner of his eye he sees the clammy forehead of the headmistress pressed against her parlour window pane.

'You're not the only one, madam!' he shouts. 'The world is stuffed with fools she's made.'

In terror, the headmistress retracts her head and the window clatters with the swing and slap of her retreating jet earrings.

The coachman knits his nervous fingers in the horse's mane for comfort. Staring at his employer, he whispers in a broken voice:

'You don't like mimosa-flower, sir? You should have said.'

· 2 ·

A Balsam called Mirabile

Take Frankincense 2 ounces; Mastick, Cloves, Gallingale, Mace,
Cubebs, each half an ounce; Aloes Wood 1 ounce; powder and
mix them with Honey half a pound; Venice Turpentine 1 pound,
and Brandy, as much as is usually required to extract a Tincture.
Distill them in Balneo; and when you have got all the clear
Water, shift your Receiver, and then you'll have next a noble red
Balsam, which rectifies . . .

Valentine Greatrakes is incapable of speech, so his driver sets off
on a circuitous route that he hopes will cool his master's hot head.
After half an hour's fruitless perambulations, without any orders
from the dumbfounded carriage, the driver is struck with inspiration and takes him to The Man Loaded with Mischief in Oxford
Street. At the sight of its painted sign – a man carrying a magpie,
a monkey and a woman with a glass of gin – Valentine disgorges
himself from the carriage without a word and slides into the familiar tavern, where he finds a companionless corner and an engaging
armchair, and sits down to think.

What does she want, herself?

This is the only thing that Valentine wishes to know.

He must force his mind to enter into the deep waters and false
channels of her own.

The actress has gulled him. She has raked up a great dunghill of
lies for him. She has taken the girl – why? To extort money? Was
it all about that, in the end? Or is it to punish him for neglecting to
marry her? Has she found out about the murder of Gervase
Stintleigh? Did she in fact love the political fop, and is it that she
now wishes to avenge him?

Valentine recalls how they had argued about Pevenche. How the actress had accused him of being twiddled by the wiles of a little girl.

A little girl! He grimaces to realise how his white lie has been exposed. Mimosina Dolcezza has now seen with her own eyes that 'Baby P.' is somewhat mature for her epithet. In fact, he reflects, Pevenche is considerably larger than her kidnapper, longways and widthways.

He takes comfort from the fact that he surely has not long to wait for an explanation. The one thing he knows – better than anyone – is that kidnappers soon reveal their requirements, and that they are usually of an urgent and financial nature.

He returns to the depository, where he is not sparing of the lights and livers in his conversations. A tremulous Dizzom, still besuited in his grey travel furs, fusses over his master until the latter sends him flying with a brusque gesture and then apologises, again and again, in an absent-minded way. He asks repeatedly, emphasising each of the five words in sequence: 'There is no ransom letter?'

Dizzom tells him of the inquiries launched, the embassies made, the messages despatched to contacts all over London and the Continent since he discovered the abduction two days after it happened.

'I was so sure,' sniffs Dizzom, 'that we would find them that I did not trouble you with the news. I hoped to tell you the problem and the solution at the same time.'

It is unlike Dizzom to put a false gloss upon things.

He is so sincere in his abjection that Valentine has no desire to punish him further. Dizzom has been doing everything that he himself would have done. He has even taken the packet to Calais to investigate all possible inns: this is where he had been on his master's return. They had missed one another by a few hapless hours.

But nothing has emerged. Nothing at all.

He tries to lose himself in work. That should sustain him until Dizzom's researches begin to bring forth results. Without Pevenche and her caprices, he has more time on his hands and he finds them full. The Venetian nostrum is making its demands: what he set in motion before his departure has now acquired an imperious momentum. Estimates of costs are starting to arrive from the bottlers and the distilleries in Venice. He needs more items to trade for the bottles.

To pay for the wool that will finance the new nostrum, he has decided to go into the anti-procreation business. For some time he has been interested in the *Capotes Anglaises*, made from the blind guts of lambs. He has Dizzom set up an experimental studio in one of the empty rooms in the depository. Daily he strides among the chattering young ladies hired for washing and drying the intestines and then rendering them soft and pliable by rubbing them between two palms anointed with bran and almond oil. Among them is Sylvia Grimpen, whose mantua business has fallen on hard times, and who is looking hungry. Remembering the incident with Pevenche at the Bond Street coffee house, he avoids her eyes, but he tells Dizzom to put a little extra something in her pay.

And still no letter arrives from Mimosina Dolcezza. He hates her and he misses her too, and he misses her viscerally, and painfully. Without her, and without news of her, he's dangling like a frayed rope in the water. He does not go to take his once-accustomed balsam at the Seven Dials. He cannot contemplate it. It does not escape him that his manufacture of devices for carefree love-making is most bitterly ironical in view of the fact that the one woman he desires is not available to him.

There is something wrong. The ransom letter should have arrived by now, unless the delay is specifically calculated to reduce him to the weakness of desperation.

It doesn't take three weeks to dip a pen in ink and put a letter on a piece of paper, does it?

Again and again, he says to Dizzom, 'I just can't understand it. What are her intentions? Does she do this to drive up the price?' Seeing Dizzom's strained face, and ashamed of his own weakness, he tries to make light of their trauma: 'Dizzom, dear friend, it's all dark as your grandfather's nostril to me.' He attempts a comical elevation of his brows, but his lip trembles underneath.

This personal frustration leads him into new professional paths with the Venetian nostrum. Out of this darkness churning inside him Valentine conjures up an inspired idea that sparkles with potential profit. Until now he has conceived the Venetian nostrum as the usual universal specific, able to cure the habitual infinite list of complaints, simply endowed with the added glamour of a beautiful bottle and alleged Venetian provenance. But in his misery Valentine has now perceived a hitherto unsupplied niche in the market. He is groping his way towards an original idea: a nostrum specific to the enhancement of the act of love.

The Venetian nostrum shall be a love potion! It shall envigour even the most depleted of libidos!

The mind of Valentine Greatrakes twirls with words for his handbill, and the title of the new creation is moulded and remoulded in his brain. He whispers aloud combinations of alluring words. By the end of the day he has dictated a list as long as his desk, and scribbled out half the attempts. By the next, he has narrowed the title down to seven key words, which he pens with a flourish in red ink:

Sovereign
Empirick
Venetian
Balsamick
The Remedy

He lays his head on the desk. When he raises it again, long minutes later, the words are staining his cheek.

Two weeks later, and he is still deliberating over titles for his Venetian nostrum, when Dizzom hands him a disintegrating letter dusted with icing sugar and smelling of marzipan. Valentine knows he should be asking questions as to the provision of the letter and the manner of its delivery but he is too feverish to be sensible. Or to listen to Dizzom's quiet urgings that something is amiss, must be explained and dealt with. It is like his first meeting with the actress herself. He wants possession unburdened with information.

He takes the letter to his lips and sniffs all along its fore-edge. He draws back in shock. Yes! Its authenticity is entire and faultless. Her every note was always perfumed with a delicate sweetness, just like this letter. Its narcotic aroma hangs around his face now. It must be from her, of her. It is only after fondling it with his lips, fingertips and nostrils that he finally looks in detail at its contents.

And looks again, in disbelief.

The letter from Mimosina Dolcezza bears no recognisable words. Somewhere on its travels it has suffered an immersion, perhaps, or the natural grease of the almond paste has invaded the ink like a cancer and replaced the words with its own vital substance. Or the ink has proved evanescent and faded prematurely. How could she economise on such an important item as ink? She must be in dire straits!

To think of her in bad circumstances! I'm sick as a small hospital just wondering what's befallen her.

Only now does he hear Dizzom's discreet cough and feel his friend's kind eyes upon his trembling back which, in response to this tragedy, has broken out in welts down which eddy long tongues of sweat.

'I believe I can help, Valentine,' murmurs Dizzom. 'Would you let me handle the letter, boy? Would you let me try?'

Valentine does not wish to hand over the letter. Not one fibre of him inclines to let go of it.

Dizzom gently prises it from his hands. Valentine Greatrakes flinches as the decayed letter is placed on a sheet of board reminiscent of the horrors of the operating theatre. He hovers, barely restraining himself from snatching it back.

Understanding how Valentine positively needs to keep touching the letter, Dizzom asks him to hold the top two corners while he performs his ministrations, and he keeps talking in a soothing voice, explaining every action before he undertakes it, like a tooth-puller who prepares his patient for the wrench.

Dizzom thoughtfully consults a cupboard, makes a selection and places a series of bottles on the table with ritualistic solemnity. He thrusts a soft tallow candle on to a pricket and lights it. Then he reaches for a large egret quill, uncorks one bottle and dips it in. He explains: 'First you cover the letters with philogisticated alkali – spreading it thus with a feather, like this, look, thin as a poor gel's shawl.'

Valentine cranes his neck, and grimaces with disappointment.

Dizzom reassures him: 'Indeed, no sensible change of colour results immediately, but just see . . . Now, with the addition of a diluted mineral acid . . . I use marine, but vitriolic and nitrous will also serve you to a nicety, my dear – and as you observe, the letters have changed very speedily to this mighty blue colour, of great and beautiful intensity, beyond comparison stronger and more vivid than it was even on the day it was written.'

As he watches this alchemy, Valentine stands with his mouth open. When the words bloom on the paper he cries out and makes to seize it, but Dizzom halts him by pointing to letters already starting to merge into one another. The blue is now out of control, threatening to eat every inch of the paper and overwhelm the words again! Valentine groans.

But Dizzom continues: 'Fear not. We have a remedy also for this. To stop this blue from spreading, we must quickly apply the blotting paper near the letters so as to imbibe the superfluous liquor.'

He dabs at the page with tiny scraps of blotting paper, which are soon speckled blue. There is frantic activity for a few minutes and then Dizzom stops and surveys his work. The letters are stable.

Valentine breathes, 'Is it safe to hold now?'

'Yes, indeed.'

And in a moment the fragile paper is snatched up and secreted in his breast, as he stumbles away to the dim privacy of his bedroom.

He reads the letter standing by the window, again sitting on his bed, and then he runs down the stairs and walks to the river, to read it again out of doors, as if natural light will verify its contents.

The denizens of Bankside watch their favourite son and see his shoulders shaking. Oblivious to their clucks and sympathetic eyes, he strides back to the depository.

The letter has made him weep. It makes him dizzy. It makes him wild. Yes, she is in Venice now – no, she was not there when he searched the town the first time – and she suggests that he makes his way in that direction again with all possible speed.

It is not the letter he expected.

· 3 ·

A Foment for the Pain of Haemorrhoids

Take Onion, Linseed, each 4 ounces; Herbs Henbane, Toad flax,
Tarrow, Mullein, each 2 handfuls; boil in Water 3 quarts to 2
quarts; in the strain'd liquid dissolve Opium 2 drams.

It relaxeth the cruel tension of the Vessels, obtunds the
Acuteness of Pain, melts down and discusses those viscid and
grumous Feculencies, that lay Obstructions and Excite Tumors:
And lastly, it repels the Inundation of the Blood.

The black humour of his situation does not escape Valentine
Greatrakes, hurtling the other way down roads he has so recently
traced homeward.

In less than three weeks he is making the same arduous journey, still beset with a cough and now with an ominous soreness
in his nether parts – and for what? On the strength of scarcely
credible words wrung from a greasy scrap of paper. Yet he's
cursing the notion that caused him to run all the way home
from Venice, only to find the gold is still waiting for him at the
wrong end of the rainbow. If only he had not lost courage and
stayed a little longer. He has worked at the timings of it – she
must have left London just days after he fled Venice. They must
have passed each other at some point on their opposite journeys,
even rested at the same inns, eaten off the same hostelry's
pewter.

*That is, of course, if she's not acting the lapwing, and leading me away
from the nest, and the girl safely stowed in London all the while?*

Mimosina Dolcezza has hinted that she has answers to more
mysteries than she has cared to name in writing.

This time, at least, he can admit that he seeks the actress. It is no

345

shame to him now to say that he is going after her. A letter like that! And she has Pevenche!

Well, the women are physically safe, he tells himself again and again. He has already resolved that the actress shall not have it all her own way. It is his turn to be in control of the timing. Having manipulated him like a marionette, she shall herself now know the agony of waiting without explanation. He has no intention of going straight to the Black Bat. *Oh no. Indeed not.* First he will find out who she really is. When he condescends to meet her at the appointed spot, he will show that he's not at all the halfwit she takes him for.

That is definite. That goes without saying. I'll not be running to her with the intention of greeting her with caressing and kind words. Not till I do it in my own time. In the meantime, if I saw the devil running down the street with her crosswise in his mouth, I wouldn't be after him to drop her.

And it does not escape Valentine that the actress has taken upon herself an awkward arrangement.

Pevenche would annoy a saint, he thinks with a smile, *the hinges of her tongue clattering away without thinking of stopping. Let the actress have the care of that one for a while, why don't I? She'll soon see the error of her harshness to me on that score.*

He smiles: *It was no great masterpiece of planning, was it? To steal the girl.*

He contemplates the unlikely scenario that Pevenche has taken to her kidnapper like a calf to the teat, that she rejoices in her company.

No, Pevenche is never well disposed to female strangers. Or men for that matter. When she's a little older something drastic will need to be done to find her a husband.

He laughs wryly at himself. Pevenche – married?

The girl hasn't the titter of a wit about her. She knows as much about being charming as a pig does about a clean shirt. She's not behind the door when it comes to telling people disagreeable things about themselves. She has not the kind of nature that dreams of love.

And her size!

Most men would be like a pimple on a hill to her.

It does not bear thinking about, Pevenche undressed for love, all those laps and dewlaps trapping moisture. He realises that she's

346

probably never been touched, never charmed a hug out of Tom since she was a baby, never seems to want one from anyone else. Perhaps she's embarrassed at her size. Perhaps no one may hug Pevenche or they'll embarrass her by discovering her topography.

He promises, *When I see her again, I myself will be giving the girl a proper hug. It's not her fault.* People always use Pevenche for their own motives. Both Tom and the actress took her up to serve themselves, not for her own sake or out of any love for her. *Is it any wonder that the girl is awkward?*

He will gather them both to himself soon enough. But the agony of impatience is upon him and he needs a distraction.

His brain is bruised with thinking about the kidnap. The going's brutal on all the roads. His eye is so tic'd with tiredness that it runs hither and thither like a fly. As the carriage rattles and pounds down the roads, grinding his tender buttocks, he turns his mind back to unravelling the mystery of Tom's death.

There have been new developments. It has come to his attention, via Dizzom's inquiries, that the dark-haired Italian man who shadowed Mimosina Dolcezza at Tom's wake has also been seen in London in his absence, and that this man has been making inquiries about the business of Valentine Greatrakes and the manner of his relations with the actress.

Dizzom sent men to intercept this Italian, but he evaded them, and the theory is that he too has now gone back to Venice, where he reports to some kind of underworld lord, some kind of Italian Valentine Greatrakes. But decked out in Venetian robes of state.

On hearing this, Valentine had summoned all those of his men who had seen the Venetian spy with their own eyes at the viewing of Tom's corpse. The memory of the scene with Cecilia Cornaro had prompted in him a stream of questions. *Neck long or short? Hair straight or curled? Eyes long or wide?*

The men, at first confused, soon fell into the game with gusto. They argued roundly among themselves, but when an answer finally came it was definitive and universally accepted. After a scant hour, Valentine had folded up a list of features so detailed that his own recollection of the man had been wonderfully refreshed. This list now lies in his valise and he will make use of it as soon as he has liberated Pevenche and . . . dealt with . . . Mimosina Dolcezza.

All the way through France, Valentine plans those dealings, sadly distracted by the pains of a crop of haemorrhoids he can no longer pretend away, especially as they burn like torches with every rasping cough. It's as if there's a pulley and trap inside him solely devoted to wrenching his neck and unscrewing his spine. That cough of his has thickened. His companions are a noisome lot, who appear not to calculate the benefits of breath-comfits or soap. The foetid air of the carriage stuffs his loaded bronchia with a fresh income of phlegm. He coughs up greenish slime with each gusty sneeze. His nostrils are so impacted that he must breathe solely through his raw throat. After a while even the cough is besieged in his lungs – except at night, when it racks his sleep with its imperative effusion. He'd never stop if he had his way, but each evening the coach disgorges him at sordid but compulsory lodgings, some pasha always occupying all the best rooms with his secretaries and blackamoor footmen.

In the carriage on the last stage, from Padua, his discomfort peaks. Someone has packed a case of china carelessly, and it rattles without cease. The clinking of the china starts to chime with the jostling of his vertebrae, and his cough wakes up and adopts the rhythm, so he's barking like a choleric puppy.

At Mestre he urges the gondola forward, first with gesticulations to the gondolier and then with imperceptible thrustings of his own body, despite the pain this occasions in his trews.

Although he remains unaware of it, Valentine communicates with great facility in Italian. He has that exuberant poetry of gesture that is normally reserved for their race. When he shrugs, it is with their fervent resignation; if he smoked, it would be with their avidity. Now that he is in a hurry, he expresses it with his hands, his feet, his nose, his eyes. The whole quayside at Mestre is alert to the fact that here is an Englishman who needs to be in Venice *this instant*, despite the distraction of a woman bewailing a case of broken china just unloaded from a carriage.

The sky is juicy, white and luminous as a blind man's eyeball. It makes his hot head ache. All the way through the oblating water he counts the three-legged *bricole* that rise up like the truncated legs of outsize wading birds. He counts the vanilla-pod gondolas behind and before him. He counts the forty shades of green and blue in the waves. He counts the church towers pinpricking the horizon. He counts the gulls crying the news of his arrival. He counts the days he has spent apart from Mimosina Dolcezza.

By the time they reach the town itself, he is clutching the sides of the gondola, for a storm has swelled up to welcome him back to town. Thick thrills of lightning illuminate the Grand Canal. Rain boils into it. Like an impatient mother, waves are combing the long-eared seaweed that grows from the banks. Two weeks of painful trotting are erased from his mind. He is back in Venice.

And there is Smerghetto, waiting magically on the landing at San Silvestro, the faintest frown detectable between his brows, because while he is always happy to see Valentine Greatrakes, he does not like the sound of that cough and he knows that it is not exactly business that has brought his master back so soon.

· 4 ·

A Draught for a Catarrh

Take Coltsfoot water 6 ounces, white Sugar Candy powder'd 6 drams; Yolks of 2 Eggs, having beat them up together, and set well.

This Draught usually gives great Relief in a (let me call it) Guttural Rheumatic and Evening Cough, caused by catching Cold, which is pretty quiet all day, but returns at Night, especially when one lies down in Bed, incessantly disturbing, and vexatiously hind'ring Rest. For by reason of its sweet unctuous Mucilage, it so defends the Larynx, that it feels not the pricking of the sharp irritating Serum, and so staves off the Cough, and dallies away the hour, 'till at length, the time of Coughing is slipp'd, and Sleep steals on.

That same afternoon he takes the list of the Italian's features to the studio of Cecilia Cornaro. The girl is dozing on her *divano* when he enters, and eyes him with a sleepy good humour, without raising her head from its yellow silk cushion.

'Ah, *Signor* Englishman, back to see me? You have something new for me?'

There is no mistaking the pleasure in her voice. Three months ago, this would have been enough to plunge Valentine in pleasant speculations, but his nerves are worn to transparency and his eyes are gritty from lack of sleep. His rear end burns, and his cough, thickset and heavy in the daylight hours, is prancing in a lively fashion now, ready for its nocturnal pillaging of his viscera. He cannot conceive of giving pleasure, so he renounces the thought of taking it. And whatever Cecilia Cornaro intends by that softly mewing voice, he will not be distracted from his primary object.

No woman has been able to do that, he reflects, since he first laid eyes on Mimosina Dolcezza.

'I – I would like you to try again with the portrait,' he says, between coughs.

'Ah,' she pronounces. She has already risen from the divan and splashed water on her face. Droplets cling to her curls and she shakes them off. 'What's so different from last time, Mister Lord Valentine Greatrakes? Exactly? Remember,' and her voice is low and dangerous now, 'I failed you before.'

He finds it hard to meet her eyes then; instead his own wander over the walls lined with painted faces. When last he came it had been night, and those faces bore the unmistakable look of sensual satiety. By contrast, in daylight, these same visages seem eager and desirous, even anxious to be about the business of love, lest it escapes them before the sun sets.

Cecilia Cornaro is awaiting his answer in no very patient manner. He knows she adores a novelty, so he offers her the new thing first.

'Now I would like you to draw a man for me. I have all the features.'

He flourishes the list like a child who has completed a laborious item of scholarship. Even that eddy of air provokes a fit of coughing. The artist turns her back on him and busies herself in a cupboard that seems to be a larder. She brings raw eggs and various powders and syrups to the table. She breaks the eggs into a goblet and stirs them vigorously. He thinks she is mixing up an egg tempera to commence the portrait, but she surprises him by thrusting it into his hand.

'Drink,' she says.

No one in the world addresses Valentine Greatrakes in this peremptory manner. Above all, he is used to more caressing tones in a woman. But he wants her to draw the murderer, so he drinks up the potion, which is loathsomely sweet and reeks of coltsfoot.

'A man?' she says, snatching up this list. 'Have you seen him yourself? Could you verify what I do?'

'Yes, indeed. I can see him even now!' Valentine is so weary that he almost thinks that the ghost of the murderous Venetian floats in front of him, transported from the scene of Tom's corpse in the depository. So carefully has he imprinted the man on his memory that it is almost impossible to evacuate the image from his mind. He takes back the sheet of paper and reads her the list, embellishing it with new inspiration. She rapidly transcribes his words into Venetian on a leaf of a blank book.

In moments, the girl has set up a piece of paper on her easel and is sketching with charcoal. Swiftly she covers the page with an outline cross-hatched with small lines. Repeatedly consulting her translation, she adds details. Her hand hovers over the sketch like a hummingbird. She asks him to read again from his own list. She is troubled with a few words of English, and he is obliged to explain them to her.

Watching the head materialising on her paper, Valentine knows that he has his man now. He is itching to rip that cruel face off her easel and to hand it to the *truncheoni* who will soon be on the trail like bloodhounds. No, those drumbling boys will never get it right. He will do it himself. The man is as good as found. In any case he doesn't dare ask Cecilia Cornaro to grind out copies of this sketch. He has another favour to ask her, a more important one, an unusual one, of the kind it gives her so much pleasure to bestow.

He knows she is fascinated by him. This makes him shy. He has already presumed on her too much, and he guesses that she will not accept mere monetary payment. He will have to think of something more unusual than that to reward her. Novelty is the wine of life to this girl.

But his own need is too great to be contained: 'I have had a thought. I presume that you keep studies of all the ladies you paint. You told me once that all the beautiful women of the city come to you while they are still lovely, so that there is a permanent memento of their beauty.'

She nods, smiling. Valentine does not realise it but he has just uttered four sentences without a cough.

He asks, 'Rich and poor?'

'Noble and gutter. The Golden Book families come to add another little face to their family tree. The poor ones, if they are beautiful, become the mistresses of rich men, who also want to immortalise the fact that they once were wealthy enough to bed such a lovely creature. A different kind of investment.'

'And do you keep studies, as I thought?'

She nods. She can see what he is seeking.

'Could we . . . could I look through them?'

'Do you realise how many women I have painted? Also, I keep here the studies of my old master, Antonio, who used to be the most famous portrait artist in Venice. Before me, that is. His studies have preserved many family likenesses that I keep for my researches when I cannot myself discover what has gone into the making of a face.'

'I have as much time as it will take.'

'*Va bene*,' she smiles. 'If she is to be found, then I am sure she will be here.'

She lights a row of candles and sets them on the table, then opens the window to monitor the water, the noise of which has risen noticeably.

'There's a high tide coming,' she tells him. 'Does anyone need to know where you are?'

He shakes his head – Smerghetto always already knows where he is – and moves to the window himself, looking down on the water that has started to steal the lower parts of the *palazzi*. He knows it is a childish thing, but Valentine has a foreign tourist's love, a child's craving for *acqua alta*. He thrills to feel the water churning up under the city, and to see it spill into the squares. He loves the drama and *confusione*. When he hears the water rising, he imagines the vagrant hands of the waves reaching out to haul themselves up to dry land. Millions of tiny hands, all grasping greedily at the inner edges of the island, as if trying to better themselves. When an *acqua alta* starts to abate he always grieves a little.

Cecilia Cornaro walks over to a huge cupboard and flings open the double doors. Floor to ceiling, Valentine beholds neatly stacked sheets of paper contained in large leather portfolios.

'So these are all the people you've painted? You and Antonio?'

She laughs. 'No, these are just some of the women!'

353

And she walks to another cupboard, and flings open its doors. 'And here are some more. And I'm not yet done.'

A fourth and a fifth cupboard are opened, all similarly stacked.

Valentine quails. He had not imagined such a work as raking through these sheaves. And he is already worried. What if looking at portraits is like sniffing at perfumes: after four or five the impression becomes blurred?

Cecilia Cornaro says: 'Are you sure?'

But what choice has he? He is determined to find his lover.

He sits at a desk and pulls three candlesticks towards him.

'How are they arranged?' he asks, wondering if some sifting might be done in advance. For example, perhaps blondes may already be separated from brunettes.

Cecilia Cornaro does not mitigate his task.

'By family, for the noblewomen and *borghese*, and by the names of their noble lovers, for the courtesans.'

He mislikes the last category, hopes that he does not need to look at such faces, or that he shall not find that of Mimosina Dolcezza among them.

'Family,' he says in a confident voice. 'Let us start alphabetically.'

And so he works his way through the Golden Book of Venice, sees all that the city has to offer in the way of blue-blooded and middle-class beauties. He finds that he likes the strong, equine style of the Civran and Flangini women, but that the Mocenigos have too much chin and the Morosinis are too heavy-lidded for his taste. The Soderinis are appallingly plain. By the time he gets to the Vendramin ladies he is worn out with lips and eyes and noses, and he is getting frightened. So close to the end of the alphabet of noblewomen and still he has not seen the face that he is seeking, or has he indeed become blind with too much seeing and already passed her by? Worse, is she to be found in the folders of the courtesans?

But when he opens the Venier folder, his breath quickens. In his very first Venier he sees a slight resemblance to Mimosina Dolcezza. He holds it up to the light. It is not her, but there is some cousinly blood running in the veins of this woman. He picks up another, and there it is again, that trace of her lineaments, something about the eyes and also about the nostrils.

354

Cecilia Cornaro, who has finished her sketch of the murderer, is watching him with interest.

'You have found something?'

'I think she's a Venier.'

Cecilia Cornaro makes a low sound at the back of her throat; it seems to indicate that she is impressed. The Veniers, she tells him, are the bluest of the blue bloods.

He lingers over every Venier portrait. Of course it may be a long time since she was painted, so she could have changed. But how? These women are uniformly elegant, suave and well informed of their own superiority. While they have approximations of her features, none of them has the febrile energy of Mimosina Dolcezza, and none has her vulnerability.

He asks Cecilia Cornaro, 'How could a Venier lady end up as an actress?'

She too is mystified. 'I never heard of such a thing.'

She bends over him as he looks, enlivening the search with scraps of personal history about the women she has painted. 'Mistress of the French ambassador,' she observes, or 'Lover of her sister's husband!'

They seem a libertine lot, the Venier women.

Valentine detests the thought.

In the end he finds her. A piece of paper slips into his hand, just like any other, but it is she, Mimosina Dolcezza, real as life, though some years younger, and he has pressed his lips to it before he can restrain himself.

Cecilia Cornaro gently asks if she might see what he has found. He has whipped it up so quickly that she was not able to look.

When he hands it to her, the artist's face darkens.

'This is one of Antonio's, but I know it well. That is Catarina Venier, from nearly twenty years ago. She was a piece of work, that girl! A melodrama every minute, would never sit still, Antonio told me. You see the blurring round the chin. She changed her expression all the time. Every time he looked up, there was a different face there. He felt as if she was making fun of him. In the end he asked for her parents to attend, and he begged them to discipline her. Like Antonio, I do not care to intervene with silly adolescent

355

girls. It is too boring: they are all precisely the same in their affectations and they all know the same amount of nothing. Anyway, Antonio explained to Ippolita and Carlo Venier that her bad behaviour was their problem, not his.'

Valentine stares at the young face of his lover. He cannot bring himself to think of her as 'Catarina'. And it is simply not possible that thirty-five is the age of Mimosina Dolcezza. That would make her just ten years younger than himself. He looks back at the sketch. Its lines are less certain than those of the other studies.

'This is not finished, is it?' he asks. She shakes her head, her expression muted.

'What happened in the end?' he wants to know.

'Ah, that is something I'm not likely to forget. Antonio often told the story. She made the most tremendous scene, an outrageous fit of hysterics, because her father asked her to wear a piece of the family jewellery. She sneered at it, and screamed that it was ugly, and she would never wear it. She said she hated diamonds. Then she clawed at her throat and ripped the necklace off her neck and threw it out of the window. It fell in the canal, and that was the end of it, of course.'

'And the end of the portrait too?' asks Valentine, flushing as he remembers the actress's reticence when presented with his diamond brooches.

'Yes. Her father bundled her out of the room, and she was never brought back.'

'Do you know what happened to her? Did she marry?'

Cecilia Cornaro's face is kind, but it is clear that she has information that will cloud rather than clear the mystery.

'Yes, she married, in a sense. She became a bride of Christ. Antonio told me that after that scene her parents put her into a convent and that she has never been seen in public again.'

'Which convent?'

'It must have been San Zaccaria,' she said in a hard voice. 'It's the richest one. That's where the Veniers bury their living daughters.'

· 5 ·

A Balsamic Bolus

Take Conserve of red Roses, Lucatellus's Balsam, each half a
dram; Balsam of Peru 3 drops, mix.

It's a prevailing Medicine against an inveterate Cough, and
recent Consumption, Spitting of Blood, Dysentery, Contusion;
and wheresoever the Vessels being opened, or broken bleed
inwardly.

While he has gazed at women's faces the tide has risen over the
stones of the city and renounced them again. He walks back
through the freshly baptised streets and he too feels reborn in this
new state, a state of information. He knows who his lover is.

In London he has no eyes, he thinks, or at least dull, insensible
organs in their place. In Venice, he sees so much more. It is as if
the city speaks to him in a purely visual language, all the clearer
because her spoken one is impenetrable to him. On this walk, illuminated by the night's events, the salt efflorescence of the bricks
speaks to him of perilous high waters that the young Catarina
Venier once watched from her *piano nobile* window, and the black
teeth of the loggias recount insupportably humid summer days
when she took refuge there. There are salt-weeping bricks in
London, and loggias too, but they are inscrutable, or passive.
Valentine never notices them.

He turns the new truth over and over in his head, like a shiny
coin in an impoverished hand.

He is not displeased – in fact, he is gratified – to learn that she
is a noblewoman, although he finds it hard to believe. He felt so
close to her: there was no distance at all. He has never mated outside his class, and had supposed the sensations would be different.

357

He did not feel instinctively deferential towards her, except in normal ways with regard to her femininity. Perhaps it is true, something he has always liked to believe: that there is a natural nobility in human beings that can transcend their births and circumstances. 'Catarina' has proved the ephemeral nature of class by floating downwards, he by rising upwards in his great material success.

It begins to rain without mercy, flaking down out of the wet heavens, so hard that small dogs must be carried, or else be swept away in the sudden rivers that still overflow the streets. His stockings are sodden, his shoes shipwrecked. He is breathing rain and choking on it. Rain is washing the pupils of his eyes faster than he can wipe it away with fingers so sodden that it is as if he is distilling teardrops from beneath his nails.

The downpour ceases abruptly, and instantly an impossible volume of birdsong is gushing from the stone city. It follows him all the way home, swelling in greeting as he enters the garden of his headquarters, nosing through the frisking butterflies still jewelled with raindrops.

Valentine takes the two portraits back to his room, and lies down on his bed. He has propped the papers up against a candelabra on the table, and he looks now from one to the other: a beautiful blonde girl and a dark, refined-looking man.

Of course they have nothing to do with one another. It was mere coincidence that placed them together in the room where Tom's blood suddenly burst from his breast. Mimosina Dolcezza – Catarina, that is – had come to seek out her lover and a sweet reconciliation after a meaningless quarrel. The murderer had come to revel in the spectacle of his handiwork, and to confirm its efficacy.

And the girl in the portrait does not look much like a nun. He asks himself again: how could a Venetian nun become an actress? The scenario is so unlikely that he can find no possible logic to it. He longs to hear her own explanation: now that he has got this far, he is sure that face to face, lip to lip, in the quiet intimacy of their bedchamber, she will soon tell him the rest of her story. He has this cherished appointment to keep at the Black Bat when the mystery is solved. Soon, surely, the wait will be over.

He turns to the man's portrait, so deftly rendered that he growls in his throat to behold it.

'I'll see you whimpering,' he tells the face aloud.

The candle drops wax on to young Catarina Venier's portrait. Swiftly he removes the candelabra and instead sets the two portraits up against the paper box that Dizzom has insisted that he bring with him, on the absurd hunch that it might provide a clue. 'This box could be a message, too, or a clue in itself, you know,' he had suggested anxiously. Dizzom often has these portentous fancies; Valentine hates to throw cold water on them, even when they are as far-fetched as this one. So merely to please Dizzom he has brought the useless box. It is a white card creation with a blue woodcut that shows a church of some kind with an angel hovering above it. It once contained some marzipan cakes and the letter from 'Catarina'.

And, he reminds himself sharply, that letter also concerns the whereabouts of his poor little ward, Pevenche.

· 6 ·

Peruvian Antihectic Lozenges

Take fine powder'd Bark of Peru 1 ounce and a half; Balsam of Capive 2 drams; Sugar of Roses (dissolv'd in compound Wormwood Water) 8 ounces; with Mucilage of Gum Tragacanth make Lozenges, each weighing 2 drams.

The Communicator of these saith, Lozenges are a pretty pleasant sort of Medicine, and fit for delicate nice Persons, that must have their Palates complimented, as well as their Distempers cured. These are good in Hectic Fevers, Consumptive Coughs, difficulty of Breathing, and the like Symptoms.

Valentine Greatrakes goes looking in churches.

He knows that he should go straight to San Zaccaria, but he cannot bring himself to do so. It is easier to furnish himself with this simpler errand. Cecilia Cornaro has told him that San Zaccaria is the oldest and noblest convent in Venice: Smerghetto now informs him that its nuns are the most corrupt and venal, the worst whores and beanflickers. A fortress of hard, clever, hoity-toity women: an incontrovertible instinct tells him not to look for her there. If she indeed once upon a time escaped from the place, this will not reflect well on those charged with the operation of the convent. They will furnish him only with obfuscations and lies, humiliating him as much as possible in the process.

Meanwhile, he knows that the simple truth of family histories is usually written in stone, particularly in the case of nobles. He goes looking for tombs, hoping to find the 'beloved father and mother of Catarina . . .' and a kind of priest who will be able to tell him the whole story of the family. He envisions the gentle man, remembering the mother's or the father's funeral, unable to forget the beauty of the daughter . . .

Valentine Greatrakes is no great God-botherer, and has not previously frequented the Venetian churches. He now finds his head swimming with the peculiar detritus of their faith and their swooning smell of warm mice and cold stone. These buildings in no way resemble the bony London churches. Each one is a knick-knackatorium of saints' fingers and toes encrusted in wax, silver or glass. His eyes hurt under the burnished fanfare of precious metals. Slanting fingers of light poke his eyes and he walks into gilded candlesticks taller than himself and low-slung censers that have the unmistakably unchristian light of the Orient about them. The merchant in Valentine sees all these things melted down and turned to uses more practical than their current ones.

The Irishman in him aches to interrupt the dismal caterwauling of the choir with a decent bit of melody.

Would you ever think of putting a tune to it? he thinks to himself, while the Venetian fathers intone their rituals.

In church after church he forces himself to examine crypts and tombs, looking for the names of Catarina's parents.

Eventually, after some hours of diligent research by Smerghetto, he learns that the Venier crypt is to be found in the convent church of SS Cosma e Damiano on Giudecca. Valentine claps his hands when he hears this news. For these two saints are, by coincidence, the most familiar to him of all in his largely unsainted world. The holy moneyless ones are the patron saints of apothecaries and medicine, a protection which Valentine has always felt extends even to those of the quack fraternity. He often adorns his handbills with their portraits and the rostrums of his quacks with their effigies in wood.

Arriving at SS Cosma e Damiano, he jumps out of the gondola, already scenting success – and not a little cat urine – in the salty air. The handsome brick and marble church is set in a frosty, verdant *campo* much prowled by cats, who rub ingratiatingly against his calves. Smerghetto addresses them with one or two firm but caressing words, and they respectfully desist.

Unobstructed, they enter the high depths of the church and stand blinking in the luminous dust of a single shaft of light streaming from the roundel above the door. The atmosphere is frigid; the silence absolute.

It is colder inside this church than outside. This is not a place to which people would hopefully come with their aching and paining of the spirit.

From a concealed door, a novice slides forth, his hands clasped together, and inquires about their business in tones that seem unwelcoming. Smerghetto confers for some minutes with the narrow-faced boy, who all the while clamps a haughty and cynical eye on Valentine Greatrakes.

With a great display of unwillingness the novice eventually ushers them into the office of the presiding cleric. They are not asked to sit down. The senior priest, pocked as a toad and endowed with a similar bass croak, answers Smerghetto's questions in harsh monosyllables. Then he turns to Valentine and fixes on him an interrogative look that stirs something greasy in his belly.

Valentine refuses to be intimidated. When he asks, via Smerghetto, about the family of Catarina Venier, eyebrows and shoulders are raised and there is a disbelieving snort. However, eventually two nuns are summoned to show him not the family vault he expects, but a singular tombstone. Smerghetto is explaining this as they converge on a dark corner of the church. Valentine feels paralysed internally, though his feet move mechanically in step with Smerghetto's. The nuns glide ahead, their feet invisible, as if rolling on wheeled platforms.

Valentine gasps with a sudden shortness of breath. He reaches into his pocket for the Peruvian lozenges he has purchased that morning from a local quack. He winces at the cloying, rose-scented sweetness only slightly mitigated by the juice of the bark. But as he sucks the lozenge he begins to breathe again. Now the nuns have stopped in front of a small plaque, already blackened with the smoke of the church candles. They turn to face Valentine, who makes a brave attempt at manifesting a mere cerebral curiosity.

He knows nothing of how Smerghetto has explained their interest. But it does appear that Smerghetto has been unusually undiplomatic – or that the case is unexpectedly polemical. The nuns regard them both with hostility and even now their frigid expressions suggest that it would be much better if the men desisted immediately from this useless mission that can bring no possible good to anyone involved.

'I want to see it,' says Valentine, notwithstanding. He steps forward and the nuns part to permit his passage to the plaque. He does not need Smerghetto's help to translate it. It is dated sixteen years before. There are no affectionate messages, no blessings. Just a name and the dates of birth and death, with so few years in between.

It is not the tomb of her parents. Cut into stone is the name of Catarina Venier herself. Valentine takes a step backwards. He does not understand. His head throbs in time with dense-packed heartbeats.

No, he tries to tell himself, *this is another Catarina Venier entirely.*

When he asks for more information, they close their faces.

'There is nothing more to be gained from talking of her,' they say.

'Her parents . . .?' he tries to ask.

In answer the nuns show another stone, bearing the names of Carlo and Ippolita Venier, who died within a year of one another, a decade ago. These are the names Cecilia Cornaro gave him. With hard faces and practised gestures, the nuns now suggest that Valentine Greatrakes might like to make an offering to their church, which has so graciously furnished him with all the answers that any *reasonable* gentleman, even a *foreign* one, might require.

Valentine notes the offertory box under the rack of candles, and pushes coin after coin into the slot until the nuns unfold their hands and lean over to whisper to each other. He takes a candle, pinches open a candle-holder, and snaps it close around the wax stem. He lifts a small taper and lights his offering.

'For the memory of Catarina Venier,' he says aloud, as if saying her name will conjure her presence. A childlike part of him insists: *she is not dead; when she hears this she will appear and tell me so!*

The nuns fall silent – in the act of clucking their tongues – and even Smerghetto gasps. For Valentine has inadvertently chosen a candle with an overgrown wick. The flame now blazes up three inches, four inches, five, while the wick writhes around in its blue epicentre. The nuns cross themselves.

The flame dazzles Valentine's overwrought eyes and his hands are tortured by long pins and needles.

He spins around to the nuns: 'Did you see that? Is there not more to say? Smerghetto, ask them . . .'

But the nuns repeat, 'There is nothing more to be gained . . .' Although Smerghetto translates the words as gently as possible, Valentine is at last defeated by the severity of their tone and he bows to thank them for their help, and indicate his acquiescence: he will not trouble them further.

He turns sharply on his heel so they will not see the liquid welling up again in his tight eyes. Too late, for he sprays them lightly with a swollen tear as he swings away.

With Smerghetto at his side, his sharp eyes carefully averted from his master's wet face, Valentine steps out into the cold, clear air.

· 7 ·

A Peruvian Epileptic Electuary

Take powder'd Bark 6 drams; Virginia Snake root 2 drams; Syrup of Piony as much as needs, mix it up into a soft Electuary.

I have Experimentally found it a most prevalent and most certain Remedy. (After due Evacuations) 1 dram may be given to adult Persons (and less a Dose to others) Morning and Evening, for three or four Months, and afterwards three or four days before change and full of the Moon, it absolutely eradicates Epileptic and Hysteric Diseases; and also those odd Epileptic Saltations called St Vitus's Dance, in which the Affected are vexed with a thousand ridiculous Gesticulations and Leapings, after the manner of those in Apulia, that are bitten by a Tarantula.

Smerghetto is ineffably discreet. Even though Valentine has not shared with him the revelations gained at the studio of Cecilia Cornaro, the Venetian makes no inquiries as to why his master is weeping over the grave of a long-dead Venier. When he ascertains that he can be of no more help, Smerghetto subtly indicates that he could usefully busy himself elsewhere. Valentine nods gratefully and the man's nebulous presence dematerialises entirely.

It has begun to snow.

Aimlessly, Valentine walks back through the light veil of snowflakes along the canal that runs beside the church. Away from the broad Giudecca canal, this inlet is still as cold broth, and smells as if it once bubbled up from somewhere ten miles below Hell. Or, he thinks, as if something crawled in and died, giving it a high flavour. He thinks of the noble corpses stowed in the crypt under the church. It is impossible to avoid the image of their effluvia trickling into the canal. Including that of Catarina Venier, whoever she is. He flinches at the thought.

The rich smell brings into his mind an image of Dizzom back in Bankside, keeping his vigils over his stinking pipettes in the depository, and his chest lurches with homesickness.

The thought of Dizzom rouses Valentine from his morbid fantasies. He has a sudden appetite for work. He hurries the gondola under snow-grizzled skies to the Riva degli Schiavoni, home of the quacks and charlatans. It is his intention to browse among the local talent, something he should have been doing all these days he has wasted on – what? All the while they pole through the icy water his head is spinning with the thoughts of Catarina Venier, who should have been Mimosina Dolcezza, but lies dead. He feels a leaden panic in his belly: it is as if the actress has also died. He has invested too much in the felicity of his discovery. He cannot throw off the certainty that the two women are one and the same, despite the cruel truth etched in stone.

He tries to tell himself that it makes no difference that Catarina Venier is officially dead. Mimosina Dolcezza has demonstrably survived her. There is no reason why these tears should be springing from his eyes like lively tadpoles, so fast and so quick that he doesn't bother to wipe them away. He doesn't know where this knowledge will lead him, for it seems he must give up his theory that Mimosina Dolcezza was once a reluctant Golden Book nun, and accept a lesser one: that she merely resembles one.

His mind ranges over its previous construction, trying to reconcile the new-known facts with imperious instincts and wild hope. Certainly aristocratic girls are known to escape from convents in these lax times. And a Golden Book daughter who took on the shabby profession of an actress might well be disowned by her parents. But would they declare her dead? How hard-hearted might an Italian mother and father become, what cruel action might they take against a wilful daughter who brought disgrace on the family? Surely not so cruel as that? She might have been dead to them, but surely they could not inter her memory in a dishonest and empty grave? And anyway, there would be documents to sign and legal observances to be made in the event of deaths among the noble classes. So it is in London, so it must be here, where the nobility are not just the ornament but the spine of the state. Without some conspiracy at the highest levels, such things could not be forged and false-witnessed. And in what way would a powerless sixteen-year-old nun merit the attention of the Council of Ten or the Inquisitors?

No, decides Valentine, *the thing is that the actress merely resembles the lovely young Catarina to an astonishing degree. Perhaps she is a natural daughter of the father, Carlo Venier?*

Even the mother, Ippolita, could have strayed before wedlock. A girl of such mixed parentage might have been renounced by the family, could have ended up on the stage, helped a little by her connections. This scenario also explains why he is so drawn to Mimosina Dolcezza: he feels intensely that she is like him, someone who has needed to make her own way in the world, who has learned to support herself from an early age. It is their previous difficulties that marry their hearts: they met at a time when both had overcome the obstacles that might have killed or depressed their ambitions: they had both made successes of their lives against the odds.

Indeed not, thinks Valentine, *she is no Golden Book girl, spoiled and privileged. Not she! I would not love a woman like that. It's frightened of her I'd be in that case, not heartbroken for the loss of her, as I am.*

Honesty compels him to reflect that he has never met a woman of that class, but nevertheless he is sure that he would find her, if not repulsive, then certainly lacking in any communality or amiability of spirit. She would be shallow and dull, poor in worldly experience, determinedly ignorant.

He thinks of the stone plaque in the church of SS Cosma e Damiano, and he clenches his fist.

When I find her I'm going to ask her if she'd do me the honour of being buried with my family in Ireland.

He is drawn from his ruminations by the noises around him on the Riva degli Schiavoni. In the animal enclosures lions are roaring and the Westphalian hogs are cracking cocoa-nuts. All the sounds are depressed in volume by the rising mantle of snow that swags all surfaces.

And the quack doctors are everywhere, jumping benches like cats leaping at pigeons.

Valentine stops to admire a great craftsman at his bench. He has noticed the man's gruesome handbills about the streets for some days and been hoping to see him at work. He's a one-man act, and might be brought to London, if he does well. By the time Valentine arrives near his pitch, the man is already at his business, drawing all eyes. He howls, performing all the epileptic saltations of St Vitus' Dance, as if possessed by a thousand demons. When he has collected his appalled circle, he brandishes a knife and flourishes a naked arm from a voluminous sleeve. He cries out with pain as he gashes the arm again and again. A torrent of blood pours down his flesh, mapping it with thick red rivers, and still he strikes at himself, while the women cross themselves and the men cry out that he must desist, in the name of God.

'You want me to stop?' asks the man, finally, both in Venetian and in hand gestures. And he nods sadly, observing, with a faraway, nostalgic look in his eyes, 'Ah yes, in the city of Gilead, and in the court at Constantinople, they also begged me.'

At least this is what Valentine can guess he is saying. He recognises the names of the towns, and he knows the formula, of course.

'Ahh,' sighs the Venetian crowd, transported, proud witnesses to these foreign conquests.

The charlatan appears to forget them and raises his arm to strike again.

'Please, please,' beg his victims, with eloquent hand movements, grimaces and moans: 'You'll surely die of this.'

And indeed the mountebank swoons a little now, sinking down to a shelf where he has placed just one bottle, fastened with a red seal and a feather. Breathing heavily, he picks it up and pulls the cork. For a long moment he stands there, considering the bottle, and then he shakes his sleeve, scattering droplets of blood on the horrified crowd.

He says nothing but upends the bottle into a snowy rag, and rubs it over the meaty arm, slowly. A stripe of white flesh emerges, and another, and another.

Soon all his terrible slicings are excised and the arm is flourished, clean and whole. For good measure, he takes a simulated swig of the contents of the bottle. And while he cures his mortal wounds, he is talking, talking, talking – with his hands and his eyes and his mouth – of the Arab steeds that have galloped across the desert to bring the precious balms contained in this nostrum, of how the dried powders have been fermented in liquors distilled from Peruvian bark scraped only in a propitious spring rain, and how the very bottle has been made on Murano, and blessed by a well-known nun who is even now expecting her beatification on her deathbed and who shall therefore never more be available to bestow her potent benediction. Supplies are infinitely finite, and almost exhausted.

If he's not saying that very thing, then it's something entirely similar.

The first customer comes forward, his arm outstretched.

But meanwhile, the quack shakes his head regretfully, apparently telling them that he did not dream of such a demand for his nostrum, and that in any case a minimum of nine weeks goes into the collection and boiling of the efficacious herbs, some of which are very rare. He cannot possibly supply everyone. Could those among them with a serious need to help a loved one please step forward and the others fall back a little, until it can be seen whether there are enough bottles to go round. And soon they are crowding around the mountebank, beseeching his attention, some even drawing to his notice fresh wounds of their own that are in need of this remedy. These he avoids until the very last minute, just before he jumps over his bench and disappears. He will not be visible when the soapy water bites into their cuts.

Valentine has amused himself with the show, but it will not work in London. The tone is not right. The bladder of animal blood is too easily detected by just one sour member of the audience. The Oriental tales, even translated into English and pronounced with an Italian accent, will not impress John Bull. They are peculiarly charming to the Venetians, who have such an affinity with the East.

Licking snowflakes from his lips, Valentine moves to leave the Riva degli Schiavoni. In that moment he notices the *calle* which leads to San Zaccaria, the convent where Catarina Venier apparently met her death. He turns into it and walks swiftly to the church complex. He stands outside, looking at the *ruota* by the gate.

He thinks he might ring the bell, and enter on some inventive pretext or another. He stares at the gate, and wills an idea to emerge from his teeming thoughts. He waits a long time, till he must shake the heavy snow from the furrows of his hat, but no inspiration comes to him for a case that might be presented in a credible manner to the nuns of San Zaccaria, who are surely not in the habit of permitting entry to foreign men lacking even the Italian to make their request. Anyway, from within he hears the choir at song: he can hardly interrupt their devotions.

He is almost losing his nerve: his every fibre cries out to go to the appointed rendezvous at the Black Bat, despite his determination not to do so until he knows all about her; at least until he knows as much about her as she now knows about him. Remembering how much that is, a flush suffuses his face. For surely Pevenche, with her unquenchable candour, has also revealed the exact nature of his business to the actress, and many more unpalatable facts besides. Mimosina Dolcezza has hinted at a more refined understanding of his circumstances in her letter.

Once again he is hardened: he can survive another day – the third since arriving in Venice – without seeing her. He knows she is safe. These days of denying her serve to put his own dignity, so damaged by her machinations, into a necessary state of recuperation.

Smerghetto has been despatched to see if a woman is to be seen in the vicinity of the Black Bat at four o'clock each afternoon on successive days. He has reported the presence of various ladies. When breathlessly questioned on their specific attractions, he has supplied cold-blooded descriptions such as could not confirm or deny the presence of Mimosina Dolcezza. There is one woman about whom he appears to hesitate, for there is something about her appearance that he seems to find hard to describe. It is at this stage that Smerghetto always delicately brings the question back round to his master: why is it that he wants to know so much about this particular woman?

· 8 ·

Splanchnic Powder

Take Ashtree rind half a scruple; Rhubarb 5 grains; Spikenard,
Saffron, each 2 grains; long Pepper 1 grain; make them into a
Powder. To which may Chalybeats be added, pro re nata.

It removes Obstructions of the Viscera, corrects depraved
Ferments, represses spasmodic Flatulencies, rouseth up a
languishing Appetite, and alleviates pain and tension of the
Hypochondria.

Preparations for the Venetian nostrum are proceeding well,
Dizzom writes. Some instinct has compelled Smerghetto to hoard
the letter until that dangerous hour that hovers around four
o'clock, when he beholds in his English master all the symptoms of
a lively fever. For this moment of maximum temptation he has
reserved the packet from London. After placing it on Valentine's
desk, he makes bat-like motions with his hands and points to his
black hair, then waves and slips out of the room before any remon-
strance can be made.

Valentine forces himself not to follow by sitting firmly in a chair
and clutching its arm with one hand while flapping open the letter
with the other. Soon he is absorbed in its contents.

Dizzom is currently working on some *Manus Christi* preparations, allegedly made from crushed pearls (sacred to Cleopatra),
and swirling with passable imitations of gold leaf. It seems that
real gold leaf might prove less expensive than some of its imita-
tors. It shakes Valentine to think that there might be some
justification in the outrageous price of the medicine. But why
not? The Venetian Balsamick nostrum is to be different in every
way from what has gone before it. And he has come to think of it

sentimentally, as the nostrum inspired by his love for Mimosina Dolcezza.

And in this case the haggling and scrimping are unacceptable, entirely.

Meanwhile Dizzom has been struck by a promising idea as to how to market the nostrum. There is a certain Dottore Velena working in Bankside whose performances easily rival those of the Venetians, he writes.

The name is ringing a bell at the back of my mind. I wish I had more of an ear for these foreign tongues.

Instead of disseminating the new Venetian Balsamick among all the quacks of their manor, Dizzom suggests that they render it more desirable by making it (at first) available through just one source, thereby building up its legend among the quack fraternity itself before news of it is broadcast to the public.

Dizzom himself has just been to see Dottore Velena perform – normally he does not concern himself with the retailing end of the business – and he is constrained to admit that the Dottore's act is unparalleled. A Scot, he paints up well as an Italian, and even peppers his act with genuine Venetian words. On being interviewed, the Dottore declared that he had been taught them by a proper Venetian woman who has lately served a short season as his cure-victim. Dizzom has no idea if the words are genuine. He has written down a few for his master to verify locally. They concern ill-health.

Valentine holds up the relevant words under the noses of the *truncheoni*, who have arrived promptly as Smerghetto left. He reads them aloud, struggling with the unfamiliar syllables: '*Ti xe mal ciapa . . . Ti xe drio . . . Tirar i spaghi.*'

The *truncheoni* cross their eyes in concentration – and eventually admit that these words are recognisable to them. But they are nudging one another, and eventually Momolo says, 'Veleno . . . POY-Zen.'

So Velena means poison? Valentine Greatrakes laughs out loud. The name has a good ring and bounce to it, and Londoners are not likely to uncover the meaning of the word. He turns back to the letter.

According to Dizzom, Dottore Velena is wildly enthusiastic, which gratifies. He would adore to take on the Balsamick. He has even suggested an additional merit for it: as well as encouraging the Venus Sports, he says that this nostrum might also be marketed as a cure for those diseases which come from them! Or those spurious symptoms which are imagined by those whose engagement with the act is more contemplative and solitary than active and intermingling: the onanists are always ready to believe that their lonely pleasures are dangerous.

Dottore Velena, Dizzom recounts, has recently positioned himself as the saviour, and indeed also the creator, of a generation of erotic hypochondriacs. Since the departure of the Venetian lady he has been obliged to diversify: her absence has bitten a hole in the profits – she really was a most notable cure-victim, able to generate tears, groans and mad delight in her audience.

Without her, Dottore Velena has turned to preying on those unfortunate young men who suffer from nocturnal emissions caused by self-abuse. The doctor knows that each young man is tortured by guilt and ignorance, and usually believes himself unique in his malady. It soon comes to a point, if carefully managed, that the youth's imagination runs on nothing much beyond his sexual organ. He is only too suggestible to the notion that these symptoms are merely the early stages of a far more serious disease.

And to help him milk these young gulls, Dottore Velena carries everywhere with him a wax model showing a man and a woman in the advanced stages of venereal disease. Recycled from his previous act, for reasons of modesty this vile prodigy is kept in a curtained cage, and viewings of it are normally strictly confined to men – men who pay considerable sums for the revelation. Then, gasping with horror, these unfortunate boobies are informed that the mild itch in their privities is but the first sign of such catastrophic ravaging, and that without the doctor's particular nostrum their fate is shortly to be as already portrayed in three lurid waxy dimensions in front of them. Dizzom has seen and handled the model, which is said to have been made in the hot laboratories of Mrs Salmon herself. It is most cleverly done. The wax effigies are of a young blue-eyed couple of handsome and sweet demeanour. Dizzom writes, 'I assure you, their very visages scream the implication: we innocents committed just one indiscretion and look!'

Dottore Velena always draws the curtains before his clients have finished looking. He can rely on their imaginations to do the rest, and more efficiently than the carbuncular dollies.

He is perfectly safe from the vengeful ire of uncured patients. He sells his nostrum only to those who are sure to die soon anyway, or to those whose healthy complexions tell him that they shall fast recover from their mild symptoms. And when word of mouth fails him Dottore Velena also runs to printed advertisements in loud lettering. His handbills are prefaced with such beckoning words as MANHOOD, MANLY VIGOUR and THE SILENT FRIEND. Other words flutter forth in many combinations: always included are allusions to certain manual practices and secret cures. These handbills are dispensed from boxes in every urinal and dark byway where a young man might find himself alone in an anxious moment. Dizzom has enclosed one of the handbills and Valentine Greatrakes peruses it with pleasure, finding much to amuse himself.

Dizzom has more to tell, for then there is Dottore Velena's honoured colleague Doctor Sniver who keeps a priapic anatomic museum near to Guy's Hospital, and profits in respectability from this geographic coincidence. The museum, to which no woman may be admitted, is far from respectable, for its exhibits are all of venery and the consequences of venery. The larger and hidden part of the premises are given over to a small manufactory for various potions that are readily bought by the trembling visitors who have seen their fill of the exhibits. Doctor Sniver has been consulted and he would be prepared to pay premium sums for a Venetian Balsamick specific to the condition of love. He knows it will bring customers to his museum, and he is confident of selling it in breathless quantities.

'In all,' concludes Dizzom, 'I would recommend this twin course for the Balsamick. But there is one thing to add, in which you may be able to help, being situated in Venice.

'Dottore Velena tells me that the woman who taught him his Venetian glossary would be the perfect cure-victim for his Balsamick "*spettacolo*". She brought him more profit than a dozen Zanies, being young and quite lovely, and yet infinitely adaptable to any kind of role and malady. He suggests that you try to find her in Venice and persuade her to return with you so that she might resume her duties with him. She is certain to render the whole exercise far more profitable.'

In fact, Dizzom continues, the good Dottore goes so far as to suggest that she is indispensable. He adds a description: she is small, pretty, hair of a variable colour, probably in the sunset years of her third decade. She has a mobile kind of face, and claimed to have come from one the most salubrious situations of Venice, but then of course she would. Dottore Velena realises that none of this will substantially aid Valentine Greatrakes in trying to locate the correct woman. It might apply to thousands of them. And nor can he supply a profession: the doctor said that she had 'spouted lies like a teapot' when asked about her training. But he has been able to offer one helpful detail: the woman rejoices in the name of Miss Jallowfiwhore, and perhaps that gives the clue to the true manner of her cultivation!

'There cannot,' writes Dizzom, 'be too many courtesans of that name, even in Venice.'

Reading this letter, Valentine moans. This is rich! He had thought he was looking for just one murderer and just one woman in Venice. Now he is set to looking for a murderer and *three* different women: Mimosina Dolcezza, Catarina Venier and Signorina Jallowfiwhore.

A truly unfortunate name, he reflects, *this last.*

Yet, I suppose she must let her clients know the nature of her business.

· 9 ·

Sternutatory Powder

Take Florentine Orris 1 scruple; white Hellebore half a scruple;
Oil of Nutmeg 1 drop, make a Powder.

Sternutatories purge and cleanse the Head, because they
irritate the Spirits nidulating in, and irradiating those Nerves
that are disseminated into the internal Membranes of the
Nostrils. For the Spirits being provok'd into Spasms and
tumultuary Transports, loosen the impacted viscous Humours,
shake them out of their Places, and eliminate them through the
Infundibulum and Pituitary Gland, out of the confines of the
Brain into the Veins.

So Valentine Greatrakes goes searching in the high-class brothels
of Venice, of which there are some several score, all now decked
bridally in a covering of snow. It is not his intention to visit as a
customer, and nor is this chore to his taste at the moment, but he
obliges himself to tour the luxurious establishments in order to find
this woman, this Signorina Jallowfiwhore, who will help with the
Balsamick nostrum. There is also the chance that information is to
be had there regarding the actress and his ward, and perhaps even
the stranger who had gloated over Tom's body in London. His
mind is open to all possibilities.

He tells each madam that he looks not for a singular act of
pleasure, but to find a courtesan with whom he might enjoy some
pleasant conversation.

'In words, you know,' he adds, with a smile that works just as
well in Venice as it does in London.

To this end, he explains to a now-captive audience that he
wishes not even to sample the merchandise in the usual way, but

merely to talk a little to the girls who might be available for such a contract.

'I pay,' he adds, with an inviting candour, 'handsomely, because I know this request is out of the ordinary.'

The madams narrow their eyes and raise their hands to indicate that such an expensive line of work can barely be paid for by mortal agency. In response, Valentine pats high mountains of imaginary coins to show just how well he understands the difficulty.

'And of course,' he apologises, 'I need someone who speaks English.'

It is at this point that he asks casually, 'Perhaps you have among your Goddesses a lady recently returned from some time in London?'

The answer to the last question is never the one he wishes for. However, the mercantile madams are charmed at this challenge, and he is presented with any number of girls who have a smattering of English among their charms. Each one is boasted of as 'fully fluent in your tongue, my Lord, and a perfect companion for an English gentleman like yourself'.

Nearly all of the girls match the physical descriptions given by Dizzom of Dottore Velena's assistant, which might also at a stretch describe Mimosina Dolcezza. This coincidence gives each visit a frisson of excitement that washes away any irritation at such a bizarre and exhausting mission. Among the Venetian courtesans the same qualities are valued both in the aristocratic marriage market and in the whorehouses: a petite frame, fair hair, regular features. The only difference is that the courtesans are expected to be barren and capable of intelligent conversation, and that the noble brides are required to be fecund and silent.

Valentine is numb about the lips from asking the questions, 'Do you know a Signorina Jallowfiwhore? Has she perhaps been a colleague of yours? Do you know where she might dwell now?'

And at each interview he has also allowed himself to utter the names of Mimosina Dolcezza and of Catarina Venier with the same questions. To the first he receives only a feathering of giggles at the name, and to the latter the invariable response is a sucking in of teeth and a widening of eyes. '*A Venier?* In a *whorehouse?* What kind of question is that?'

He had hoped for better gleaning. With every failure he weakens against the temptation to go to the Black Bat anyway, never mind the mysteries, and claim Mimosina Dolcezza for his own. Every day at four in the afternoon, it becomes harder to sit at his table and watch Smerghetto depart for the apothecary. But every day he just manages to control himself. He sits firmly at the desk and plans his nightly itinerary of brothels.

He adds to his repertoire of questions for the whores, but no further clues emerge. He does better when he produces the portrait of the murderous man. Several girls in assorted establishments have nodded with minimal enthusiasm. Yes, indeed that man has visited. But half the time he wanted only *information*. He was not a good customer. And if he traded in their habitual commodity, he took his pleasure cruelly and paid poorly. They fall into charming faraway smiles and sit silent, allowing Valentine to follow their drift. He responds by tucking an extra coin into a bodice or sleeve, and making a prompt exit, so as not to parley wastefully with their time. No one is a greater enemy to the losing of time than Valentine Greatrakes, after all.

None of them can name the murderer, or even remember in credible detail the shape and style of the man, even those who got to see the whole man, as it were. There's not a mole or a scar to identify him. It seems as if he makes a profession of his anonymity.

Impatiently, Valentine makes the rounds of all the *casini*, consuming his evenings in empty investigations, working his way down a list that Smerghetto has, of course, produced in immaculate order.

It is at the fourteenth *casino* that he finds something of interest.

This is a luxurious establishment, discreetly entered from the Calle Balloni just behind San Marco. Once inside, the style and purpose of the place are unmistakable. The first reception room boasts a large painting of a banana tree, of whose fruit pleasure-bent women are supposed to be extraordinarily fond. Beneath its shadow disport large numbers of ladies in a state of aggravated undress, all contending for windfalls with open mouths, and litigating violently over custody of the fruits of the greatest lengths.

The comical painting, the ripe yellow velvet hangings, and an abundance of candlelight give the place a cheery air.

Nor does the madam stint in her hospitality. She tells him that all her girls have English, as her establishment is the one most in demand with the British quality visiting Venice. Unlike others, she does not ration him to one girl at a time for his parleys, but allows her entire domestic stock to enter the Banana Room, and he presents the drawing of the murderer to the assembled harlots, with the usual query.

Instantly, on seeing the portrait, one young girl gasps.

The madam nods and makes a subtle movement with her hand. The other girls file out, to be ready for more gainful employment. She looks significantly at Valentine and he lays a gold coin casually on one of the ornate desks. Eyeing it, she smiles, and leaves, closing the door behind her.

The girl has commenced to weep. In strongly accented English she tells him: 'That is a very evil man, my lord! Take care if you have dealings with him!'

'You know who he is?'

'He's called Mazziolini. He's some kind of state agent. Two years ago, he came as a client. I thought he'd chosen me for the usual reasons' – she runs a distracted hand over her breasts – 'but he was very desultory in that department. Afterwards he became much more alert, asked a lot of questions. I suspected nothing – boasted of my brother, who used to trade a little in, well, traded a little with the English wool merchants. The next day my brother was denounced by this Mazziolini, for consorting with foreigners, and was sent into exile. It was merely a business matter, not political. This Mazziolini knew, but he had scalps to take. And when my brother returned before his allotted time, for the funeral of our mother, he was murdered. Mazziolini had sworn it would be so, and it was so. And at his hand, there's no doubt.'

The girl breaks down and sinks to her knees. She lays her head on his lap. He is embarrassed but strokes her hair abstractedly and wipes her eyes with his handkerchief. It comes away stained with paint.

At last Valentine has a name and a proof of the murderous nature of the man he saw at the viewing of Tom's body at Bankside. He feels a small sense of relief, a sense of light glowing through a fresh slit in the black blanket of ignorance that has been wrapped around his head since Tom's death. He has more questions for the girl.

She doesn't want to answer them. She has another chapter of her own story to tell.

Mazziolini, it seems, had the brazen face to return to this *casino* even after killing her brother. Naturally he asked for another girl, her own uses having expired.

'But she is my dearest friend. She'd die a thousand times for me. And when she saw who he was, she finished his visit with a little dose of Sternutatory Powder while he dozed. It was a risk, but he suspected nothing. He thought his waking spasms some natural affliction' – she grins at the memory – 'even when he sneezed so much that the blood came pouring out of his nose.'

She giggles: 'The madam made him pay extra for staining the sheets and she charged him a small fortune for the damask napkin he was still clutching to his nose when he left.

'That part I was sorry to see because we know that the right amount of Sternutatory can kill. If you rupture enough vessels the bleeding never stops, and the brain bursts! We wanted him to die. I wanted it with all my heart. It's what he deserves.'

Her face is alight with hatred. She hisses, 'If you're looking to do him a damage, you'll need all your wits, and more than them too. A foreigner like you has little hope of finding the likes of him. If you do, and aim to do him harm, then I wish you well. But be careful. It is a known thing that he hates Englishmen worse than arsenic.'

Valentine thinks of the words in Smerghetto's report of Tom's death, those words that have thrashed in his head for so many weeks.

He asks her urgently, 'Is the man a sadist? Does he kill – in – special – ways? Did he disturb – ruin – the remains of your brother?'

380

Suddenly she looks afraid. Her face closes. Clearly, she has been struck by the suspicion that she has made a fatal mistake, that this foreigner is perhaps another Mazziolini sent to exterminate her family. She will not be drawn any further. When he persists she suddenly lunges out and tugs on a silken cord. A bell rings somewhere below and two large men enter the room. Valentine smiles ingratiatingly and offers purses all round. It is to no avail. He is forced to leave, a strong arm on each elbow. He is effervescent, however, and cannot wait to set Smerghetto on the case.

At the depository he finds that Smerghetto is waiting for him with information that turns everything to dust.

'The woman you want: we know where she is,' Smerghetto whispers, in a grave voice. 'It is not good news.'

Which woman I want?

Through a haze of disbelief, Valentine absorbs what Smerghetto evenly recounts. One of the women whom Smerghetto has been observing at the Black Bat failed to materialise that afternoon. This had alerted him to her particularity. He was already favouring her as the prime candidate, despite the fact that . . . Here, he hesitates a moment and seems about to describe her condition in more detail, but clearly thinks better of it, or judges it immaterial to the main business in hand, or possibly calculated to drive his master out of his wits.

Her disappearance gave him occasion to make inquiries inside the Black Bat. Her daily visits there had not gone unmarked. The apothecary had news of the incident that had removed her from the scene, for indeed it is the kind of story relished by his customers, two of whom had happened to witness it, and had rushed back to tell him.

In a full crowd, in San Marco, she has been seized and taken into custody in one of the dim *palazzi* kept by agents of state for their prisons.

At this point a network of informants have filled in the rest of the picture for Smerghetto, who is all this time pouring a glass of wine, setting it in front of his stupefied master, and gently directing him towards a chair.

Valentine Greatrakes stares dumbly as Smerghetto explains that this *palazzo* is the kind of place from which few prisoners are liberated. Her crime is unknown to Smerghetto's informants, but it is surely serious. There is no way into her cell via bribery, no matter what the price.

Smerghetto's face is telling him the truth, though it won't spill from his mouth: that he wouldn't take a lease on her life, if she's locked up in there.

Valentine erupts in agony, 'But *which* one of the women is it? Signorina Jallowfiwhore, Catarina Venier . . . or . . . Mimosina Dolcezza?'

His hand is on the lapels of Smerghetto's jacket, his breath comes in short bursts. His eyes are staring and his hands prickle unbearably.

He reads the answer that he dreads in Smerghetto's face.

Valentine sags on his feet. He has come so close to her, only to have her snatched away. All this time he has wasted looking for the Signorina Jallowfiwhore, while sitting on his pride, insisting on meeting on his own terms the one woman whom he really needs, the one woman he cannot do without.

Smerghetto tells him: 'I think you must sit down. There is much to tell you.'

Then Smerghetto explains, slowly and clearly, that this dramatic evening a number of facts have supplied the missing pieces of the fractured picture that has eluded their mutual comprehension. He mentions that there has been no sign of the young English girl who was supposed to be with the woman.

But Valentine Greatrakes is keening, 'The one woman, the one woman, haven't I come back here again precisely and just for her?'

He thumps his hand on the table.

'One woman,' whimpers Valentine.

Smerghetto now tells him, slowly and in simple words, that he may in fact triple that number, and yet still come up with the same – singular – woman.

Who is now in peril of her life.

Part Seven

A Balsamic Lohoch

Take Balsam of Tolu (powder'd, searced and subacted with Yolk of an Egg) half an ounce; Lohoch Sanans 1 ounce; Balsam of Peru 4 drops; Syrup of Coltsfoot flowers, as much as needs, mix.

It entirely possesses all the Virtues that are after to be rehearsed, of the Balsamic Electuary, but with this advantage, that being much more grateful to the Palate; it may be more commodiously offer'd to the Nice and Nauseous, that abhor the Oiley bitterness of Capive.

This morning I buried the incriminating ring in the orchard of Sant'Alvise.

On reflection I don't want to damage poor old Jaune-Fleur in Uncle Valentine's too-credulous eyes. I'm not bitter, and forgiveness is a virtue, one of a number I am cultivating at the moment.

I asked the other girls about Mimosina Dolcezza – they laughed at the name. Dolcezza means 'sweetness', apparently. If she is from Venice, she is definitely not Golden Book, anyway. And quite possibly one of those ladies who depends on the public for support. She could be an embarrassing connection.

Better the devil you know, eh, and particularly the one that you have under your thumb. Better Miss Jaune-Fleur than Mimosina Dolcezza, the Ice Maiden, who stole my Christmas dinner.

All these disgusting thoughts of mating and pairing! How animal it is. How crude. How much lovelier are the bosom friendships between women, how much more couth and yet how much more satisfying.

Still no visit from Uncle Valentine, who needs to be informed of my decision to stay here. He will try to dissuade me, of course, because his heart is set upon my joining him when he arranges his domestic situation. I am sorry, but my plans are of a higher nature, and I must disappoint him.

When he comes, I plan to take him to the well in the centre of the cloister for our painful little interview. I want to let the other nuns see what kind of lover I might have, should I ever change my mind. For I believe that it was a near thing with my Uncle Valentine. He could not have helped falling in love with me, over time, and I might in the end have taken pity on him.

But No – It Can Never Be – for I have decided to betroth myself to Someone Else entirely.

Venice, March 1786

· 1 ·

Chalybeate Syrup

Take white Wine 1 pint and a half; filings of Iron 1 ounce and a half; powdered white Tartar 6 drams; Cinnamon, Nutmeg each 1 dram and a half; Mace, Cloves, each half a dram; make a warm infusion 4 days in a large open Glass (else it will burst asunder); or (which is better, if time will permit) let them stand cold 14 days; decant the clear Wine through a strainer; and having added to 1 pint of it fine Sugar 1 pound, make a Syrup.

My interlocutor was pacing around the room. All his former composure had evaporated, as had his dry delivery. There was none of the cynical amusement I had read in his younger face and voice all those years ago, and none of the indulgence.

I lay silently on the table, my head immobile, my lowered eyes following him covertly. I did not put it past him to strike me unexpectedly. Now that the worst thing had happened, and the imagined sophistication of my plans had been exposed as feeble, my fears were base and simple. I was afraid that he would beat me. He looked bitter enough to do so.

The other men had filed away, and we were alone.

'Of course you knew who she was! You must have known the moment you saw the father's corpse. You must have recognised your old lover, even after all these years. You can count. Don't tell me you did not know in that instant exactly who *he* was. Mazziolini says that you grew pale as glass when you saw the body. How do you explain that?'

'Any woman of normal sensibilities would react in that way to the sight of a corpse,' I said as levelly as I could. 'Bleeding like that.'

'But you are not such a woman,' murmured my interlocutor. 'We have reason to know that it is a long time since you showed honest behaviour in any respect.'

He gestured contemptuously at my pregnancy apron, destroying my faint hope that my supposed condition would gain me more merciful treatment.

'If that is the case, you have made me this way,' I said bitterly. 'And as you know everything, you must be aware of the fact that I knew him by a different name in Venice. He did not tell me the truth. I myself went by a different name then, my real name.'

'This is immaterial. I maintain that you knew who he was when you saw his body, and at that moment, if not before, you realised that the ward of your low-life paramour Valentine Greatrakes was none other than your own daughter. That is why you were so shocked. That is why you broke your bond with us, escaped from Mazziolini, returned to London and kidnapped her.'

'I told you! She's someone else's daughter! I do not think the man who came to San Zaccaria lacked for mistresses: I was not the only one who could have mothered the girl. But that's not the point. The thing is: I do not have a daughter! I never had a daughter. I had a son! And he was murdered by the man-midwife. I never even saw the body.'

Except in my imagination, of course. How often had I pictured the crushed skull and the forceps pulling the limp and mangled baby out of me as I lay delirious on my pallet. The facts that they were asking me to believe now – that Pevenche was the creature whom I had conceived and carried, and that she had been born alive, had lived and that my first lover had taken her away to raise her – these things were too incredible to absorb. I had never even acted in a play that spun its plot on such a preposterous premise.

'It was a little boy,' I whispered again, feebly. 'He died.'

Real tears ran down my cheeks and between my open lips. I did not know if I was weeping for the dead baby or for myself, disbelieved and helpless to make my interlocutor understand the truth.

'So you insist. But the nuns at San Zaccaria say otherwise. They say that you were delivered of a healthy girl, and that you rejected her. You would not even take her to your breast. They insist that you were wild with anger at your treatment by her father. You refused to have anything to do with her. You told them that if she remained in the convent you would hunt her down and put an end to her.'

'These are lies, the most incredible and outrageous lies. You know what they are like, the sisters at San Zaccaria. They are whores, liars, all of them. They hated me. How can you give any credence to what they said to you? If they did not kill the baby inside me with that instrument, why have I never conceived again?'

But there was no gainsaying him.

'The nuns were instructed by your lover, and informed by their own good instincts about the best way to deal with a lewd little troublemaker like you. After the birth, certain instruments were used to ensure that you would not stray into that kind of mischief again.'

When I thought of all that had been taken from me in that short period of unconsciousness I suddenly felt savage with grief for the misuse I had suffered. A girl of sixteen, what chance had I then with the forces ranged against me, the callousness of my lover, the venality of the nuns, the power of the drugs and the swift hands of the doctor exterminating my fertility? I had been rifled and robbed by everyone, and left to a deceived and blighted life. I had not been innocent, but my crimes paled in comparison with this abuse I had suffered, starting from the moment I snatched the first candied fruit from a tree in the orchard of San Zaccaria. My tears continued to flow, slicking my cheeks and dripping off my chin. They raised no compassion whatsoever in my interlocutor, who plied me with more and more indigestible tales.

'And so they gave the baby girl to the father and he took her back to England, quite willingly, I may say,' he added with a vicious kind of quietness, 'so long as he did not have to take you too.'

'But she is too old, too gross,' I moaned. 'This happened only sixteen or at most seventeen years ago – that great big girl must be twenty if she's a day.'

'She is sixteen years old, though large with it, our reports say. On the English diet even a girl with Venetian blood can run to fat. I can scarcely be surprised at your lack of maternal tenderness, but you can deceive neither us nor yourself about her true age. It seems you were happy to keep her amused with childish toys, when it suited you.' He gestured towards Pevenche's ukulele, evidently ransacked from my rooms and now displayed upon a velvet cushion on his desk.

I had nothing to say to this – I had never actually asked her about her age – so he continued.

'Why do you think we kept you out of Venice as much as possible? We know what kind of woman you are. We were afraid that you would find the Englishman who had betrayed you and make trouble with him, and then we would have had a diplomatic incident on our hands. We were able to hush up the scandal of the nun you blinded – she was not Golden Book, fortunately. But a foreign businessman – no! And now that he has got himself killed in any case – it is worse than we thought. It seems he was mixed up in a criminal community of a type that insists on a primitive English kind of rough vengeance. It is all we can do to contain the situation.'

He had grown distracted, thinking of problems that no longer concerned me. I watched his shoulders rise and fall. Suddenly he turned back to me, clearly harnessing his feelings and his intellect for one last effort to reason with me.

He said softly: 'It was a most unfortunate chain of circumstances that brought you into contact with that corpse.'

He waited for this sugared offering to open my mouth; when it did not, he abandoned all pretence of sympathy.

'You are that kind of hellbrand who will not let the sins of the past die, to pass away if not be forgiven. No, not you. As soon as you knew that the father of your daughter was dead, it infuriated you to be robbed of your chance of revenge. I suspect you took the daughter because you wanted to punish her for your own

392

pains. God alone knows what other plans you were formulating against her and would have carried out, if we had not caught you. When we put you back in San Zaccaria, you can be sure that there will be no more lapses of security.'

So this was it, then – my worst fears confirmed. I was to be incarcerated in the convent again. As my interlocutor stared grimly out of the window into the blank *calle*, I fell to wondering what they wanted from me and why I was not already chained to a bed in a cell at San Zaccaria.

Suddenly I realised that they were probably looking for Pevenche. They would want to appease the English criminals, as he had put it, by handing back the girl to her guardian. A stolen English girl in Venice could certainly cause difficulties. Withholding that information was the only way to keep myself out of San Zaccaria for the moment, until I thought of a better plan. It was imperative to muddy the trail that might lead to Pevenche, and so I dared to hiss: 'It is strange how in this supposedly godly city everyone sees a life spent in piety as the worst kind of torture.'

He made a sharp movement with his hand, but controlled himself at the last second. He was not interested in anything I might observe, unless it was to throw light on the situation, he told me.

I remained silent. I knew that if I spoke of Pevenche I'd be opening my grave with my mouth.

And so I protected my secret. He grew bored, and gave orders for me to be locked away.

I lay on a plank in a ground-floor cell, and listened to the impatient scratching of the rats. Despite the bleak nature of the accommodation, I was relieved to be alone. It had been too much to absorb, the story I had been told. I pictured Pevenche happily snoring in her comfortable quarters at Sant'Alvise, and tried to summon some motherly feeling towards her. Surely it was better to have a living child, even one like her, than a murdered infant? The truth was that I felt nothing except shock, and a great longing for the arms of Valentine Greatrakes. *He* felt like family, like home, like refuge; Pevenche felt foreign to me in every way.

393

One does not become a mother merely by receiving news of it. But when my lover discovered the truth, would it endear me to him? Given his own tortured feelings about the girl even before this latest revelation, now he would surely find me more problematical than palatable.

Then I laughed bitterly at myself, for such projections of the future were entirely in vain. If I did not prove co-operative, my employers would have no reason to keep me alive, despite the threat of San Zaccaria. I was already a disappeared woman, officially deleted from their record books. It would be the merest thing to dispose of me, and to rest a last piece of paper in my dossier.

And I remembered, with a storm of palpitations in my breast, that it was yet easier than that for them to dispose of me. For of course, in the eyes of the world, Catarina Venier was already dead, and buried near but not inside the family crypt on Giudecca.

· 2 ·

A Cataplasm of Webs

Take Venice Turpentine 2 ounces; juice of Plantain 1 ounce and a half; Figs 3; the yellow paring of Orange Rind 2 drams; Bolus 1 dram and a half; Soot half an ounce; Pigeon's Dung 1 ounce and a half; large Spider Webs 6; black Soap 4 ounces; Vinegar enough to unite it.

To drive an Ague, tie this about the Wrists, so as to make it bear hard upon the Pulses, two hours before the Fit.

My cell faced a *calle* that was not frequented, probably being blocked from the street. I could smell and hear the waves nearby but no canal was visible, except for the teasing reflection of water that sometimes lit a tiny corner of my ceiling when the sun shone. I lay on my plank and watched the muscular wriggles of light, following each radiant sinew to its conclusion. Those were my short stories, my plays and my songs with which I beguiled the untold hours.

They allowed me to wash and brought me clean clothes. Each day I refastened the pregnancy apron over my chemise. It made lying face-down on the hard bench just a little more tolerable. My stomach continued with its cruel distempers and ventiferous humours, encouraged not a little by the direful pap they brought me to eat.

I was conscious of the dye fading from my hair. I felt my skin sagging on my poor rations. Hourly I expected a summons to the noose or the arrival of hard-faced women with a bottle and a tube. I lived my death continuously until it was life itself that seemed the other side of a cloudy pane.

Of course it was not the first time that I had endured solitary confinement. The difference was that this time I had known true companionship, both with Valentine Greatrakes and also, I had to admit, with Dottore Velena and the Zany, and the remembered affection of these three friends threw my current isolation into an ever crueller relief. For all their tricks and monkeyshines, in each of those men was the soul of decency. And they had all shown me the human warmth that I craved for now, more than food, more than light, more than air.

I took to talking to them under my breath, with my eyes squeezed shut. I used my skill as an actress to mimic their answers. Even the Zany took his part in these little playlets I performed. When I fell asleep I sometimes curled up as if in my basket at the Feathers, and when I dreamed, they were London dreams, in English. Or London nightmares infected by Venetian memories.

I longed for gin, and there was none to relieve me. I was shocked to see how I had come to rely on a dreamy tide of the spirit rising in my blood to protect me from unhappiness. It was hard to lose consciousness without a glass of its cooling fire. Without it, I dreamed more vividly, when I finally fell asleep.

One night I fell into a dream that on waking could be traced to a story I had heard at Bankside. The Zany had come rushing into the Feathers with the news of a baker who had rid himself of a troublesome apprentice girl by pushing her into the bread oven at the peak of its heat. In my sleep the London sojourn was erased, in the way of dreams, and I saw myself among the capacious ovens in the kitchens of San Zaccaria once more. Faceless nuns surrounded me and, deaf to my screams, started to strip me of my clothes. When I was naked, they basted me with olive oil and butter and wrapped my head in muslin, like a pudding. Trembling and blind, I felt them grab at my slippery limbs and lift me up. The heat snapped closer and closer to my flesh. I heard the slow shriek of the oven door opening. Then I was gagging on my own screams and they were pushing me through the maw of the oven. The flames licked my skin, found it to their liking, and fastened themselves upon me. I writhed in the ashes, devoured by the flames. The muslin bag on my head was burned away, and then I watched my own skin melt and perish in the fire.

It was a dream with the sound all drained out of it: in a roaring silence I felt and smelled myself roasting, and saw the flesh fall off my bones like that of a joint on a spit. I awoke gasping and weeping to see the red rim of dawn stripe the window-sill of my cell. I took scant comfort from this reality. For all I knew, it would be my last dawn. For all I knew, just such a fate as I had dreamed awaited me at San Zaccaria. When they gave me back to the nuns, there would be no one to protect me from their vengeful plans.

That dream brought all the pities welling up, all the cruel things that had ever hurt me. I wept for them all, from the day my parents abandoned me to the time when my former lover, the father of my murdered baby – no! – the father of Pevenche! – first began to abuse me. All these things came to rack me with fresh tears. Other griefs came too, ones I thought long buried, until I was wheezing sobs in the back of my throat. I remembered the day, ten years past, when Mazziolini came to me with a miniature Brustolon carving of three chained blackamoors holding up a marble tabletop. Their eyes of vitreous paste glared at me, forcing me to remember where I had seen them last – in one of the reception rooms of my parents' *palazzo*, where a life-size edition of the same design dominated the room.

'My parents are dead then, I suppose?' I said in a toneless voice, 'and this is my inheritance.'

I did not ask how they died; there were tales of typhus in Venice at that time.

Mazziolini had whispered, 'A dead woman cannot inherit. Even a Golden Book corpse may not live off the family spoils.'

I realised then how much humble-born Mazziolini hated me. This was the only emotion I had inspired in my sole companion of the last decade and a half, and I could barely conceive of what trouble he must have put himself to in order to extract the Brustolon and taunt me with it.

Even Mazziolini, I realised, had his miseries. He too was exiled from his beloved Venice to serve as ignominious guard to a woman he despised.

And these cruel fates reminded me yet again of my own, and I wondered when they would come to kill me, and began to hope that I would not be left long to contemplate it, for surely this fear was worse than death.

And lastly I thought of Valentine Greatrakes, and how I had failed to win his enduring love. Instead, with me, he had merely sent his heart out in holiday dress, for a little recreation. Just as it is said the French queen plays at being a shepherdess in prettified pretend-humbleness at Le Petit Trianon, so this false English gentleman had gone a-slumming with a Venetian actress for a while, little dreaming of my noble birth. I thought I had seen love in his eyes – perhaps I had. Perhaps I had made a cull of all my hopes by concealing too much from him. Could it be that he had scented my dishonesty? Maybe he could not believe in my love, sensing something awry?

If only I had confessed the whole truth to him when there was an opportunity to hold his hand while doing so, and to appeal to all his faculties for clemency! Those precious weeks together in London, when we might have lived in an atmosphere of truth, I had hidden the real events from him. And why? Because to tell him the truth of my birth would entail other confessions of a less palatable nature. And I had not trusted his love sufficiently to make him the companion of my clean, confessed heart.

Would I have won him with the truth? Would he have returned the compliment? Did I at that time have heart enough to accept him for what he was?

I did not know. I would never know.

When the fearful thing happened, it came not from the door to my cell but from the snow-lined window-sill.

It was in the early hours of the fourth night that four huge hands appeared on the grilles that strained the light. A few seconds later those hands had hoisted two large and stupid heads up to the window-sill from where they regarded me with a manifest delight. It was evidently a near thing that they had found the right cell.

'Momosina Gentilcuore?' mumbled one of them, in a brutish *terraferma* accent. A smell suggestive of *pancetta* and garlic suddenly enriched the air of my cell.

From this name, however muddled, I was filled with the hope that these men came from Valentine Greatrakes, and that they meant to take me away with them. I leapt to my feet, gathering my shawl.

It seemed that I was both right and wrong. Yes, they explained, in a dim-witted chorus, they had come from the English *Lord* (they too, I sighed!) Great Rakes. But it was not possible to bear me away in this instant. They gestured briefly at the bars, as if I might not have noticed them.

Steeling myself to be patient, I asked, 'Then why have you come?'

For a moment this befuddled them, and they looked at one another in some desperation. Then one of them fumbled a bottle out of his pocket. This he placed carefully on the window-sill before giving up on the battle to stay aloft. He slipped down from view, closely followed by his companion. I flinched as the walls reverberated with the impact of their landings. I heard their running footsteps and then the sound of their huge bodies clambering over a barricade.

This was followed by a sharp scratch of whispers and one angry groan which sounded to my eager ears something like the voice of Valentine Greatrakes. I craned my neck upwards but I could see nothing.

One of the idiots lumbered back over the barricade. His fat palm gripped a bar and his face swung into view.

'We forgot to tell you. Use what's in the bottle on these bars. A bit each day. Just two bars. Enough to let you out. Don't drink it.'

Having gabbled this message in a monotone he slipped out of sight. In spite of my plight, the Zany's voice rose up inside my head: 'You sordid Hunks. You niffy-naffy persons! Come back, you idiots, don't leave this half-done.'

I reached up and carefully pulled the bottle down to me. I opened the stopper and sniffed it. A stench of sulphur assaulted me. I slammed it down on the window-sill.

I sat on my plank and cried.

Was this how they planned to rescue me? After the years it would take to corrode the inch-thick bars with drops of acid? Did they really think that the Inquisitors would allow me to live that long? I would almost rather die immediately than wear out my strength with this pathetically comic plot. I lay on my back and thought of drinking what was in the bottle.

But soon the moon came up to push fingers of white light through the cell. In that eerie radiance the contents of the bottle glowed with a potency that seemed credible.

I picked it up and stood on tiptoe by the window. I chose two bars and irrigated their bases with a splash of the liquid. I heard a faint fizzing and immediately pulled with all my strength, to absolutely no effect.

I almost flung the bottle out of the window then. But instead I hid it carefully in a dusty corner and went back to my plank, where I slept.

· 3 ·

Unguent for Shrinking of the Sinews

Take Nerve Ointment 1 ounce; Neats-foot Oil, Oil of Earth-worms, Bullocks-fat Marrow (that droppeth out of a boil'd Marrow-bone) each half an ounce; fine Turpentine 2 drams; liquid Storax, Spermacetti each 1 dram; Oil of Aniseed 12 drops: Mix up an Unguent.

When a Limb, struck with a dead Palsie, begins to grow cold, waste away, lose its motion, and shrink up: In this difficult Case, such a remedy as this, used with good friction, sometimes is helpful. For by means of its suppling, oily Substance, it mollifies and relaxes the dry, hard, contracted, carneous Fibres; by means of its Balsamic, and Aromatic Parts, it revives and roborates the benumbed, weak, nervous Fibres. And lastly, when good rubbing is added to the rest, one may well hope, that the Blood, and Spirits may be drawn more plentifully into the part; and that natural Heat, and Tone, and Nourishment may be restored to the Member again.

Three days later I still could not discover the slightest effect of my acid irrigations on the bars. I had seen nothing more of the idiots, heard no more of my lover's voice. If the bottle were not secreted in the padding of my apron to allay such thoughts, it would have been easy to imagine the whole episode a dream.

On the eighth night of my imprisonment the idiots visited me again.

'Good evening, Momosina,' they smiled. 'Griet Lord Rikes sends his . . . something . . . regards perhaps.'

'Please tell him that I long to see him,' I responded fervently. 'Please tell him that I love him with my entire heart. That I adore him.'

401

The idiots frowned and blushed, covering their embarrassment by testing the bars. With all their strength they produced just the merest movement. We all stared at the black metal with hatred, they from their side, I from mine.

They dared not say anything to me, but silently slid down and made their usual noisy progress over the barricades where I heard more angry whispering.

One of them came back: 'More from the bottle, ten times a day, just a little bit. And make holes in the wood above and below the bars. Little ones.' They handed me a long nail.

I nodded.

I was mortified that Valentine Greatrakes himself did not come to see me. Why had he chosen such crude messengers? Why did he send no message of love? The idiots did not even ask, on his behalf, how I did! He was prepared to save me from my prison, but he wanted me to know that he would take no personal risks to do so. He was of course angry with me for the abduction of Pevenche. Perhaps, like my employers, he was keeping me alive only so as to be able to extract information as to her whereabouts.

My mind had previously skittered away from the subject. But I now spent a great deal of time thinking about the girl. My captors left me strictly alone: I had ample hours for reflection. The more I thought about her the less I could conceive that the flinty chit once quickened in my belly. And yet, and yet, when I pictured her face, I knew that there were elements of it that were not unlike my own. Buried in that barely animate porridge were lineaments I had seen in my own mirror: the shape of her nostrils, the curve of her brows. There was more. She had my own gift for histrionics; my own sweet tooth. And the deception that prized her from me at birth, the cruel lie about the cranioclast, *that* was so very like her father. I could not think of another man who would devise such a plot. Between us we might well have sired such a brute as Pevenche. I began to accept that my interlocutor had told me the truth, and the full irony of the situation flooded through me.

Now I remembered things that my lover had told me about his ward; of how her father had been entranced by the baby but

402

how he had soon lost interest. Yes, the span of my first lover's attention had been by no means generous, when it came to sentimental attachments. So Pevenche too, though but a tiny child, had known the inexplicable waning of his affection, and no doubt she had felt his noxious choler too. I would not be surprised if he had beaten the child. Probably, all her ridiculous pretensions to juvenility could be traced back to a desire to return to that infant state when her father had truly seemed to love her. The same with the clothes – Tom had always insisted on picturesque, if gaudy, dressing. And the food! My lover had tried to tell me how Tom had encouraged her naturally large appetite, for satirical motives. He had fashioned her as a monster for his own amusement. How confusing it must have been for her, and she without the sense of a flea to start off with. The comfort of a warm belly must have won out in the end, further consolidated by that surprising talent of hers in the kitchen.

This was the girl I had regarded as an enemy. Now I saw her as purely pathetic. But I could not warm to her. And nor would the world. The trouble being that pity is more easily evoked by beauty and delicacy than by disgust and a dark desire to sneer, the only human responses to Pevenche's grotesqueries. She had no natural melody of character to counteract them.

'Did you not see the tragedy of the thing?' Valentine had asked me in London, reproaching me for my lack of compassion for the then-unmet Pevenche.

Yes, but still no maternal affection rose in me for the girl, and little compassion. I could not sentimentalise her: my actual experience of her was too fresh. Her situation was sad, I acknowledged, but mine was perilous, and of course much more compelling for me.

I continually wondered if Valentine Greatrakes now knew the truth too. Or how much he had discovered. If he knew that Pevenche was my daughter, then he would also know that his precious Tom had once upon a time been my lover. And he would know that I had concealed this very salient fact after seeing the corpse. How would that make him feel? Betrayed by me, certainly. But would he be disgusted to share a woman in that way? Or would it, as I hoped, raise me in his estimation? Some men are so intimate in their friendships that sharing a lover only unites them more. Perhaps he would now think that my abduction of Pevenche was a wild expression of unconscious motherly love. How very wonderful, and how very convenient if that could be true.

Now that I knew he meant, however hopelessly, to rescue me, I could not refrain from warming speculations that his feelings for me had survived the shock of what I had done and what I had dissembled. When I thought about it clearly, I knew that my own affection for him had remained untainted and that I cared as much about seeing him again as I did about saving my life and escaping this prison. Perhaps more. If he felt what I felt, or even a fraction of it, all was not lost.

Diligently, I watered the bars with acid, as if they were precious orchids and I was sprinkling the Balm of Gilead about their roots. I fancied that I saw a discoloration at the base of the metal. I imagined that when I shook the bars myself a little tremor of looseness rewarded me. But it remained well beyond my strength to extract them from their wooden casings. These too I bored with dozens of tiny holes. Every night I awaited the idiots in such a high state of suspense that I felt as if I lay a full inch above my pallet.

When they finally came, they leapt on the bars without ceremony, swinging all their weight, so that at last the groan of metal rent the air. A shuffle in the corridor announced the curiosity of a guard, and I motioned to them to disappear. When the guard peered into my cell I was giving a notable performance of sweet slumber. He stared at me for hateful moments, and finally disappeared. I waited until I had heard his footsteps turn a corner before I ran to the bars and whispered to the idiots: 'Come back!'

This time they were quieter but more determined. There was no doubt that the bars were starting to buckle, but try as they might, they could not bend them enough to allow me a clear passage out. Their contorted faces showed me they were close to tears, when they finally slid down the wall and fumbled away.

I sank to my knees, retching dry, ugly sobs, nothing like the silent, decorous teardrops I had for years conjured up professionally.

A few moments later they were back, and from the number of footsteps it seemed to me that they were reinforced in numbers. I hoped against hope that I might now see the dear face of Valentine Greatrakes. Instead a pale and ugly countenance was lifted up to the bars. It resembled that of Dizzom, except that the man was Venetian. He nodded to me and inspected the bars. Then he slipped below and consulted in whispers with the others.

A new pair of hands appeared at the bars. And I knew those long fingers. I knew them by heart.

· 4 ·

Restorative Caudle

Take Tent Wine 2 quarts; White Sanders, Acorn Cups, each half
an ounce; candy'd Eryngo Roots, Dates, Figs, each 4 ounces;
Nutmegs sliced thin half an ounce; Archangel 2 handfuls; boil to
1 quart, strain it and while it is yet a little warm, add the Yolks of
4 Eggs, white Sugar Candy 1 ounce: mix all. To these may be
added shavings of Harts-horn, Ivory, Priapus of the Sea-Horse,
Calry, &c. give it warm for Breakfast every day.

The wood supporting the bars, fatally weakened by the holes I
had made, soon gave way with four of them at work. I was out
of the cell in a very few minutes and then passed hand by hand
over the barricade to a *calle* where a gondola waited to bear us
away.

The idiots and the Venetian Dizzom saw us safely into comfortable quarters at the back of a familiar noble *palazzo* at Rialto.

Then our companions tactfully left us. A fire was tickling in
the grate and on the table glowed a decanter of wine surrounded
by fine glasses. But neither of us moved towards these comforts.
We stood staring at each other. I did not dare to embrace him,
though I starved for his touch. His face was iced with anger, and
he made no tender motion towards me.

Despite having risked his life to save mine, my lover seemed
not much inclined to sweet reunions. I guessed that he required
his pound of flesh still, the affront was too gross, that my letter
had not proved sufficient to pacify him. How hard he seemed to
me then, how much like a man grudgingly cut out of stone. His
dry anger appeared unmitigated even by nostalgia for our time
together or by simple kindness, such as he might show a dog he

had rescued. Just for a moment, he reminded me of the man I must now learn to call 'Tom'.

It seemed too much, after the last months, after the past few hours, that I must still sing for my supper, grovel more for my deliverance. Stealing corner glances at his agate eyes, which roamed the room lighting on anything but me, I feared he had it in him to cast me aside even now. It seemed that he had taken me from my employers because I was *his* booty and not theirs. For him, the robbery of me was just one more act of free-trading, one more manifestation of the creed of that hard little kingdom of his, comprising the low life of both London and Venice. He would extract the information he required about Pevenche and then throw me friendless into the street, or deliver me back to my employers. Or hand me over to those two thugs who had contributed their brute force to my liberation. He might wish to do more than humiliate me. He might wish me hurt.

I had asked too much of that single letter. I had also depended too much on the hope that his own feelings for me had some true depth. Instead, it seemed at that moment as if he had made use of me, perhaps even more than I had made use of him.

So, having delivered me to his apartments, my lover did not wrap his arms around me or seek to blot out our individual and mutual alarms with a kiss that might at least have sapped the terrible tension from the room. Instead he now washed his hands, without offering me the same facility, and sat at his desk, where he lifted one paper after another. He did not quite keep his back to me, as if to show that he did not trust me, but neither did he show any interest in my presence or my welfare.

I threw back my shoulders and took deep, professional breaths. Then, in the complete silence, I began to recite in my head the first lines from the first opera I ever performed. I recited not just my lines but also the responses of the other performers until I reached the end of the first act, and then the second. Still my lover kept me tangentially in his view, and did not offer me a seat, or a word.

I felt my feet growing numb. I had begun to sway slightly. It had been hours since I had eaten or drunk anything, and the drama of the day was beginning to take its toll. My lover had risen, some time during the second act, and barked down the stairs for some food. The idiots had arrived soon after with a great plate of bread and cheese, which he fell upon and emptied, without offering me a morsel. He washed it down with unwatered red wine. While my own lips parched and my tongue grew furred, I still thought: *Good, good, drink more. Drink is good for softening.*

An hour later I was reaching the end of the first act in the fourth opera I had performed. I was so tired now that I did not bother to infuse my silent recital with any feelings. I spoke the words inside my head as if I was reciting numbers. But I was feeling better. To exercise control over the time by choosing my work and the speed at which I performed it gave me a calming sense of power. To be engaged in an activity of which he knew nothing also helped salvage my sense of self.

Two hours later I was not even mid-repertoire and he was still at his desk, nodding slightly from the wine.

When he finally broke down, it was to say; 'Why did you not tell me that you were expecting our child?'

He stood up, pigeon-toed, grimacing with an effort not to burst into tears, and was pointing at my false belly with all the despair of a good man who has been comprehensively betrayed.

And suddenly it was clear to me: this was the reason for all his sulking. He was angry that I had hidden the greatest news of all from him. It was his own supposed act of propagation that obsessed him. The other issues – Pevenche, my true identity, Tom even – were minor, compared with the apparent genesis and burgeoning of an issue from his own seed!

He clearly believed that he and no one else must be the father of the putative child. It had not occurred to him to doubt my fidelity.

I must work with this, I thought.

For the first time, I dared to approach him. I moved towards the desk and sat myself on its corner, as close to him as I could contrive without actually touching him.

'My darling,' I said seriously, 'I would give my own eyes for it to be true. There is nothing that I would desire more than to bear your child. Nothing that would give me greater honour than that.'

And my interior thoughts were even more fervent, for to them was added the piteous knowledge that, damaged as I was by the doctor's instruments, I would never have his child.

His eyes moistened now.

I gestured towards the pregnancy apron and said, 'But I confess that this belly is not my own. It is merely a disguise that I assumed to try to save me from discovery in Venice. Sadly it did not serve, and you know the rest.'

His shock was entire. He moved his blanched lips silently.

I was in agony. Was this the moment when I might touch him? Would this be the moment when he would surround me with his arms? Or must I still bear entire the burden of managing this scene, steering us through the dangers to a happy conclusion? I was sure that when he touched me, he would not be able to resist the pull of memory. His skin, if not his brain, would remember what pleasure was to be had in the holding of me. I was aching to feel his hands on me, to taste his breath, to touch his hair.

I decided to trust that instinct.

'Test it for yourself,' I whispered, knowing that he would not see this as a climbing down from his great height: after all, it would be a mere examination of the evidence and his dignity would lose nothing by it.

I did not lift my skirt or show him where to find the ribbons. I lifted my arms and allowed him to fumble around the sash and mantle himself. I stood as if crucified while he put his hand first on the outer padding of the apron, and then inserted it underneath that he might feel my own flat stomach beneath the wads of linen.

At the touch of his hand, tears exploded from my eyes. Then, at last, I raised my face to kiss him, letting him taste the genuine salt and know the truth and substance of my great regret.

· 5 ·

A Pacific Foment

Take Vine and Willow leaves, Lettuce, each 2 handfuls;
whitewater Lily flowers, red Roses, each 1 handful; white Poppy
heads (with the seeds) 2 ounces; boil in Water 1 gallon to 2
quarts; in the strain'd dissolve Opium 2 drams.

Use it warm with a Sponge, to the Temples, Forehead, whole
Head and the Feet. It deserves to be employ'd, where 'tis not
altogether safe to give Hypnotics; namely in Fevers that rage
Impetuously, with Fervour, and pulsing pain of the Head,
pertinacious Watchings, and danger of a Delirium: For by its soft
Cherishment, kindly Warmth and temperate Humidity, it
humects, mitigates and appeases acrious, boiling Juices, and drives
them from the Head, either by Perspiration or Circulation, and
so disposeth the weary, worn-out Spirits to rest and procureth
placid Sleep.

It was only two days later that I remembered Pevenche. My
lover had not remembered her at all. How I envy men those
strange membranes round their brains that make them impervious to anything that is not convenient!

'What shall we do about your war . . . my daughter?' I asked
him that morning, my bare thigh cosseting his.

'My God! Pevenche!' He leapt up and paced naked in front of
me, a most appealing picture of self-reproach. 'How could I have
forgotten about her?'

I wanted to say, 'Because it was such a pleasure to do so,'
especially while my eyes roamed over the fine, firm tracts of his
breast and limbs.

But I answered, with equal sincerity, 'I have been entirely

410

lost in you. I was not able to think of anyone else. How selfish I have been!'

'No, no!' He sat beside me and stroked my hair. I hoped his feet would not meet the bottle of gin I had ordered while he slept and had hidden under the bed. 'Think of the shocks you have endured. And you are not accustomed to thinking of her as your daughter. It will take you some time to absorb your joy.'

'My joy?' I repeated faintly.

'That your child survived and was not murdered by the doctor and the nuns! That Fate put her back in your hands. You know, I have long suspected that it was some kind of veiled maternal instinct that drew you to her.'

'Yes, darling, perhaps it was like that. I did always have a strange feeling about her.'

As I said these words I wished with all my heart to make them true. For the sake of Valentine Greatrakes, I wanted to learn to love Pevenche.

'I knew it!' he said, elated. 'And of course *my* unconscious eye realised the resemblance but my brain was not absorbent to it – that was why I caused Cecilia Cornaro to draw her face instead of yours!'

If I had not loved Valentine Greatrakes for his shapely limbs and ideally creased face, I would have loved him for his optimism. Truly, to wake up beside that man was to feel every morning the first day of an exceptionally promising spring.

Logically, my lover should now have been rushing to dress and to make for the convent of Sant'Alvise to liberate his little ward. I saw that he did not do so. It was sad to watch the struggle in him, between duty and desire, and worse, to see him realise for himself that he did not crave her company or look forward to seeing her again. His eyes closed up and his shoulders hunched.

It was then that I thought of a way to help both him and myself in this.

'There is something about Pevenche that you should know,' I said quietly, toying with his fingers.

'She is quite safe, yes, isn't she?' he gabbled, in a panic at my tone.

'Oh she is indeed safe and happy, just as I told you. The point is that she is so happy at Sant'Alvise that I believe that we would be doing her a cruelty to take her away from the place where she is at last content.'

My honest feelings were catching up with my words, even as I spoke them.

'You and I must decide if we shall sacrifice our own happiness for hers. I mean our natural desire to have her with us always' – his eyes contracted with misery at this vision – 'must be countered by the felicity she has unexpectedly found for herself.'

He followed my words with a boundless eagerness, as I told him about her astonishing talent with the pastries, about her ease and indeed pre-eminence at Sant'Alvise. Some of her creations, I said, were destined to become famous. I had tasted them myself. They were causing a stir in Venice, bringing unsuspected wealth to Sant'Alvise.

I declared, 'If Pevenche were not a woman, she could command a ducal stipend. She would be sought after by any court. At last, her energies are channelled into their God-sent purpose. All that strange behaviour of hers – why, it was frustration that she could not express herself in sugar, as she does now.'

My lover took this in, straining to believe me. My eye fell on the blue cake box which had housed my letter to him. I rose from the bed and walked to it, not insensible of the effect of my naked form. I brought it back to the bed, and refocused his attention on it, by remarking, 'Could we not involve Pevenche and the convent in a little quiet business, as couriers for some of your own items? We have seen that as a discreet method of transportation, it certainly functions. I was wondering about the Venetian Balsamick . . .?'

He said nothing, but he fingered the box thoughtfully.

He was already persuaded, really, but I wanted to make sure that he would never regret the decision we were taking.

I had heard from the nuns and seen with my own eyes that Pevenche showed particular kindness to one of the younger girls.

'It is a very delicate matter, and I barely know how to tell you.'

His brows furrowed instantly. 'Tell me what?'

'You see, something a little unusual has come to my attention regarding your – my – Pevenche.'

He leaned over towards me.

'You know that I am very aware of the way that nuns live and conduct themselves? I of all people know that many nuns have no true vocation of their own. They are unwilling brides of Christ. If the sacrifice of chastity is not made willingly, then . . . well, then there are ways around hated vows made under force.'

'You mean the child has escaped, and taken a lover!' he exclaimed.

My voice was a little steely when I said: 'She is not a child. Nor did she escape. Pevenche did not need to escape in order to find a lover.'

'I don't understand.'

'She has all the lovers she needs around her. From what I hear, she has already made a selection.'

'You mean . . .?' he gasped.

'Yes, I believe that Pevenche prefers her own kind. That is what I meant by the felicity she has found. At the convent she may discreetly pursue her own nature. Outside it, she would be ostracised or misunderstood.'

The Zany's voice rattled my inner ear: 'What a load of spiced brown trout!'

And yet I wondered – Pevenche was without doubt superlatively comfortable in the company of women, and showed no interest in men except as objects of derision. I remembered how intimate she had seemed with the girl who accompanied her at the convent.

My lover was striding about the room in an agony of indecision. I could see what he was thinking: perhaps it was our responsibility to rescue her from the depravity of the nunnery and to take it upon ourselves to educate these tastes of hers that ran against nature. Kind as he was, he wished for her to sample

413

some of the joys we two knew together. Thinking of Pevenche, I doubted if they would impress her.

I did not feel guilty. She had shown me quite clearly that she was abundantly content where she was, as sole queen of her narrow kingdom, the object of reverence and fawning. And it was true, cooking made her happy on her own terms. She would not be willing to do what was necessary to obtain and keep a man in her life. And she would not find it easy to attract one in any case. Outside the convent, Pevenche would be only an object of mockery wherever she went for her vanity, corpulence and pretensions to juvenility. Inside the convent she was safe from the sneers of the world. Her father's blood made her competitive and aggressive. Her incarceration in Mistress Haggardoon's Academy had already atrophied her emotional development. She would always have the maturity of a thirteen-year-old. She was a natural nun! Even if her God was sugar. None of this, of course, could I articulate to my lover, but I trusted his intelligence to draw the obvious conclusion.

To test him, I suggested: 'Perhaps you are right. We should go and seize her, even against her will, and drag her away from there and confine her in some quarters with us. I expect that eventually we shall tame her anger. We can teach her some more ladylike skill than cooking. Flower-painting, perhaps. It may take years, but we shall persevere, no matter how fiercely she fights us.'

His eyes were dull with grief at this desecration of our happiness, so new and so hard won.

I imagined Pevenche lying, as I had once done, on the cold marble of the church floor, happily ignorant of the vow she was making, thinking only to ennoble herself to the rank of the Golden Book nuns, and preserve her dominion in the kitchen. I saw the priest struggling to force the large ring on her fat finger. I saw her spread-eagled from above, a lumpen black figure, agreeing, without comprehending, to a living death.

I ran to my lover and flung myself into his arms. 'Tell me what to do, my love,' I sobbed. 'I just do not know what is the right thing for her.'

414

And so I let him persuade me to leave Pevenche in the convent.

How surprised she would be when we went there to take her the triple good tidings of her own situation, my true identity, and our imminent marriage.

· 6 ·

An Alexiterial Julep

Take Alexiterial Milk Water, black Cherry Water, each 4
ounces; Rue Water 3 ounces; Epidemial 2 ounces; Tincture of
Saffron (extracted in Treacle water) 1 ounce; Syrup of Gilly-
flowers 2 ounces; Goa, and Contrayerva Stone, each 1 dram;
Confection of Alkermes 2 drams, mix.

It's useful and necessary in putrid and malignant Fevers, where
the Spirits are overborn, and almost slain, by a deleterious and
mortifying Venom, namely, to give them a lively brisk
Expansion, and to rouse 'em up, and make 'em able to recover the
due Mixture of the Blood, vanquish the Venom, and expel it.

Ah, the relief of *confession*! Of honesty! When I had told my –
husband – of all that I had done in the pay of the Venetian
Inquisitors, I felt the sordidness of my employment expunged
from me.

He forgave me everything, and every note of my confession
was waylaid by his endearments; even my pitiful account of the
blinding of the cruel nun accidentally impaled on the icicle.

It had been a risk. He might have found me sullied by what I
had done. Instead, he chose to see me as a victim of the cruel yet
impersonal machinations of the Venetian state. He chose to
know that I never loved any of those men I was sent to seduce,
and that it had revolted me to behave with them as I did. He
declared that my true purity had not been touched. This was all
proved to him by the fact that when for the first time I truly fell
in love, it was with *him*, someone forbidden by my employers.

With astonishing optimism, he decried any disappointment
that I had not such a large stock of virtue as he had thought:

perhaps in his mind he traded it against certain damaging discoveries I had made about himself. I did not draw his attention to all that I now knew about his past, and his present. Instead I told him the truth: it had come to mean nothing to me. I cared not if, for example, those diamond brooches were acquired in a fully legal manner: I loved the romance of the gesture. It was true. I still simply liked the *style* of the man, gentleman or not, and all my inbred Golden Book scruples could not make me dislike him simply for not being a nobleman. I had proved renegade to my class, after all, and turned actress. Could not a London criminal rise above his station and become in life and habit noble? And in this way did we not meet exactly in the middle of some nationless, classless amorphous pool?

After hearing this he stood in silence for some moments. Then there were other matters to consider, melancholy ones, but much mitigated by our turtle billing and mutual caresses.

He did not like to blame his beloved Tom for anything, of course, but I could see that he too wished to build a solid base on which to proceed. So he even admitted that it was Tom's usage of me that set me on the terrible path I was forced to take.

In this way, he forgave me everything, from beginning to end. He found goodness and transparency in all my motives, and reasonableness in all my responses.

It is, I reflected, listening to his words, *possible to see very clear things that are not true.*

'And so,' he asked me, tenderly, 'you never saw Tom again, after that terrible time in San Zaccaria? All those times he was in Venice, and you never once came across him?'

I shook my head.

'And you never sought him out to avenge what he had done to you?'

His eyes were soft and moist while he marvelled at my gentleness. I looked at him with satisfaction. He was so exceedingly well made! Such long legs and such slim, shapely thighs, and a torso with enough meat on it to be manly but not enough to lose a sliver of useful flexibility.

With lowered eyes, I reminded him that most of the time I had been abroad, on my 'missions'. Tom had been in Venice only occasionally. It was very unlikely that our paths should cross here. Anyway, my employers kept me under close supervision. I met no one they did not put in my path.

'And I never felt anything but regret for him,' I said. 'When I saw him in his coffin, I felt nothing but shock. I loved him once, but by then I was yours. For the residue of our lives, I am yours.'

He pressed my fingers, one by one, his handsome face fixed on mine.

There was one last question from my lover.

'Can you think who would have wished to kill him?'

I shook my head again, sadly.

'Such a beautiful man, so full of life.' I added quickly, 'So he must have been, even after all those years.'

Then he surprised me. 'I always thought that the man who followed you – Mazziolini – must have had something to do with it.'

'Because Tom started bleeding when he was in the room? You thought Mazziolini came all the way to London to gloat over the murder he had done?'

My lover hung his head, ashamed to put credence both in the superstition and in such a far-fetched theory. He said, defensively, 'Well, it is a known thing in murderers to be drawn to the corpses they have made.'

He then recounted the story of the whore and the Sternutatory Powder, concluding: 'Mazziolini could have done it. He has it in him to kill. And the timing *was* possible. After all, your troupe did not leave for London until after Tom died.'

It was true. Our living bodies had travelled more expeditiously than Tom's dead one, held up by customs officers, by paperwork, by unwilling porters and even adverse weather. We had sprinted ahead, arrived in London nearly two months before his preserved remains did.

'What would be Mazziolini's motive though?' I asked.

'Perhaps he knew about you and Tom. Perhaps the man loved you? Following you around for years, how could he not? Perhaps he was jealous?'

I said sincerely, 'Mazziolini feels nothing like love. Believe me, I have known him these sixteen years. He feels only hate. He merely serves, without relish and with distaste. I believe his affectionate feelings were cauterised in the womb. He's an automaton for the Council of Ten. There is no goodness in him.'

Unlike myself. I did not know if I was a good woman or not. It had hardly been my choice to make, between virtue and evil, the way I saw it, not since I was forcibly confined in the convent at the age of fifteen. Until now Fortune had thwarted any laudable intentions or instincts on my part and had drawn me towards the cruel path I had taken. The flaws of my disposition were on a natural convergence with the route of the greatest evil, otherwise I should not have done anything blameworthy. Though swarming with faults, like every other human being, I never did, or only once did, something bad that was not a forced choice between extremities, finely calculated to save my life or my sanity.

But it would be better to close the subject of Tom between us. It was too painful for my lover. I mused, 'Of course *my employers* might have set Mazziolini to do it.'

'But why?'

'Think of all the mischief Tom was making in Venice. I don't mean what he did to me. I mean the little "businesses", the free-trading. They would not endear Tom to them.' I reminded him: 'They hinted as much during my interrogation.'

'They would have him killed for such a little motive?' My lover found this reason unpalatable. If Tom was killed for reasons of commerce, then he himself had sent his friend to his death. Tom had died on his behalf.

I saw no reason to torture him further. He was miserable enough, missing his friend. A sad husband is a dull affair.

So I suggested: 'It could perhaps have been because of his cavalier treatment of me. A Golden Book daughter. A Venier! When a noble is slighted, the whole of Venice is humiliated. In their perverse logic it might have become a matter of state honour.'

He nodded with relief. 'That's likely, isn't it? That they were angered by it, and that Tom was killed because of that. They

419

bided their time, waited until he felt secure, and then struck. That is the way of the Venetians, is it not?'

I reassured him it was entirely likely that Tom was killed for this reason and in this way.

'So this Mazziolini killed Tom. So I must kill Mazziolini,' he said, with a quiet steadfastness as if promising to remember a saint's day or some dietary observance.

Mazziolini was a dead man then.

The more I thought about it, the more satisfactory was this conclusion. I kissed my new husband.

And that was an end of it.

Epilogue
Venice, March 1787

Powder of Crabs Eyes Compound

Take Crabs Eyes ground on a Marble 1 dram; Cream of Tartar half a dram; Salt of Wormwood, Prunel, each 12 grains; Salt of Amber 6 grains; make all into a Powder for 6 Doses, to be given twice or thrice a Day.

It restoreth the ferment of the Viscera and Blood, when almost lost and gone. Fuses thick Blood, promotes the Secretion of Febrile Matter, and by way of Precipitation, throws it off into the Emunctories.

Dear Signore Mazziolini,

It is many months now since I first set my mind to solving the mystery of my father's death.

Certain items of the subsoil I have pieced together from fragments of fact. Smerghetto has been useful, without realising it. So have Momolo and Tofolo. For other matters, too dark to be noised about even over a bulging glass of a racy Canary, I have relied on my instincts and my wits.

It is my opinion that it started on a Thursday.

An icebound winter's night in a narrow alley behind San Marco. That's where she lodged; that's where she left the drunken maid asleep, in those precious days of freedom when you had gone ahead to London to set up rooms and servants. Remember?

This is how I see it, in my mind's eye, a year ago now, before I myself ever came to Venice, the city I now know like the veins of my wrist, perhaps better, because of course the place is in my blood.

The bird-framed Venetians stumble past one another, bundled in shawls and capes, slipping on the ice, grazing their hands on window-sills and door-knockers in an effort to stay upright.

In that eerie frostbound light, a woman and a man collide. He is bulky and tall. She is small and finely made: she falls on her back. When he reaches down to help her, his apologies sound heartfelt.

423

But something in his accent – foreign – and in his face – handsome – causes the woman to recoil.

'Don't be afraid,' he says, kneeling down to meet her eyes.

But when he sees her face, he too recoils.

'Catarina,' he whispers, 'I thought you were . . .'

He does not finish the sentence because she has fastened her lips on his.

So two lovers have found one another again, after a decade and a half apart. What matters now, it seems, is not what separated them but what apparently brings them together: it is the same desire, the same unexpired heat, the same thing that made me.

My mother must have had her reasons for embracing my Pa, for letting him lift her up and half-carry her to his gondola where he cradles her in his arms until they arrive at the landing stage near San Silvestro.

My Pa leads my mother through the remembering gates and up the stairs to his bedchamber where they stay locked in each other's arms for two nights and days, eating nothing, drinking only stale water from the ewer and never once putting on the clothes they discarded that first hour.

So then it is Saturday.

This is when things must have started to go bad.

On the third evening, he must have told her that he had to attend to certain business affairs. His eyes are vague; perhaps it is exhaustion. She lies centred in the listless bed without saying a word while he calls over-heartily downstairs for hot water, and then pinions the door shut against prying eyes with a dextrous ankle when a discreet scuttling announces its arrival. He turns his back on her and washes, dresses and gathers together a sheaf of papers into a goatskin pouch.

No doubt he tries to joke, something typically crude about being an empty goatskin himself – she has drained him of all his vital juices, but it comes out badly – as it so often did – and she does not smile. It is already night again and her eyes, yellow in the candlelight, follow him around the room like those of an ancestral portrait.

He does not tell her to stay and wait for him. He does not tell her

424

when he will be back. He does not ask where she lives or request another appointment. He looks at her clothes, blossoming in circular heaps on the floor, and then back at her.

So now she must understand that this was all he wanted. To renew the pleasures of an old acquaintance and leave it at that. She nods her head, letting him see that she has understood. She too looks at the pools of skirt and petticoat on the floor, recognising the need to put them on and leave. After all, this is not a place where she has any right to be unless her presence is specifically sanctioned by him. I imagine the merest sign from her: her breath catching in her throat, as if to acknowledge that she is also dispossessed of the right to breathe in this room once he leaves it. My mother would never betray her true feelings in a natural manner: in this alone she would have made a worthwhile nun; otherwise she is no loss to the vocation.

While he retires to the *necessario* downstairs, she leaps out of bed, extracts the papers from the pouch and fans them out. She nods and smiles. She dips a quill in ink to amend an address on the uppermost one. It's subtle as a sigh but she has perhaps changed '1st' street on the left to '4th' and made assorted tiny amendments of this style and minute substance. The ink is dry and the paper back inside the pouch before he returns to gather his possessions.

She is lying in the bed, clutching the blanket to her breasts.

'I'll leave you to dress,' he says, embarrassed. It is the first conversational phrase he has used in two days. All this time he has moaned and whispered words of passion. The prosaic now falls heavily, and he knows it.

She nods again. Her eyes are still. Her mouth inclines neither up nor down.

He leaves, closing the door behind him. He does not pause on the threshold. There comes the noise of his heavy but agile steps on the stairs and then the opening and closing of a door below. A snake's breath of cold surges up the stairs and under the door of the bedroom.

But the naked woman is already dressed, and in a moment her light step murmurs down the stairs. No one saw her arrive and no one sees her leave. Not even the man she now follows under the ghost-limed beams of the Sotoportego de la Pasina and across the empty Campo San Silvestro, where she ducks behind the stone well for a moment, until he has passed beyond her sight. She runs the remaining diagonal, skirting the *campanile*.

Watching her darting figure it would be hard to say what she seeks. Perhaps she wants to know what business calls him from the bed they have shared, and why it should do so in this late hour of the evening. Perhaps she merely cannot bear to be apart from him after the intense intimacy of the last days. It seems that the latter is the case, because she draws closer and closer to him, and the expression on her face is avid, though the detail of what it is she craves is not clearly inscribed on her features.

The unwinking moon follows her progress with a baleful eye. A sudden wind flaps her skirt up like a sail, revealing cruelly bare legs. There was no time to pull on her stockings nor tie their bows. They are thrust in her pocket. She continually tugs at the chafing brocade at her neck, for nor had she waited to whisper her silk and lace chemise over her head. It still lies on the floor in the apartment. The thought of this freezes her for a moment in reflection.

Now the Rialtina chimes in the *campanile* of San Giovanni Elemosinario, so it must be some time between nine and ten at night.

He walks slowly, breathing in the gelid air, flexing his shoulders. She trips along lightly, looking from left to right at frequent intervals, up into doorways, down into stairwells where weeping pipes have sent long fingers of ice to seek but not quite find the ground.

They pass into quiet streets. At the Calle del Stivaleto, where we nuns go to have our boots fitted, my father stops for a moment to pull a paper from his goatskin pouch, and scans it, perhaps confirming some directions. When she sees this, my mother looks pleased. They move on, down the Calle del Paradiso, towards the water.

It is there that she notices one stalactite that has formed itself with elegance so that it resembles nothing more than a slim white dagger. It is hanging from the grating of an ironclad window. (There is a broken pipe there – it's still unfixed, and leaks profusely.) She tiptoes up and snaps it off. The length of the ice shard in her hand is twelve inches.

At the tinkle of ice my Pa looks around but she is already in the shadows, clutching her prize. She kneels quickly and rubs the blade of ice in the filth of the street. When she raises it again the ice has lost its transparency beneath a sheath of dust compounded of particles of ordure, detersives, dressings and other nameless, rampant toxins.

At the Calle del Cinque, my Pa frowns, puts the paper back in the pouch, and moves uncertainly to his right, stops again.

She seems to know exactly where he is going. She no longer needs to shadow him but instead trails him obscurely, in parallel lines and circles that meet with his.

So while he crosses the Campo San Giacomo, she turns down the orange-scented path of the Naranzaria and runs along the Sotoportego de l'Erbaria. And when he paces through the Casaria, sniffing the remnants of the day's trading in cheese and oils, she slips along the Fabbriche Nove, and waits at the edge of the Campo de la Pescaria until he has passed into the shadows beyond it. Then she crosses his wake into the Calle de la Donzela, turns right into the Ruga dei Spezieri and right again into the Calle de la Becarie. She makes her way along the façades of the bread shops until they no longer provide protection. She pauses in the shadows, her quarry again in sight. Now he is mounting the steps of the bridge that leads to the Fondamenta de l'Ogio. When he reaches the peak of its humpback, he descends and disappears. She counts off his footsteps on the fingers of her hands.

At this point she darts across the street and hides herself behind the wall at the foot of the bridge, facing the deserted Ca' Rampani, first ascertaining that the Poste Vecie tavern has bedded down for the night. She flinches when she sees that smoke still belches from its funnel-shaped chimneys, but the lamps, voices and music are all long extinguished. She turns her back on the Poste Vecie, crouches down and appears to be listening intently.

A footstep can be heard from the other side of the bridge. My mother counts under her breath. *One, two, three . . .* at sixteen she pauses, and my Pa's full silhouette is visible at the top of the bridge.

He is squinting at his piece of paper and back again at the Ca'
Rampani. He looks confused. He swivels round and starts to walk
down the steps back in the direction of the market. Again my
mother counts, under her breath. When she reaches 'eleven' she
surges up blindly from her hiding place. She is standing a breath
away, behind him.

Then she is upon him; the ice raised and falling like a bird of
prey.

When he turns back to see her, he does not scream or even raise
his voice. He smiles weakly, foolishly, as if he understands that all this
is his own fault, or perhaps in one last attempt to ingratiate himself.

He is twice her size, a huge man, but her first quick blow has
punctured his neck and the blood pulses out from between the fingers he clutches to it.

He raises one hand up to the moonlight to look at the black ribbons of blood that lace his fingers. Then he looks at her and at the
dark-tipped weapon that has wounded him. He raises an eyebrow:
this is to show that the ice knife has impressed him, both in concept
and execution. He would have been proud to be the author of its
invention, a murder weapon that shall never be produced in evidence against the murderer. He acknowledges it as a righteous tool
of his own trade.

She has drawn back and watches him.

He is suddenly very tired, not just from the wound but from the
past days of love-making and perhaps also from the weight, suddenly thrust upon him again, of all that passed between them
sixteen years before. It is as if he cannot bring himself to enter
into one more conflict with her, not even to remonstrate or beg for
mercy. He does not even tell her about me.

He sinks to the ground, rolls and rolls with effort until he is
lying on his back. In doing so he has involuntarily wedged himself
behind the balustrade of the bridge in the far corner of the Campo
de la Pescaria among the refuse of fruit and fish merchants who
have purified their shops for the holy day. She crouches over him
and looks up again quickly to ascertain that neither of them can be
seen now, not even if some unlikely passer-by should enter the
deserted quarter of the market.

428

Clutching the ice dagger, she looks down into his face. She pulls aside the lapel of his frock coat, strips open his shirt and deftly inserts the dripping ice into a space between his ribs, and then pushes it slowly in until it disappears from her fingers and the flesh closes. He gasps and swallows. His eyes do not leave her face.

Then, while he lies quietly, in an apparent effort to slow the progress of the ice dagger through his flesh, she pulls the leather pouch from under his arm, takes up the note that has fallen from his hands and lies soaking up his blood. She shakes the liquid from it and slides it back inside his goatskin pouch.

The man cannot move. Yet with his eyes he lets her know that he appreciates the cleverness of this false clue, which will lead any investigation down a blind alley.

I will never be avenged now, his eyes tell her. *You have been too brilliant. They will not discover you.*

A small moan escapes from him as the icicle plunges deeper through the forks of his body.

Surely this is enough, ask his eyes, now gaunt in their sockets. *You have killed me with coldness. I see what you mean.*

But no, while he still lives, she has more metaphors to lay out on him.

It is Saturday night, the leavings of the fruit market lie stewing with the fish offal. Peel, bone, shell and fish flesh mingle, picked over by the rats. She rakes through the mound of rubbish and throws the first handfuls over his body, pausing to read the dawning understanding on his contorted face.

She nods, *Yes, it is as you fear.*

He does not cry out for help. He does not grovel or make his excuses. He does not request her forgiveness. After all, she has just extracted the apology of her choice.

Now she works fast, covering him entirely in the stinking detritus, leaving his face till last.

From time to time she checks that he still breathes. When she ascertains that he does, she nods.

When his body is entirely buried, she picks through the mound with discriminating fingers, gathering a diverse tribe of objects in her lap.

429

She checks him again for signs of life. Finding them still apparent, she bends over his face.

First she plugs his nostrils with cod bones still garlanded with soft offal. Then she stops up his ears with rotting octopus, pushing the tentacles in with her little finger until he grunts an acknowledgement of his pain. Lastly she places the carcass of a large rat-gnawed crab over his mouth, driving it inside his lips with a sudden blow so sharp that a fine spray of blood bursts from his face. And then she backs away a little, looking at him intently. The crab rises and falls with his breath, but diminishingly. She wrenches it out, and replaces it with a fish, so the tail protrudes stiffly from his lips.

Now he can never tell her about me.

Historical Notes
London and Venice, Winter 1785/6

QUACKERY

All the major characters in this novel are invented, although some of their names are borrowed or adapted from historical sources, several from the colourful world of quackery. There was a real Valentine Greatrakes: a famous, ringleted late-seventeenth-century Irish 'stroker', a healer who was reputed to cure scrofula merely by the laying on of hands. Pervenche was the name of the heroine in one of the moral fairy tales written in the late nineteenth century as a selling aid for the cocaine-based 'restorative', Vin Mariani.

'Tabby Runt' was the maid in Christopher Anstey's *New Bath Guide*, 1766, the story of a family visiting the city. The unfortunate Tabby is treated by the famous doctor Sir John Hill:

> He gives little Tabby a great many Doses
> For he says the poor creature has got the chlorosis,
> Or a ravenous pica, so brought on the vapours
> By swallowing Stuff she has read in the papers . . .

The majority of recipes for medicines that begin the chapters come from the *Pharmacopoeia Extemporanea* compiled by Thomas Fuller in 1710.

The Zany's song is based on *The Infallible Mountebank*, a popular broadside printed at Blackfriars.

There really was a London dental quack who drove a white pony painted with purple spots and brandished a female femur: 'Dr' Martin van Butchell also kept his first wife's body embalmed in his parlour until the advent of a second Mrs van Butchell. The recipe for embalming Mrs Butchell is the one I have used for Tom's corpse.

'Doctor' James Graham did indeed set up his Temple of Health and Hymen in Adelphi Terrace in 1779, a little late for Pevenche's conception, even if it had happened there. His 'Celestial Bed' may in fact have been charged with electricity to produce tickling sensations in the occupants. Graham preached that the human ovum was fertilised by electrical currents which are naturally generated by the friction of the sexual act. Graham was assisted in his ministrations by a beauteous 'Goddess of Health and Hymen'. Several sources have since claimed that this 'Vestina' was the artist's model who would one day become the notorious Lady Emma Hamilton. So popular was the Temple of Hymen that nine hundred people were turned away on the first three nights of its opening, but by 1784 its attractions had waned and it was closed down by Graham's creditors.

Most quacks produced elaborate handbills of the kind described in this novel, especially after 1762 when the hanging of street signs, once a dangerous feature of London's windswept streets, was banned.

As the scholar David Gentilcuore has remarked, it was a safety measure for the quacks to advertise the application of their nostrums to dozens of different illnesses: *someone* who bought the medicine was sure to get better.

The symptoms that cause Mimosina to be sure that she had conceived a son are based on popular wisdom prevalent in Italy from medieval times. Such advice was frequently published in marriage manuals.

LONDON

Valentine Greatrakes's rant against unjust duties reflects Adam Smith's writings on the same subject. Between 1775 and 1785 the American War of Independence was raging, and the state justified the plethora of duties – over four thousand of them – by citing the war effort.

The 'free-trading' activities of Valentine Greatrakes would not have faced much opposition from the law. Watermen and smugglers, in league with corrupt watchmen, were seldom troubled by the forces of order until the establishment of the Thames Police in 1798.

One of several great frost fairs was held on the Thames in 1789, when the incident of the City of Moscow breaking away from the shore occurred. I have set it a few years earlier, however. The year 1785 also saw a severe winter, with one hundred and fifteen days of frost.

The Venetian theatre troupe that brings Mimosina Dolcezza to London is invented, though Italian companies did go there, the first appearing in 1726. Italian theatre was a taste that Londoners only gradually acquired: the slapstick and tickle style of the *commedia dell'arte* at first received much censure. Individual Italian performers, however, were very popular. Both singers and dancers were engaged by London impresarios and gradually created a demand for Italian light opera.

The entertainments to which Valentine Greatrakes treats Pevenche were all available in London around that time, except for Signor Cappelli's Cats, who were not to be seen until 1832. I have also taken a liberty with Vauxhall – the gardens were normally open only in the summer months.

The London Bridge of today little resembles the one of this story. The famous 'falling-down' buildings upon it had already been demolished between 1757 and 1761. The huge railway arches which dominate Stoney Street and the Borough Market today would not be constructed until the 1830s.

In the 1780s, Bankside's Stoney Street was a picturesque road of half-timbered buildings. At the northern end an archway led through to Clink Street and straight to St Mary Overie's Stairs at the edge of the Thames. Now the blue building known as Little Winchester Wharf, built around 1816, blocks the river from sight. Fifty yards to the east one can still see the remnants of St Mary Overie Dock. These days it shelters a reproduction of Drake's *Golden Hinde*, but in the eighteenth century the dock must have been crowded and noisy, for it served as the main landing point for the malt, hay, fuel and other necessities for the key local industry of brewing. In Clink Street the notable tavern was the Bell, a haunt of watermen, smugglers and press-gangs ready to prey on the likes of Smollett's eponymous hero Roderick Random. It was also a warehouse for saltpetre. The street was cobbled, as it is today, but then it was lined with the establishments of millers, lightermen, coal, wood and ivory merchants.

At the west end of the street, in 1785, stood – and still stand – the ruins of the notorious Clink Prison, destroyed when Lord George Gordon's rioters turned their attention to it in 1780. It never again served as a prison and today is a grim museum with banquet facilities. Just west of the prison is Bank End, site since 1774–5 of the Anchor Inn, still a popular riverside pub. It is indeed full of concealed and unexpected staircases.

Modern-day Park Street was then known as Deadman's Place, possibly because of the nearby burial grounds ('Cross Bones'), resting place of many thousands of plague victims from medieval times onwards.

Dr Sniver's priapic museum is an invention – such anatomical museums did not flourish until the nineteenth century. My mention of homoeopathic techniques is also somewhat in anticipation of their development.

Even as this book was being researched, Bankside was undergoing one of those revolutions that periodically transform the fortunes of inner-city villages. Until a few years ago the area had been condemned as unsavoury and dismal: now the presence of the reconstructed Shakespeare's Globe Theatre, Tate Modern art gallery and the renewal of the epicurean Borough Market (which dates from the twelfth century) have quite suddenly conferred upon Bankside a rough kind of glamour, complete with restored lofts, converted railway arches and café life.

It would be almost unrecognisable to the protagonists of this novel.

VENICE

The old convent of San Zaccaria is now a military zone, the regional headquarters of the Carabinieri. The convent was closed down by Napoleon, as one of his measures to suppress powerful Venetian institutions. It stood disused for some time until the Austrians took it over and transformed it into offices. It was probably then that all traces of the convent's enclosure were removed. The *ruota* and *parlatorio* no longer exist, but from the inside it is still possible for a privileged visitor (with military escort) to see the two cloisters, one by Codussi and one by Gambello, and the beautiful raised loggia just behind the church.

The church too has changed. The interior walls, which were once perforated with the grilles through which the nuns sang and observed the world, are now hung with paintings. But there is still a representation of the nuns, in a painting by Antonio Zonca (1652–1723), that shows the annual visit of the Doge to the convent, among a series of pictures depicting the important events in the life of San Zaccaria. The nuns are shown fresh, plump and pink-faced behind their grille, interested but not straining to see the outside world; self-contained without needing any other kind of enforced confinement. The abbess has the prime position in the large aperture where two bars, vertical and horizontal, have been removed to make an opening four times the size of the other fifty-two holes.

Nor can the modern visitor to Venice enter the church of SS Cosma e Damiano on Giudecca. It is deconsecrated and derelict now, though the façade retains its handsome late renaissance brick and marble. Its former convent, however, has been restored and is used for art exhibitions during the Venice Biennale.

Sant'Alvise, in contrast, is still a working convent, today inhabited by just twenty-three white-clad sisters of the Canossian order. If 'dressed adequately', a visitor may roam among the echoing corridors of cells and the gardens. The brick cloister is these days enclosed in glass and part of the convent is now run as a school. The atmosphere, peaceful and friendly, is of another world, miles and centuries away from the tourist hub of Venice.

By one of those coincidences that invariably and felicitously befall the historical novelist, quite late in the writing of this book I discovered that the church of Sant'Alvise was endowed by an ancient member of the Venier family. In 1388, Antonia Venier had dreams in which Saint Louis (Sant'Alvise in Venetian) of Toulouse appeared to her. He told her that God wished him to be venerated in Venice also. Sant'Alvise even showed her where the church was to be situated.

The musicals seen by Valentine Greatrakes in his pursuit of the actress were those performed in the relevant theatres of Venice in the 1780s. Domenico Cimarosa's comic opera *L'Italiana a Londra* was composed in 1778. The heroine, Livia, comes to London under a false identity, searching for an English lord with whom she once shared a romance, but who could not be persuaded to marry her. The other details of the plot have been slanted to suit this story.

Modern Venice is still remarkably like eighteenth-century Venice. You have to stay up very late at night to understand the major difference between the Grand Canal of 1785 and today. The difference is silence. Today the Grand Canal is a motorway: by day the symphony of a hundred different boat engines dominates every aural sensation. Only late at night can you hear just the waves lapping for more than a few minutes at a time. And then you can also hear the rare sound of a gondola prow slapping the water, and footsteps echoing over bridges.

MEANS OF DEATH

Hangings of condemned prisoners from London and Middlesex still took place at Tyburn gallows, near modern-day Marble Arch, until the end of 1783. But the crowds became too restive and the executions were transferred to the yard of Newgate Prison. Like the Clink, Newgate was destroyed by the Gordon rioters. But it was quickly rebuilt, unlike the Clink.

Mimosina's technique for breaking out of her prison is based on one used by the notorious eighteenth-century London escape-artist Jack Shepherd. He made small holes in the wood that framed the bars of his Newgate cell; in this way he weakened the window and was able to pull the whole structure loose.

Popular belief in cruentation dates back to the Middle Ages, and is even mentioned in Shakespeare's *Richard III*.

Catarina's dream of being roasted alive at San Zaccaria reflects a true story: an instance of a London baker throwing his apprentice girl into an oven was recorded in 1787.

Pasteur's work on bacterial infections was not undertaken until the 1860s. Eighteenth-century physicians were unaware of the existence of micro-organisms. Gangrene, also known as mortification of the flesh, was seen as a natural and usually fatal result of wounds but its processes were not understood.

Casanova, who suffered a lifelong weakness for nosebleeds, records in his memoirs that a Milanese countess tried to murder him with Sternutatory Powder.

Glass stiletto daggers were indeed a deadly export of Venice.

AUTHENTICITY

Every historical novelist faces the problem of how to spice their story with the picturesque aspects of the past without embalming the characters in the equivalent of museum cases, through which their emotions may only be dimly viewed, at a distance. I have tried to paint the London and Venice of the eighteenth century, in all their flavours, but more importantly to bring to life two personalities with whom the modern reader can identify. Incorporating historical research in a novel makes for a difficult balance – like decorating a home – contriving how to add an agreeable amount of interesting clutter without obscuring what's important.

For example, popular misconception sees the entire Georgian period costumed in exaggerated panniers and hoops and towering wigs. It is true that these styles were fashionable for a time in the later eighteenth century but by the mid-1780s, when this novel is set, hairstyles were simpler and the architectural nature of dresses had softened. Hair was often still powdered with a mixture of flour, nutmeg, starch and, at times, gold dust. A powder containing arsenic or flat white lead was sometimes painted on to the face to render it fashionably – deathly – pale . . . Six hundred Italian men were said to have died of inhaling the fatal complexions of their women. Lips were rouged with a powder of red plaster. False eyebrows made of mouse fur were applied to shaved brows. But it was possible to choose to be subtle, and naturalistic, and for this reason

I have not made a point of describing such things to the point of boredom.

I have not discovered any reference to the Venetian state employing actresses as spies. But espionage was the time-honoured way for the Republic to keep a finger on Continental politics. And this was a state that in its time even employed Casanova as a spy.

SMALL OBJECT LESSONS

Pevenche's 'ukulele' is anachronistic by a hundred years (the name was given to a small guitar-like instrument brought by Portuguese immigrants to Hawaii) – she would have had access to a miniature mandolin, however. These instruments were very popular in the eighteenth century and many composers, such as Vivaldi, included them in their orchestration. Handel, working in London, also made use of mandolins.

The story of Hansel and Gretel is of antique origin. It was published in the Brothers Grimm's *Kinder- und Hausmärchen*, issued in two volumes (1812–15). The Grimms wrote down most of the tales from oral narrations, collecting the material mainly from peasants in Hesse.

The sculptor Andrea Brustolon was indeed commissioned to produce numerous boxwood and ebony sculptures for the Venier family. A large number of them, including the blackamoors with eyes of vitreous paste, can still be seen at Ca' Rezzonico, the museum of eighteenth-century life in Venice.

Acknowledgements

I have countless reasons to be grateful for the wit, warmth and tact of both my editor, Jill Foulston, and my agent, Victoria Hobbs at A. M. Heath.

In London, I would also like to thank Karen Howell, the curator of the Old Operating Theatre Museum, for her help and enthusiasm; William Helfand and Vladimir Lovric for reading the manuscript with expert medical eyes; John Waite and Melissa Stein for helping me to eliminate anachronisms and other blights; Jim O'Brien for purging the manuscript of 'Hong Kong Paddyisms'; Kristina Blagojevitch and Jane Birkett for their editorial assistance; Dave Fennell for his historical delvings in the Clink Street area; Paola de Carolis for her good advice; Ornella Tarantola and Clara Caleo-Green for keeping an eye on my Italian. As always, I thank the staff of the British and London Libraries.

In Venice I would like to thank Carole Satyamurti for allowing herself to be murdered repeatedly on the bridge at the Fondamenta de l'Ogio; Lucia Spezzati and her family for their hospitality at Ca' Zenobio; the kind sisters at Sant'Alvise for permitting me to wander round their beautiful convent; Colonello Ilio Ciceri of the Comando Provinciale, Carabinieri di Venezia, for personally showing me around the military zone that now occupies the former convent of San Zaccaria. As always, I thank Graziella, Emilio, Fabrizio and all at da Gino in San Vio for the 6 a.m. *cappuccini*. I really should pay rent for my alfresco 'desk' there. Finally, a thank-you to Sergio and Roberta Grandesso for their constant kindness, expressed both in words and in *prosecco*.

Also by Michelle Lovric

THE FLOATING BOOK

'A richly textured tale of love and learning, lust and superstition that is at turns heartwarming and heartbreaking, exhilarating and terrifying . . . prose as luminous as a Venetian dawn.'
Philadelphia Inquirer

Venice, 1468. Sosia Simeon, a free-spirited sensualist, is the lover of many men in the fabled city, though married to one she despises. On the edge of the Grand Canal, Wendelin von Speyer sets up the first printing press in Venice and looks for the book that will make his fortune. When he tempts fate by publishing Catullus, the poet whose desperate and unrequited love inspired the most tender and erotic poems of antiquity, a scandal is set in motion that will change all their lives for ever.

'Opulent and ravishing – you find yourself thinking about the nature of obsession . . . about witchcraft . . . about Judaism, about the effects of the plague, prostitution, medicine . . . hypocrisy, betrayal, loyalty and disgrace. In short, fifteenth-century Venice slowly comes alive'
Washington Post